MARCUS EMERSON

RECESS WARRIORS

HERO IS A FOUR-LETTER WORD

ROARING BROOK PRESS

New York

Published by Roaring Brook Press

Roaring Brook Press is a division of Holtzbrinck Publishing Holdings Limited Partnership

175 Fifth Avenue, New York, New York 10010

mackids.com

Library of Congress Control Number: 2016942446

Our books may be purchased in bulk for promotional, educational, or business use.
Please contact your local bookseller or the Macmillan Corporate and Premium Sales Department
at (800) 221-7945 ext. 5442 or by e-mail at MacmillanSpecialMarkets@macmillan.com.

First published in 2014 as *Totes Sweet Hero* by Emerson Publishing House

First Roaring Brook Press edition 2017
Book design by Andrew Arnold
Printed in China by Toppan Leefung Printing Ltd., Dongguan City, Guangdong Province

1   3   5   7   9   10   8   6   4   2

FOR MY KIDS . . .

EVIE, ELIJAH, PARKER & FINN

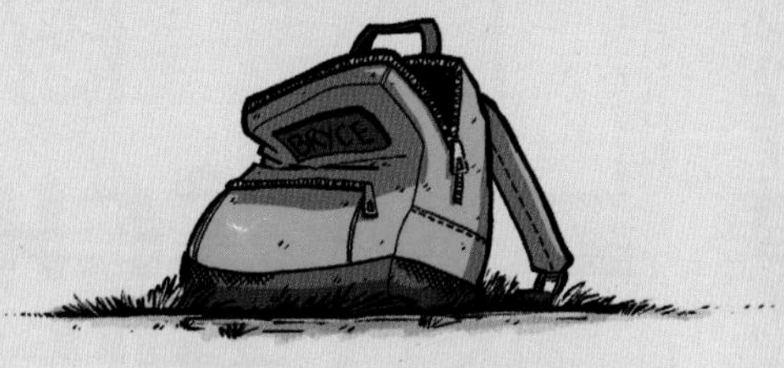
BRYCE

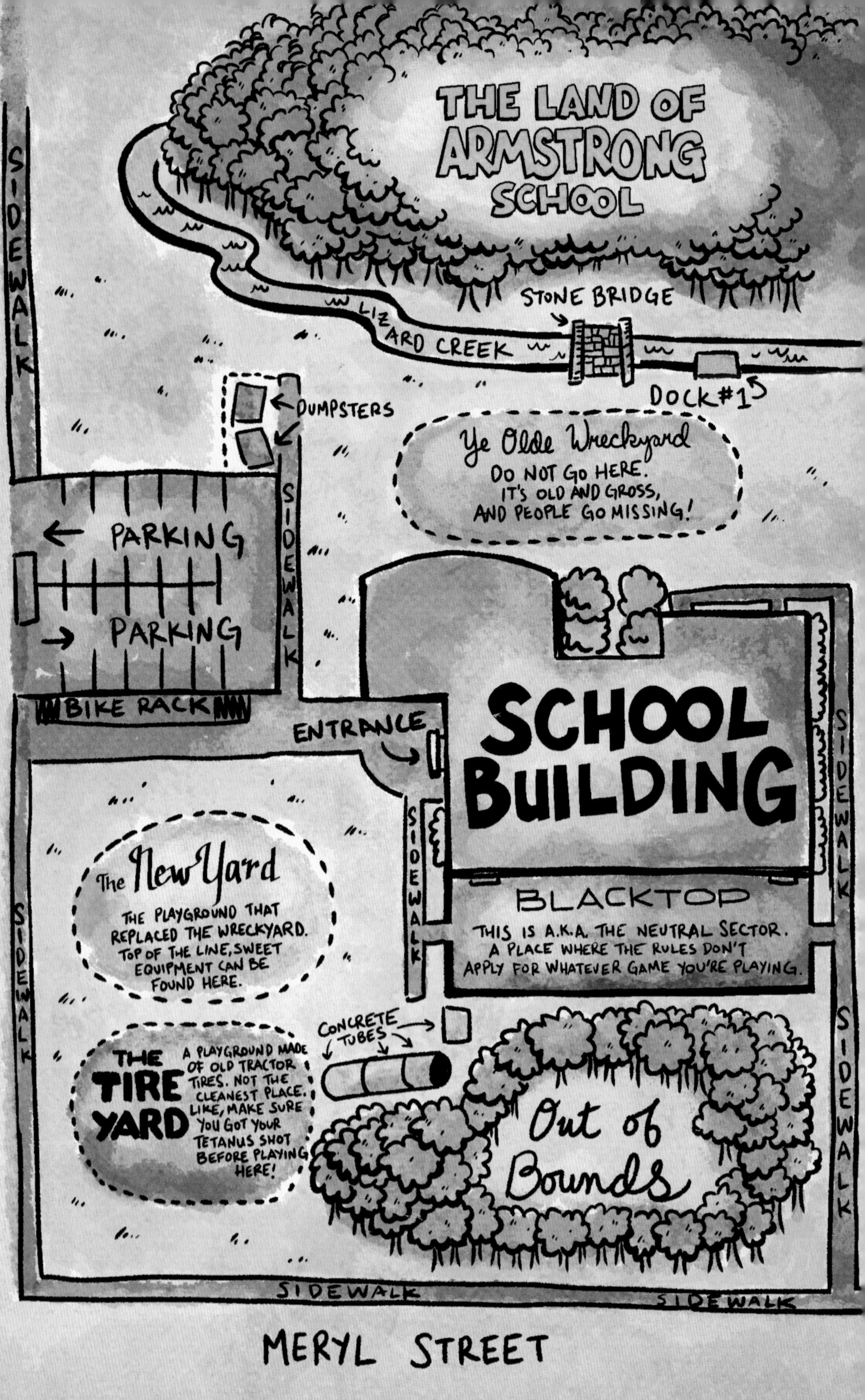

THE LAND OF ARMSTRONG SCHOOL
SIDEWALK
STONE BRIDGE
LIZARD CREEK
DOCK #1
DUMPSTERS
Ye Olde Wreckyard
DO NOT GO HERE. IT'S OLD AND GROSS, AND PEOPLE GO MISSING!
PARKING
PARKING
SIDEWALK
BIKE RACK
ENTRANCE
SCHOOL BUILDING
SIDEWALK
SIDEWALK
The New Yard
THE PLAYGROUND THAT REPLACED THE WRECKYARD. TOP OF THE LINE, SWEET EQUIPMENT CAN BE FOUND HERE.
BLACKTOP
THIS IS A.K.A. THE NEUTRAL SECTOR. A PLACE WHERE THE RULES DON'T APPLY FOR WHATEVER GAME YOU'RE PLAYING.
SIDEWALK
CONCRETE TUBES
THE TIRE YARD
A PLAYGROUND MADE OF OLD TRACTOR TIRES. NOT THE CLEANEST PLACE. LIKE, MAKE SURE YOU GOT YOUR TETANUS SHOT BEFORE PLAYING HERE!
Out of Bounds
SIDEWALK
SIDEWALK
SIDEWALK
MERYL STREET

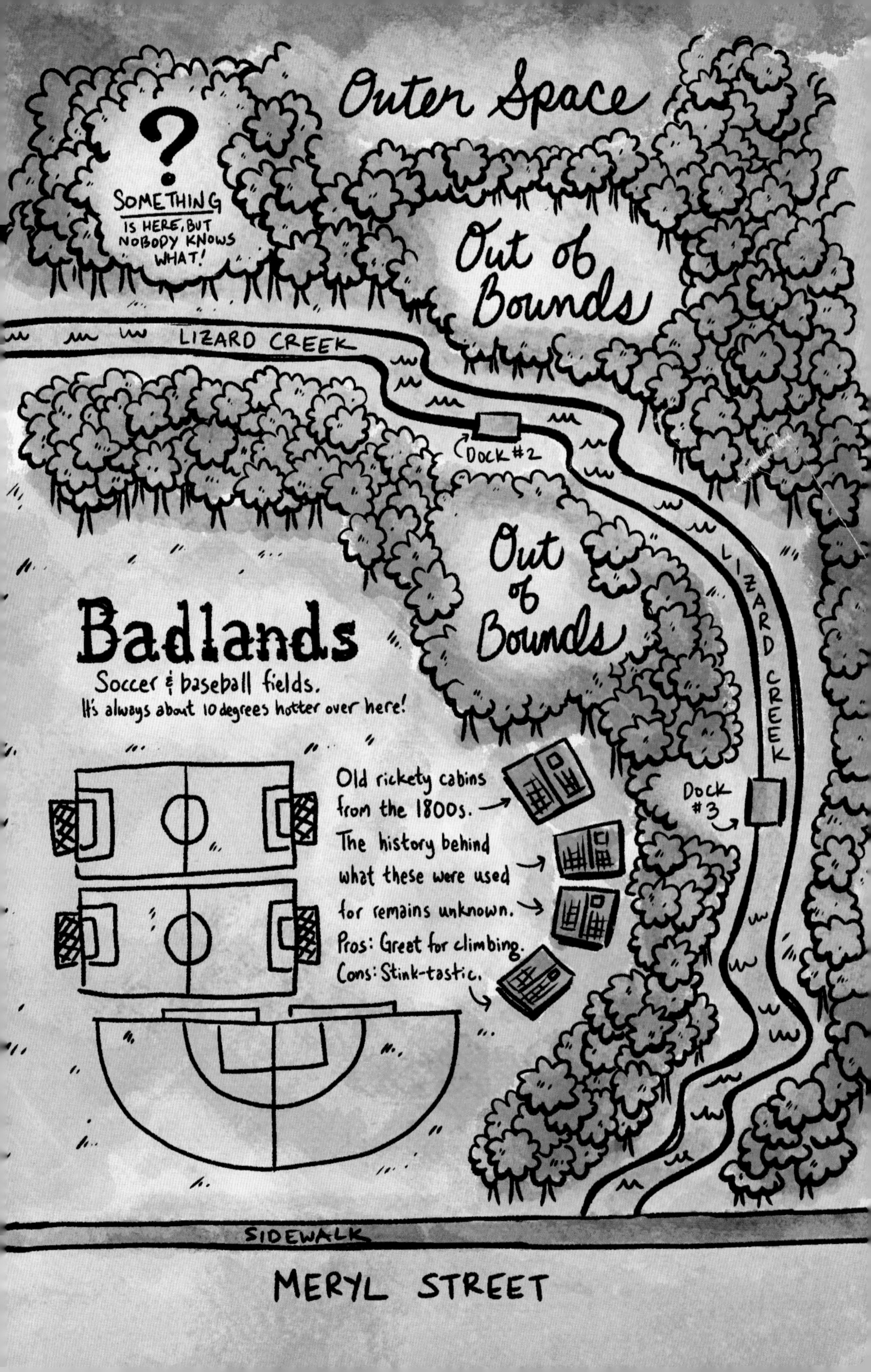
Outer Space
?
SOMETHING IS HERE, BUT NOBODY KNOWS WHAT!
Out of Bounds
LIZARD CREEK
DOCK #2
Out of Bounds
LIZARD CREEK
Badlands
Soccer & baseball fields.
It's always about 10 degrees hotter over here!
Old rickety cabins from the 1800s.
The history behind what these were used for remains unknown.
Pros: Great for climbing.
Cons: Stink-tastic.
DOCK #3
SIDEWALK
MERYL STREET

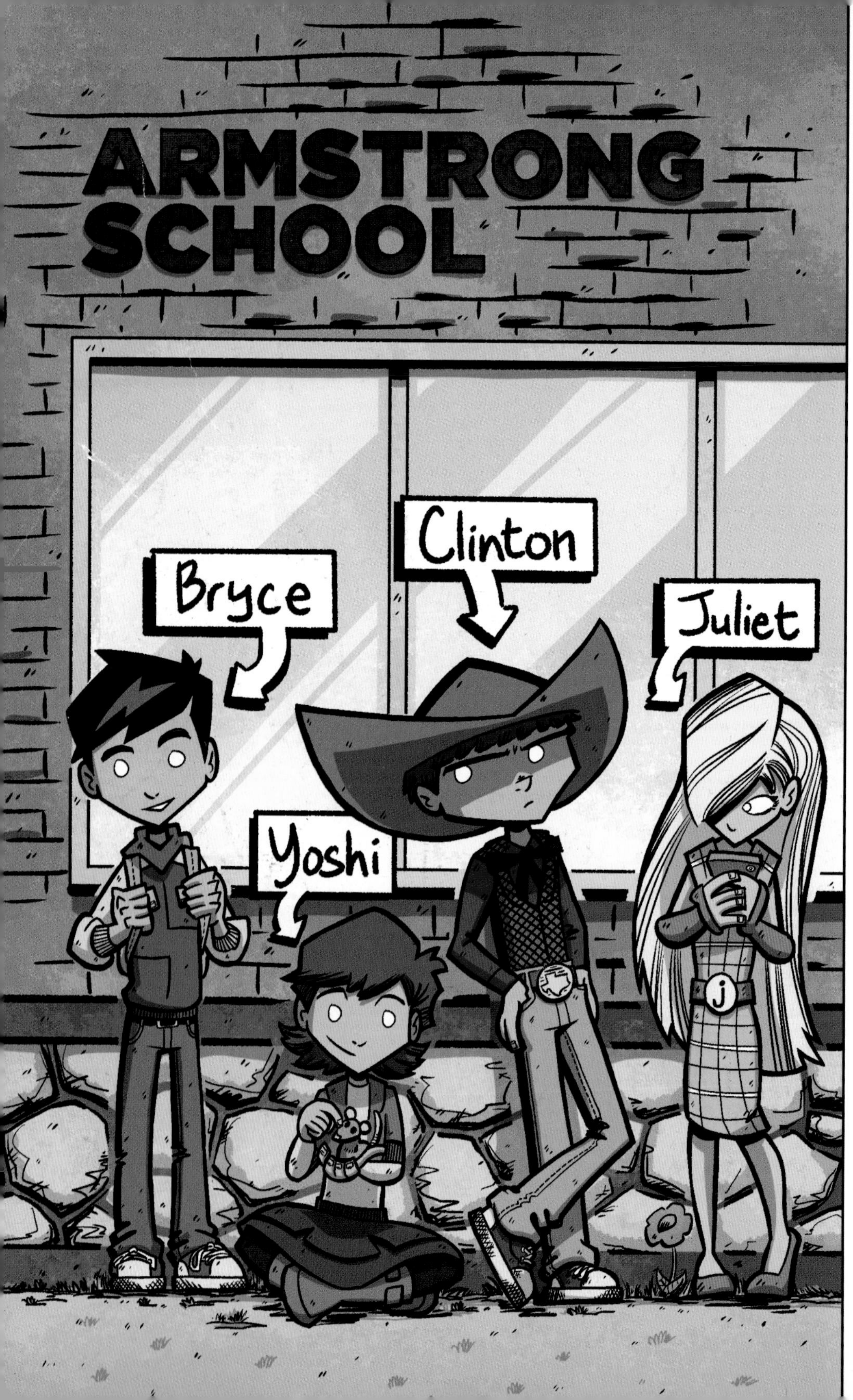
ARMSTRONG SCHOOL
Bryce
Clinton
Juliet
Yoshi

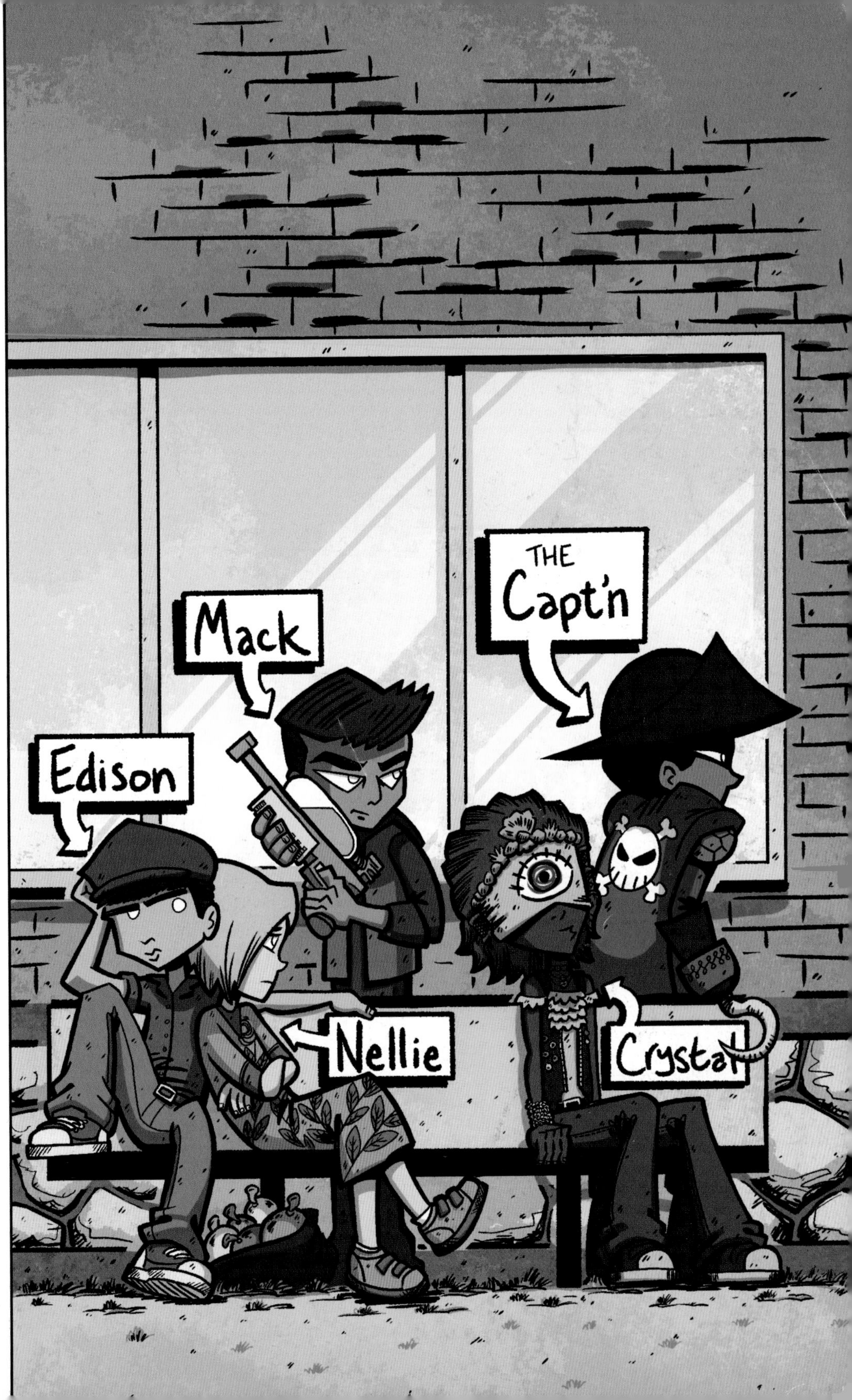
THE Capt'n
Mack
Edison
Nellie
Crystal

00 THE PROLOGUE

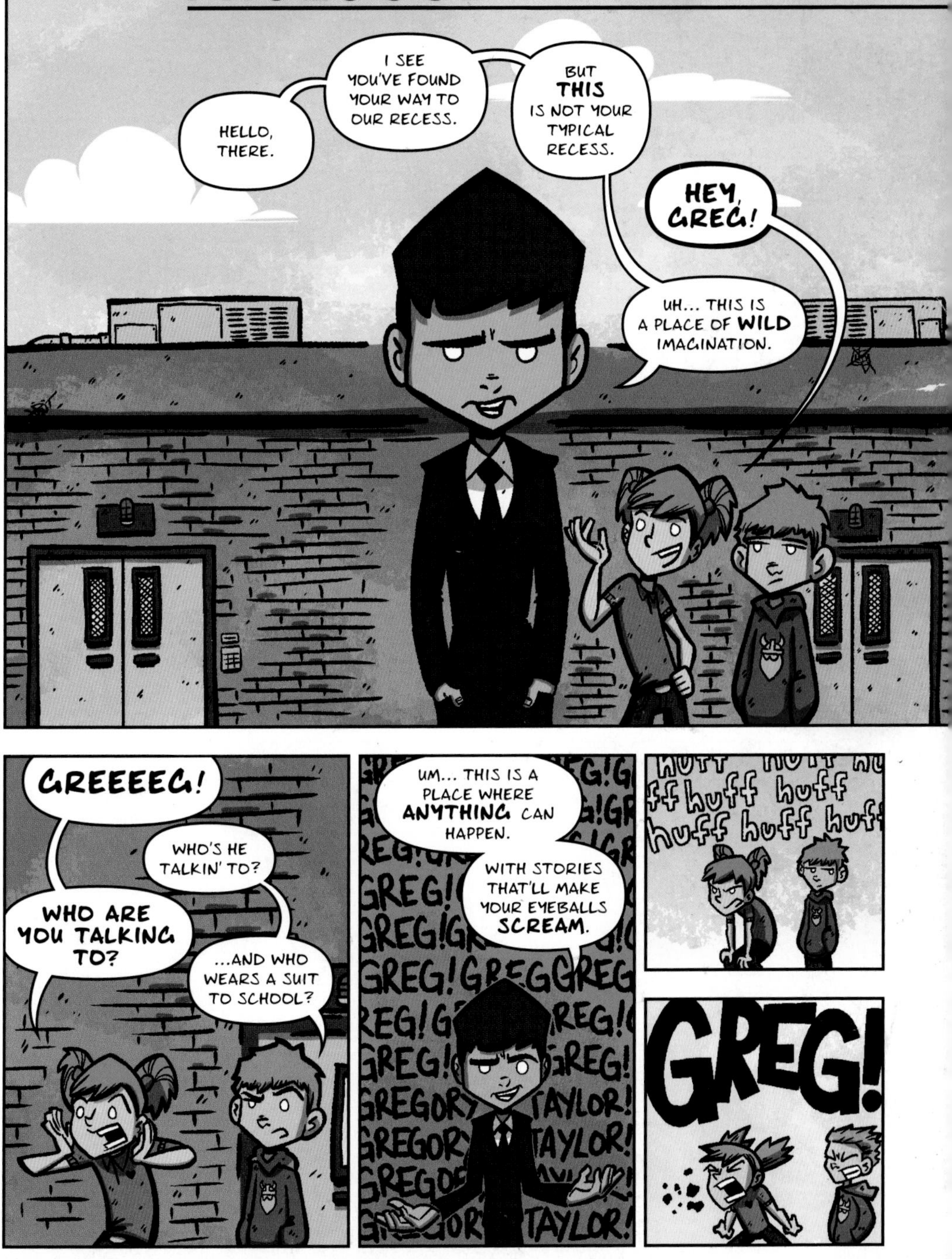

HELLO, THERE.
I SEE YOU'VE FOUND YOUR WAY TO OUR RECESS.
BUT THIS IS NOT YOUR TYPICAL RECESS.
UH... THIS IS A PLACE OF WILD IMAGINATION.
HEY, GREG!
GREEEEG!
WHO'S HE TALKIN' TO?
WHO ARE YOU TALKING TO?
...AND WHO WEARS A SUIT TO SCHOOL?
UM... THIS IS A PLACE WHERE ANYTHING CAN HAPPEN.
WITH STORIES THAT'LL MAKE YOUR EYEBALLS SCREAM.
GREG! GREG! GREGORY TAYLOR!
huff huff huff huff huff
GREG!

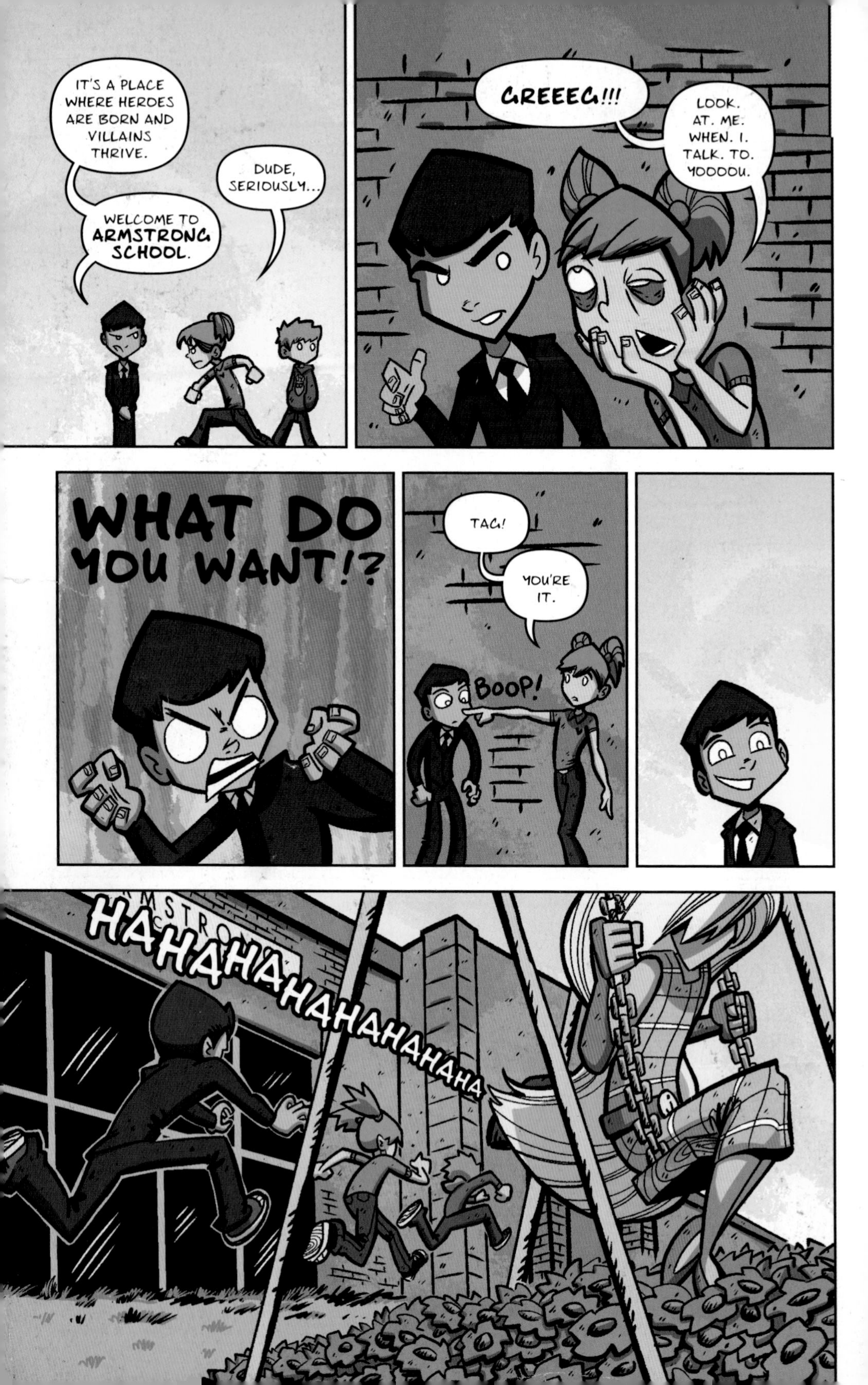
IT'S A PLACE WHERE HEROES ARE BORN AND VILLAINS THRIVE.
WELCOME TO ARMSTRONG SCHOOL.
DUDE, SERIOUSLY...
GREEEG!!!
LOOK. AT. ME. WHEN. I. TALK. TO. YOOOOU.
WHAT DO YOU WANT!?
TAG!
YOU'RE IT.
BOOP!
HAHAHAHAHAHAHAHAHA

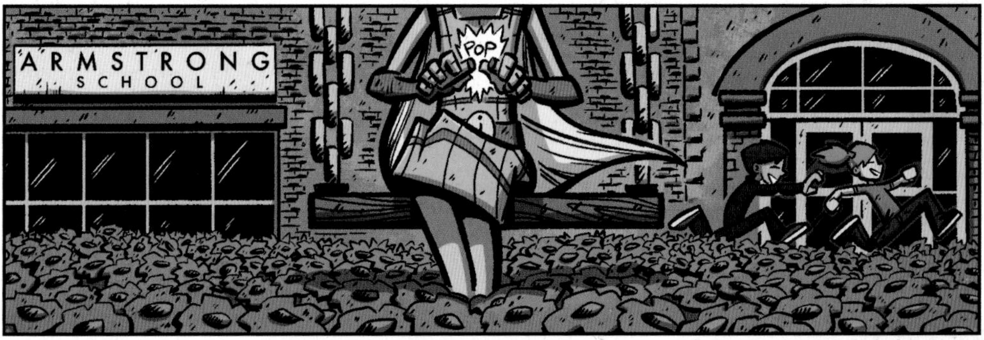
ARMSTRONG
SCHOOL
POP

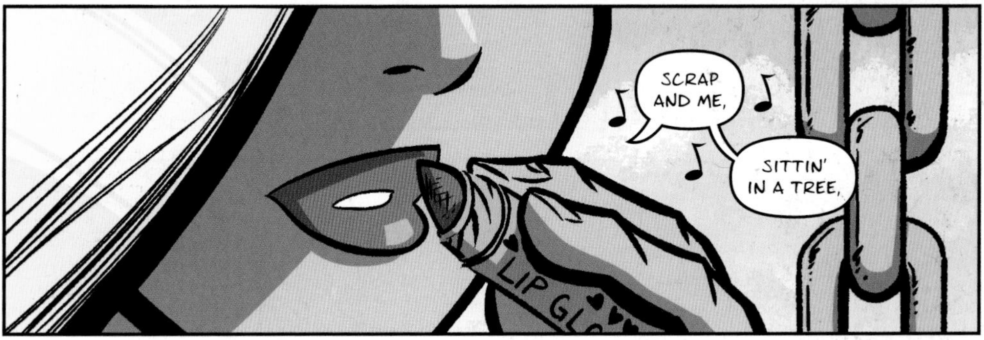
SCRAP AND ME,
SITTIN' IN A TREE,

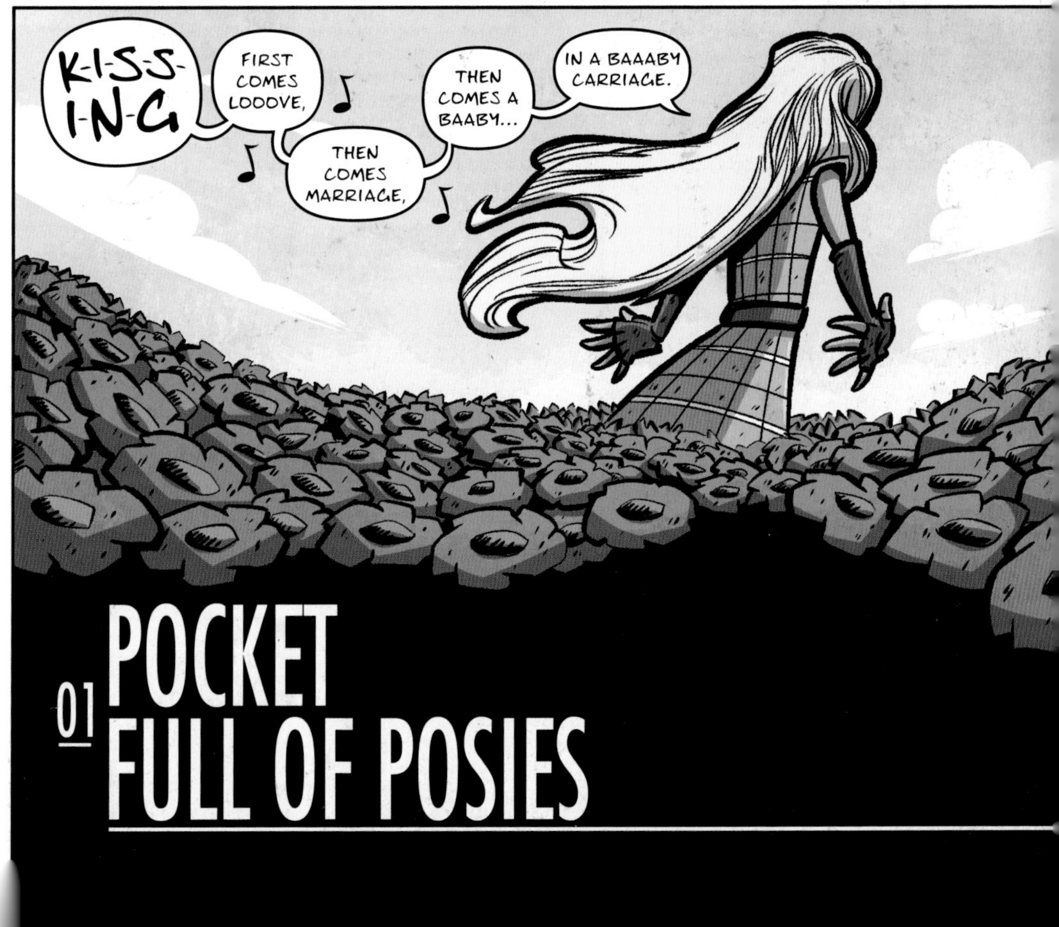
K-I-S-S-I-N-G
FIRST COMES LOOOVE,
THEN COMES MARRIAGE,
THEN COMES A BAABY...
IN A BAAABY CARRIAGE.

01 POCKET FULL OF POSIES

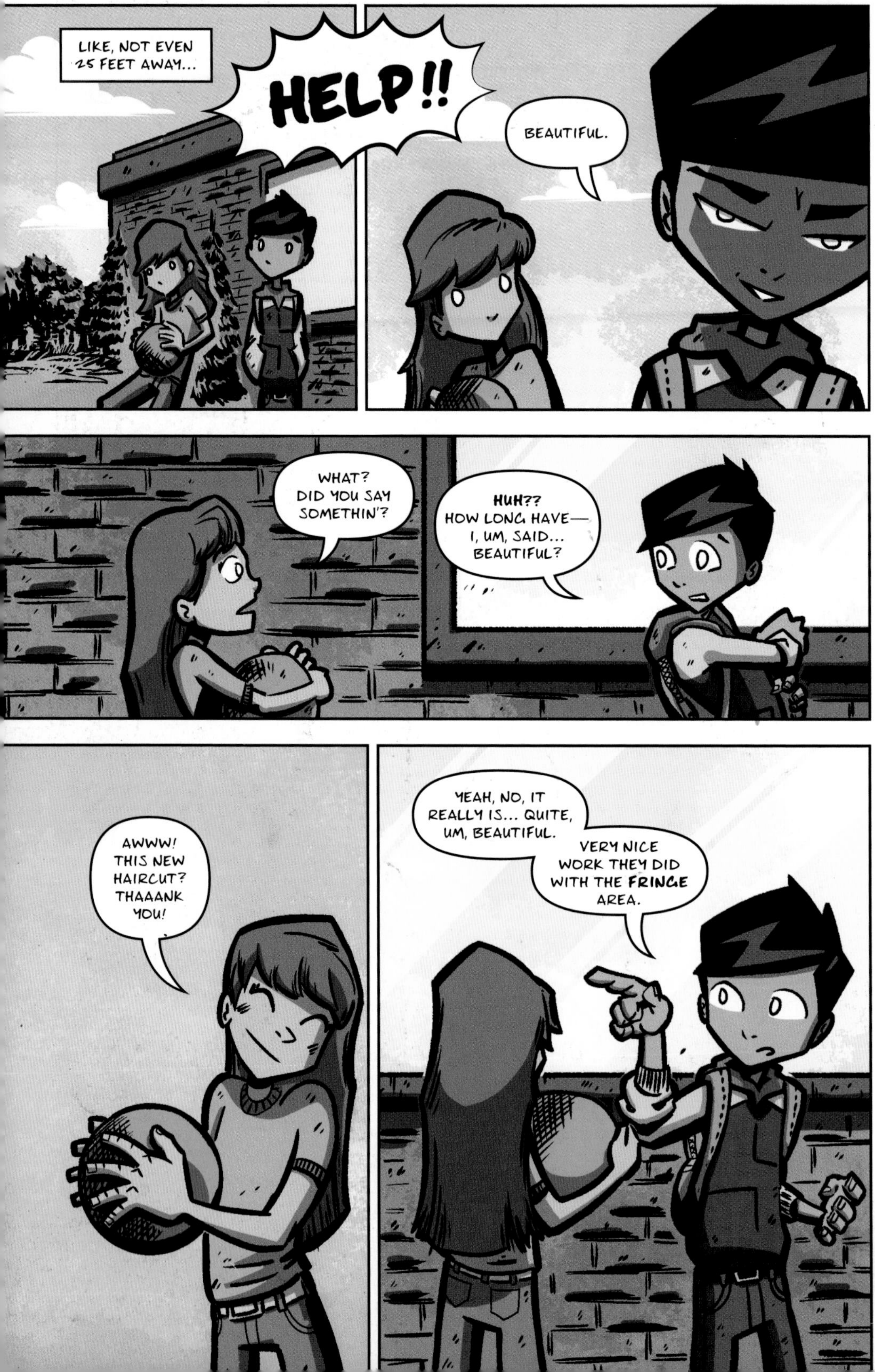
LIKE, NOT EVEN 25 FEET AWAY...
HELP!!
BEAUTIFUL.
WHAT? DID YOU SAY SOMETHIN'?
HUH?? HOW LONG HAVE— I, UM, SAID... BEAUTIFUL?
AWWW! THIS NEW HAIRCUT? THAAANK YOU!
YEAH, NO, IT REALLY IS... QUITE, UM, BEAUTIFUL.
VERY NICE WORK THEY DID WITH THE FRINGE AREA.

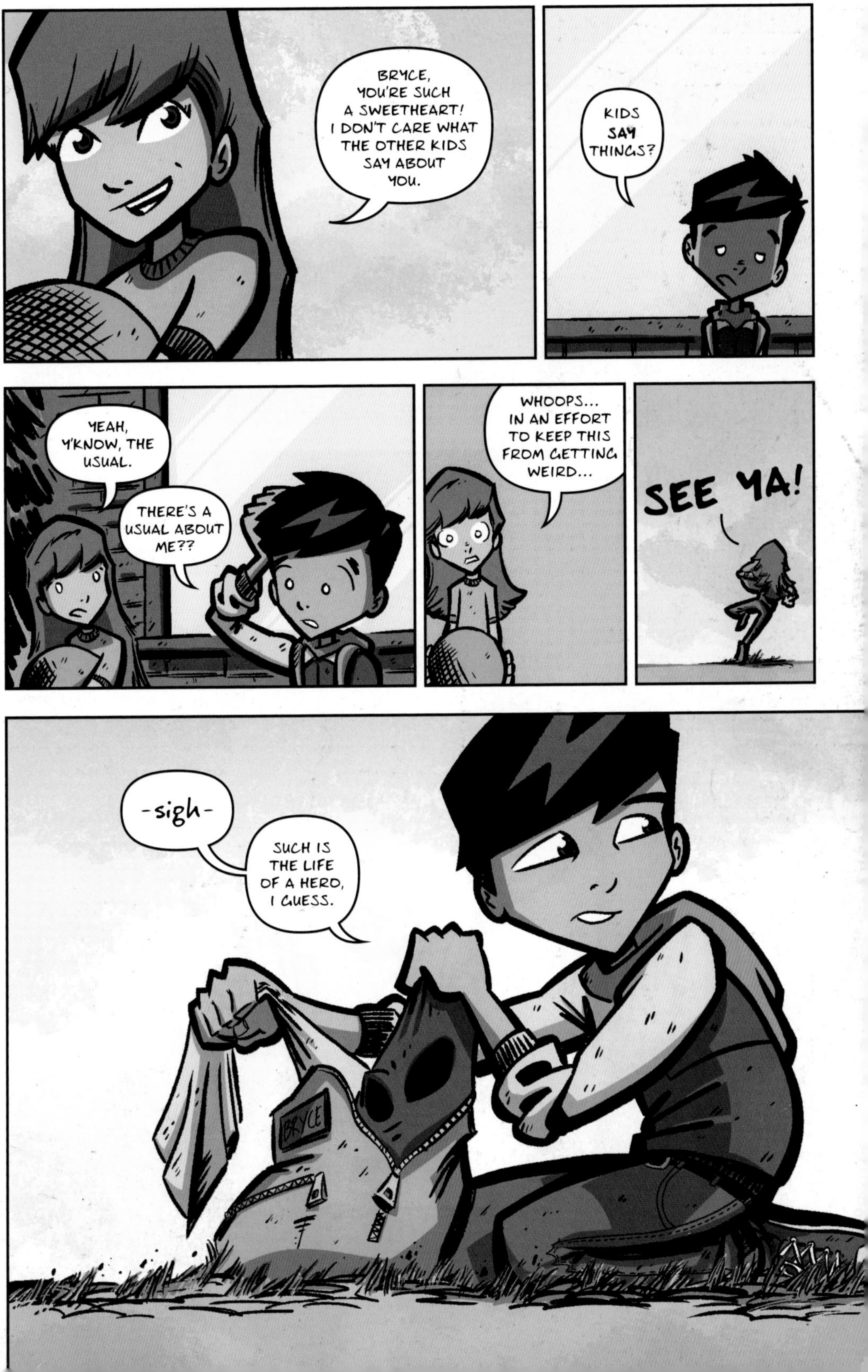
BRYCE, YOU'RE SUCH A SWEETHEART! I DON'T CARE WHAT THE OTHER KIDS SAY ABOUT YOU.
KIDS SAY THINGS?
YEAH, Y'KNOW, THE USUAL.
THERE'S A USUAL ABOUT ME??
WHOOPS... IN AN EFFORT TO KEEP THIS FROM GETTING WEIRD...
SEE YA!
-sigh-
SUCH IS THE LIFE OF A HERO, I GUESS.
BRYCE

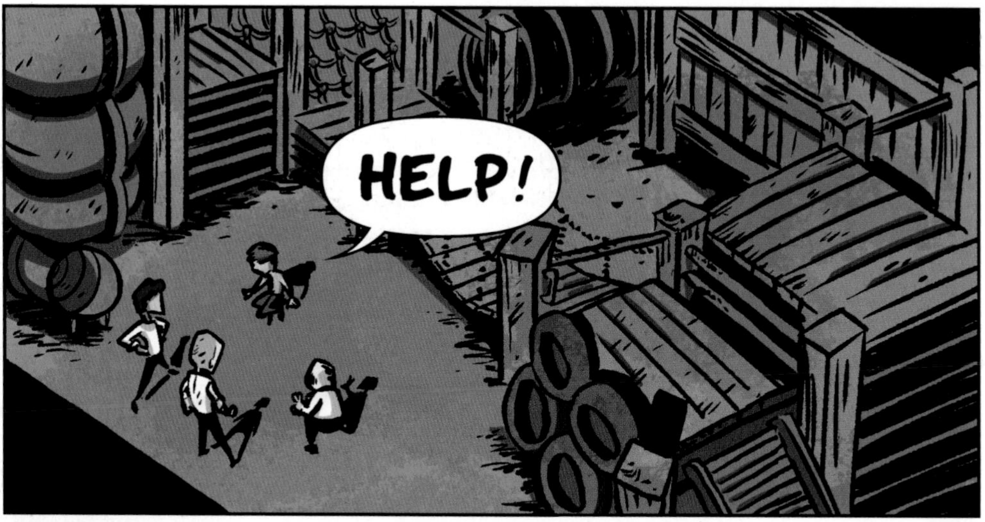
HELP!

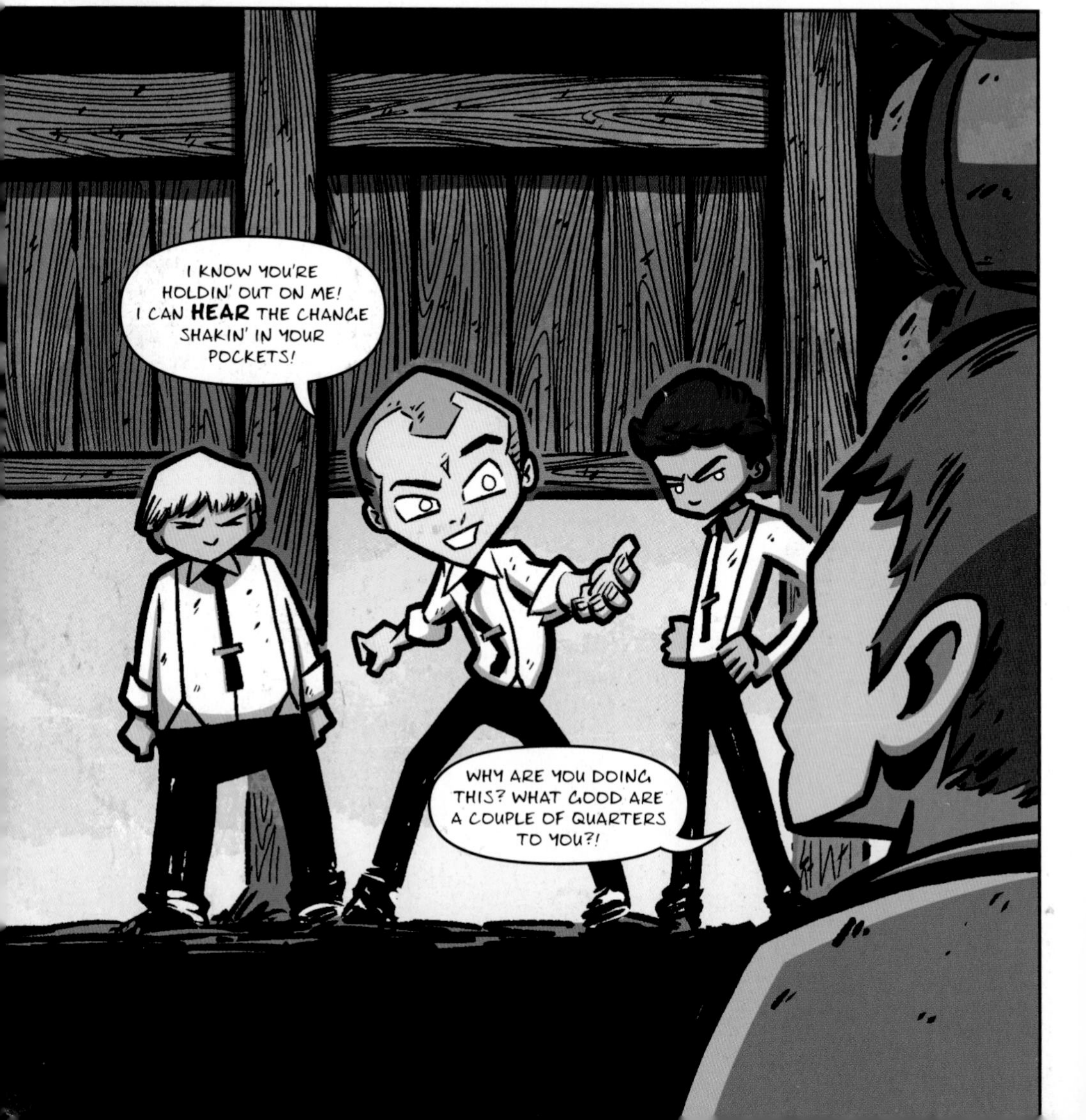
I KNOW YOU'RE HOLDIN' OUT ON ME! I CAN **HEAR** THE CHANGE SHAKIN' IN YOUR POCKETS!
WHY ARE YOU DOING THIS? WHAT GOOD ARE A COUPLE OF QUARTERS TO YOU?!

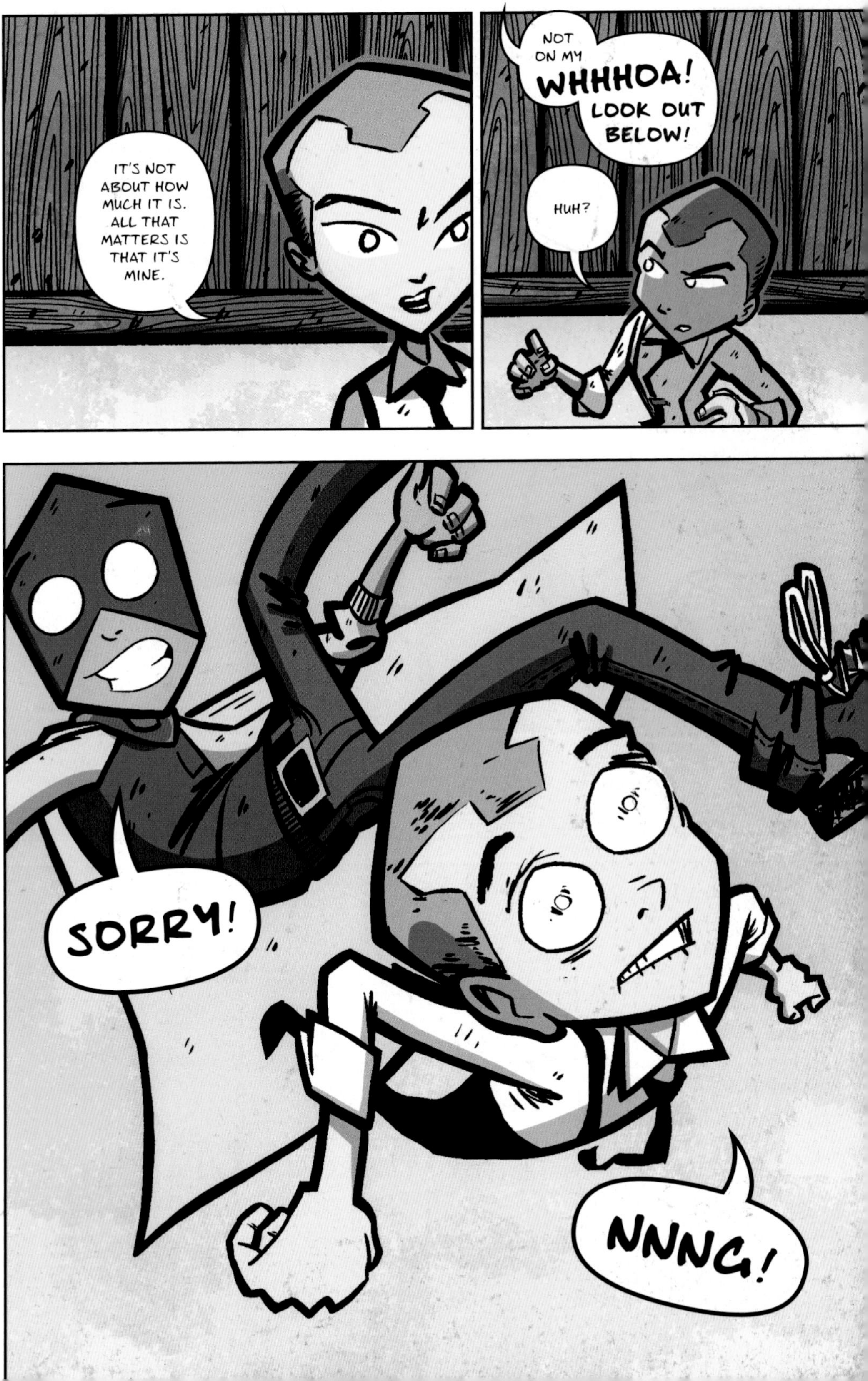
IT'S NOT ABOUT HOW MUCH IT IS. ALL THAT MATTERS IS THAT IT'S MINE.
NOT ON MY WHHHOA! LOOK OUT BELOW!
HUH?
SORRY!
NNNG!

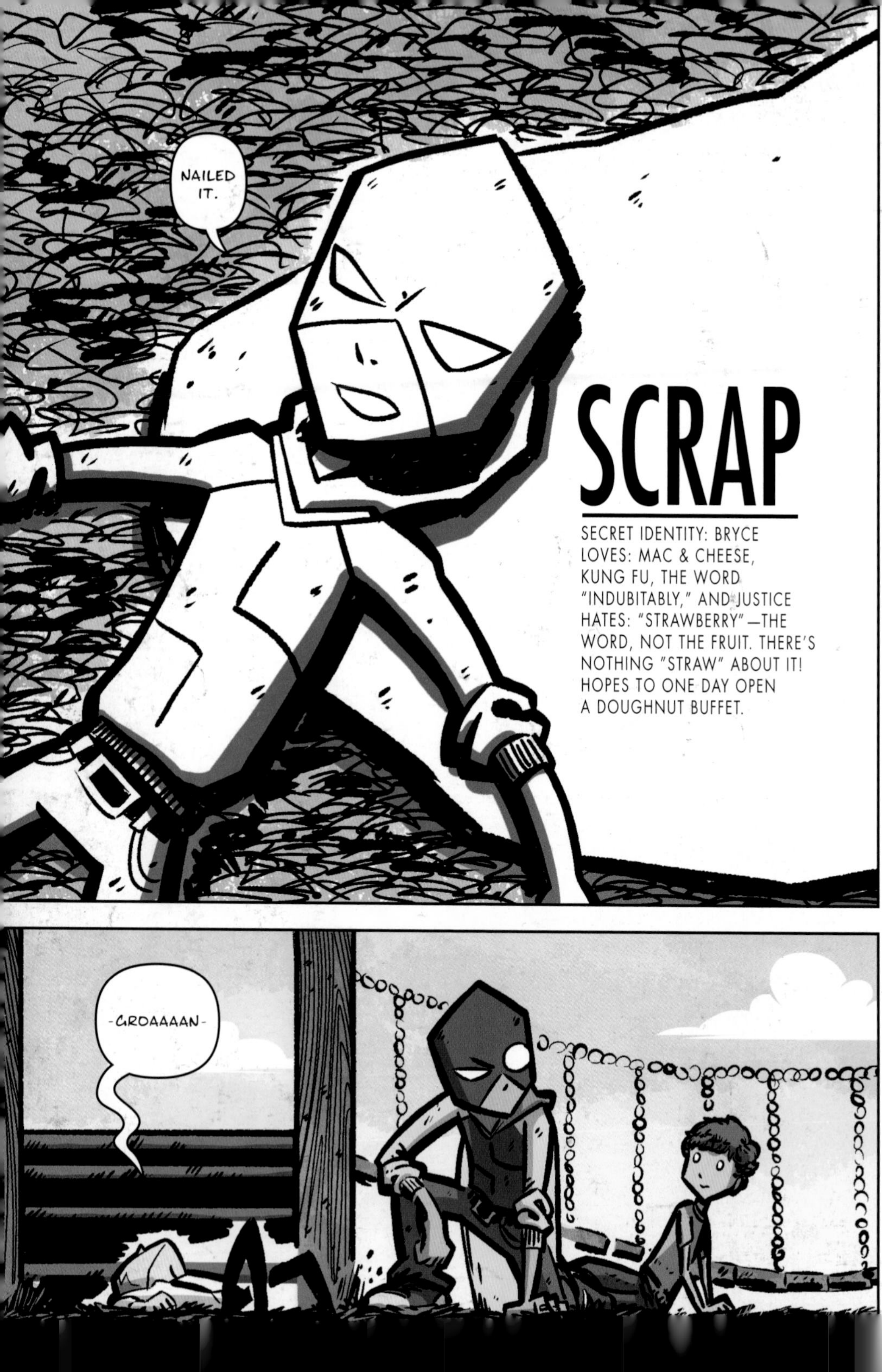
NAILED IT.
SCRAP
SECRET IDENTITY: BRYCE
LOVES: MAC & CHEESE, KUNG FU, THE WORD "INDUBITABLY," AND JUSTICE
HATES: "STRAWBERRY"—THE WORD, NOT THE FRUIT. THERE'S NOTHING "STRAW" ABOUT IT!
HOPES TO ONE DAY OPEN A DOUGHNUT BUFFET.
-GROAAAAN-

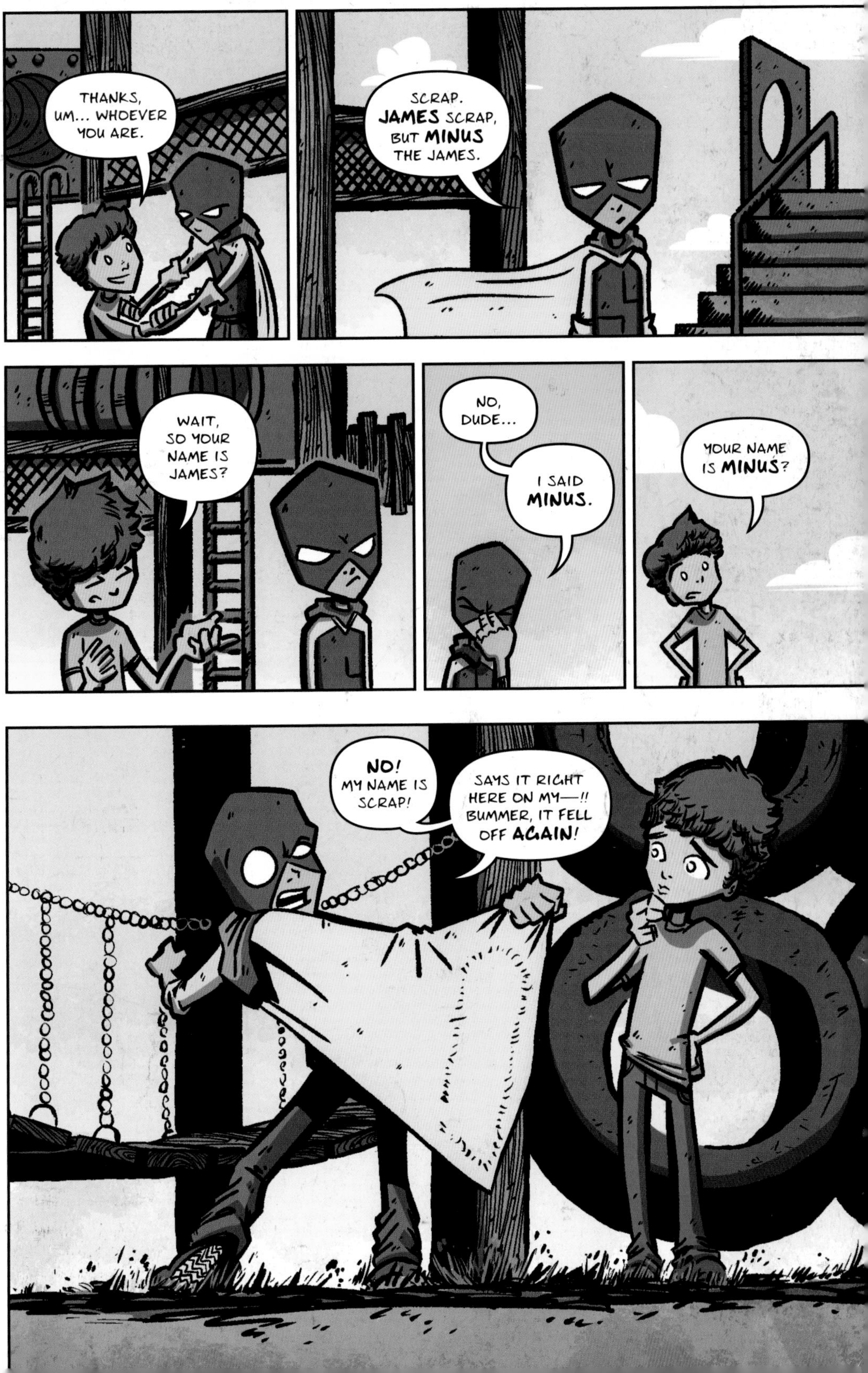
THANKS, UM... WHOEVER YOU ARE.
SCRAP. **JAMES** SCRAP, BUT **MINUS** THE JAMES.
WAIT, SO YOUR NAME IS JAMES?
NO, DUDE...
I SAID **MINUS.**
YOUR NAME IS **MINUS**?
NO! MY NAME IS SCRAP!
SAYS IT RIGHT HERE ON MY—!! BUMMER, IT FELL OFF **AGAIN**!

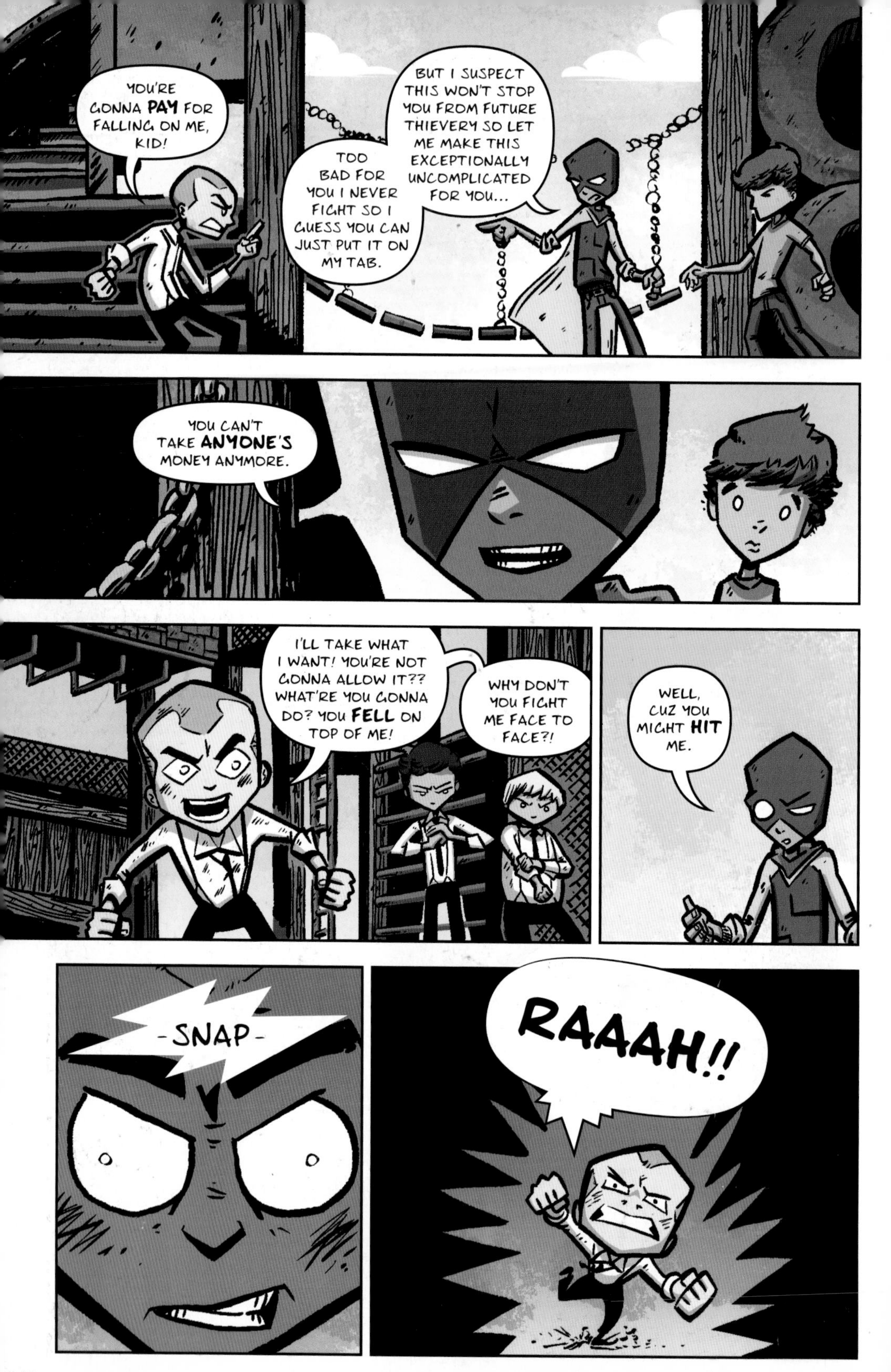
YOU'RE GONNA PAY FOR FALLING ON ME, KID!
BUT I SUSPECT THIS WON'T STOP YOU FROM FUTURE THIEVERY SO LET ME MAKE THIS EXCEPTIONALLY UNCOMPLICATED FOR YOU...
TOO BAD FOR YOU I NEVER FIGHT SO I GUESS YOU CAN JUST PUT IT ON MY TAB.
YOU CAN'T TAKE ANYONE'S MONEY ANYMORE.
I'LL TAKE WHAT I WANT! YOU'RE NOT GONNA ALLOW IT?? WHAT'RE YOU GONNA DO? YOU FELL ON TOP OF ME!
WHY DON'T YOU FIGHT ME FACE TO FACE?!
WELL, CUZ YOU MIGHT HIT ME.
-SNAP-
RAAAH!!

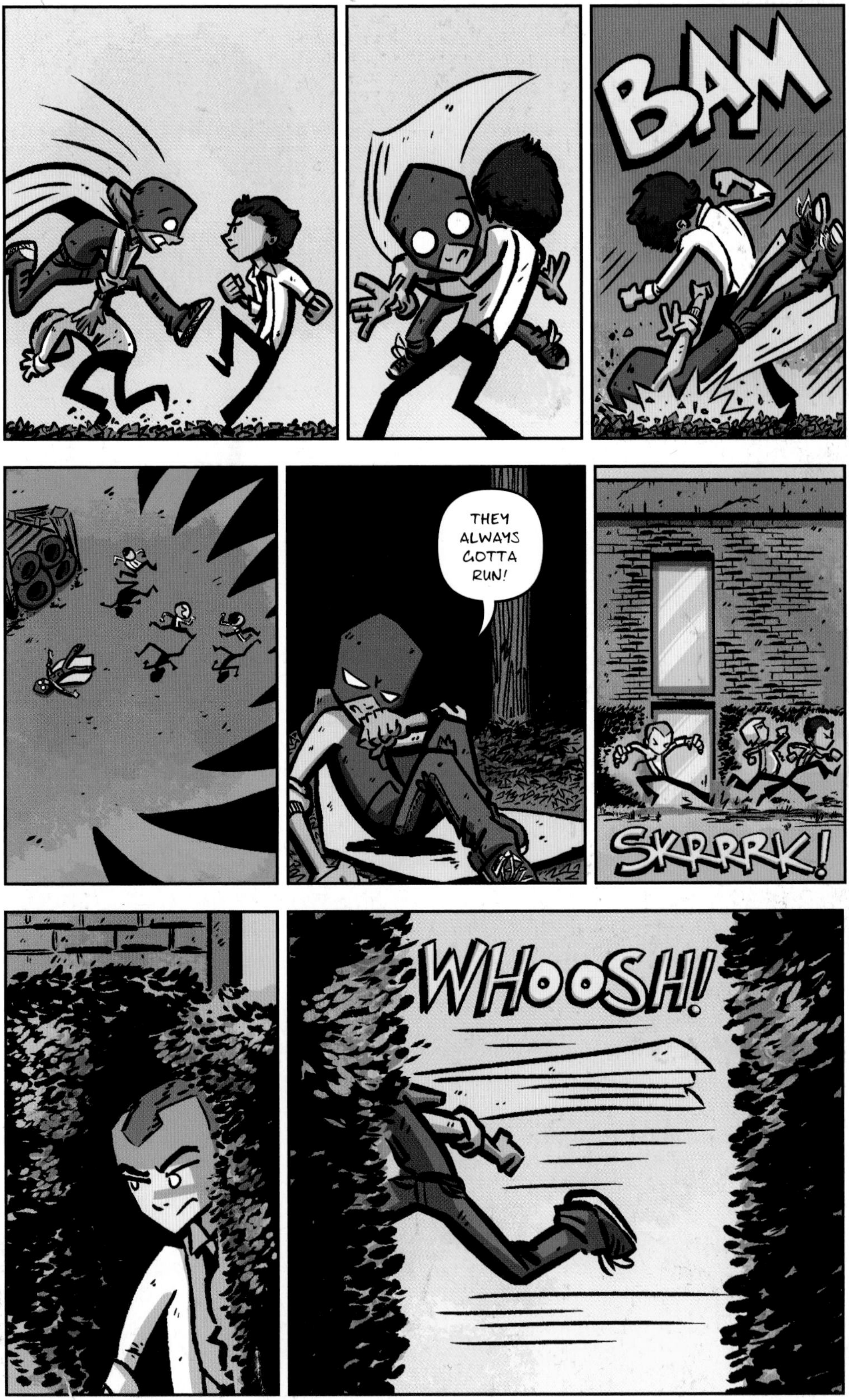
BAM
THEY ALWAYS GOTTA RUN!
SKRRRK!
WHOOSH!

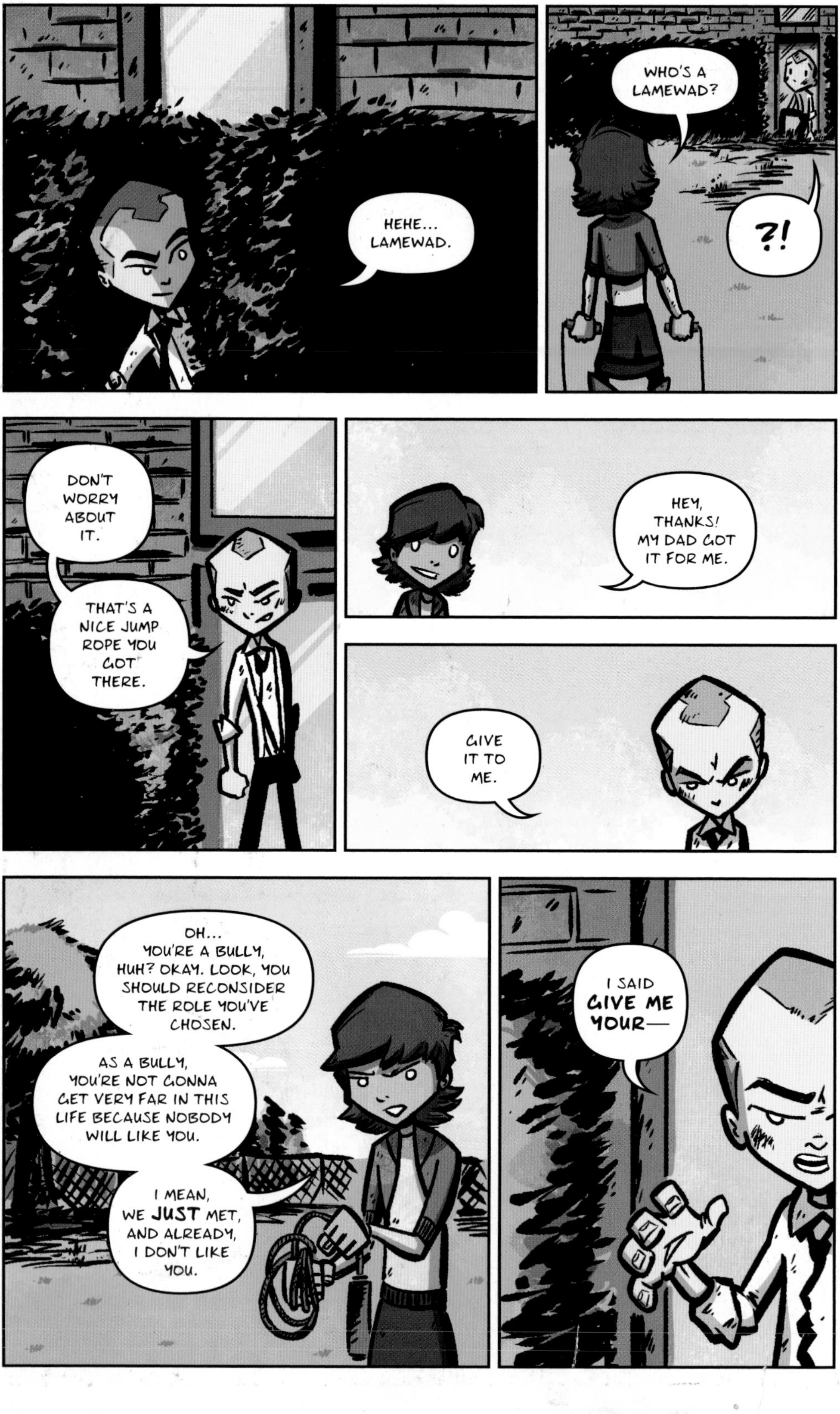
HEHE... LAMEWAD.
WHO'S A LAMEWAD?
?!
DON'T WORRY ABOUT IT.
THAT'S A NICE JUMP ROPE YOU GOT THERE.
HEY, THANKS! MY DAD GOT IT FOR ME.
GIVE IT TO ME.
OH... YOU'RE A BULLY, HUH? OKAY. LOOK, YOU SHOULD RECONSIDER THE ROLE YOU'VE CHOSEN.
AS A BULLY, YOU'RE NOT GONNA GET VERY FAR IN THIS LIFE BECAUSE NOBODY WILL LIKE YOU.
I MEAN, WE **JUST** MET, AND ALREADY, I DON'T LIKE YOU.
I SAID **GIVE ME YOUR—**

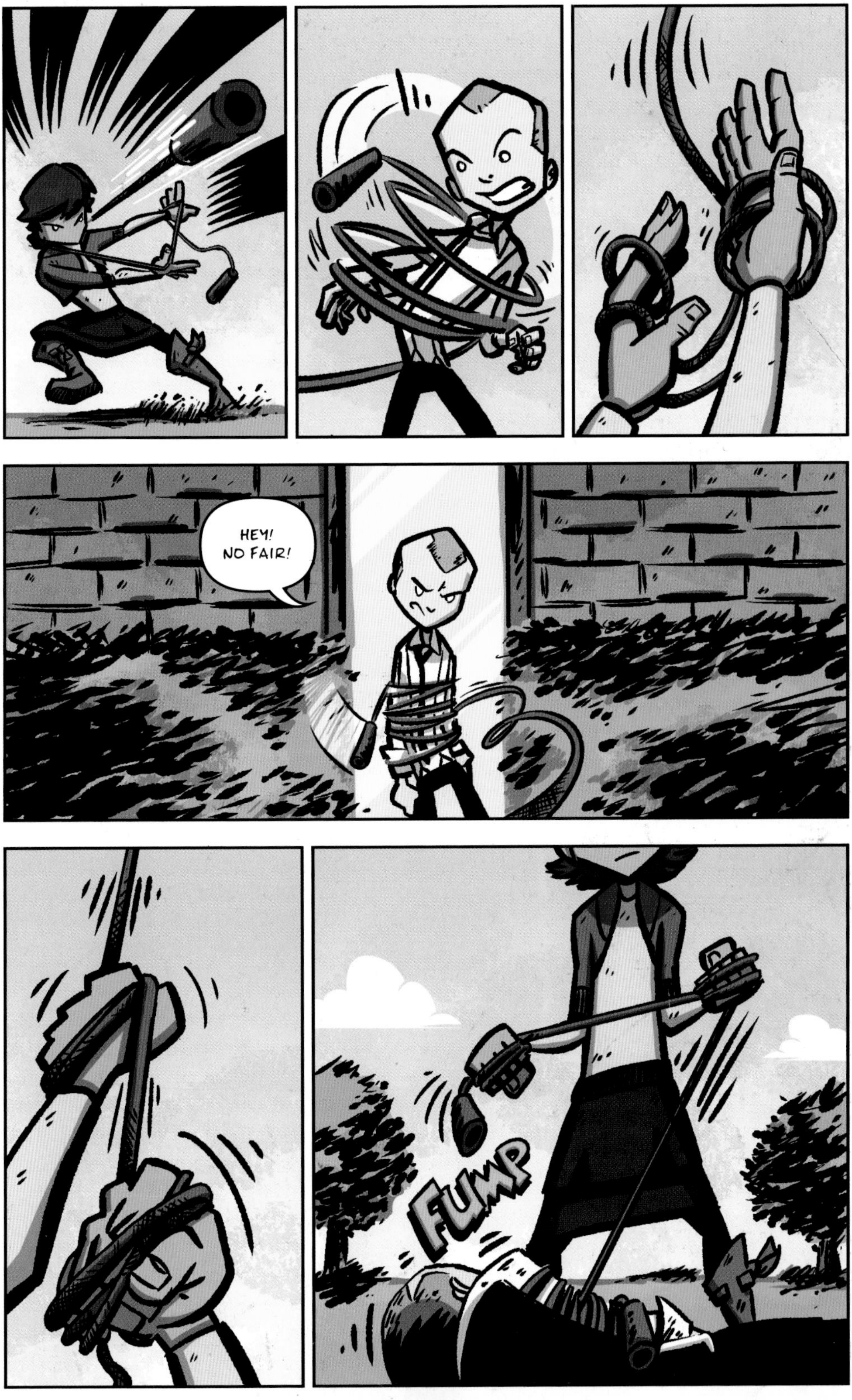
HEY!
NO FAIR!
FUMP

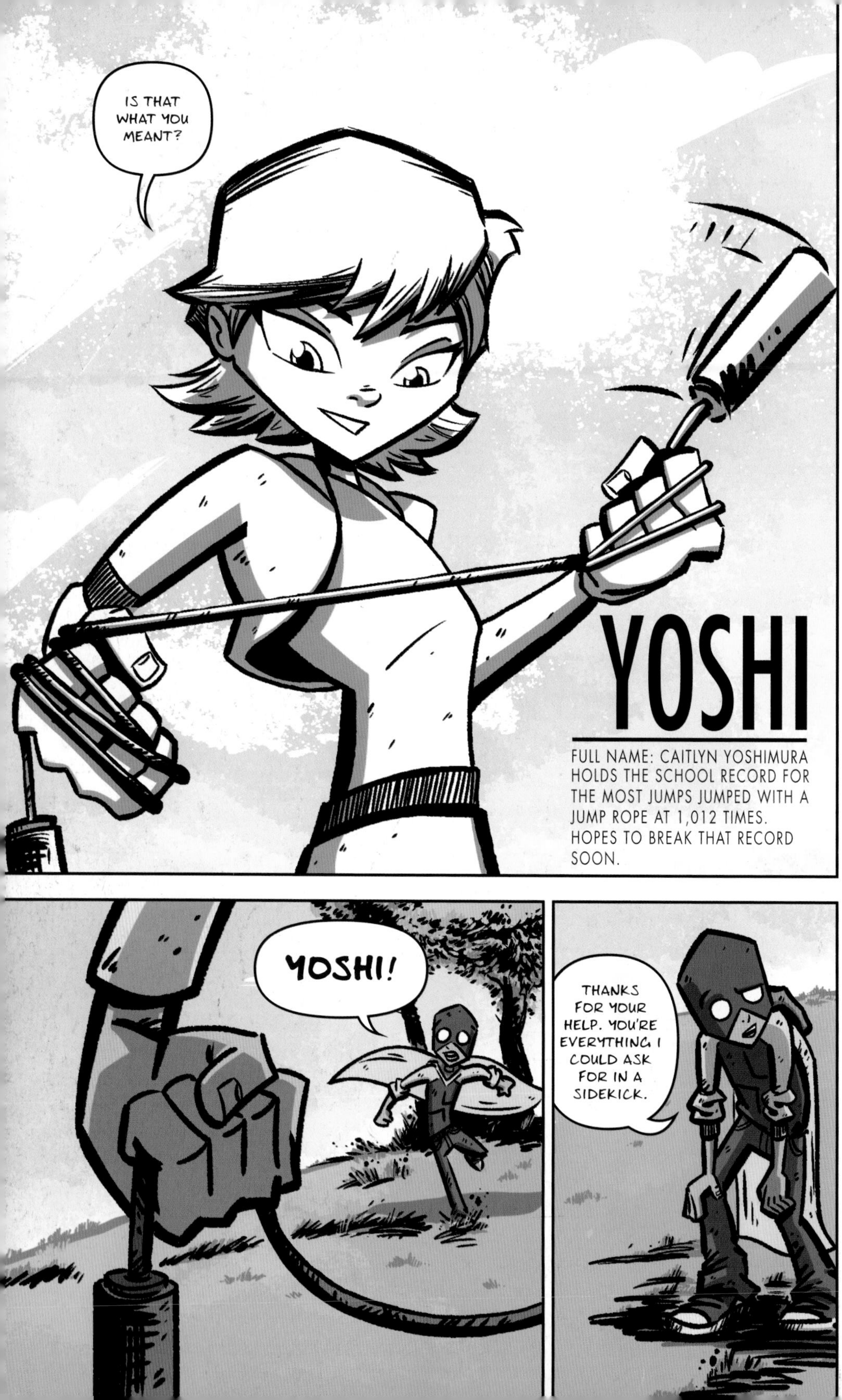
IS THAT WHAT YOU MEANT?
YOSHI
FULL NAME: CAITLYN YOSHIMURA
HOLDS THE SCHOOL RECORD FOR THE MOST JUMPS JUMPED WITH A JUMP ROPE AT 1,012 TIMES. HOPES TO BREAK THAT RECORD SOON.
YOSHI!
THANKS FOR YOUR HELP. YOU'RE EVERYTHING I COULD ASK FOR IN A SIDEKICK.

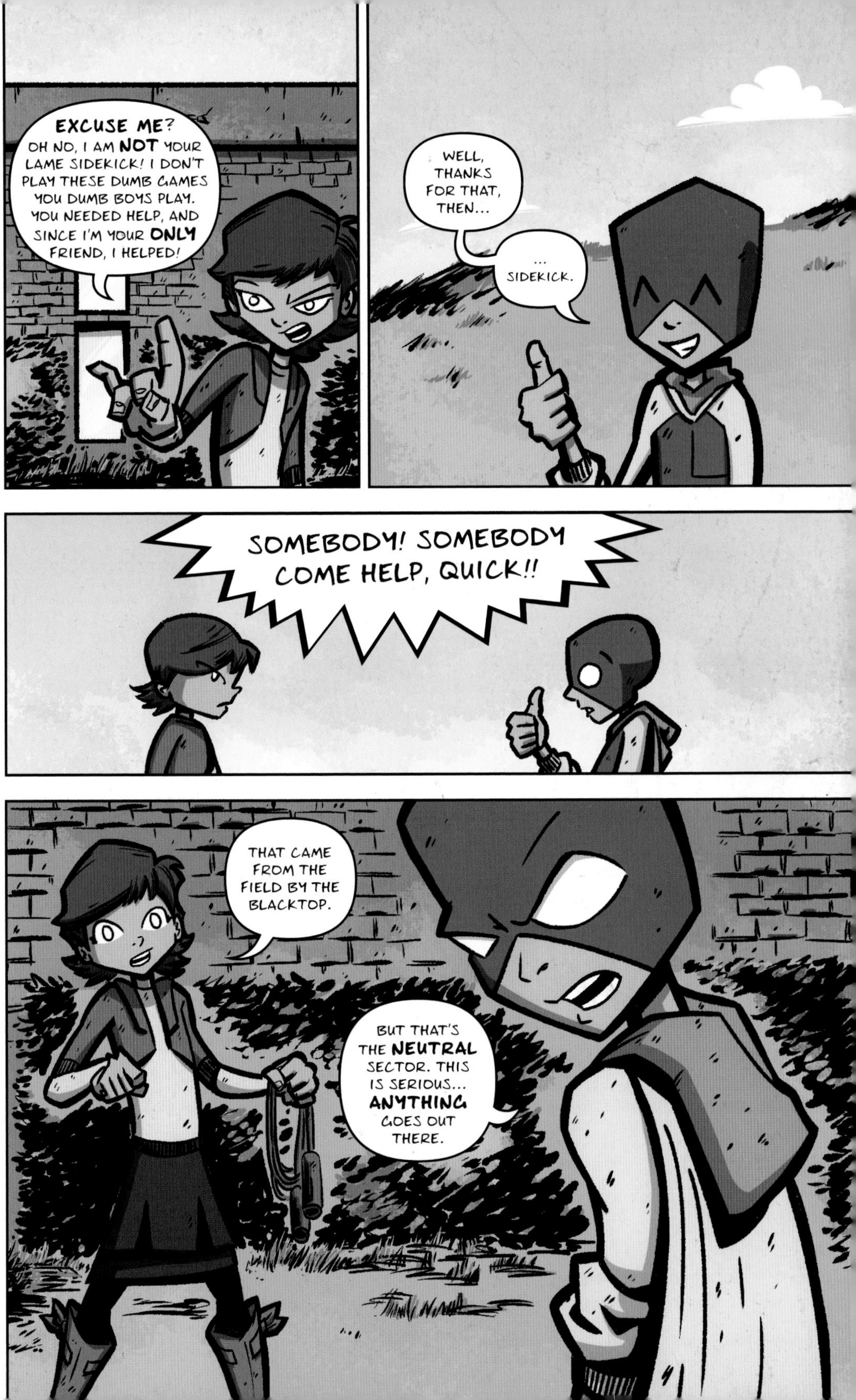
EXCUSE ME? OH NO, I AM NOT YOUR LAME SIDEKICK! I DON'T PLAY THESE DUMB GAMES YOU DUMB BOYS PLAY. YOU NEEDED HELP, AND SINCE I'M YOUR ONLY FRIEND, I HELPED!
WELL, THANKS FOR THAT, THEN...
...SIDEKICK.
SOMEBODY! SOMEBODY COME HELP, QUICK!!
THAT CAME FROM THE FIELD BY THE BLACKTOP.
BUT THAT'S THE NEUTRAL SECTOR. THIS IS SERIOUS... ANYTHING GOES OUT THERE.

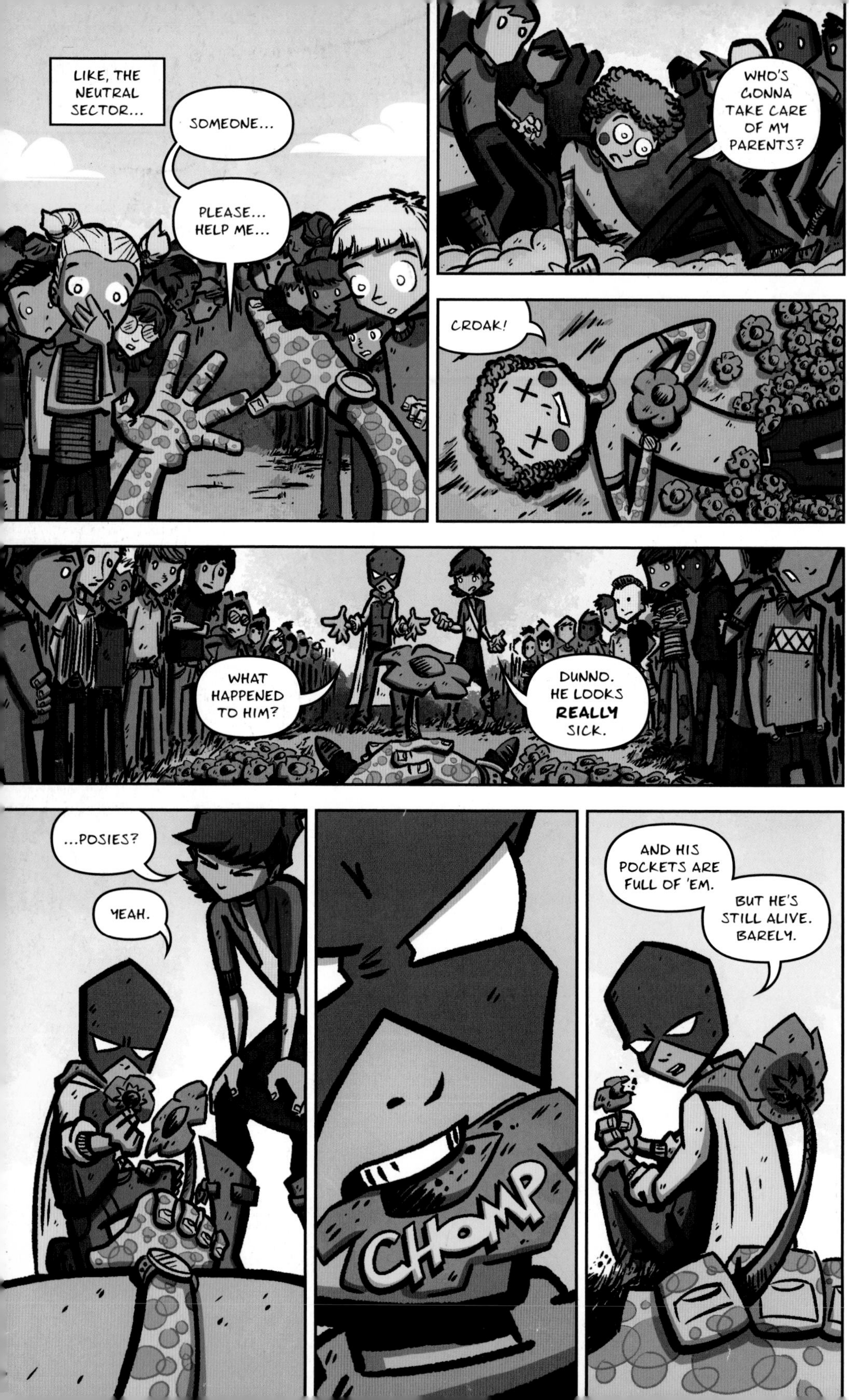
LIKE, THE NEUTRAL SECTOR...
SOMEONE...
PLEASE... HELP ME...
WHO'S GONNA TAKE CARE OF MY PARENTS?
CROAK!
WHAT HAPPENED TO HIM?
DUNNO. HE LOOKS **REALLY** SICK.
...POSIES?
YEAH.
CHOMP
AND HIS POCKETS ARE FULL OF 'EM.
BUT HE'S STILL ALIVE. BARELY.

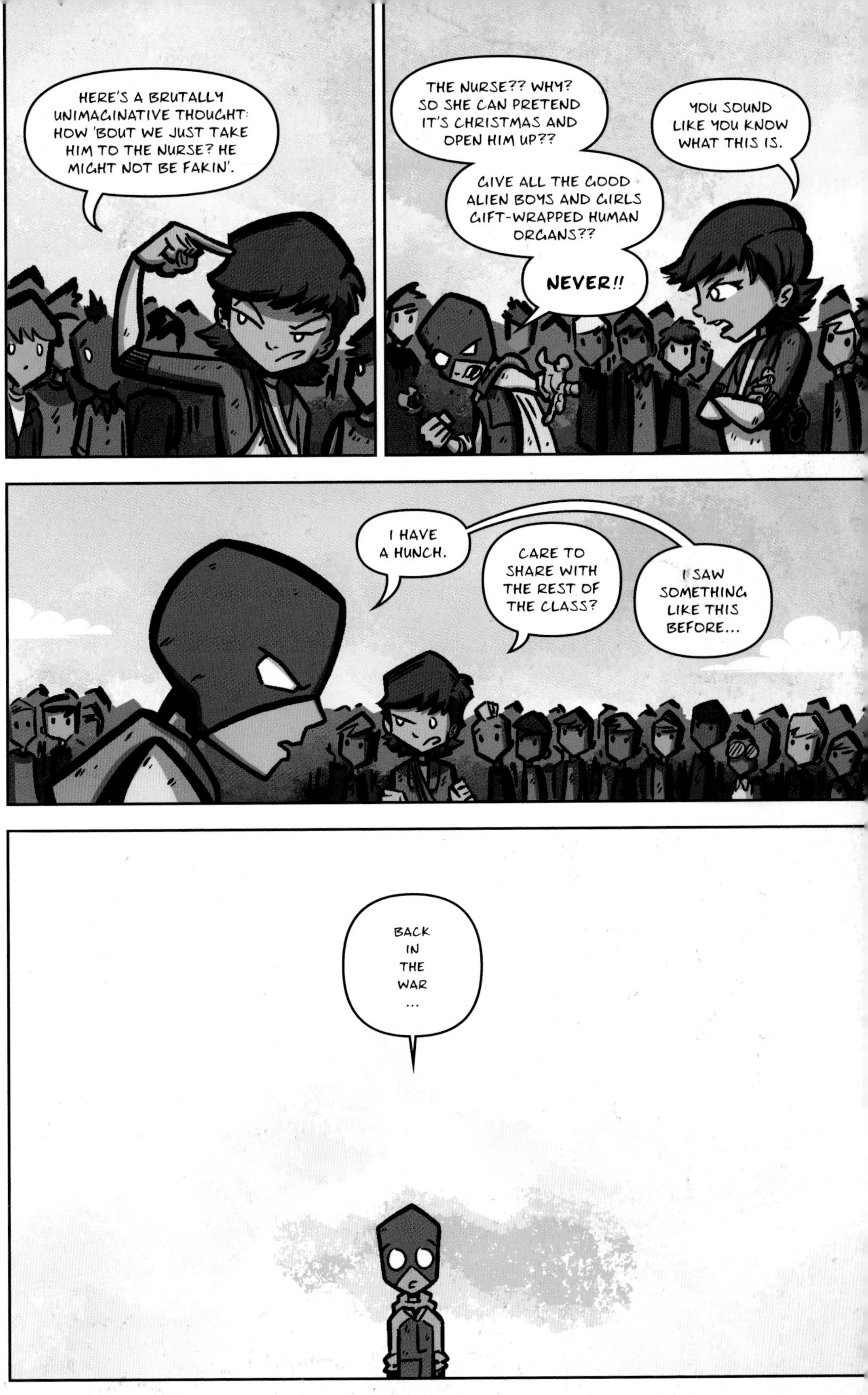
HERE'S A BRUTALLY UNIMAGINATIVE THOUGHT: HOW 'BOUT WE JUST TAKE HIM TO THE NURSE? HE MIGHT NOT BE FAKIN'.
THE NURSE?? WHY? SO SHE CAN PRETEND IT'S CHRISTMAS AND OPEN HIM UP??
GIVE ALL THE GOOD ALIEN BOYS AND GIRLS GIFT-WRAPPED HUMAN ORGANS??
NEVER!!
YOU SOUND LIKE YOU KNOW WHAT THIS IS.
I HAVE A HUNCH.
CARE TO SHARE WITH THE REST OF THE CLASS?
I SAW SOMETHING LIKE THIS BEFORE...
BACK IN THE WAR ...

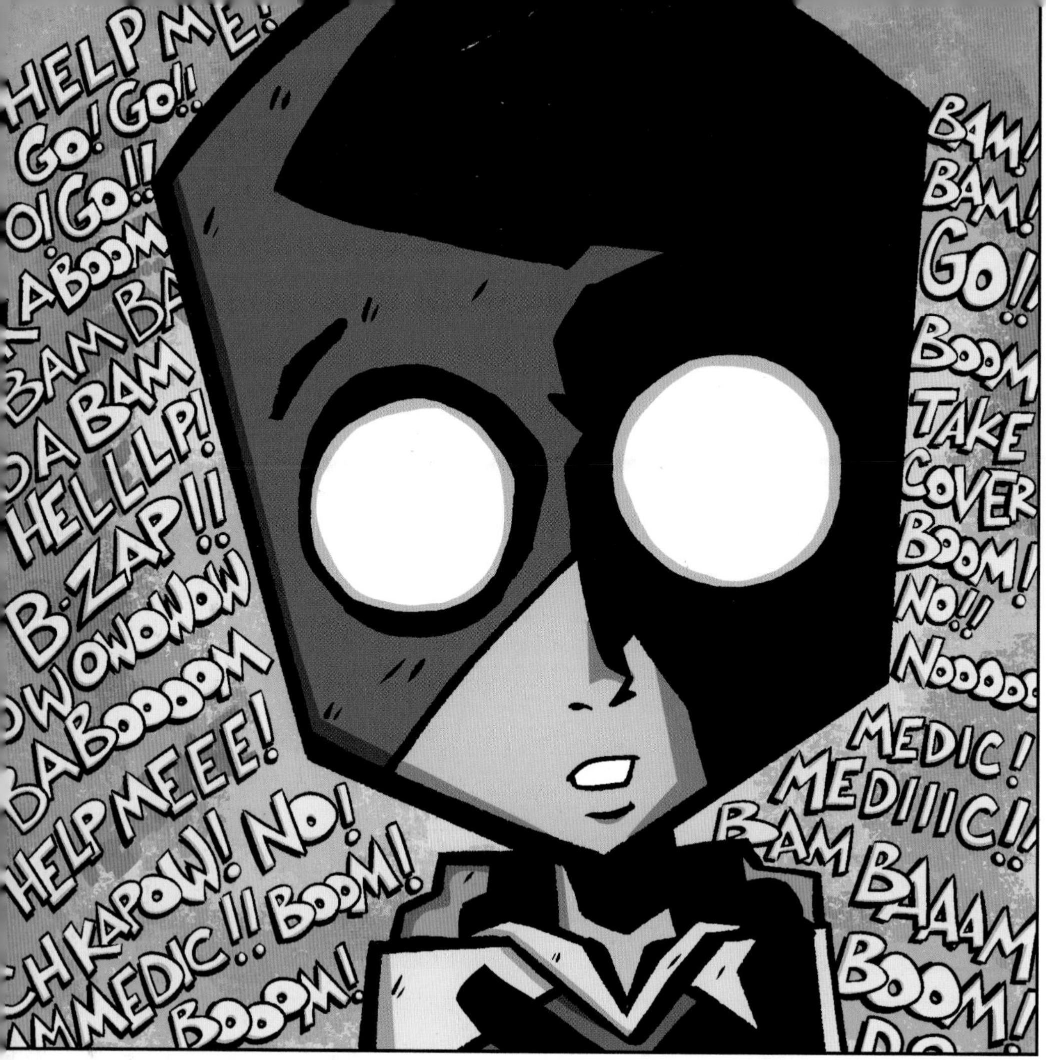
HELP ME!
GO! GO!!
GO!!
BAM
HELLLP!
ZAP!!
B-ZAP
OWOWOW
HELP MEEEE!
KAPOW! NO!
MEDIC!! BOOM!
BOOOM!
BAM!
BAM!
GO!!
BOOM
TAKE COVER
BOOM!
NO!!
MEDIC!
MEDIIIC!!
BAM BAAAM
BOOM!

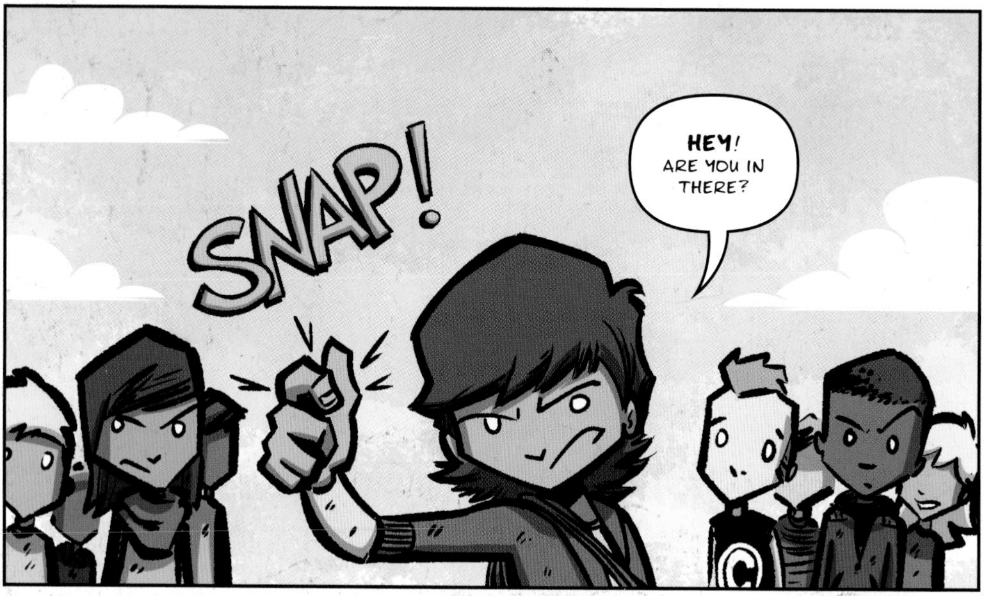
SNAP!
HEY! ARE YOU IN THERE?

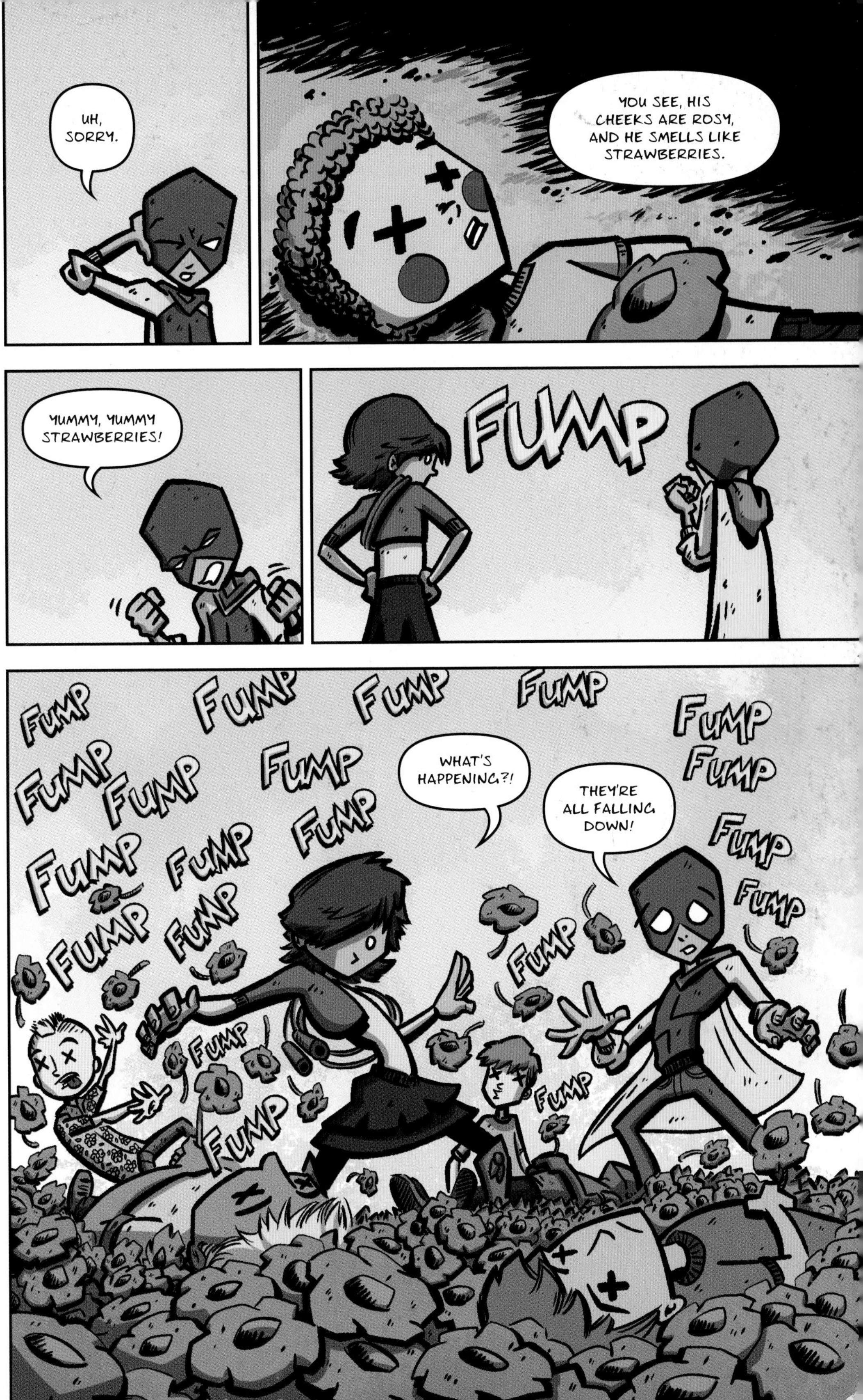
UH, SORRY.
YOU SEE, HIS CHEEKS ARE ROSY, AND HE SMELLS LIKE STRAWBERRIES.
YUMMY, YUMMY STRAWBERRIES!
FUMP
FUMP
FUMP
FUMP
FUMP
FUMP
FUMP
FUMP
FUMP
WHAT'S HAPPENING?!
THEY'RE ALL FALLING DOWN!
FUMP
FUMP
FUMP
FUMP
FUMP
FUMP
FUMP
FUMP
FUMP
FUMP
FUMP
FUMP

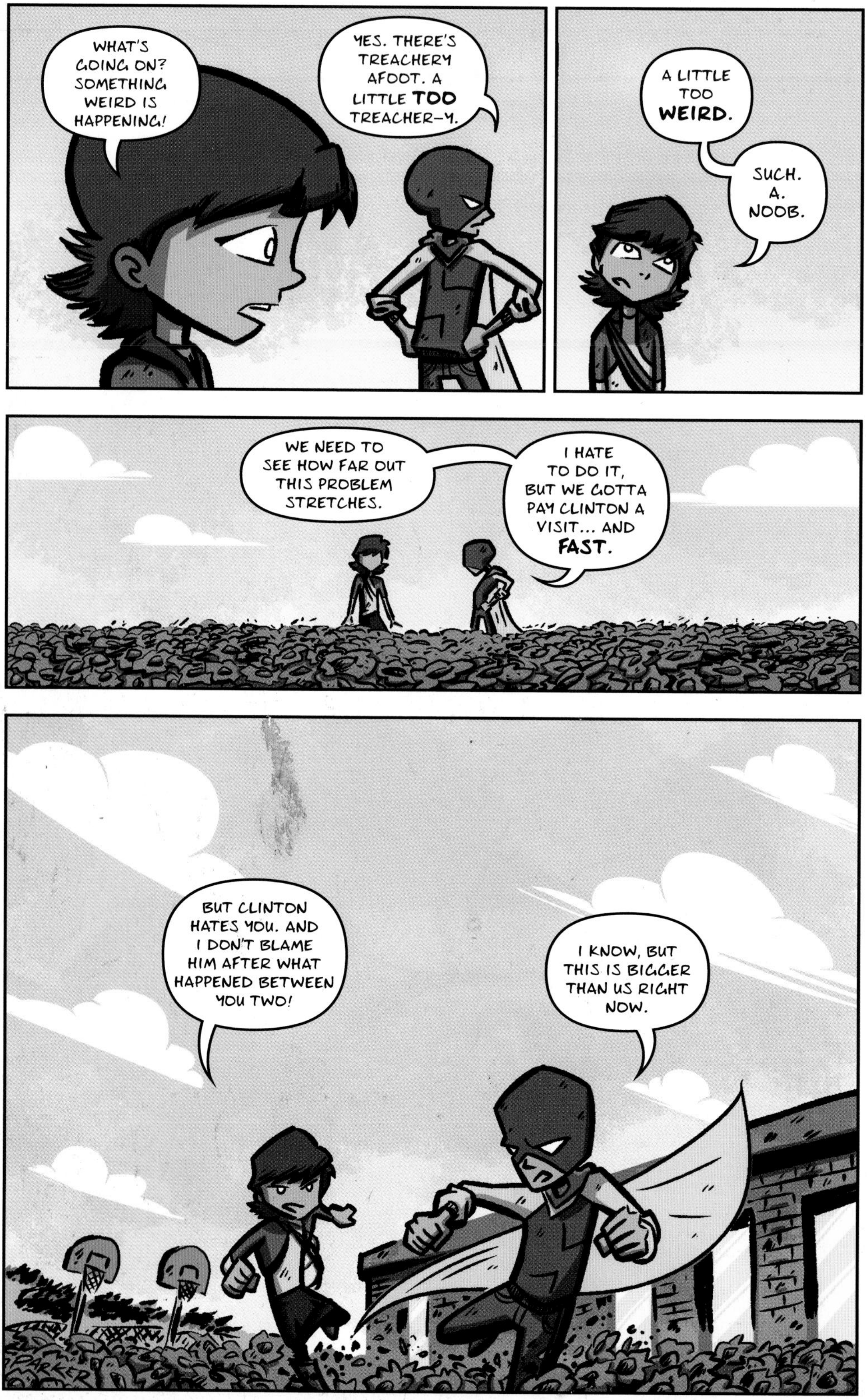
WHAT'S GOING ON? SOMETHING WEIRD IS HAPPENING!
YES. THERE'S TREACHERY AFOOT. A LITTLE **TOO** TREACHER-Y.
A LITTLE TOO **WEIRD.**
SUCH. A. NOOB.
WE NEED TO SEE HOW FAR OUT THIS PROBLEM STRETCHES.
I HATE TO DO IT, BUT WE GOTTA PAY CLINTON A VISIT... AND **FAST.**
BUT CLINTON HATES YOU. AND I DON'T BLAME HIM AFTER WHAT HAPPENED BETWEEN YOU TWO!
I KNOW, BUT THIS IS BIGGER THAN US RIGHT NOW.
PARKER

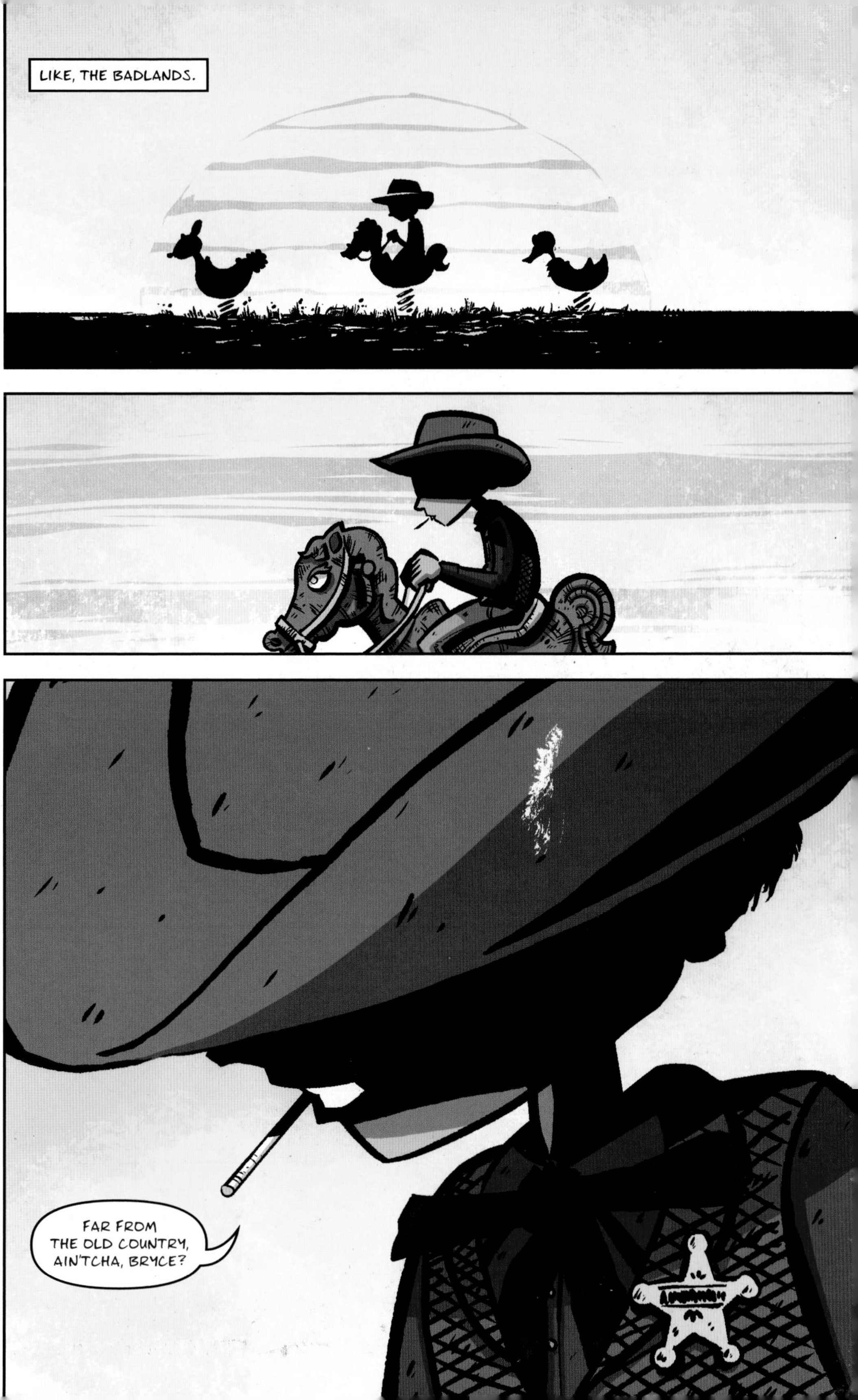
LIKE, THE BADLANDS.
FAR FROM THE OLD COUNTRY, AIN'TCHA, BRYCE?

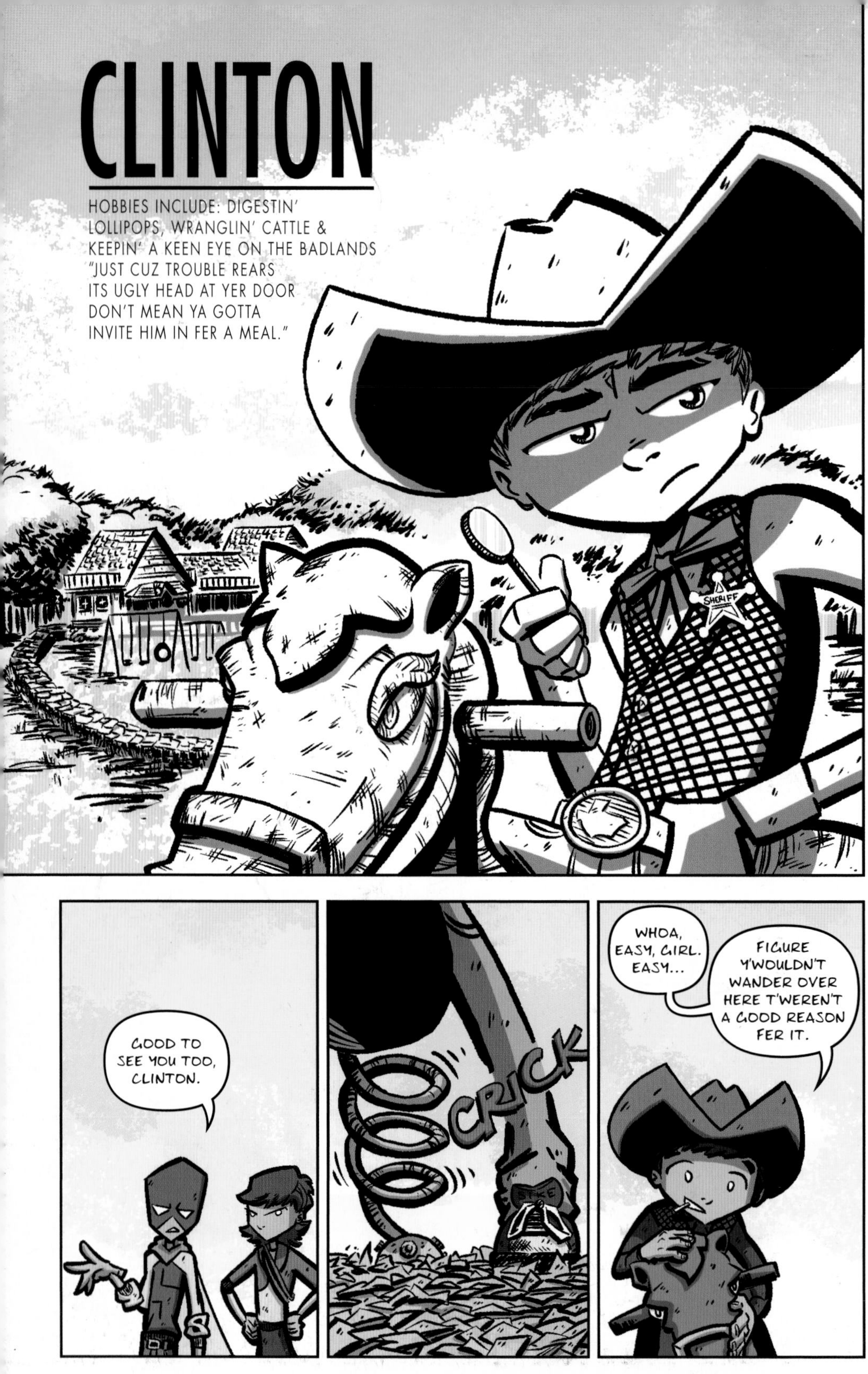
CLINTON
HOBBIES INCLUDE: DIGESTIN' LOLLIPOPS, WRANGLIN' CATTLE & KEEPIN' A KEEN EYE ON THE BADLANDS
"JUST CUZ TROUBLE REARS ITS UGLY HEAD AT YER DOOR DON'T MEAN YA GOTTA INVITE HIM IN FER A MEAL."
SHERIFF
GOOD TO SEE YOU TOO, CLINTON.
CRICK
WHOA, EASY, GIRL. EASY...
FIGURE Y'WOULDN'T WANDER OVER HERE T'WEREN'T A GOOD REASON FER IT.

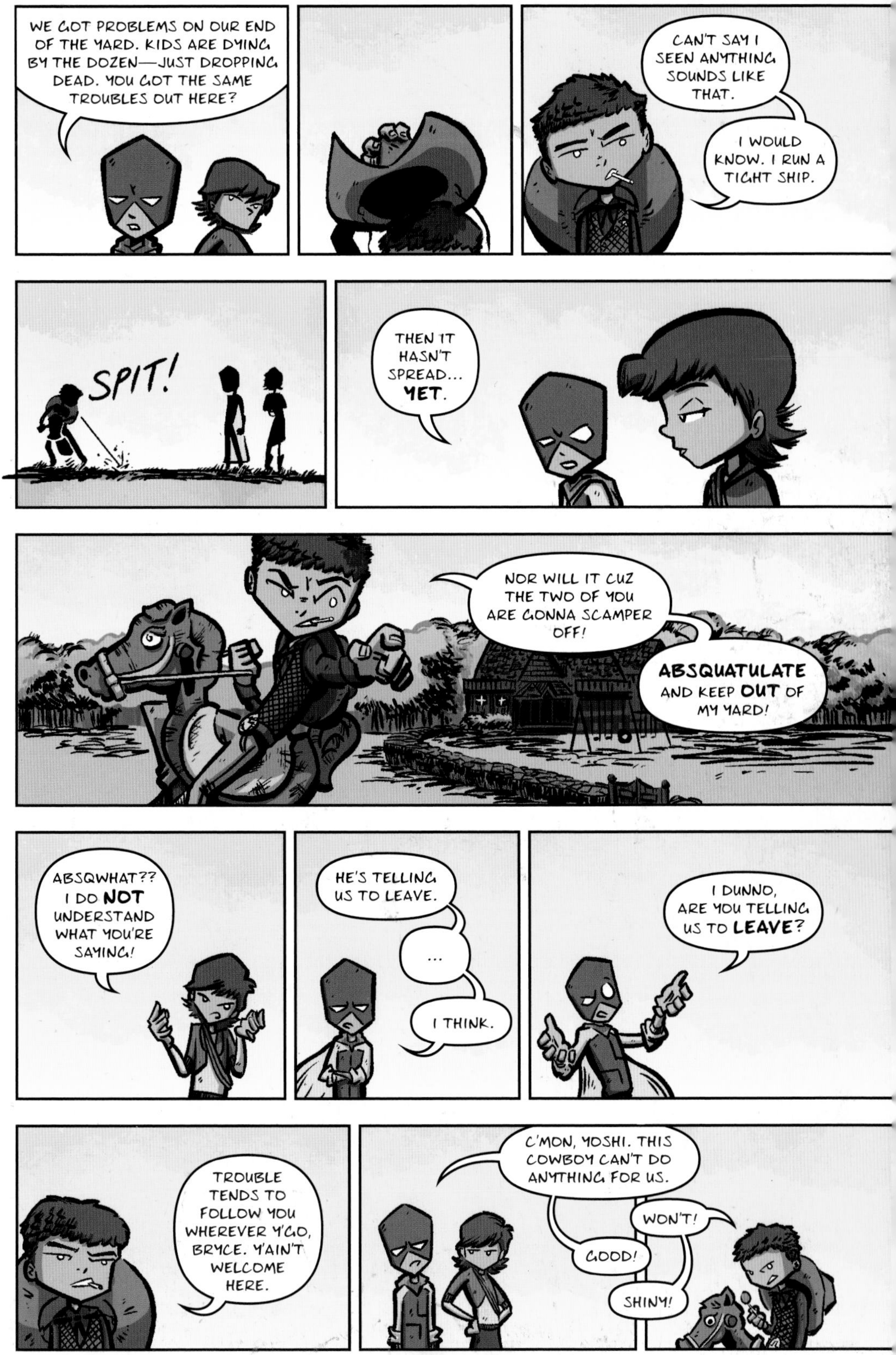
WE GOT PROBLEMS ON OUR END OF THE YARD. KIDS ARE DYING BY THE DOZEN—JUST DROPPING DEAD. YOU GOT THE SAME TROUBLES OUT HERE?
CAN'T SAY I SEEN ANYTHING SOUNDS LIKE THAT.
I WOULD KNOW. I RUN A TIGHT SHIP.
SPIT!
THEN IT HASN'T SPREAD... YET.
NOR WILL IT CUZ THE TWO OF YOU ARE GONNA SCAMPER OFF!
ABSQUATULATE AND KEEP OUT OF MY YARD!
ABSQWHAT?? I DO NOT UNDERSTAND WHAT YOU'RE SAYING!
HE'S TELLING US TO LEAVE.
...
I THINK.
I DUNNO, ARE YOU TELLING US TO LEAVE?
TROUBLE TENDS TO FOLLOW YOU WHEREVER Y'GO, BRYCE. Y'AIN'T WELCOME HERE.
C'MON, YOSHI. THIS COWBOY CAN'T DO ANYTHING FOR US.
WON'T!
GOOD!
SHINY!

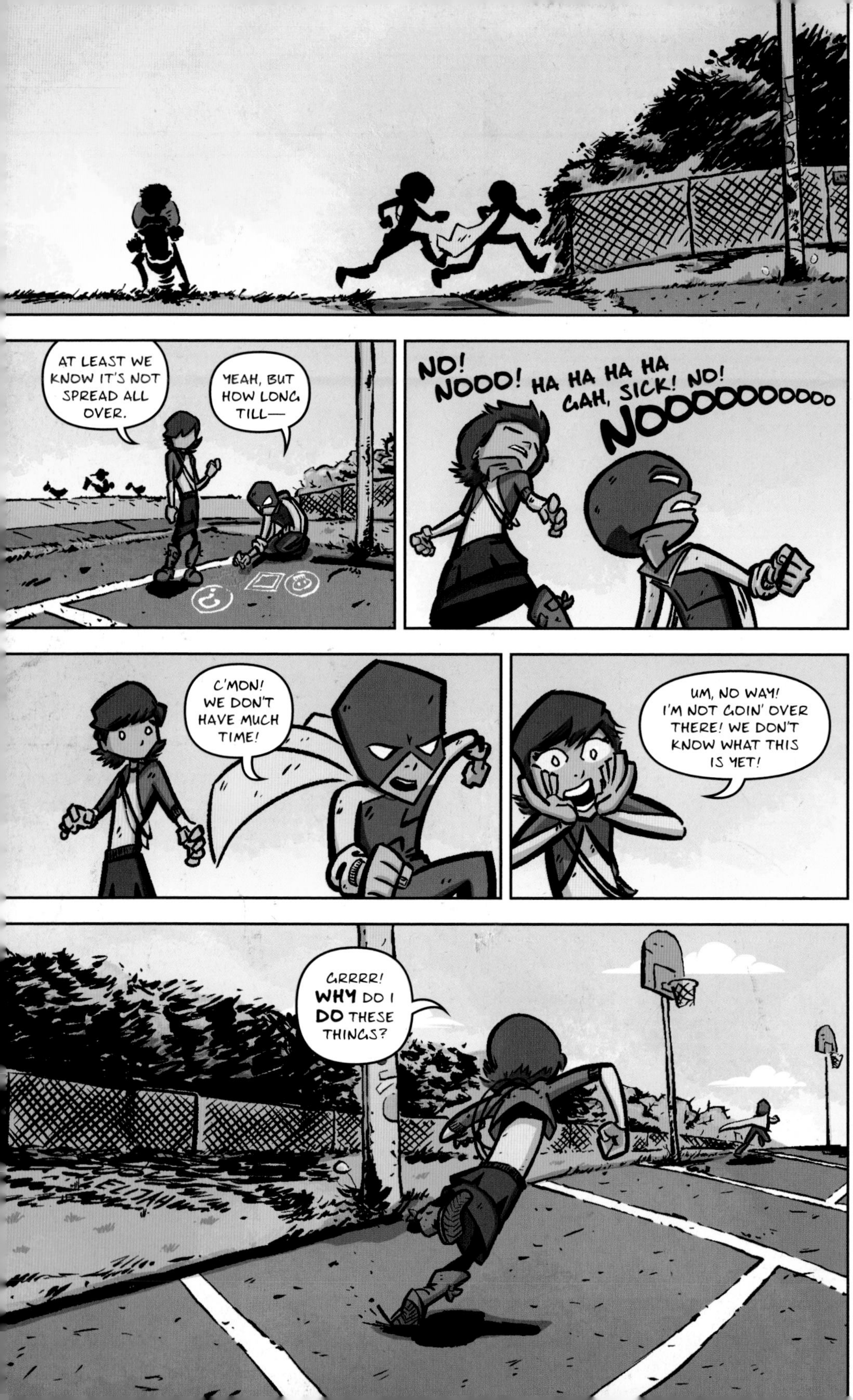
AT LEAST WE KNOW IT'S NOT SPREAD ALL OVER.
YEAH, BUT HOW LONG TILL—
NO! NOOO!
HA HA HA HA
GAH, SICK! NO!
NOOOOOOOOOOO
C'MON! WE DON'T HAVE MUCH TIME!
UM, NO WAY! I'M NOT GOIN' OVER THERE! WE DON'T KNOW WHAT THIS IS YET!
GRRRR! WHY DO I DO THESE THINGS?

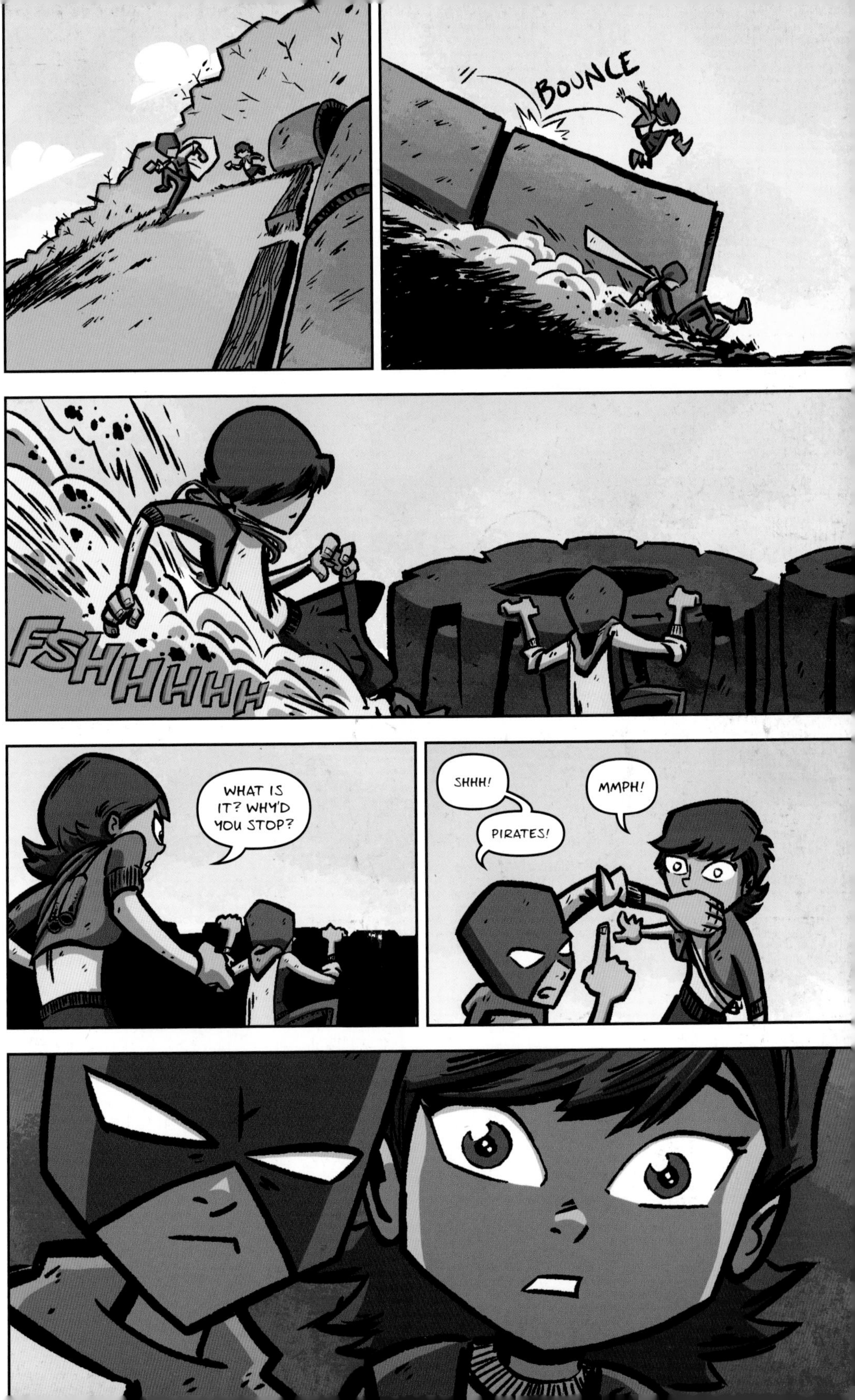
BOUNCE
FSHHHHHH
WHAT IS IT? WHY'D YOU STOP?
SHHH!
PIRATES!
MMPH!

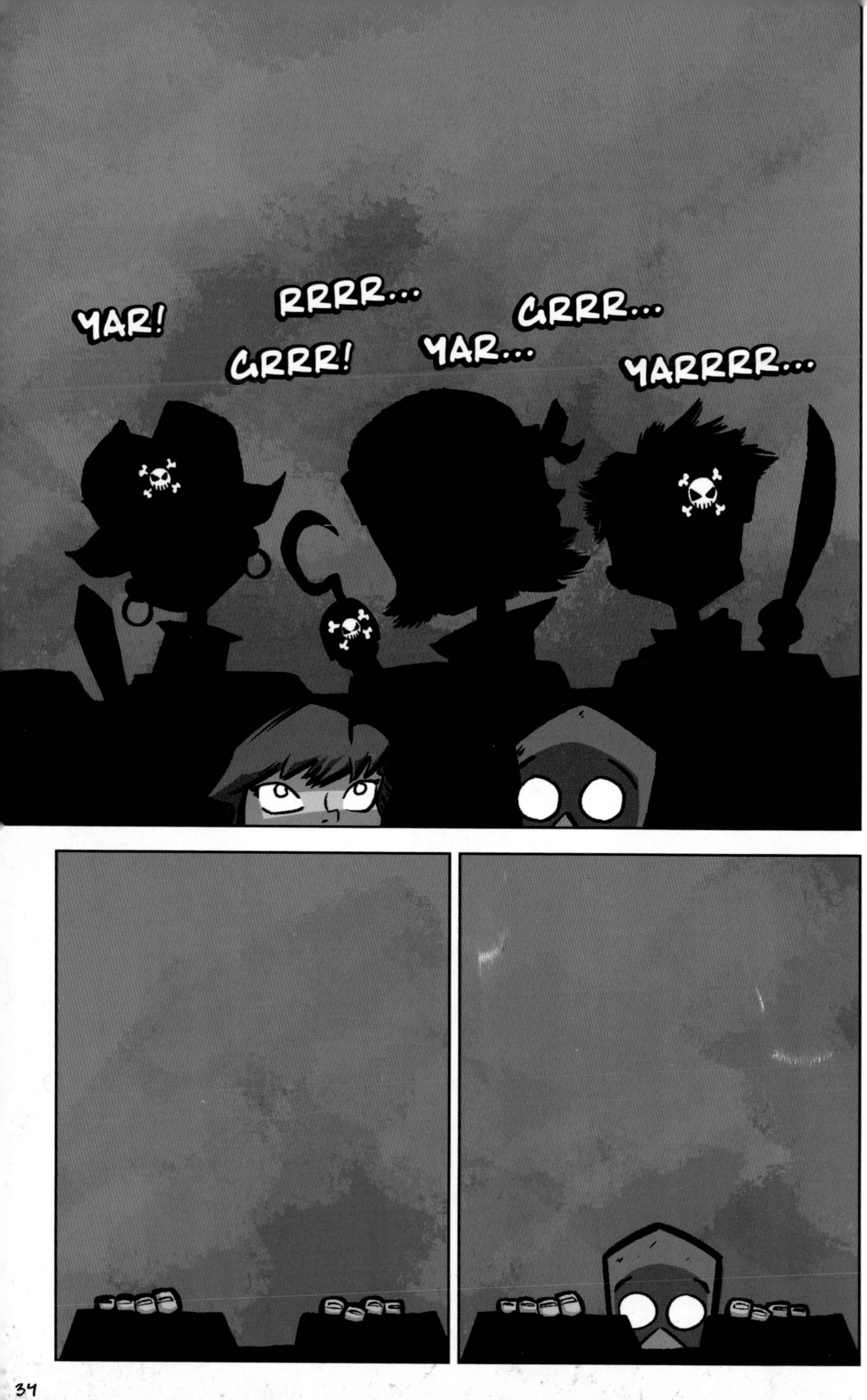
YAR!
RRRR...
GRRR!
YAR...
GRRR...
YARRRR...

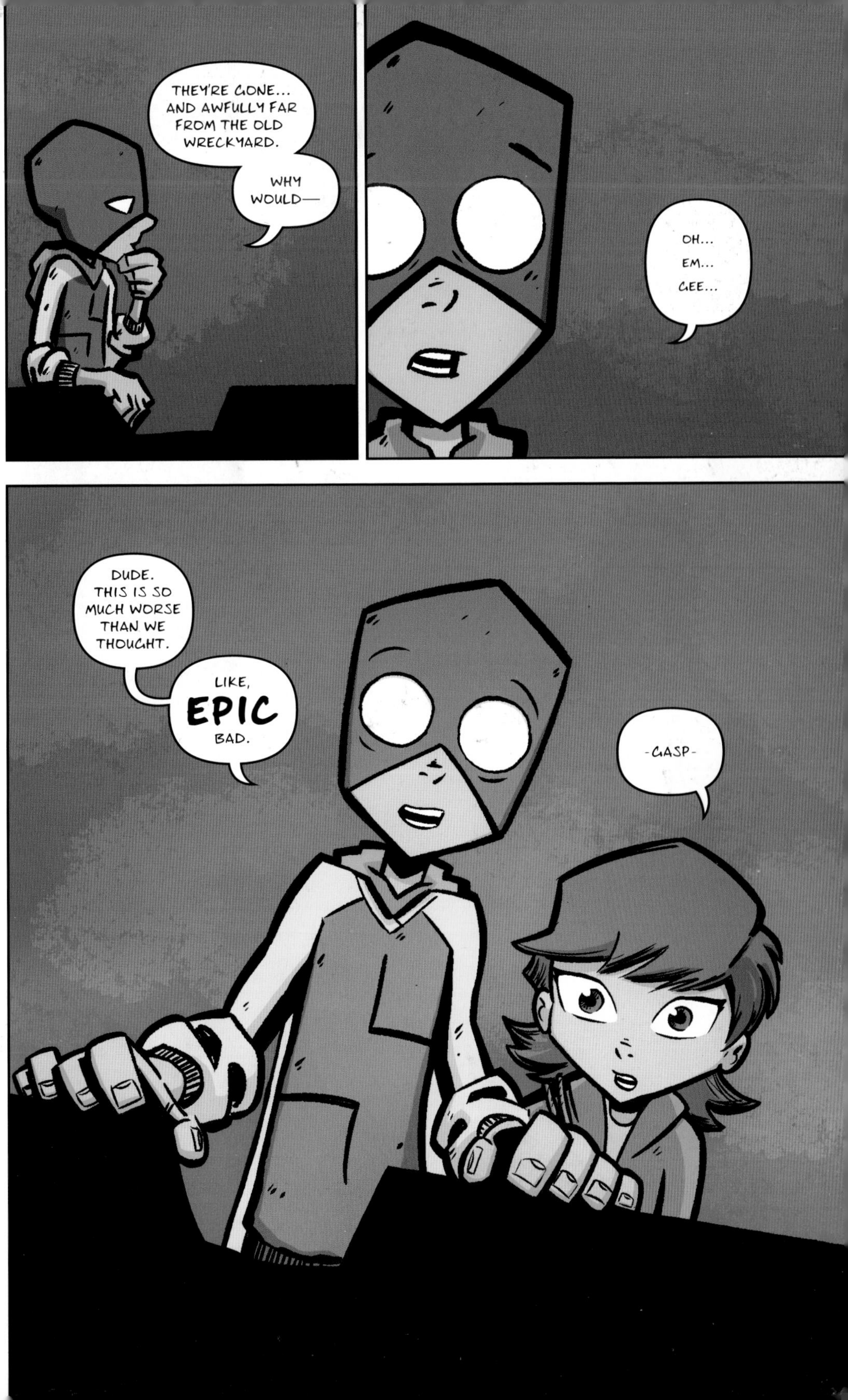
THEY'RE GONE... AND AWFULLY FAR FROM THE OLD WRECKYARD.
WHY WOULD—
OH... EM... GEE...
DUDE. THIS IS SO MUCH WORSE THAN WE THOUGHT.
LIKE, EPIC BAD.
-GASP-

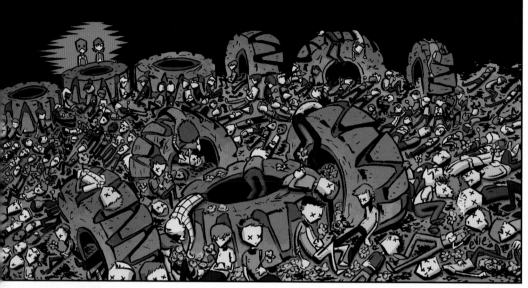

ARE THEY **DEAD**??

NO, BUT THEY **ARE** INFECTED, SO THAT MEANS DEATH IS CLOSE.

AND THEN FOR ALL OF US... SOMETHING MUCH WORSE.

WHAT IS THIS? I'VE NEVER SEEN THIS BEFORE.

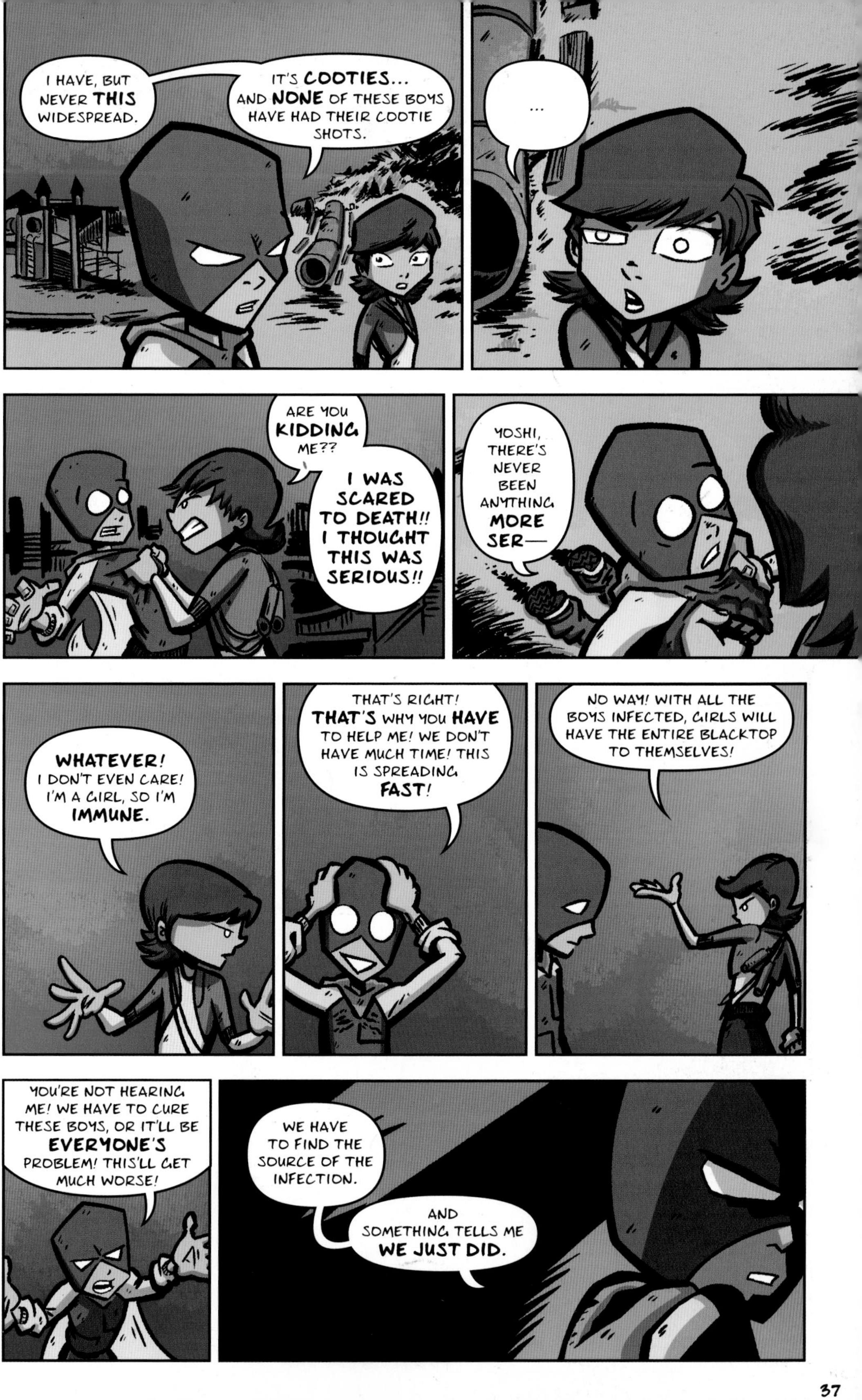
I HAVE, BUT NEVER THIS WIDESPREAD.
IT'S COOTIES... AND NONE OF THESE BOYS HAVE HAD THEIR COOTIE SHOTS.
...
ARE YOU KIDDING ME??
I WAS SCARED TO DEATH!! I THOUGHT THIS WAS SERIOUS!!
YOSHI, THERE'S NEVER BEEN ANYTHING MORE SER—
WHATEVER! I DON'T EVEN CARE! I'M A GIRL, SO I'M IMMUNE.
THAT'S RIGHT! THAT'S WHY YOU HAVE TO HELP ME! WE DON'T HAVE MUCH TIME! THIS IS SPREADING FAST!
NO WAY! WITH ALL THE BOYS INFECTED, GIRLS WILL HAVE THE ENTIRE BLACKTOP TO THEMSELVES!
YOU'RE NOT HEARING ME! WE HAVE TO CURE THESE BOYS, OR IT'LL BE EVERYONE'S PROBLEM! THIS'LL GET MUCH WORSE!
WE HAVE TO FIND THE SOURCE OF THE INFECTION.
AND SOMETHING TELLS ME WE JUST DID.

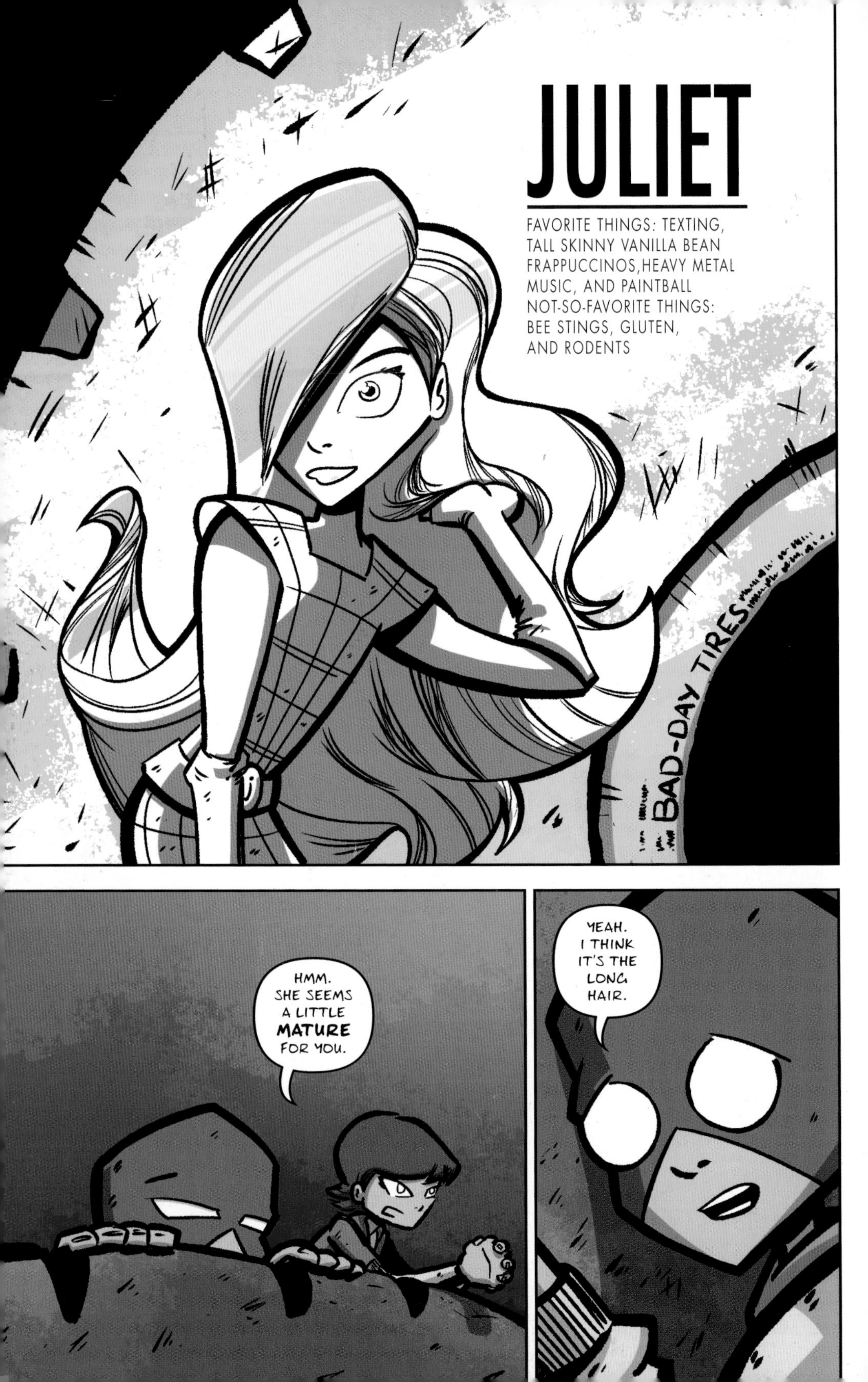
JULIET
FAVORITE THINGS: TEXTING, TALL SKINNY VANILLA BEAN FRAPPUCCINOS,HEAVY METAL MUSIC, AND PAINTBALL
NOT-SO-FAVORITE THINGS: BEE STINGS, GLUTEN, AND RODENTS
BAD-DAY TIRES
HMM. SHE SEEMS A LITTLE **MATURE** FOR YOU.
YEAH. I THINK IT'S THE LONG HAIR.

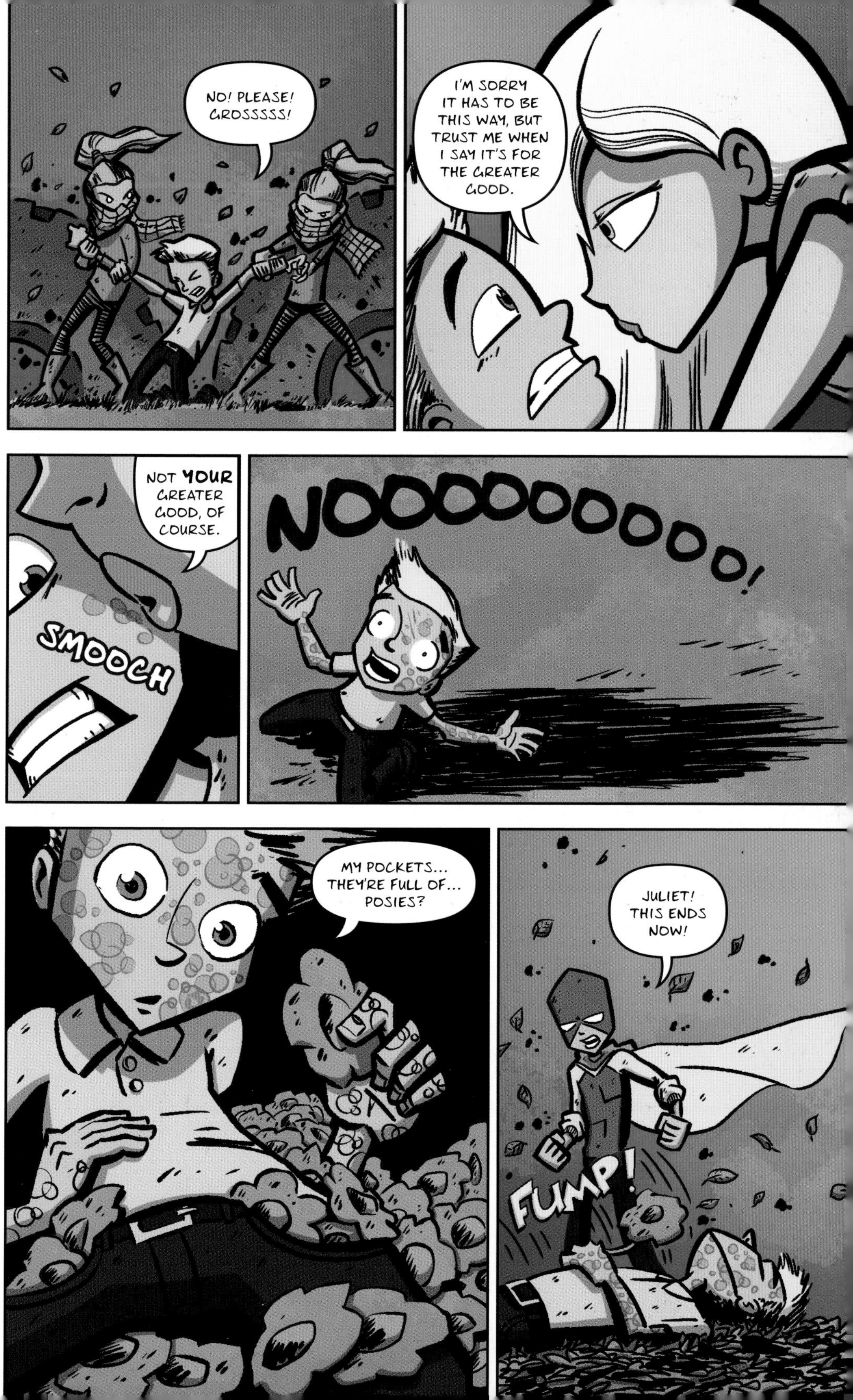
NO! PLEASE! GROSSSSS!
I'M SORRY IT HAS TO BE THIS WAY, BUT TRUST ME WHEN I SAY IT'S FOR THE GREATER GOOD.
NOT YOUR GREATER GOOD, OF COURSE.
SMOOCH
NOOOOOOOOOO!
MY POCKETS... THEY'RE FULL OF... POSIES?
JULIET! THIS ENDS NOW!
FUMP!

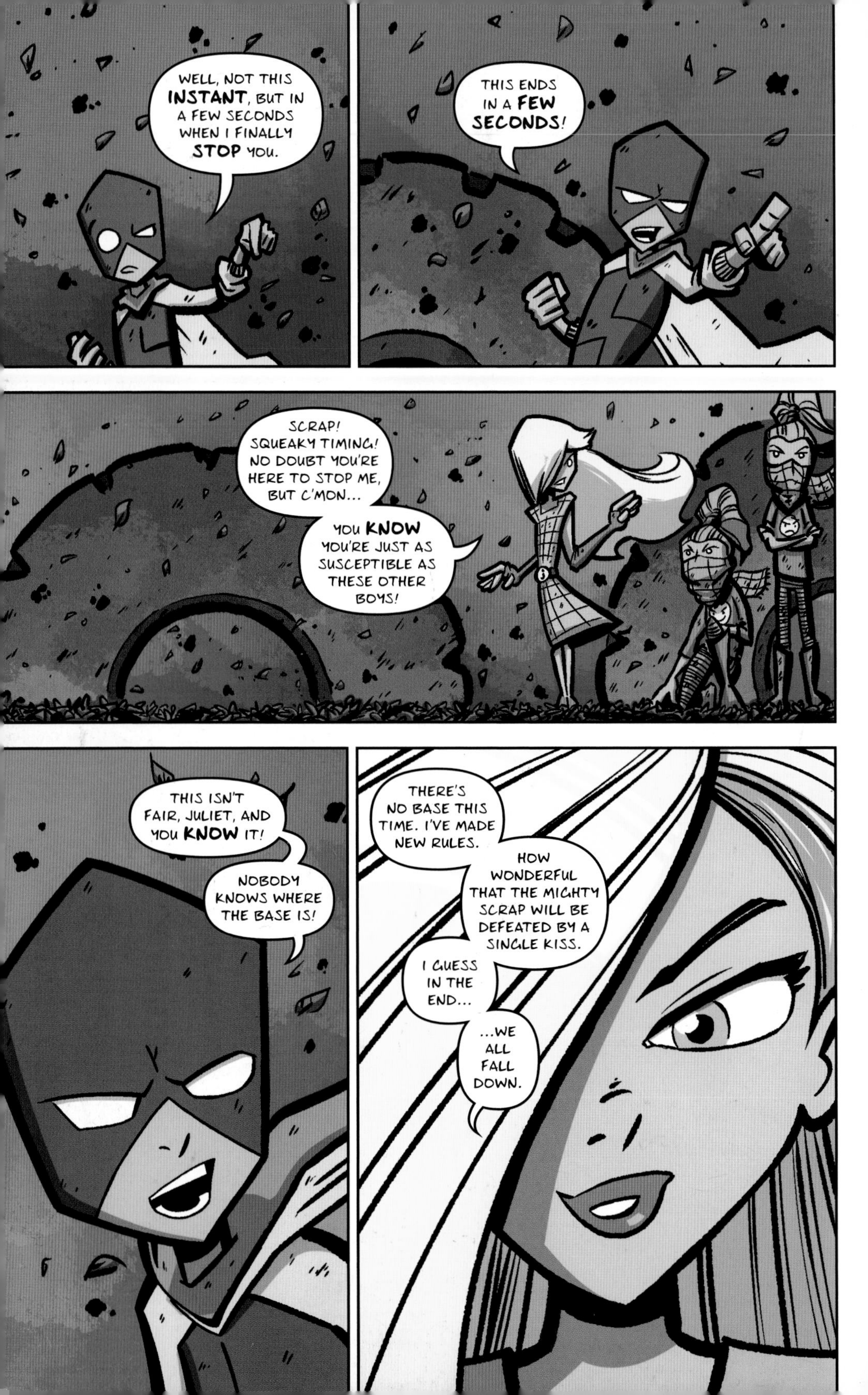

WELL, NOT THIS INSTANT, BUT IN A FEW SECONDS WHEN I FINALLY STOP YOU.
THIS ENDS IN A FEW SECONDS!
SCRAP! SQUEAKY TIMING! NO DOUBT YOU'RE HERE TO STOP ME, BUT C'MON...
YOU KNOW YOU'RE JUST AS SUSCEPTIBLE AS THESE OTHER BOYS!
THIS ISN'T FAIR, JULIET, AND YOU KNOW IT!
NOBODY KNOWS WHERE THE BASE IS!
THERE'S NO BASE THIS TIME. I'VE MADE NEW RULES.
HOW WONDERFUL THAT THE MIGHTY SCRAP WILL BE DEFEATED BY A SINGLE KISS.
I GUESS IN THE END...
...WE ALL FALL DOWN.

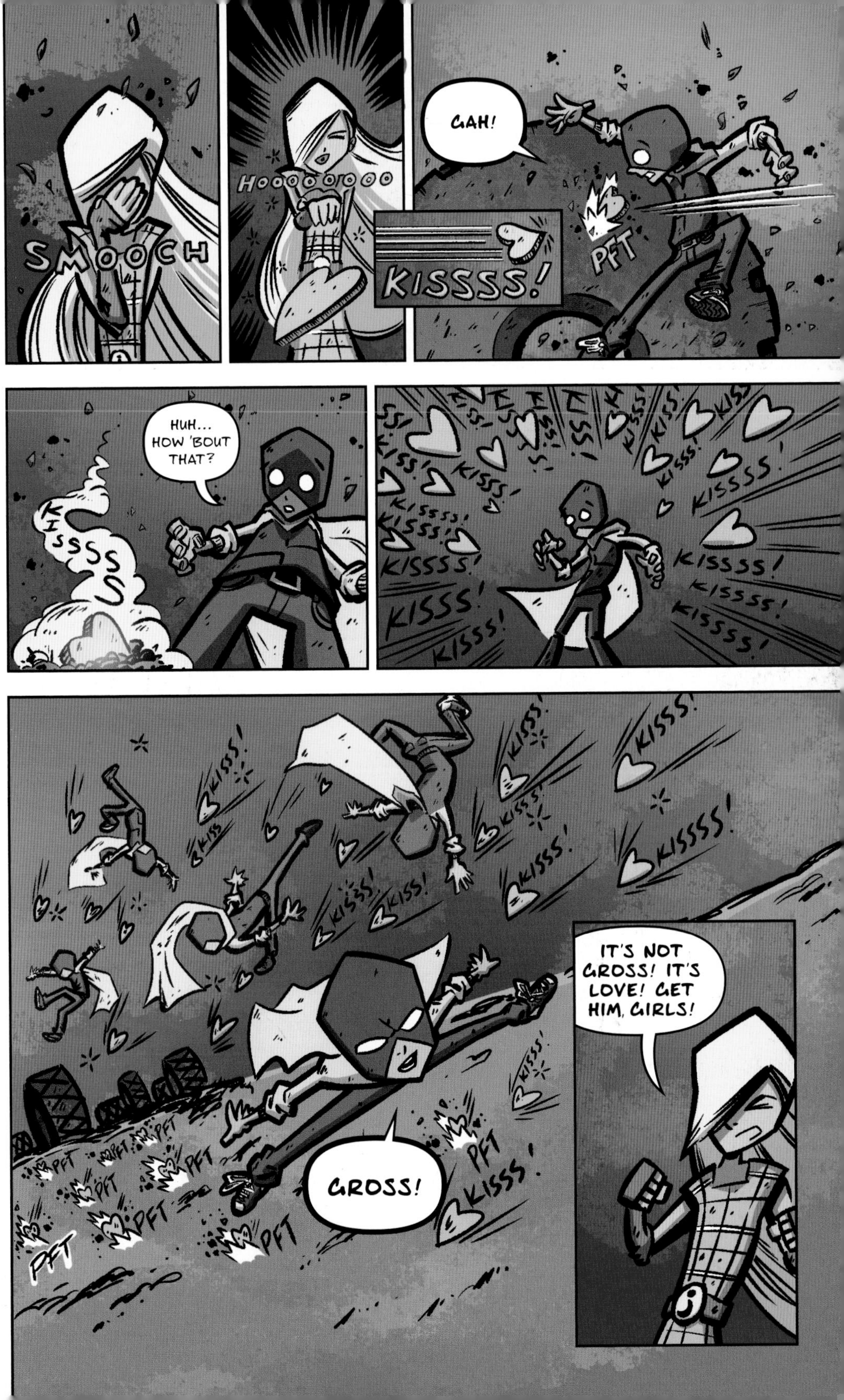

SMOOCH
HOOOOOOOOO
KISSSS!
GAH!
PFT
HUH... HOW 'BOUT THAT?
KISSSSS
KISSSSS!
KISSSS!
GROSS!
IT'S NOT GROSS! IT'S LOVE! GET HIM, GIRLS!

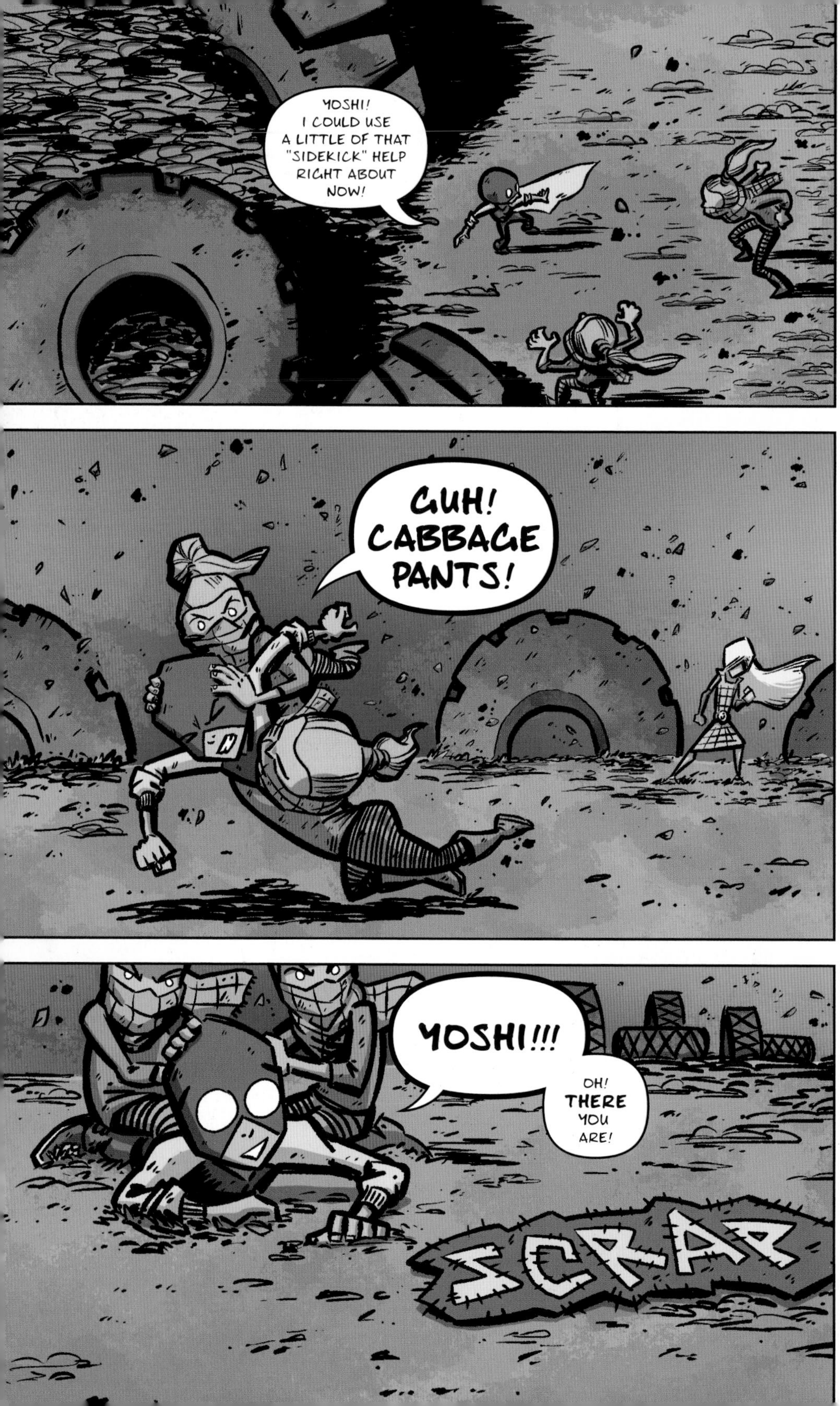
YOSHI! I COULD USE A LITTLE OF THAT "SIDEKICK" HELP RIGHT ABOUT NOW!
GUH! CABBAGE PANTS!
YOSHI!!!
OH! THERE YOU ARE!
SCRAP

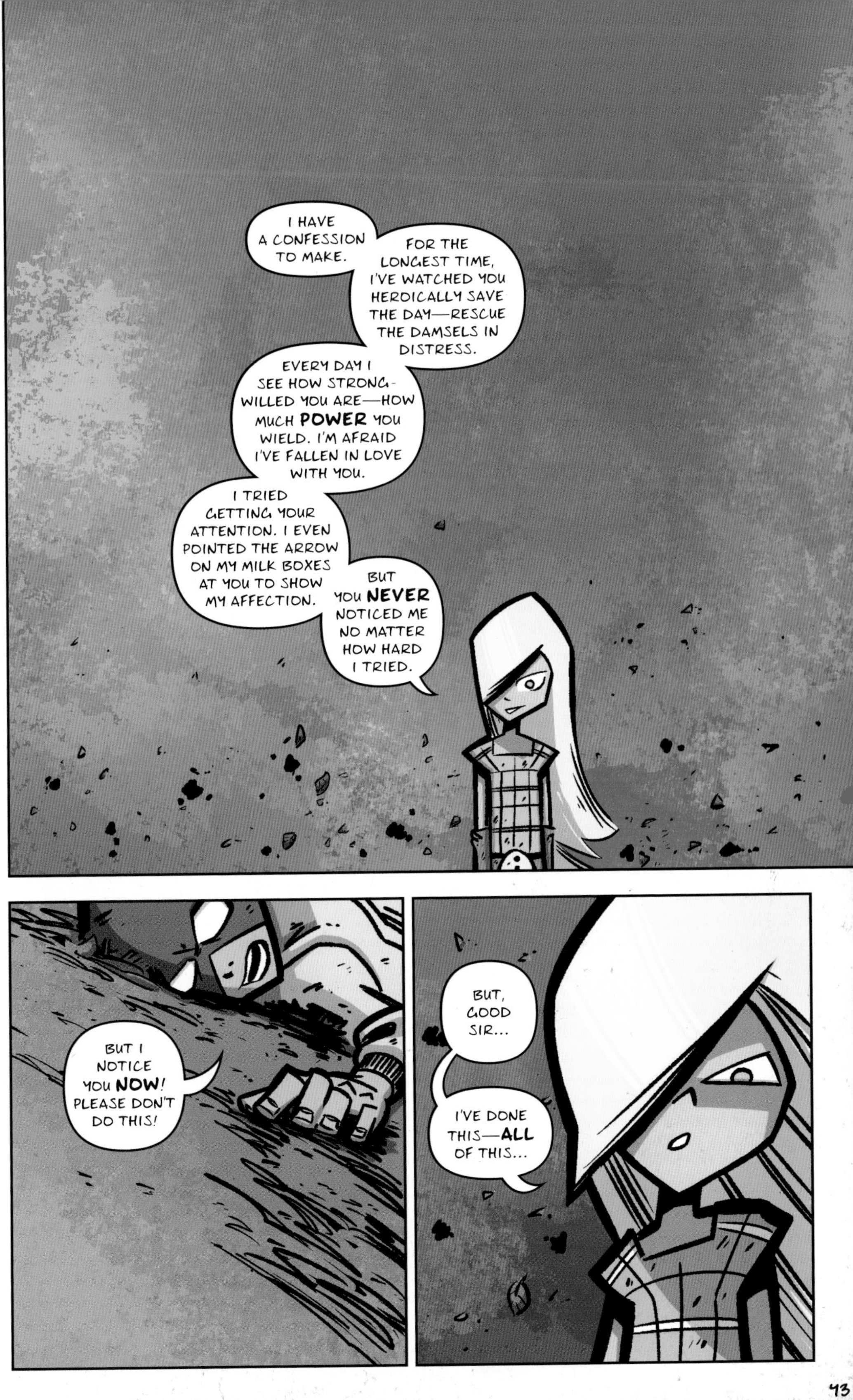
I HAVE A CONFESSION TO MAKE.
FOR THE LONGEST TIME, I'VE WATCHED YOU HEROICALLY SAVE THE DAY—RESCUE THE DAMSELS IN DISTRESS.
EVERY DAY I SEE HOW STRONG-WILLED YOU ARE—HOW MUCH **POWER** YOU WIELD. I'M AFRAID I'VE FALLEN IN LOVE WITH YOU.
I TRIED GETTING YOUR ATTENTION. I EVEN POINTED THE ARROW ON MY MILK BOXES AT YOU TO SHOW MY AFFECTION.
BUT YOU **NEVER** NOTICED ME NO MATTER HOW HARD I TRIED.
BUT I NOTICE YOU **NOW**! PLEASE DON'T DO THIS!
BUT, GOOD SIR...
I'VE DONE THIS—**ALL** OF THIS...

...FOR YOU.

YOU FINALLY SEE ME. **SCRAPPY** ACCOMPLISHMENT, ISN'T IT?

YOU SEE WHAT I DID THERE?

YOU'RE A MONSTER...

NOPE, I'M JUST IN LOVE.

AND I HAVE A **SPECIAL** COOTIE SHOT.

JUST. FOR. YOU.

THE FIRST GIRL TO KISS YOU AFTER THIS SHOT IS ADMINISTERED WILL BECOME THE GIRL YOU FALL MADLY IN LOVE WITH FOR **ETERNITY**.

WE'LL FINALLY BE TOGETHER, K-I-S-S-I-N-G-ing **FOREVER!**

HOLD HIM TIGHT, LADIES.

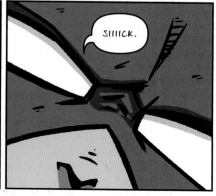

SIIIICK.

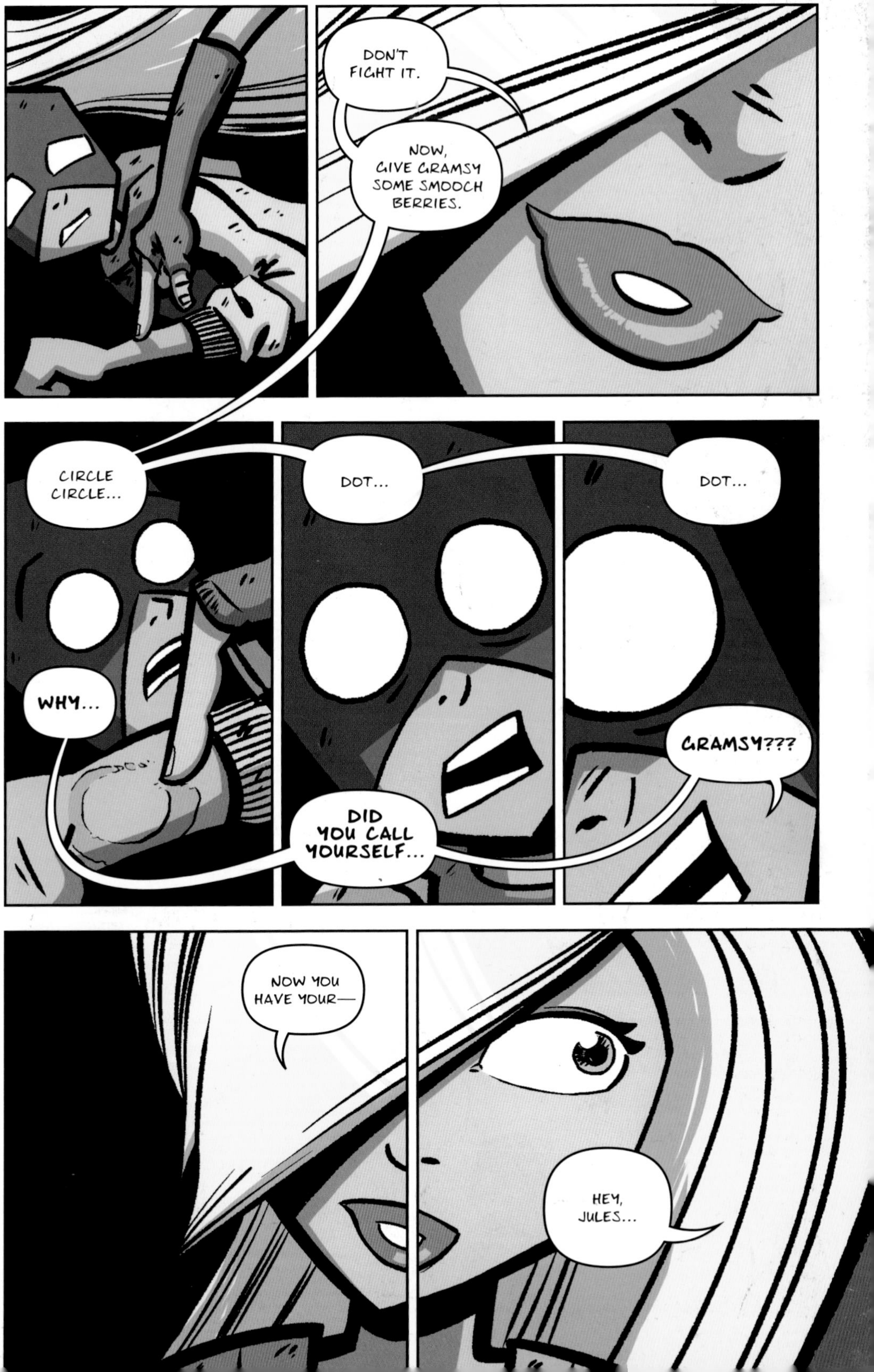

DON'T FIGHT IT.
NOW, GIVE GRAMSY SOME SMOOCH BERRIES.
CIRCLE CIRCLE...
DOT...
DOT...
WHY...
DID YOU CALL YOURSELF...
GRAMSY???
NOW YOU HAVE YOUR—
HEY, JULES...

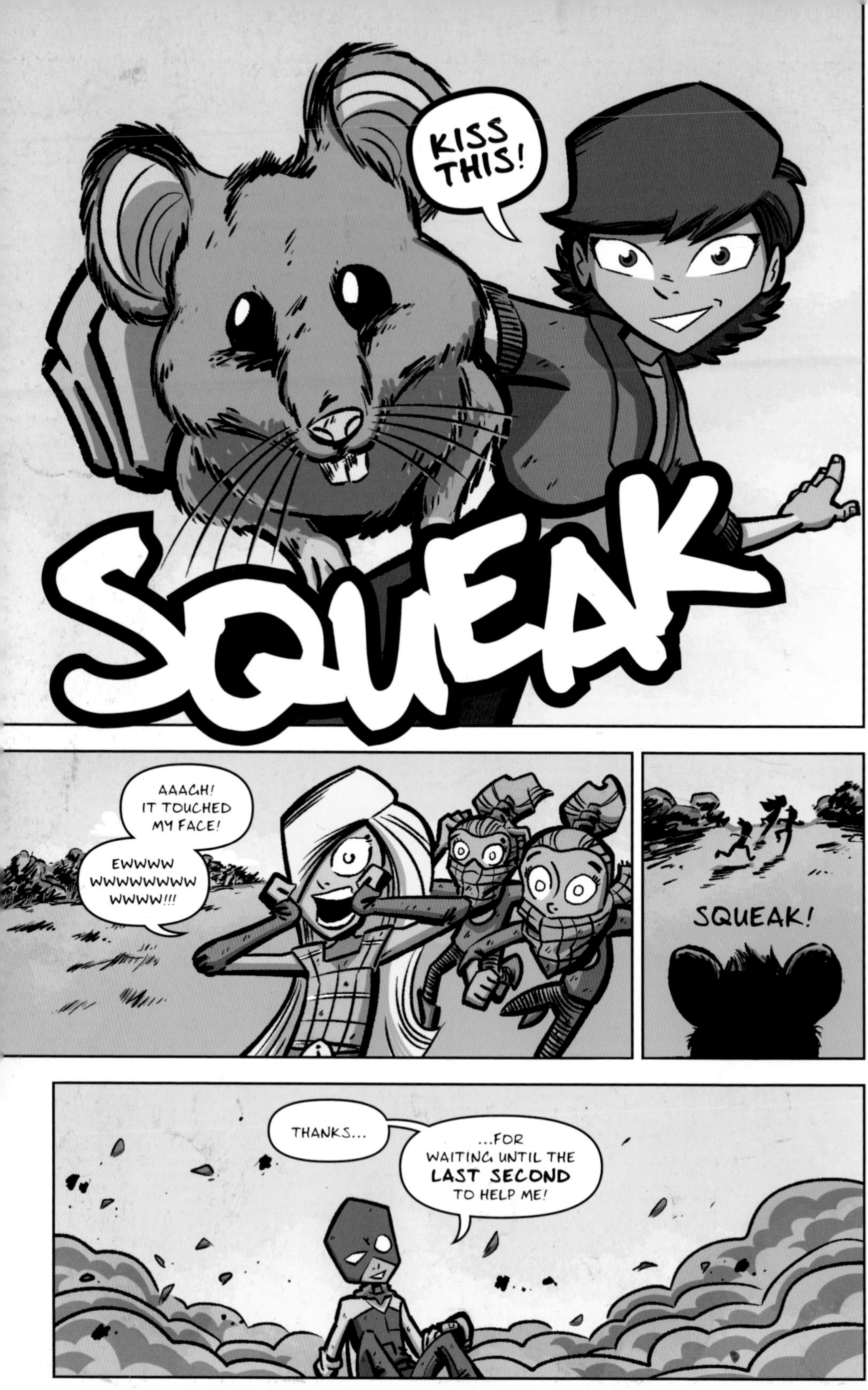
KISS THIS!
SQUEAK
AAAGH! IT TOUCHED MY FACE!
EWWWW WWWWWWWW WWWW!!!
SQUEAK!
THANKS...
...FOR WAITING UNTIL THE LAST SECOND TO HELP ME!

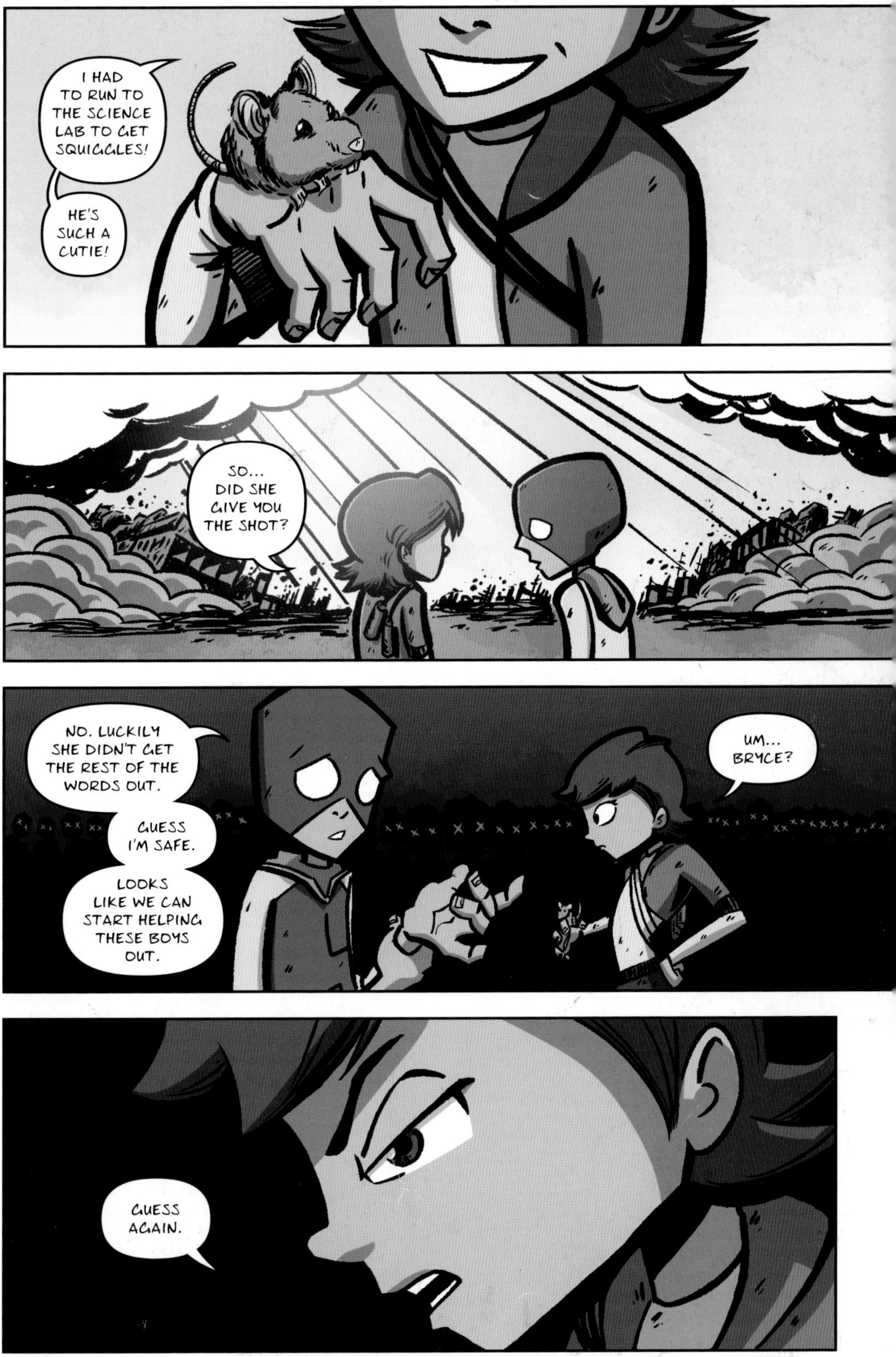
I HAD TO RUN TO THE SCIENCE LAB TO GET SQUIGGLES!
HE'S SUCH A CUTIE!
SO... DID SHE GIVE YOU THE SHOT?
NO. LUCKILY SHE DIDN'T GET THE REST OF THE WORDS OUT.
GUESS I'M SAFE.
LOOKS LIKE WE CAN START HELPING THESE BOYS OUT.
UM... BRYCE?
GUESS AGAIN.

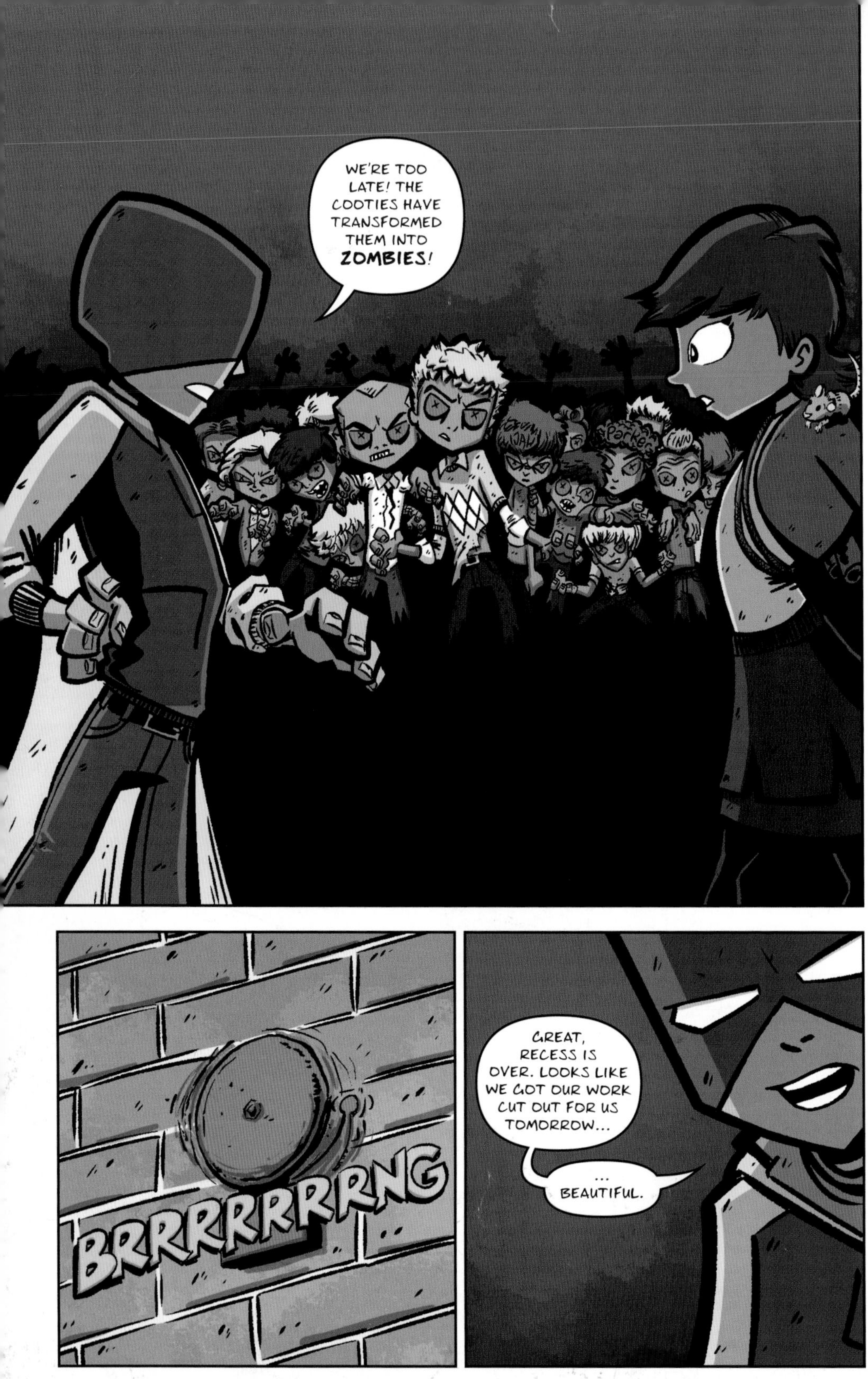
WE'RE TOO LATE! THE COOTIES HAVE TRANSFORMED THEM INTO **ZOMBIES**!
BRRRRRRRNG
GREAT, RECESS IS OVER. LOOKS LIKE WE GOT OUR WORK CUT OUT FOR US TOMORROW...
... BEAUTIFUL.

02 DAY OF THE UNLIVING ALIVE

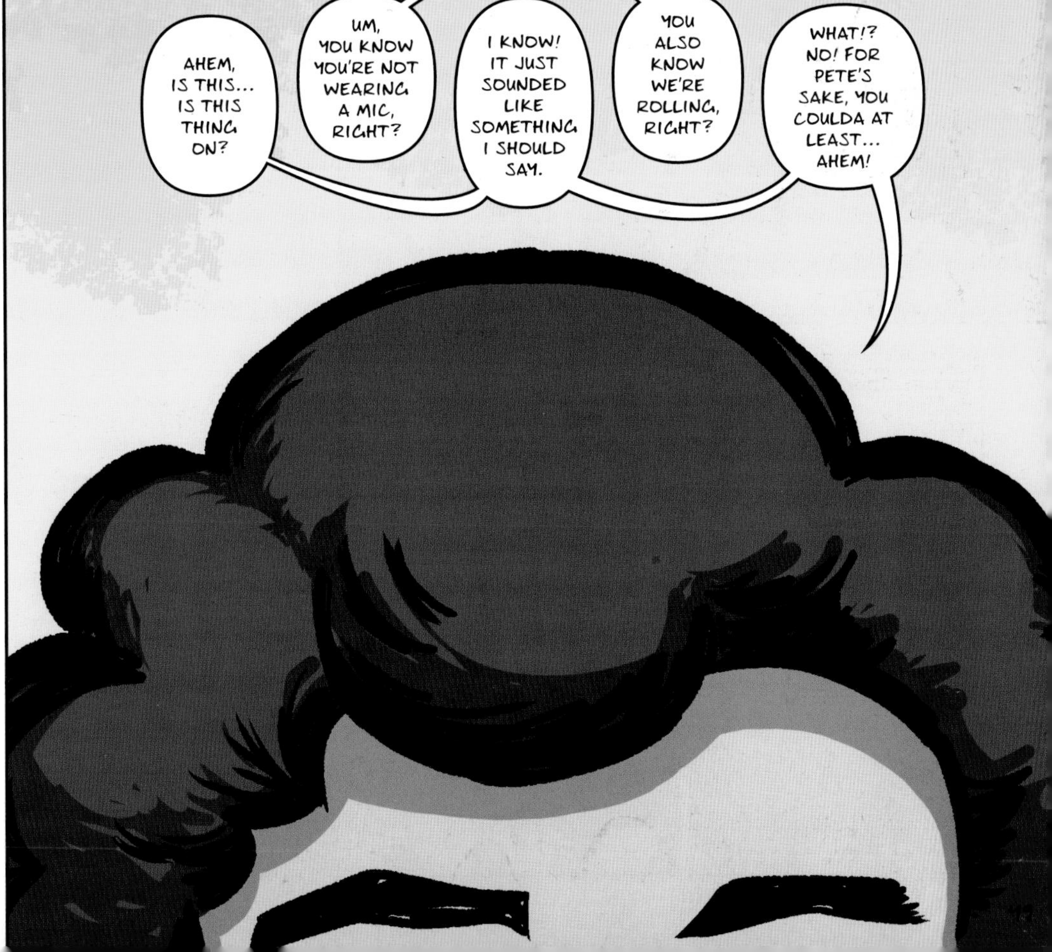

AHEM, IS THIS... IS THIS THING ON?
UM, YOU KNOW YOU'RE NOT WEARING A MIC, RIGHT?
I KNOW! IT JUST SOUNDED LIKE SOMETHING I SHOULD SAY.
YOU ALSO KNOW WE'RE ROLLING, RIGHT?
WHAT!? NO! FOR PETE'S SAKE, YOU COULDA AT LEAST... AHEM!

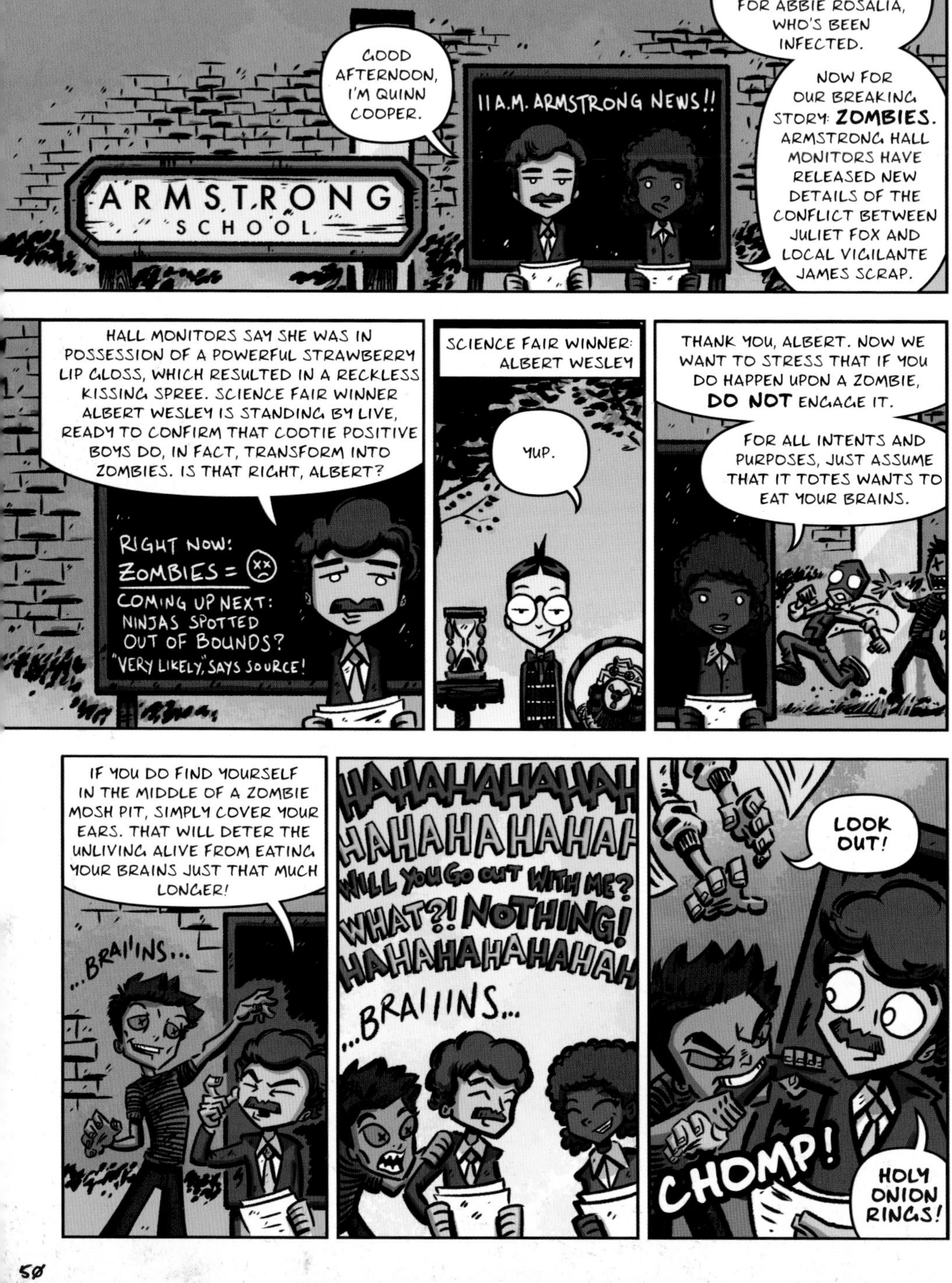
GOOD AFTERNOON, I'M QUINN COOPER.
11 A.M. ARMSTRONG NEWS!!
ARMSTRONG SCHOOL
AND I'M CHRISTABEL AUGUSTINA, FILLING IN FOR ABBIE ROSALIA, WHO'S BEEN INFECTED.
NOW FOR OUR BREAKING STORY: ZOMBIES. ARMSTRONG HALL MONITORS HAVE RELEASED NEW DETAILS OF THE CONFLICT BETWEEN JULIET FOX AND LOCAL VIGILANTE JAMES SCRAP.
HALL MONITORS SAY SHE WAS IN POSSESSION OF A POWERFUL STRAWBERRY LIP GLOSS, WHICH RESULTED IN A RECKLESS KISSING SPREE. SCIENCE FAIR WINNER ALBERT WESLEY IS STANDING BY LIVE, READY TO CONFIRM THAT COOTIE POSITIVE BOYS DO, IN FACT, TRANSFORM INTO ZOMBIES. IS THAT RIGHT, ALBERT?
RIGHT NOW: ZOMBIES =
COMING UP NEXT: NINJAS SPOTTED OUT OF BOUNDS? "VERY LIKELY," SAYS SOURCE!
SCIENCE FAIR WINNER: ALBERT WESLEY
YUP.
THANK YOU, ALBERT. NOW WE WANT TO STRESS THAT IF YOU DO HAPPEN UPON A ZOMBIE, DO NOT ENGAGE IT.
FOR ALL INTENTS AND PURPOSES, JUST ASSUME THAT IT TOTES WANTS TO EAT YOUR BRAINS.
IF YOU DO FIND YOURSELF IN THE MIDDLE OF A ZOMBIE MOSH PIT, SIMPLY COVER YOUR EARS. THAT WILL DETER THE UNLIVING ALIVE FROM EATING YOUR BRAINS JUST THAT MUCH LONGER!
...BRAIINS...
HAHAHAHAHAHAH
HAHAHAHAHAHAH
WILL YOU GO OUT WITH ME?
WHAT?! NOTHING!
HAHAHAHAHAHAH
...BRAIINS...
LOOK OUT!
CHOMP!
HOLY ONION RINGS!

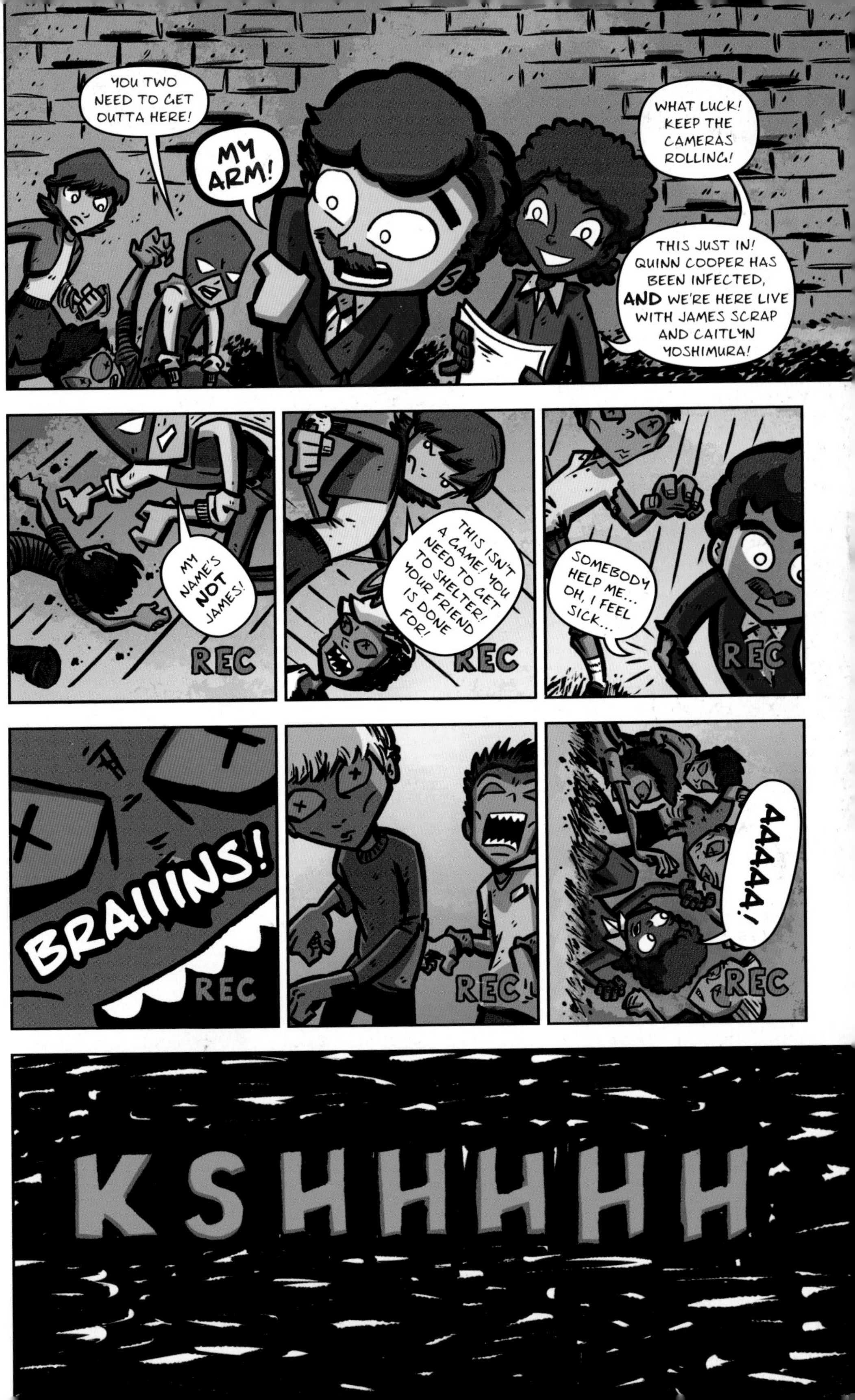
YOU TWO NEED TO GET OUTTA HERE!
MY ARM!
WHAT LUCK! KEEP THE CAMERAS ROLLING!
THIS JUST IN! QUINN COOPER HAS BEEN INFECTED, AND WE'RE HERE LIVE WITH JAMES SCRAP AND CAITLYN YOSHIMURA!
MY NAME'S NOT JAMES!
REC
THIS ISN'T A GAME! YOU NEED TO GET TO SHELTER! YOUR FRIEND IS DONE FOR!
REC
SOMEBODY HELP ME... OH, I FEEL SICK...
REC
BRAIIINS!
REC
REC
AAAAAA!
REC
KSHHHHH

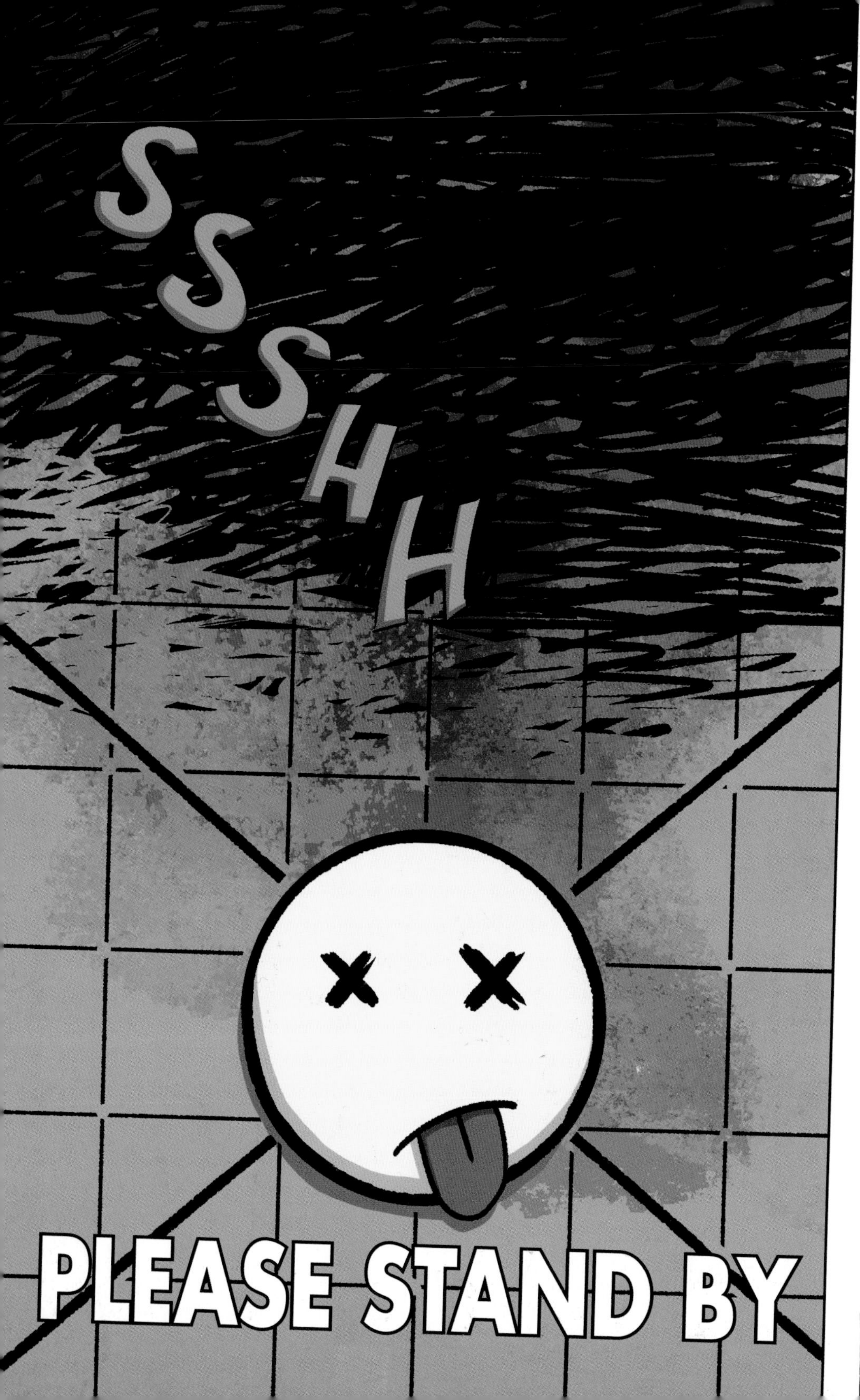
SSSHH
PLEASE STAND BY

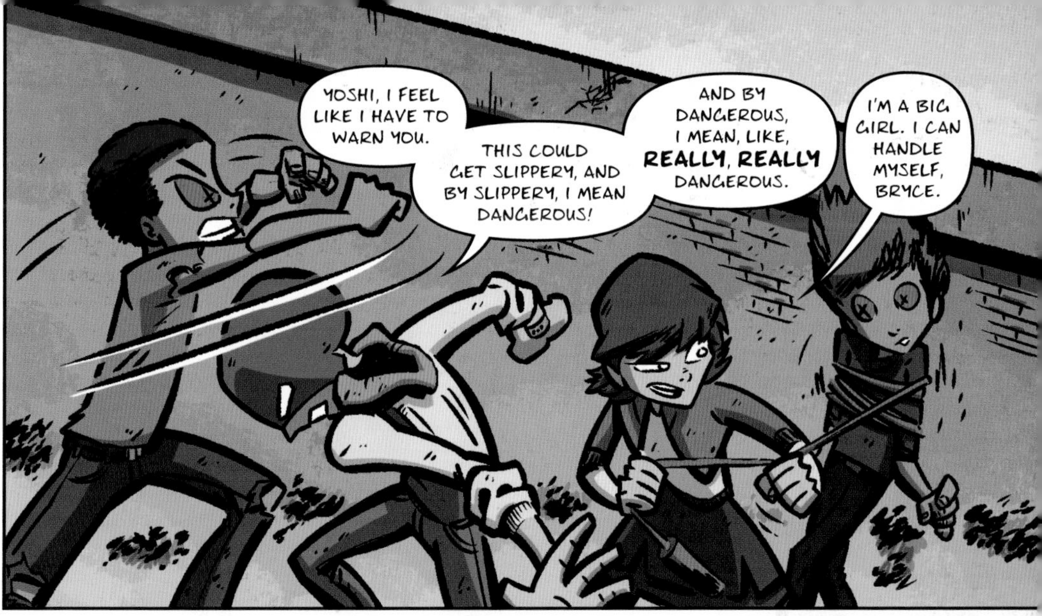
YOSHI, I FEEL LIKE I HAVE TO WARN YOU.
THIS COULD GET SLIPPERY, AND BY SLIPPERY, I MEAN DANGEROUS!
AND BY DANGEROUS, I MEAN, LIKE, REALLY, REALLY DANGEROUS.
I'M A BIG GIRL. I CAN HANDLE MYSELF, BRYCE.

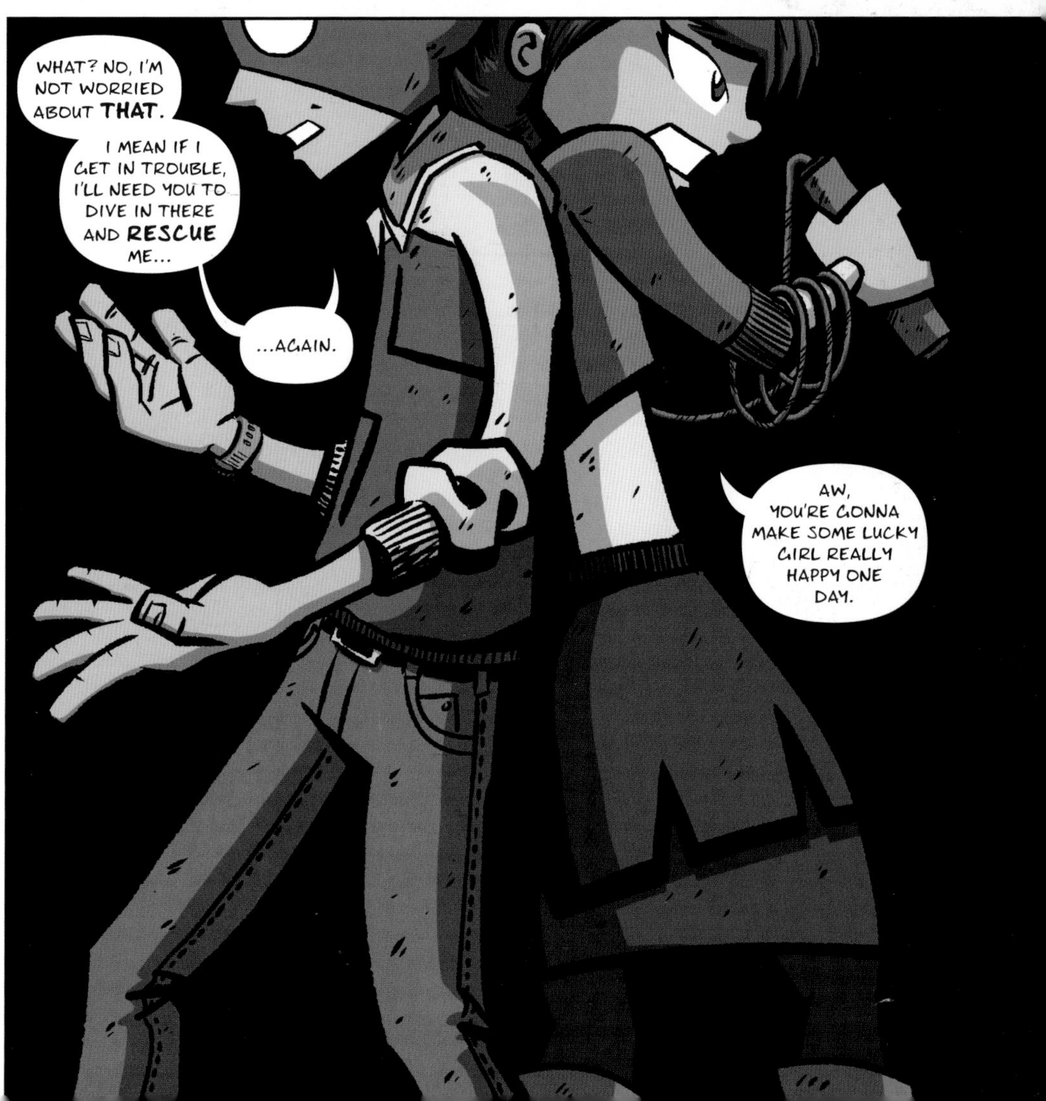
WHAT? NO, I'M NOT WORRIED ABOUT THAT.
I MEAN IF I GET IN TROUBLE, I'LL NEED YOU TO DIVE IN THERE AND RESCUE ME...
...AGAIN.
AW, YOU'RE GONNA MAKE SOME LUCKY GIRL REALLY HAPPY ONE DAY.

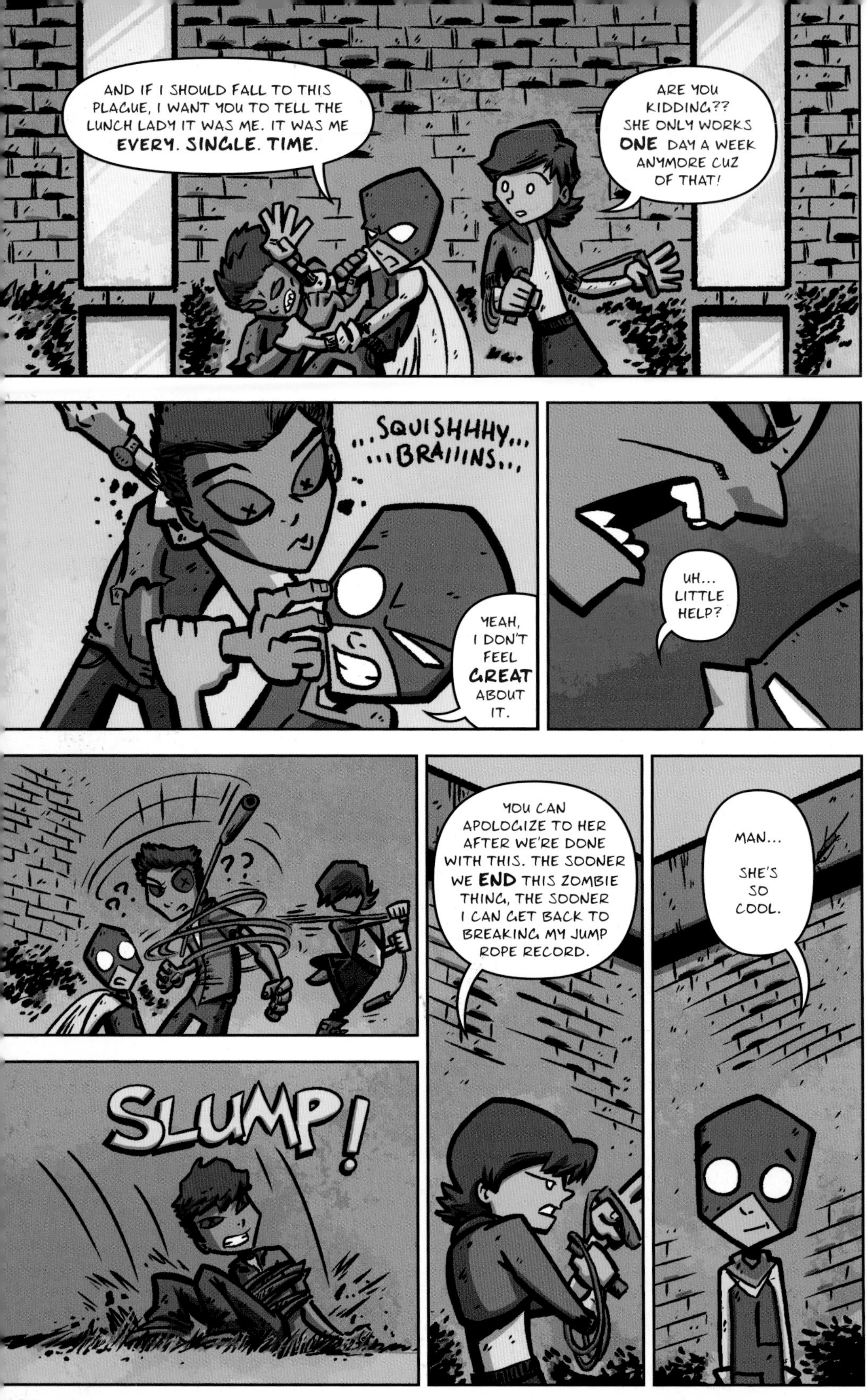
AND IF I SHOULD FALL TO THIS PLAGUE, I WANT YOU TO TELL THE LUNCH LADY IT WAS ME. IT WAS ME EVERY. SINGLE. TIME.
ARE YOU KIDDING?? SHE ONLY WORKS ONE DAY A WEEK ANYMORE CUZ OF THAT!
...SQUISHHHY... ...BRAIIINS...
YEAH, I DON'T FEEL GREAT ABOUT IT.
UH... LITTLE HELP?
??
SLUMP!
YOU CAN APOLOGIZE TO HER AFTER WE'RE DONE WITH THIS. THE SOONER WE END THIS ZOMBIE THING, THE SOONER I CAN GET BACK TO BREAKING MY JUMP ROPE RECORD.
MAN... SHE'S SO COOL.

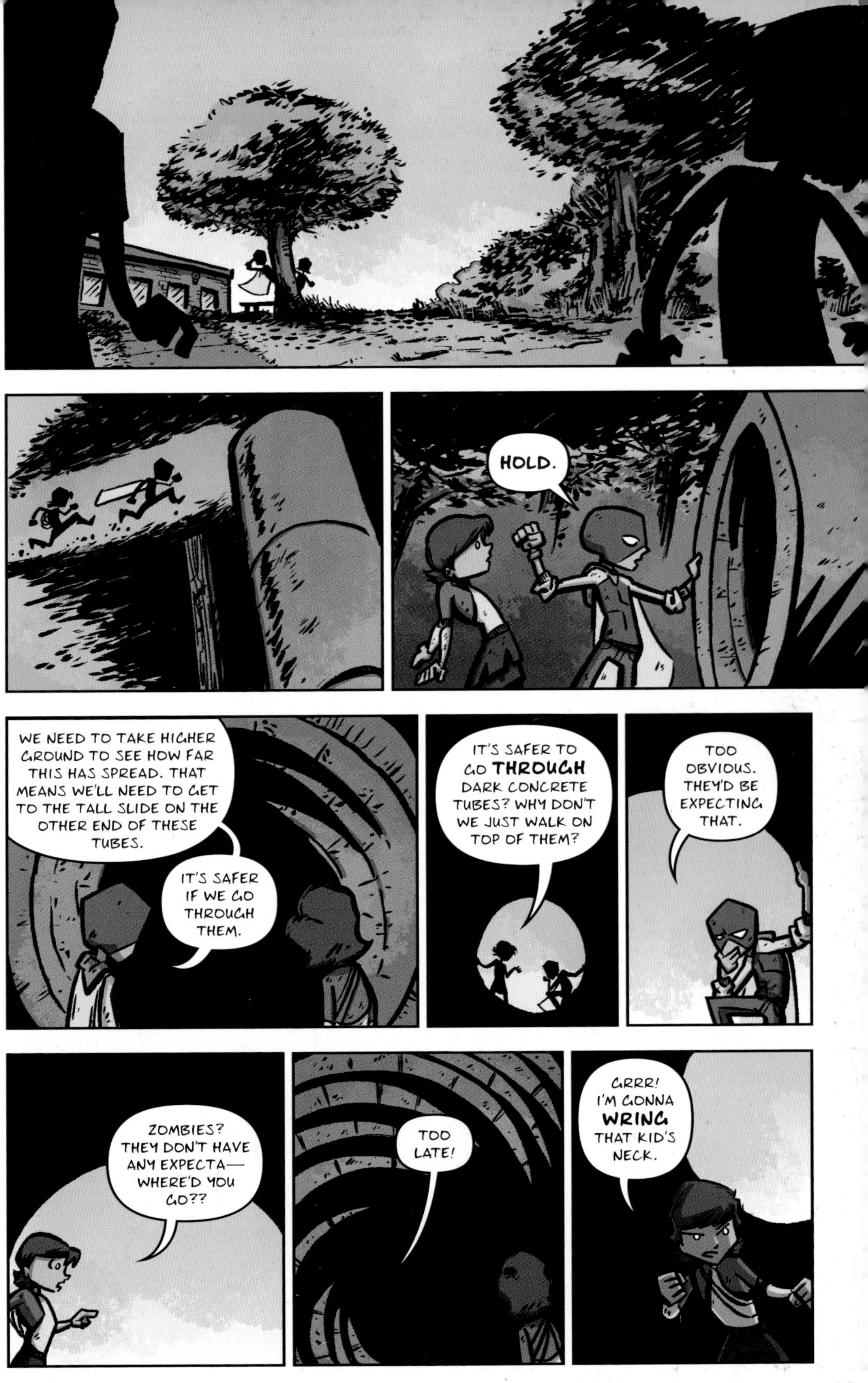
HOLD.
WE NEED TO TAKE HIGHER GROUND TO SEE HOW FAR THIS HAS SPREAD. THAT MEANS WE'LL NEED TO GET TO THE TALL SLIDE ON THE OTHER END OF THESE TUBES.
IT'S SAFER IF WE GO THROUGH THEM.
IT'S SAFER TO GO **THROUGH** DARK CONCRETE TUBES? WHY DON'T WE JUST WALK ON TOP OF THEM?
TOO OBVIOUS. THEY'D BE EXPECTING THAT.
ZOMBIES? THEY DON'T HAVE ANY EXPECTA— WHERE'D YOU GO??
TOO LATE!
GRRR! I'M GONNA **WRING** THAT KID'S NECK.

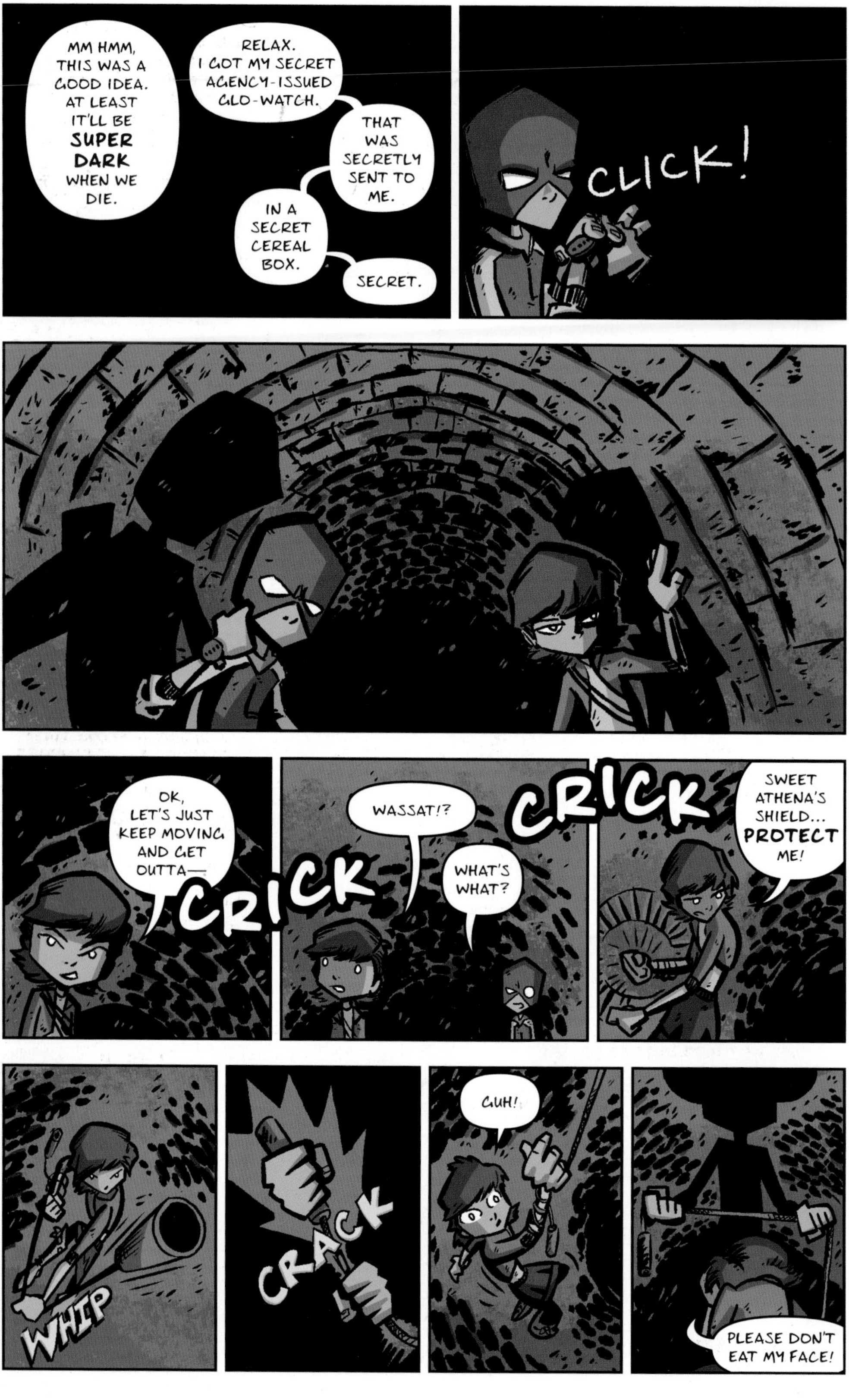
MM HMM, THIS WAS A GOOD IDEA. AT LEAST IT'LL BE SUPER DARK WHEN WE DIE.
RELAX. I GOT MY SECRET AGENCY-ISSUED GLO-WATCH.
THAT WAS SECRETLY SENT TO ME.
IN A SECRET CEREAL BOX.
SECRET.
CLICK!
OK, LET'S JUST KEEP MOVING AND GET OUTTA—
CRICK
WASSAT!?
WHAT'S WHAT?
CRICK
SWEET ATHENA'S SHIELD... PROTECT ME!
WHIP
CRACK
GUH!
PLEASE DON'T EAT MY FACE!

C'MON NOW! HOBBLE YOUR LIPS!

I COULD HEAR YOU EGGHEADS COMIN' A MILE AWAY!

CLINTON! THANK HEAVEN IT'S ONLY— WAIT!

WHAT'RE **YOU** DOIN' IN **MY** YARD?

LOOKIN' FER THE TWO A YOU!

IN HERE?

OH, YEAH, AIN'T THIS THE PLACE TO GO FOR A PICNIC?

I GOT CHASED BY SOME ZOMBIE FOLK 'N' DUCKED IN HERE 'FORE THEY COULD SEE. WHAT'RE YOU TWO DOIN' IN HERE?

KISSIN'!

GROSS. NO, BRYCE THOUGHT IT WAS A GOOD IDEA TO PASS THROUGH THESE RATHER THAN OVER.

KISS KISS!

STOP THAT!

GOOD THINKIN'. THEY'D BE EXPECTIN' THE LATTER.

REALLY??

SO, WHY US?

WELP, FIGURE A WHOMPER-JAWED SITUATION LIKE THIS? JUST FER TODAY, PUT OUR PAST BEHIND US AND SADDLE UP TOGETHER.

THE THREE OF US CAN TRY 'N' **FIX** THIS. WHATEVER **THIS** IS.

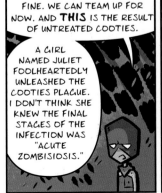

FINE. WE CAN TEAM UP FOR NOW. AND **THIS** IS THE RESULT OF UNTREATED COOTIES.

A GIRL NAMED JULIET FOOLHEARTEDLY UNLEASHED THE COOTIES PLAGUE. I DON'T THINK SHE KNEW THE FINAL STAGES OF THE INFECTION WAS "ACUTE ZOMBISIOSIS."

NOW, WHY WOULD SHE GO AND DO A CRAZY THING LIKE THAT?

SHE WANTED TO MARRY BRYCE!

COURSE THIS IS CUZ A YOU. TROUBLE FINDS YOU, BRYCE.

TROUBLE **ALWAYS** FINDS YOU.

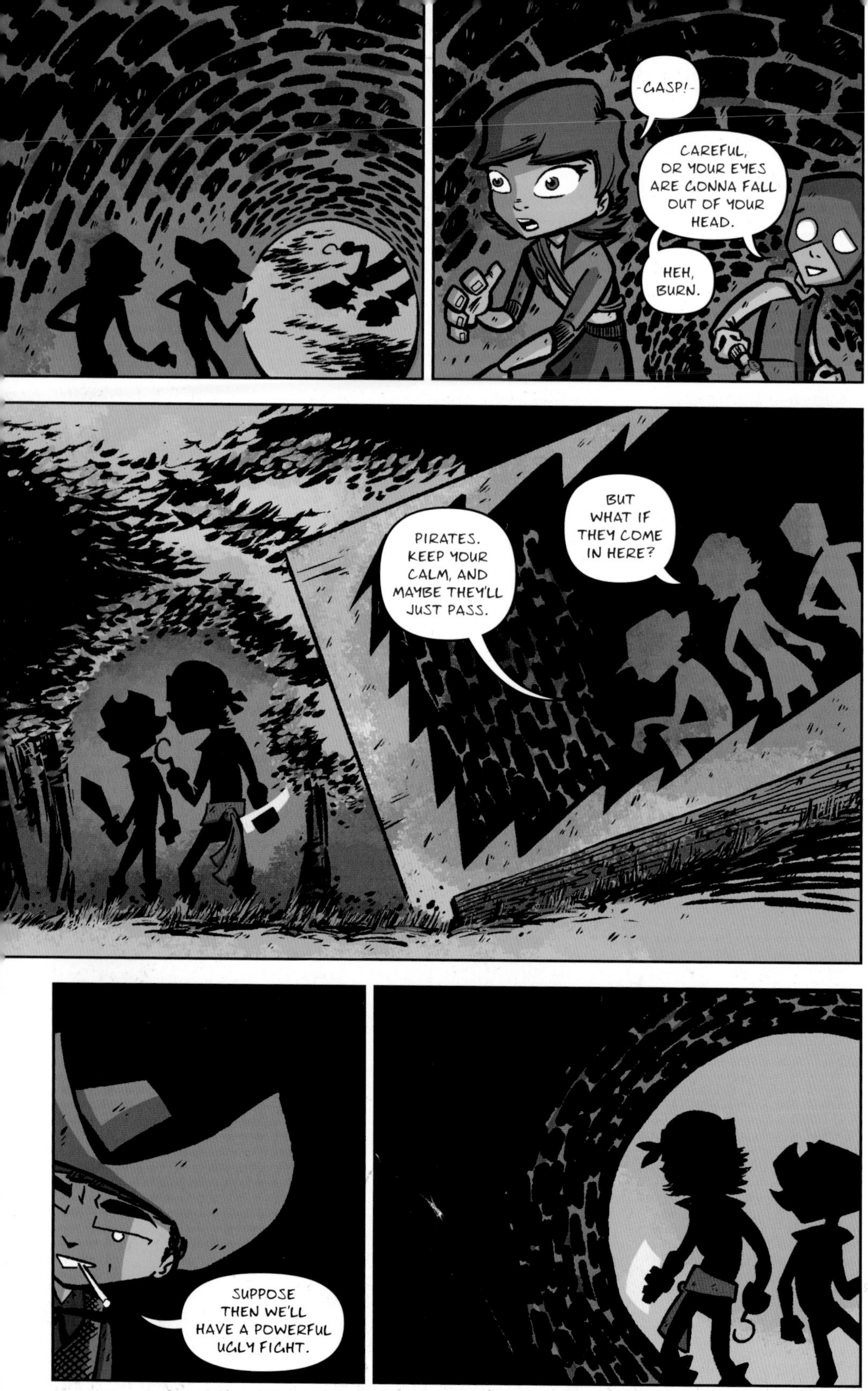
-GASP!-
CAREFUL, OR YOUR EYES ARE GONNA FALL OUT OF YOUR HEAD.
HEH, BURN.
PIRATES. KEEP YOUR CALM, AND MAYBE THEY'LL JUST PASS.
BUT WHAT IF THEY COME IN HERE?
SUPPOSE THEN WE'LL HAVE A POWERFUL UGLY FIGHT.

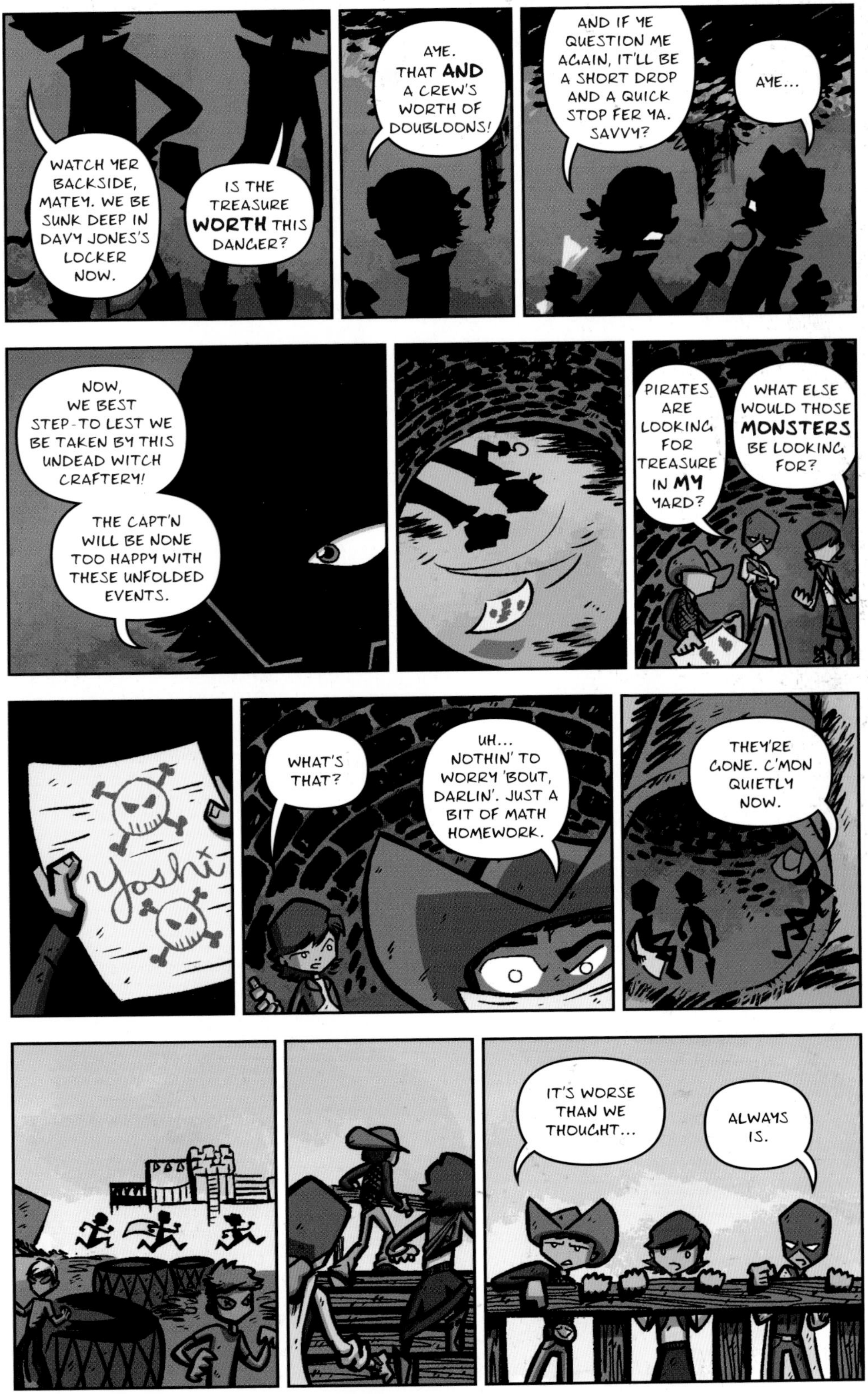
WATCH YER BACKSIDE, MATEY. WE BE SUNK DEEP IN DAVY JONES'S LOCKER NOW.
IS THE TREASURE WORTH THIS DANGER?
AYE. THAT AND A CREW'S WORTH OF DOUBLOONS!
AND IF YE QUESTION ME AGAIN, IT'LL BE A SHORT DROP AND A QUICK STOP FER YA. SAVVY?
AYE...
NOW, WE BEST STEP-TO LEST WE BE TAKEN BY THIS UNDEAD WITCH CRAFTERY!
THE CAPT'N WILL BE NONE TOO HAPPY WITH THESE UNFOLDED EVENTS.
PIRATES ARE LOOKING FOR TREASURE IN MY YARD?
WHAT ELSE WOULD THOSE MONSTERS BE LOOKING FOR?
Yoshi
WHAT'S THAT?
UH... NOTHIN' TO WORRY 'BOUT, DARLIN'. JUST A BIT OF MATH HOMEWORK.
THEY'RE GONE. C'MON QUIETLY NOW.
IT'S WORSE THAN WE THOUGHT...
ALWAYS IS.

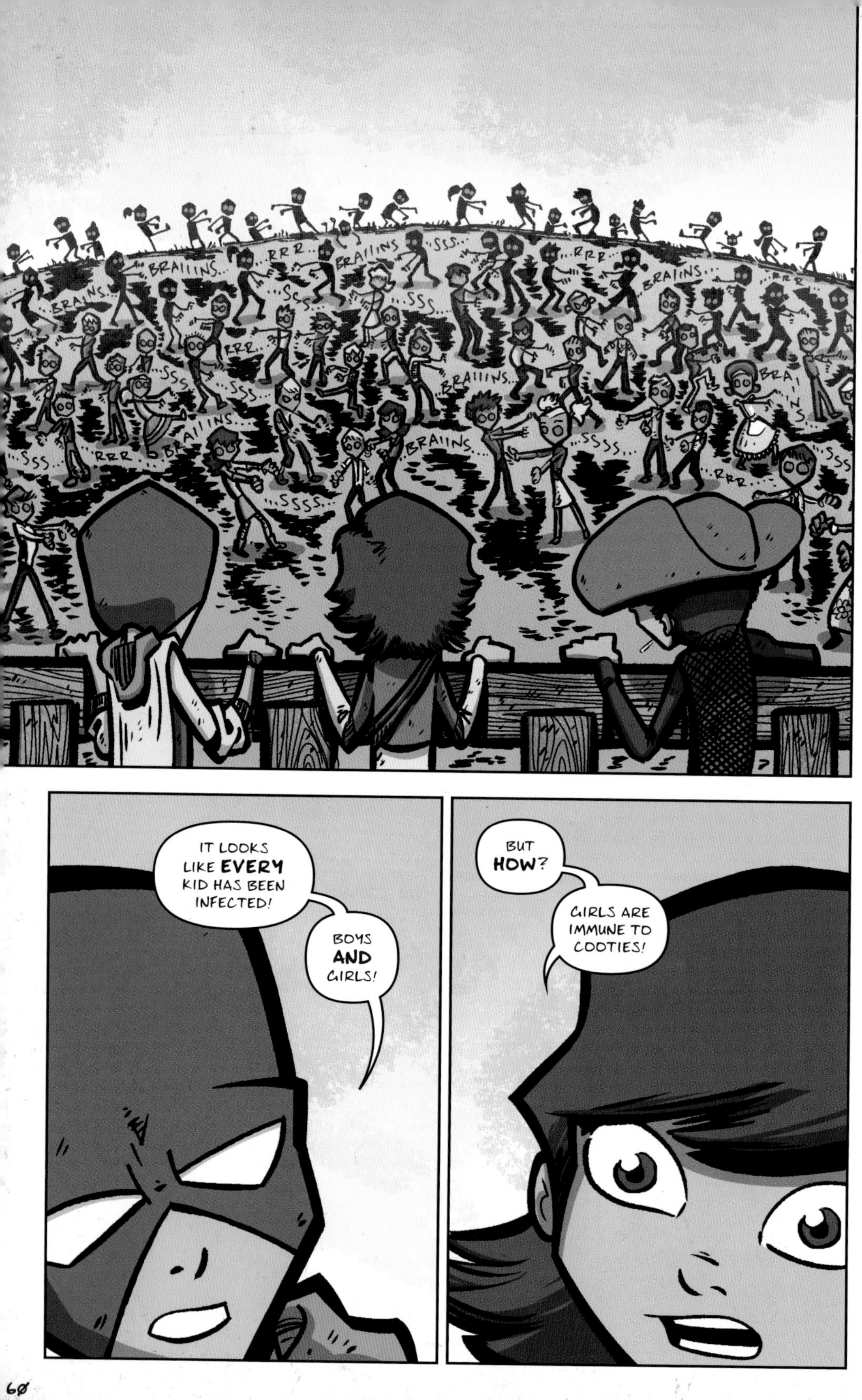
...RRR...
BRAIIINS...
...SSS...
BRAIIINS...
...RRR...
BRAIIINS...
BRAIINS...
...SSS...
...SSS...
...RRR...
...RRR...
...SSS...
...SSS...
BRAIIINS...
BRAIIINS...
BRA
INS...
...SSS...
...RRR...
BRAIIINS...
BRAIIINS...
...SSSS...
...RRR...
...SSS
...SSSS...
IT LOOKS LIKE EVERY KID HAS BEEN INFECTED!
BOYS AND GIRLS!
BUT HOW?
GIRLS ARE IMMUNE TO COOTIES!

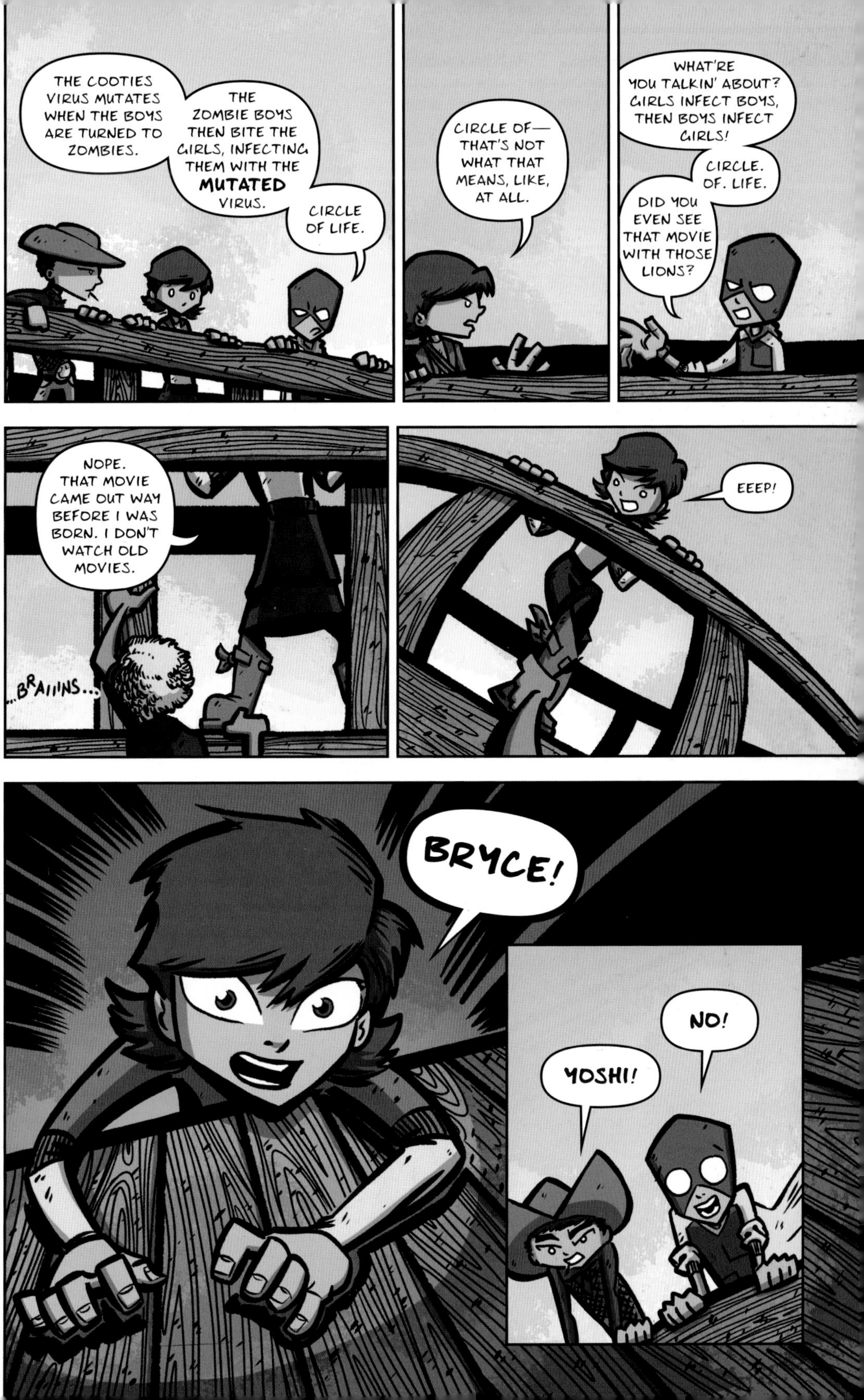
THE COOTIES VIRUS MUTATES WHEN THE BOYS ARE TURNED TO ZOMBIES.
THE ZOMBIE BOYS THEN BITE THE GIRLS, INFECTING THEM WITH THE **MUTATED** VIRUS.
CIRCLE OF LIFE.
CIRCLE OF— THAT'S NOT WHAT THAT MEANS, LIKE, AT ALL.
WHAT'RE YOU TALKIN' ABOUT? GIRLS INFECT BOYS, THEN BOYS INFECT GIRLS!
CIRCLE. OF. LIFE.
DID YOU EVEN SEE THAT MOVIE WITH THOSE LIONS?
NOPE. THAT MOVIE CAME OUT WAY BEFORE I WAS BORN. I DON'T WATCH OLD MOVIES.
...BRAIINS...
EEEP!
BRYCE!
NO!
YOSHI!

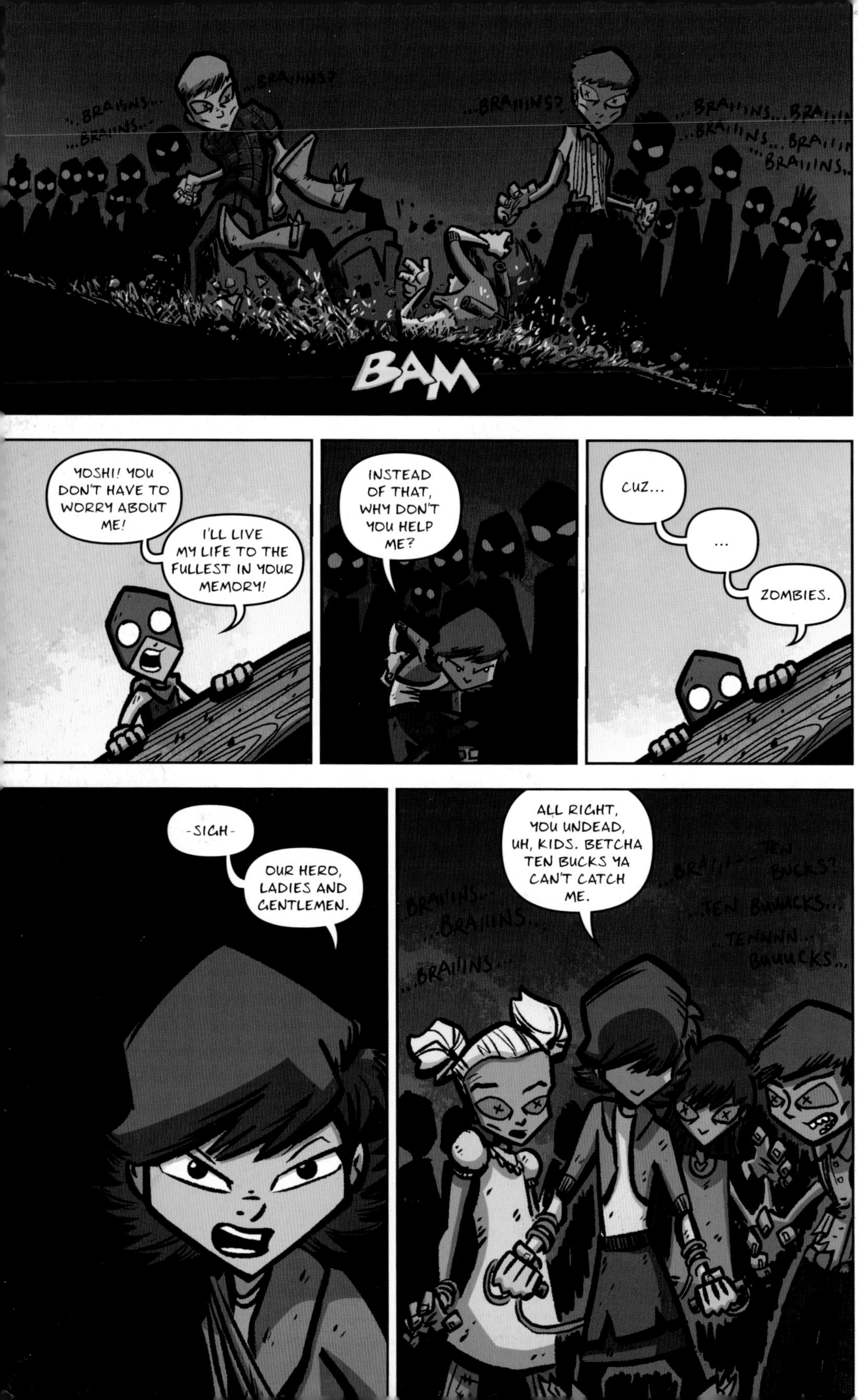
...BRAIIINS...
...BRAIINS...
...BRAIIINS?
...BRAIIINS?
...BRAIIINS... BRAIIINS...
...BRAIIINS... BRAIIINS...
BRAIIINS...
BAM
YOSHI! YOU DON'T HAVE TO WORRY ABOUT ME!
I'LL LIVE MY LIFE TO THE FULLEST IN YOUR MEMORY!
INSTEAD OF THAT, WHY DON'T YOU HELP ME?
CUZ...
...
ZOMBIES.
-SIGH-
OUR HERO, LADIES AND GENTLEMEN.
ALL RIGHT, YOU UNDEAD, UH, KIDS. BETCHA TEN BUCKS YA CAN'T CATCH ME.
BRAIIINS...
...BRAIIINS...
...BRAIIINS...
...BRAIIINS? TEN BUCKS?
...TEN BUUUCKS...
...TENNNN... BUUUCKS...

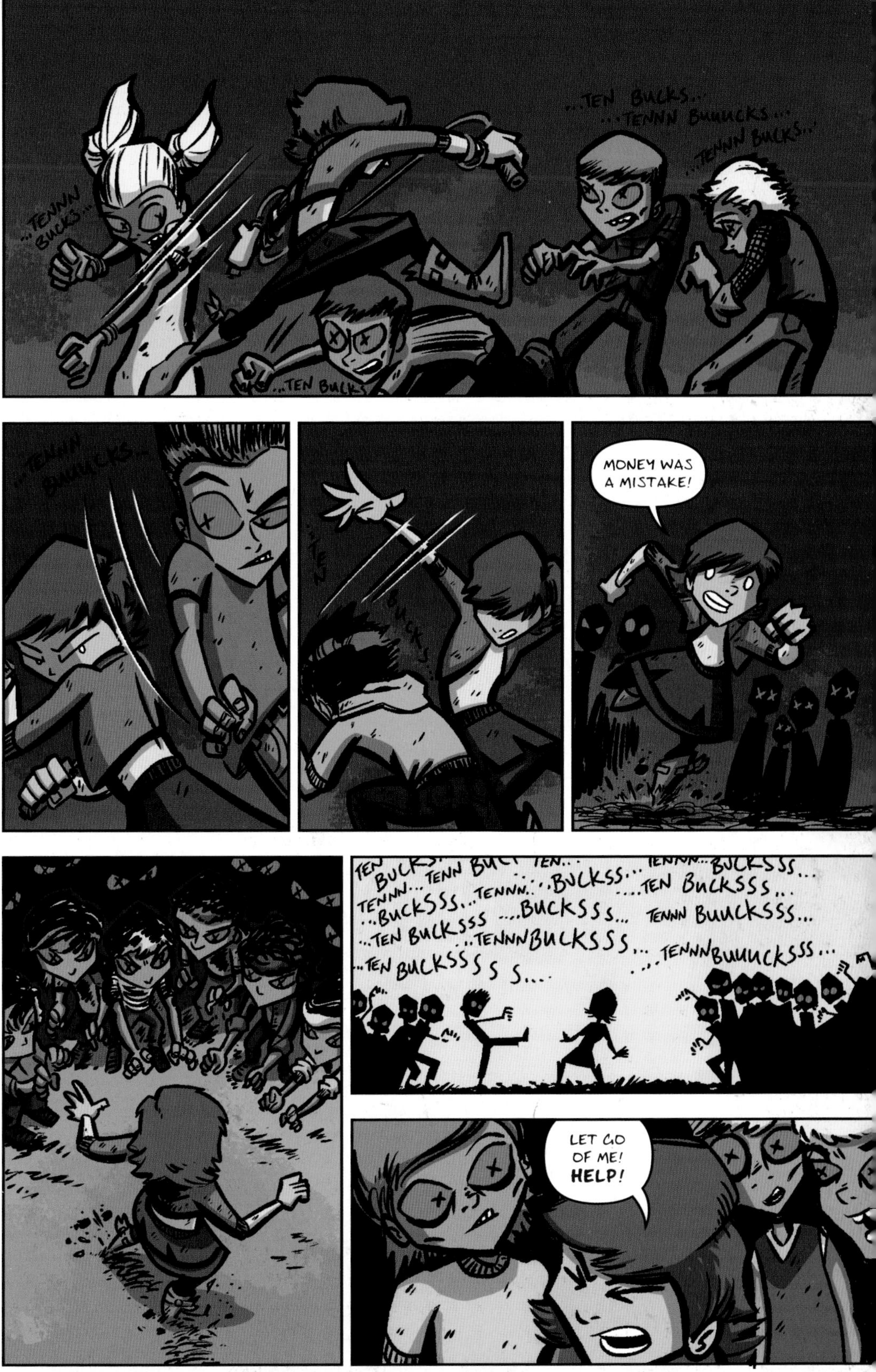
...TEN BUCKS...
...TENNN BUUUCKS...
...TENNN BUCKS...
...TENNN BUCKS...
...TEN BUCKS
...TENNN BUUUCKS...
...TEN BUCKS
MONEY WAS A MISTAKE!
TENNN... TENN BU
TENNN... ...BUCKSS... ...TEN BUCKSSS...
...BUCKSSS... ...BUCKSSS... TENNN BUUUCKSSS...
...TEN BUCKSSS ...TENNNBUCKSSS... ...TENNNBUUUCKSSS...
...TEN BUCKSSSS...
LET GO OF ME! **HELP!**

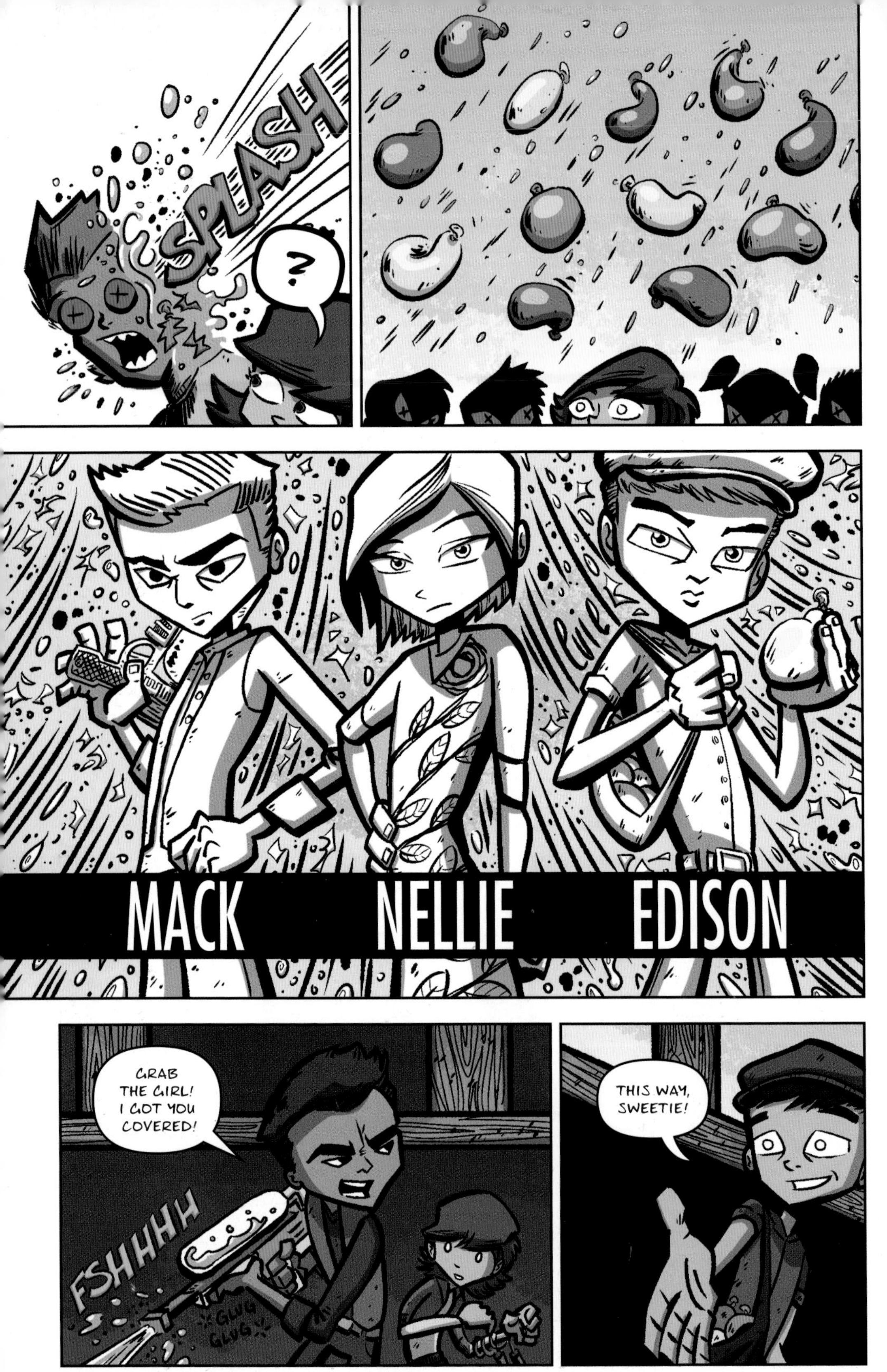
SPLASH
?
MACK
NELLIE
EDISON
GRAB THE GIRL! I GOT YOU COVERED!
FSHHHH
GLUG GLUG
THIS WAY, SWEETIE!

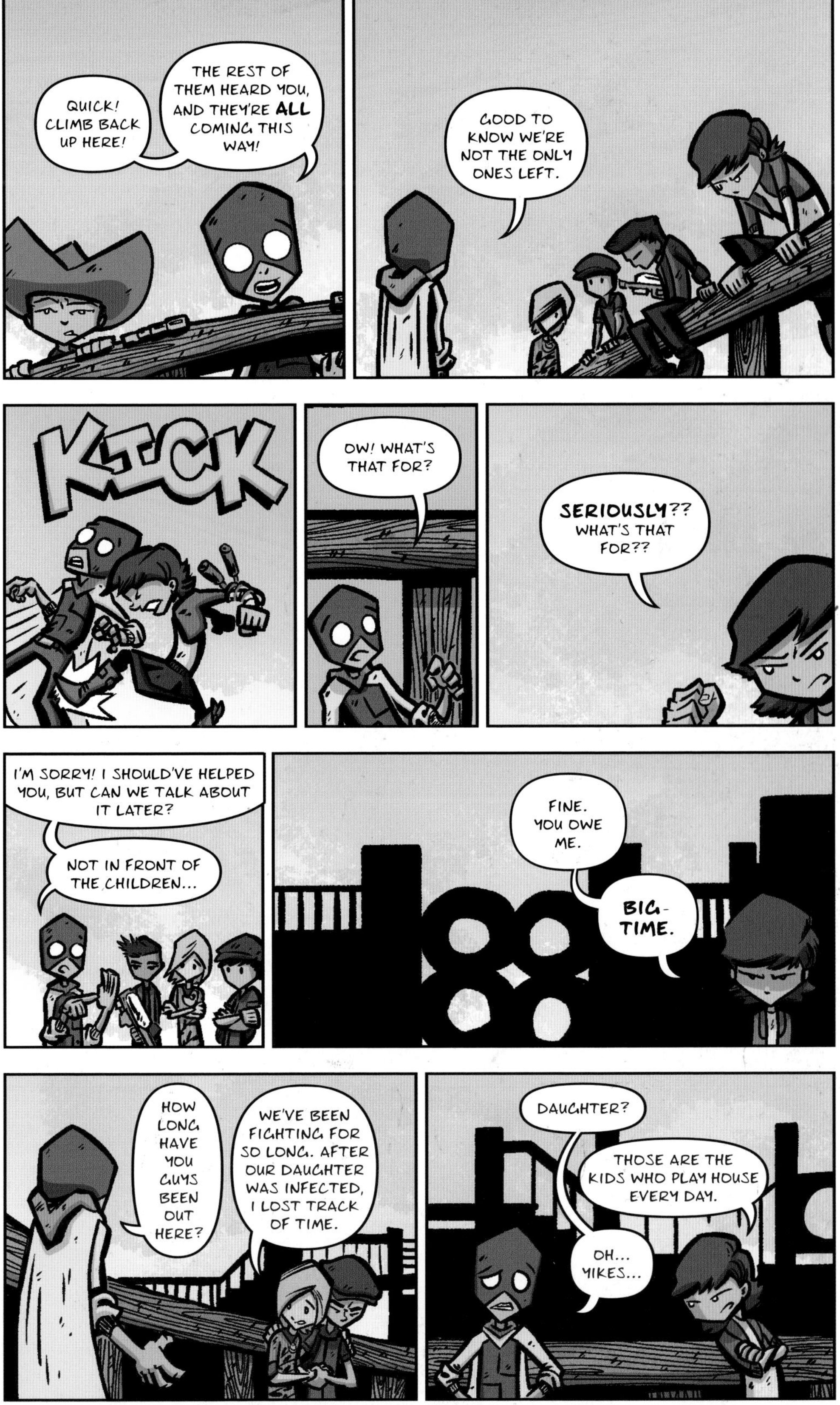
QUICK! CLIMB BACK UP HERE!
THE REST OF THEM HEARD YOU, AND THEY'RE ALL COMING THIS WAY!
GOOD TO KNOW WE'RE NOT THE ONLY ONES LEFT.
KICK
OW! WHAT'S THAT FOR?
SERIOUSLY?? WHAT'S THAT FOR??
I'M SORRY! I SHOULD'VE HELPED YOU, BUT CAN WE TALK ABOUT IT LATER?
NOT IN FRONT OF THE CHILDREN...
FINE. YOU OWE ME.
BIG-TIME.
HOW LONG HAVE YOU GUYS BEEN OUT HERE?
WE'VE BEEN FIGHTING FOR SO LONG. AFTER OUR DAUGHTER WAS INFECTED, I LOST TRACK OF TIME.
DAUGHTER?
THOSE ARE THE KIDS WHO PLAY HOUSE EVERY DAY.
OH... YIKES...

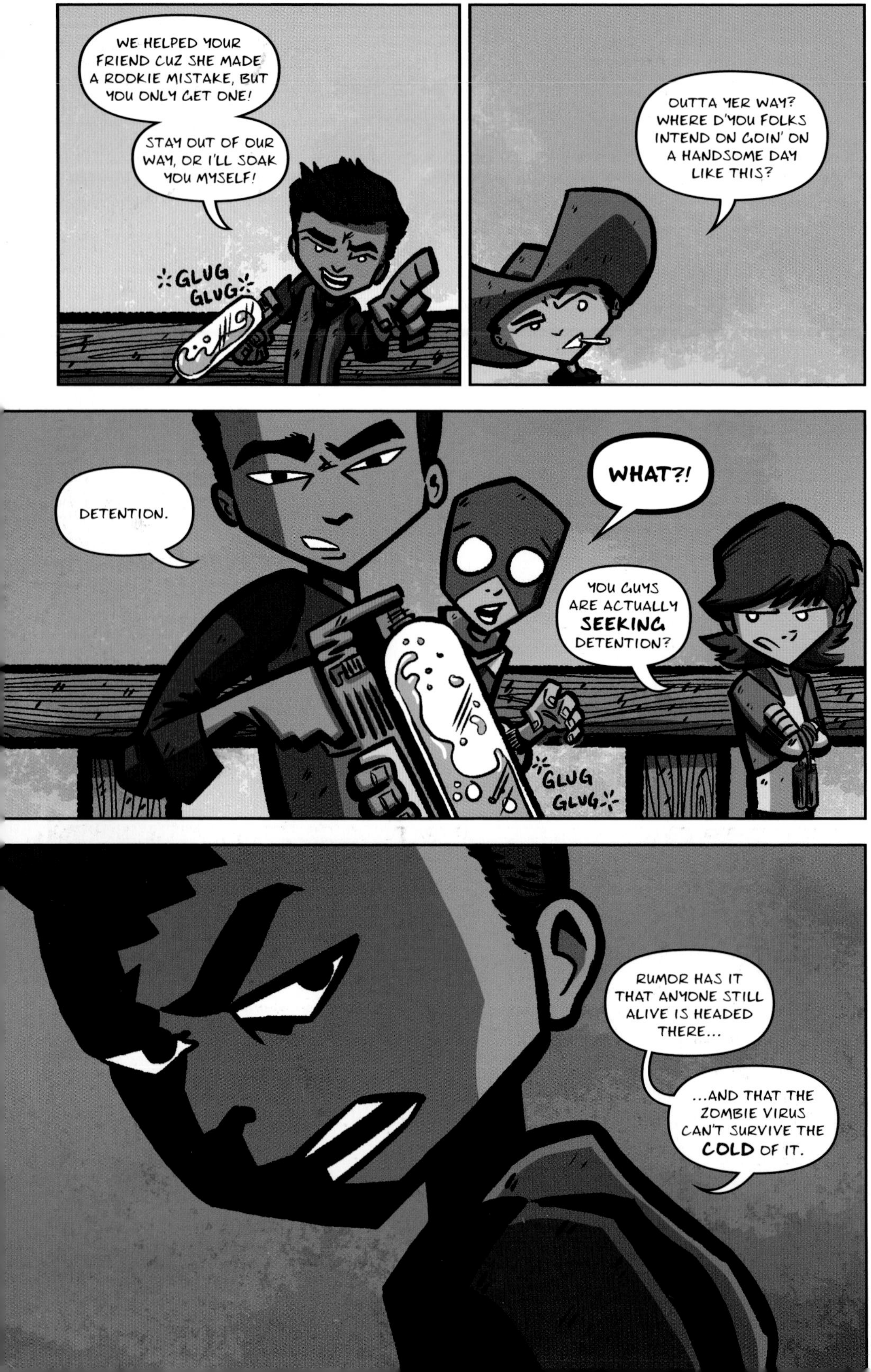
WE HELPED YOUR FRIEND CUZ SHE MADE A ROOKIE MISTAKE, BUT YOU ONLY GET ONE!
STAY OUT OF OUR WAY, OR I'LL SOAK YOU MYSELF!
GLUG GLUG
OUTTA YER WAY? WHERE D'YOU FOLKS INTEND ON GOIN' ON A HANDSOME DAY LIKE THIS?
DETENTION.
WHAT?!
YOU GUYS ARE ACTUALLY **SEEKING** DETENTION?
GLUG GLUG
RUMOR HAS IT THAT ANYONE STILL ALIVE IS HEADED THERE...
...AND THAT THE ZOMBIE VIRUS CAN'T SURVIVE THE **COLD** OF IT.

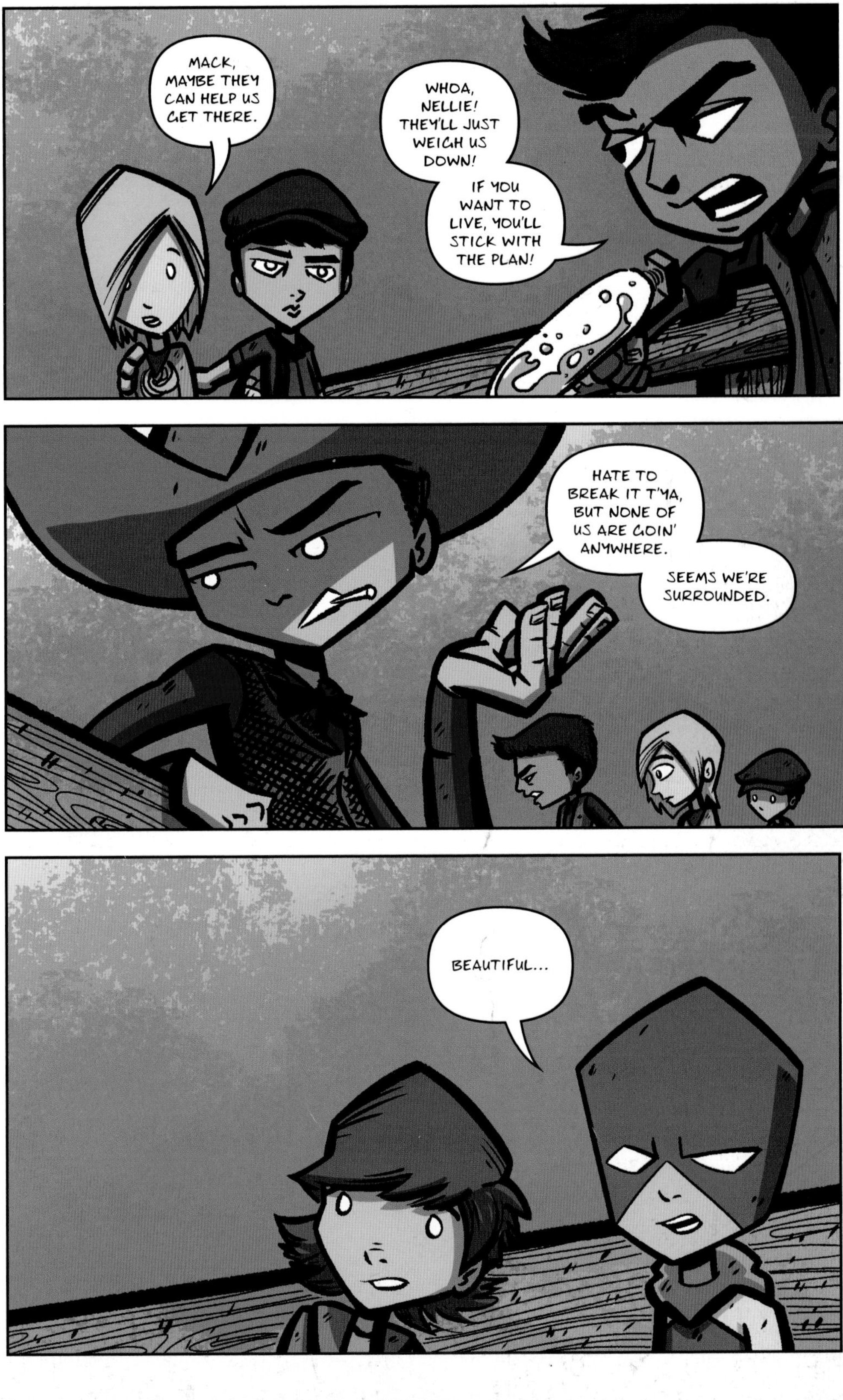
MACK, MAYBE THEY CAN HELP US GET THERE.
WHOA, NELLIE! THEY'LL JUST WEIGH US DOWN!
IF YOU WANT TO LIVE, YOU'LL STICK WITH THE PLAN!
HATE TO BREAK IT T'YA, BUT NONE OF US ARE GOIN' ANYWHERE.
SEEMS WE'RE SURROUNDED.
BEAUTIFUL...

BR...
BRAIIINS... BRAIIINS... BRAIIINS... BRAIIINS... BRAIIINS... BRAIIINS... ''INS... BRAIIINS... BRAIIINS... BRAII
INS... BRAIIINS... BRAIIINS... BRAIIINS... BRAIIINS... BRAIIINS... BRAIIINS... BRAIIINS... BRAIIINS... BRAIIINS
INS... BRAIIINS... BRAIIINS... BRAIIINS... BRAIIINS... BRAIIINS... BRAIIINS... BRAIIINS... BRAIIINS
BRAIIINS... BRAIINS... BRAIIINS... BRAIIINS... BRAIIINS... BRAIIINS... BRAIIINS... BRAIIINS...
BRAIIINS... BRAIIINS... BRAIIINS... BRAIIINS... BRAIIINS... BRAIIINS... BRAIIINS... BRAIIINS...
AIIINS... BRAIIINS... BRAIIINS... BRAIIINS... BRAIIINS... BRAIIINS... BRAIIINS... BRAIIINS...
BRAIIINS... BRAIIINS... BRAIIINS... BRAIIINS... BRAIIINS... BRAIIINS... BRAIIINS... BRAIIINS...
INS... BRAIIINS... BRAIIINS... BRAIIINS... BRAIIINS... BRAIIINS... BRAIIINS... BRAIIINS...
RAIINS... BRAIIINS... BRAIIINS... BRAIIINS... ''BRAIIINS...
RAIIINS... BRAIIINS...

THIS IS **YOUR** FAULT!

I SHOULDA LET THE ZOMBIES SCARF YOUR BRAINS! I OUGHTA SOAK YOU RIGHT HERE!

YOU SNAKE IN THE GRASS!

PUMP PUMP PUMP PUMP

BEST PUT THAT GUN DOWN, BOY.

DON'T TELL ME WHAT TO DO!

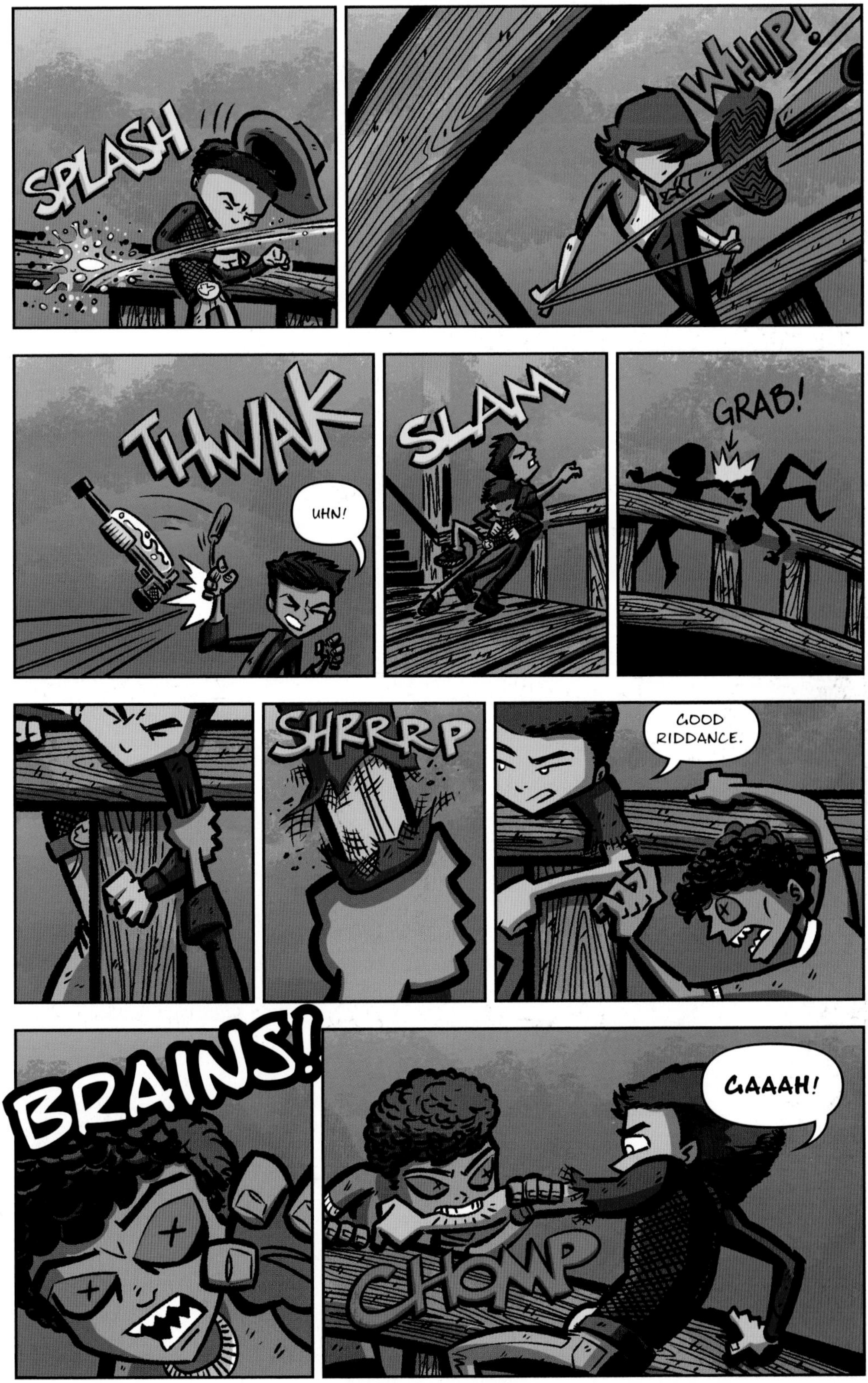
SPLASH
WHIP!
THWAK
UHN!
SLAM
GRAB!
SHRRRP
GOOD RIDDANCE.
BRAINS!
GAAAH!
CHOMP

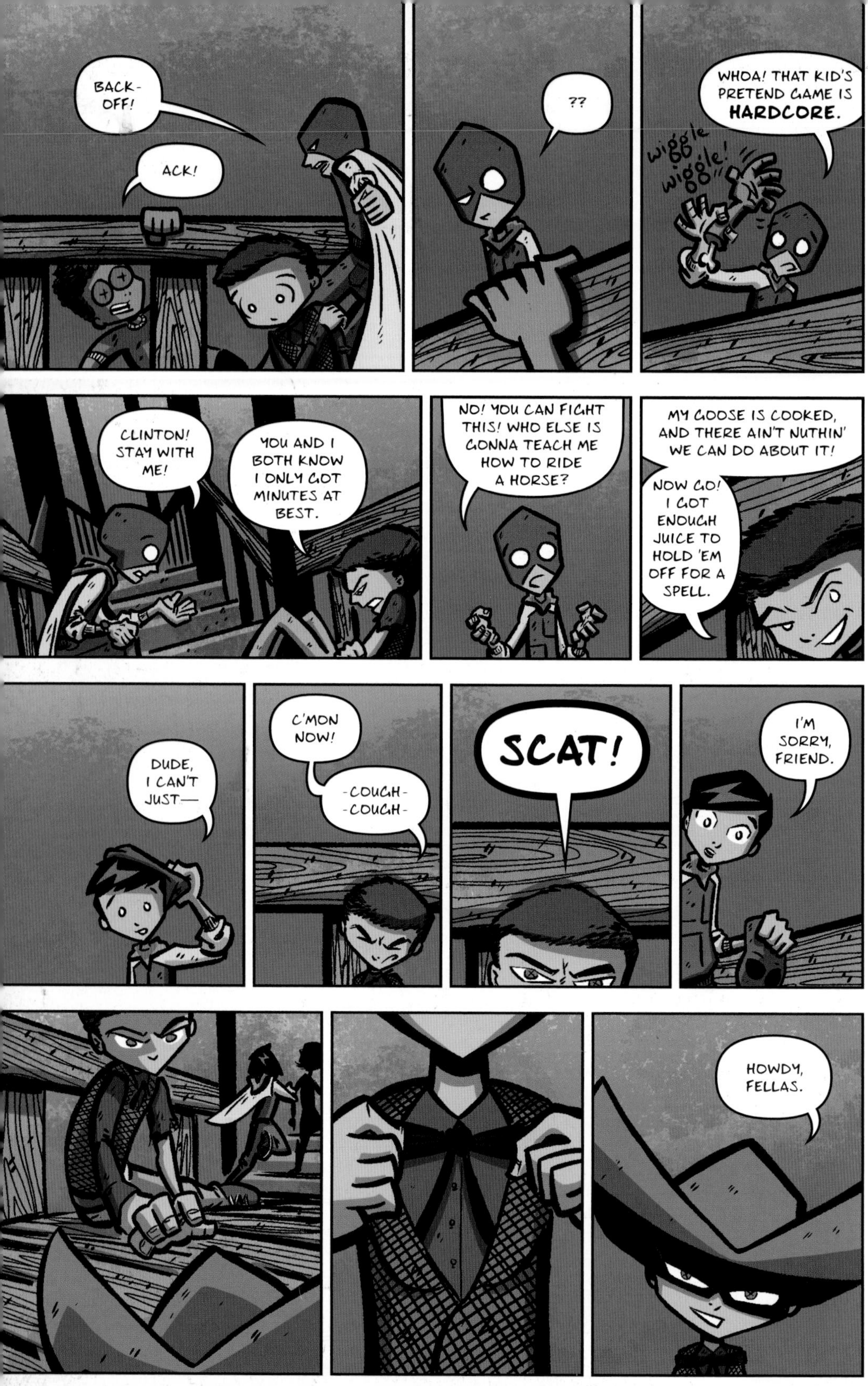
BACK-OFF!
ACK!
??
WHOA! THAT KID'S PRETEND GAME IS **HARDCORE.**
wiggle wiggle wiggle!
CLINTON! STAY WITH ME!
YOU AND I BOTH KNOW I ONLY GOT MINUTES AT BEST.
NO! YOU CAN FIGHT THIS! WHO ELSE IS GONNA TEACH ME HOW TO RIDE A HORSE?
MY GOOSE IS COOKED, AND THERE AIN'T NUTHIN' WE CAN DO ABOUT IT!
NOW GO! I GOT ENOUGH JUICE TO HOLD 'EM OFF FOR A SPELL.
DUDE, I CAN'T JUST—
C'MON NOW!
-COUGH- -COUGH-
SCAT!
I'M SORRY, FRIEND.
HOWDY, FELLAS.

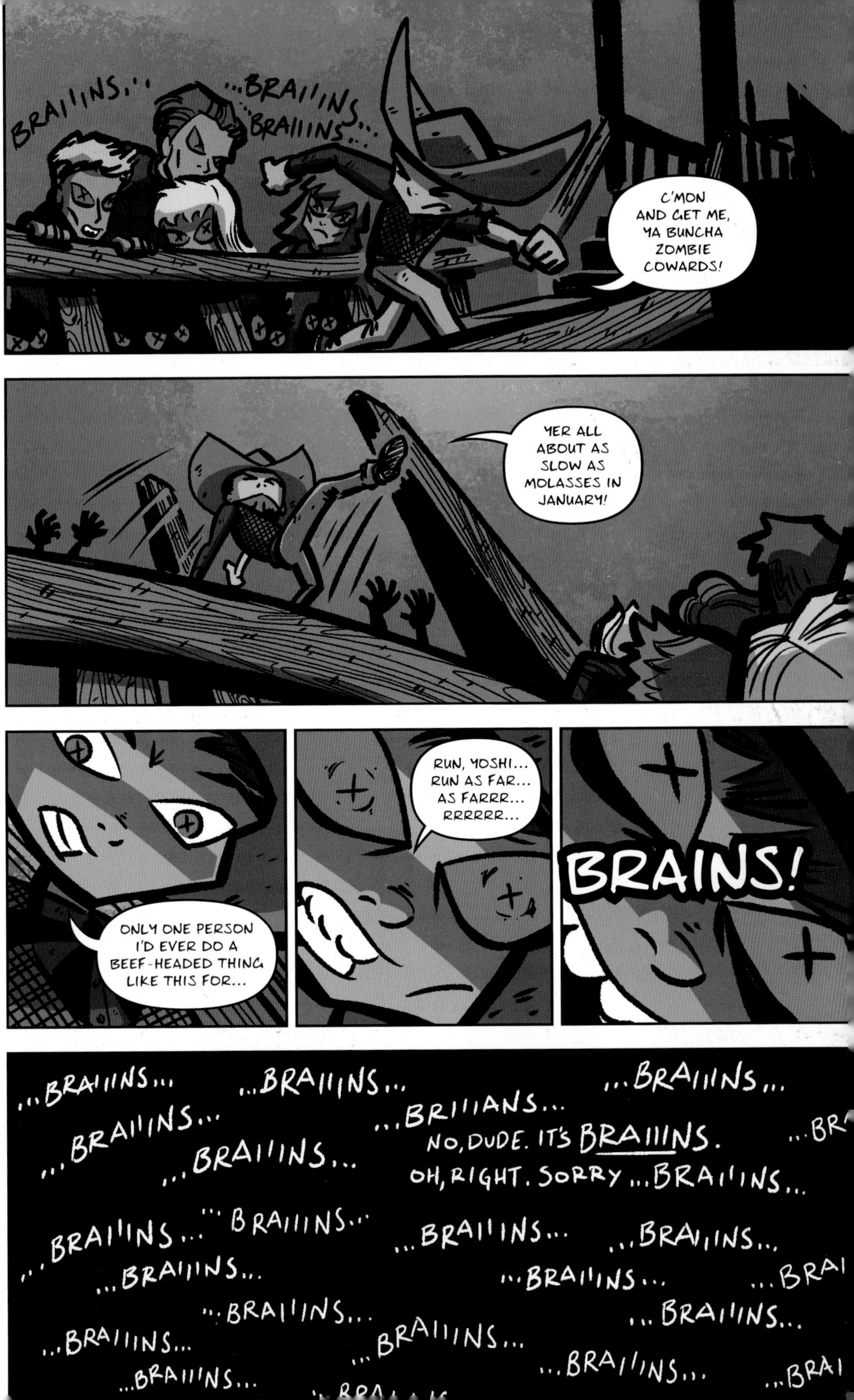

BRAIIINS...
...BRAIIINS
BRAIIINS...
C'MON AND GET ME, YA BUNCHA ZOMBIE COWARDS!
YER ALL ABOUT AS SLOW AS MOLASSES IN JANUARY!
ONLY ONE PERSON I'D EVER DO A BEEF-HEADED THING LIKE THIS FOR...
RUN, YOSHI... RUN AS FAR... AS FARRR... RRRRRR...
BRAINS!
...BRAIIINS...
...BRAIIINS...
...BRAIIINS...
...BRAIIINS...
...BRIIIANS...
...BRAIIINS...
NO, DUDE. IT'S BRAIIINS.
OH, RIGHT. SORRY ...BRAIIINS...
...BRAIIINS...
...BRAIIINS...
...BRAIIINS...
...BRAIIINS...
...BRAIIINS...
...BRAIIINS...
...BRAIIINS...
...BRAIIINS...
...BRAIIINS...
...BRAIIINS...
...BRAIIINS...
...BRAIIINS...
...BRAIIINS...

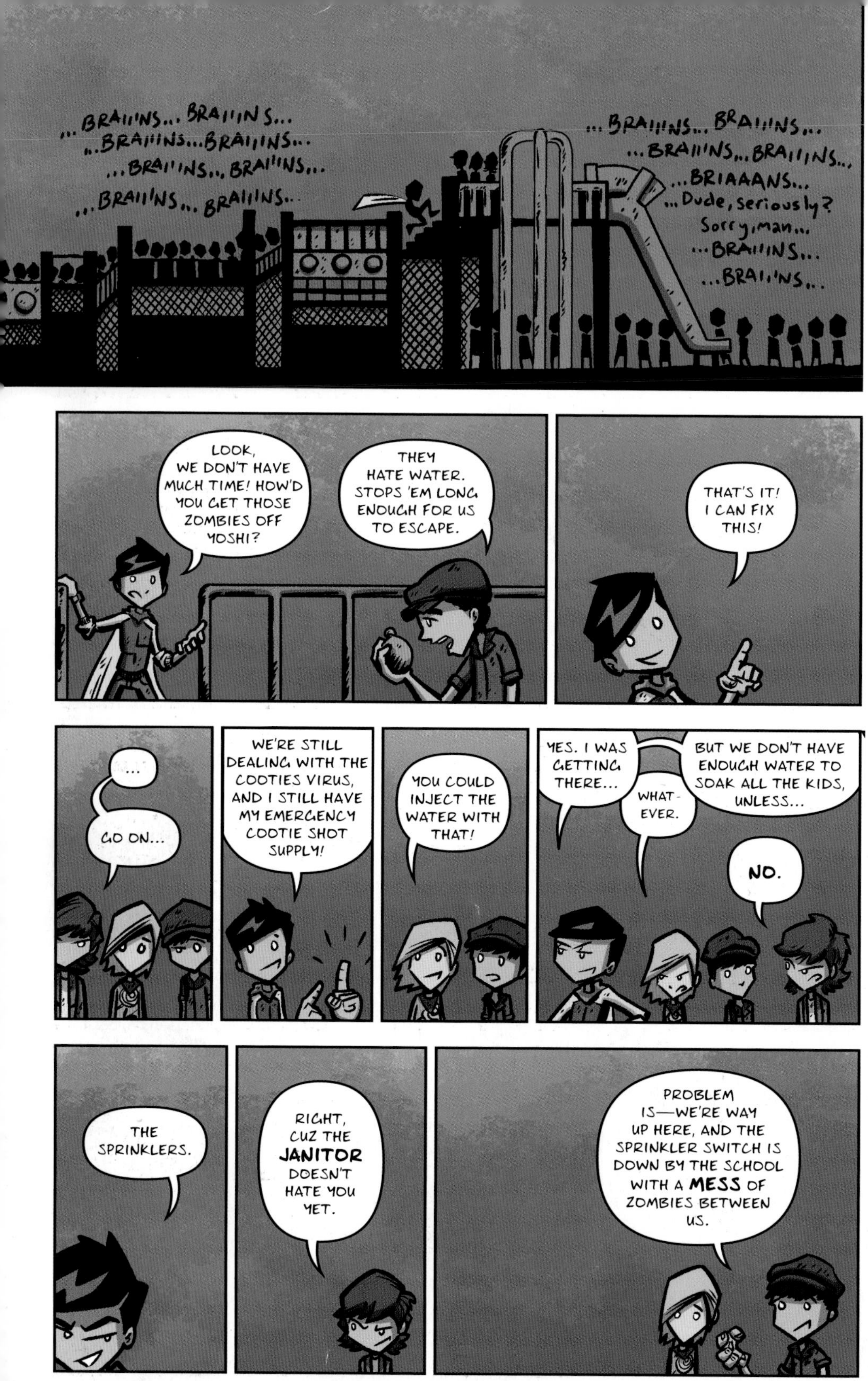
...BRAIIINS... BRAIIINS...
...BRAIIINS...BRAIIINS...
...BRAIIINS... BRAIIINS...
...BRAIIINS... BRAIIINS...
...BRAIIINS... BRAIIINS...
...BRAIIINS... BRAIIINS...
...BRIAAANS...
...Dude, seriously?
Sorry, man...
...BRAIIINS...
...BRAIIINS...
LOOK, WE DON'T HAVE MUCH TIME! HOW'D YOU GET THOSE ZOMBIES OFF YOSHI?
THEY HATE WATER. STOPS 'EM LONG ENOUGH FOR US TO ESCAPE.
THAT'S IT! I CAN FIX THIS!
...
GO ON...
WE'RE STILL DEALING WITH THE COOTIES VIRUS, AND I STILL HAVE MY EMERGENCY COOTIE SHOT SUPPLY!
YOU COULD INJECT THE WATER WITH THAT!
YES. I WAS GETTING THERE...
WHAT-EVER.
BUT WE DON'T HAVE ENOUGH WATER TO SOAK ALL THE KIDS, UNLESS...
NO.
THE SPRINKLERS.
RIGHT, CUZ THE JANITOR DOESN'T HATE YOU YET.
PROBLEM IS—WE'RE WAY UP HERE, AND THE SPRINKLER SWITCH IS DOWN BY THE SCHOOL WITH A MESS OF ZOMBIES BETWEEN US.

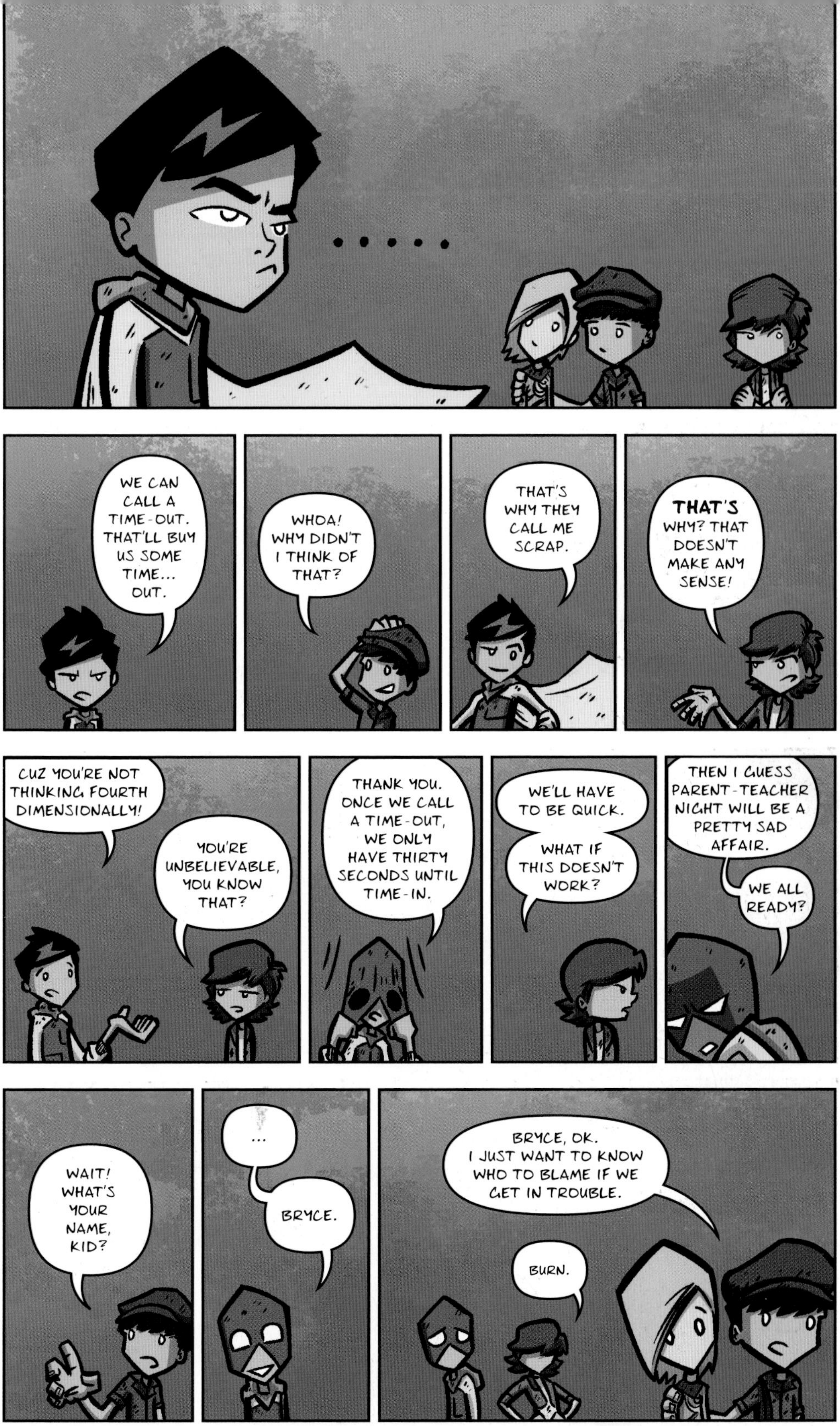
.....
WE CAN CALL A TIME-OUT. THAT'LL BUY US SOME TIME... OUT.
WHOA! WHY DIDN'T I THINK OF THAT?
THAT'S WHY THEY CALL ME SCRAP.
THAT'S WHY? THAT DOESN'T MAKE ANY SENSE!
CUZ YOU'RE NOT THINKING FOURTH DIMENSIONALLY!
YOU'RE UNBELIEVABLE, YOU KNOW THAT?
THANK YOU. ONCE WE CALL A TIME-OUT, WE ONLY HAVE THIRTY SECONDS UNTIL TIME-IN.
WE'LL HAVE TO BE QUICK.
WHAT IF THIS DOESN'T WORK?
THEN I GUESS PARENT-TEACHER NIGHT WILL BE A PRETTY SAD AFFAIR.
WE ALL READY?
WAIT! WHAT'S YOUR NAME, KID?
...
BRYCE.
BRYCE, OK. I JUST WANT TO KNOW WHO TO BLAME IF WE GET IN TROUBLE.
BURN.

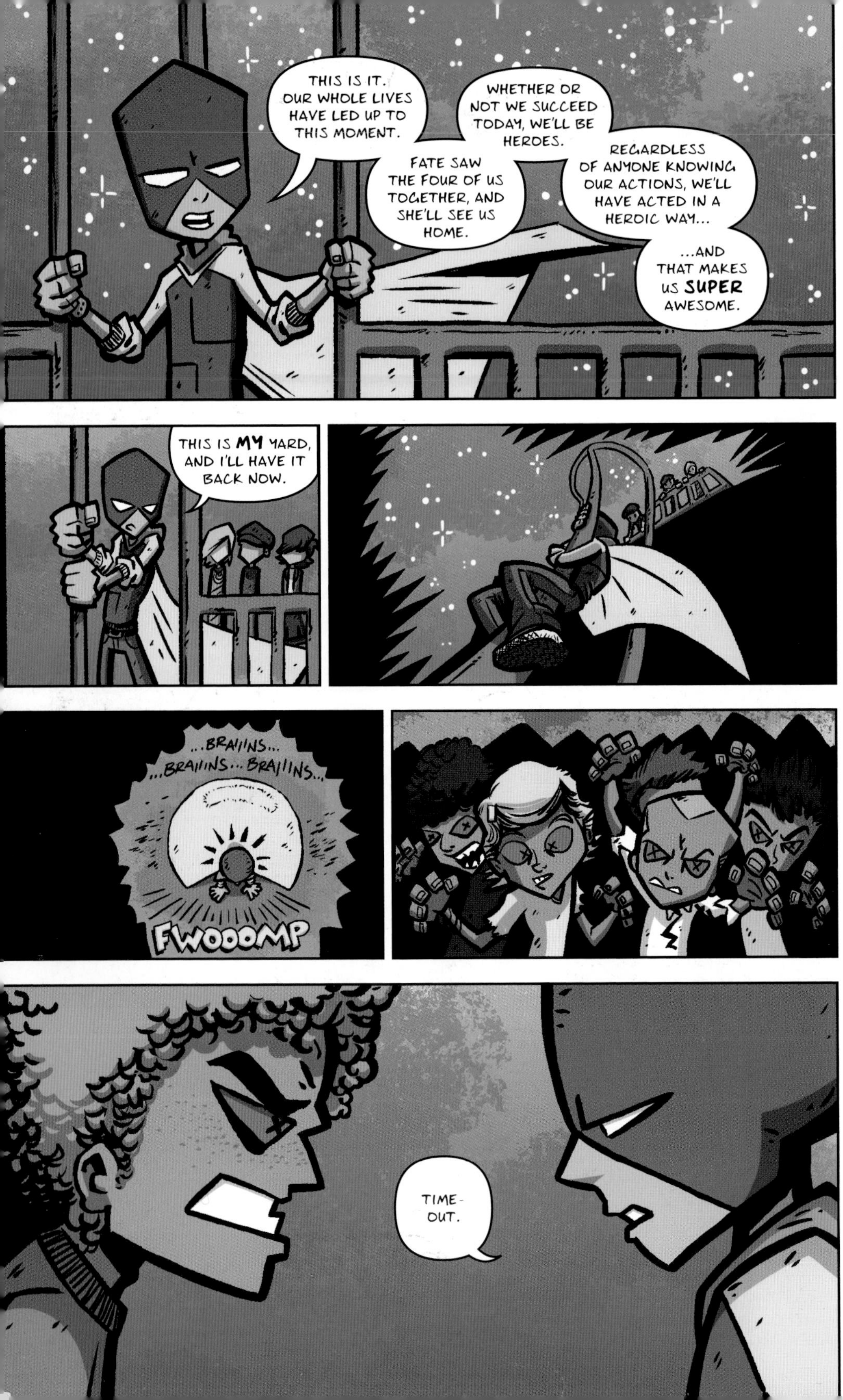

THIS IS IT. OUR WHOLE LIVES HAVE LED UP TO THIS MOMENT.
WHETHER OR NOT WE SUCCEED TODAY, WE'LL BE HEROES.
FATE SAW THE FOUR OF US TOGETHER, AND SHE'LL SEE US HOME.
REGARDLESS OF ANYONE KNOWING OUR ACTIONS, WE'LL HAVE ACTED IN A HEROIC WAY...
...AND THAT MAKES US **SUPER** AWESOME.
THIS IS **MY** YARD, AND I'LL HAVE IT BACK NOW.
...BRAIIINS... ...BRAIIINS... BRAIIINS...
FWOOOMP
TIME-OUT.

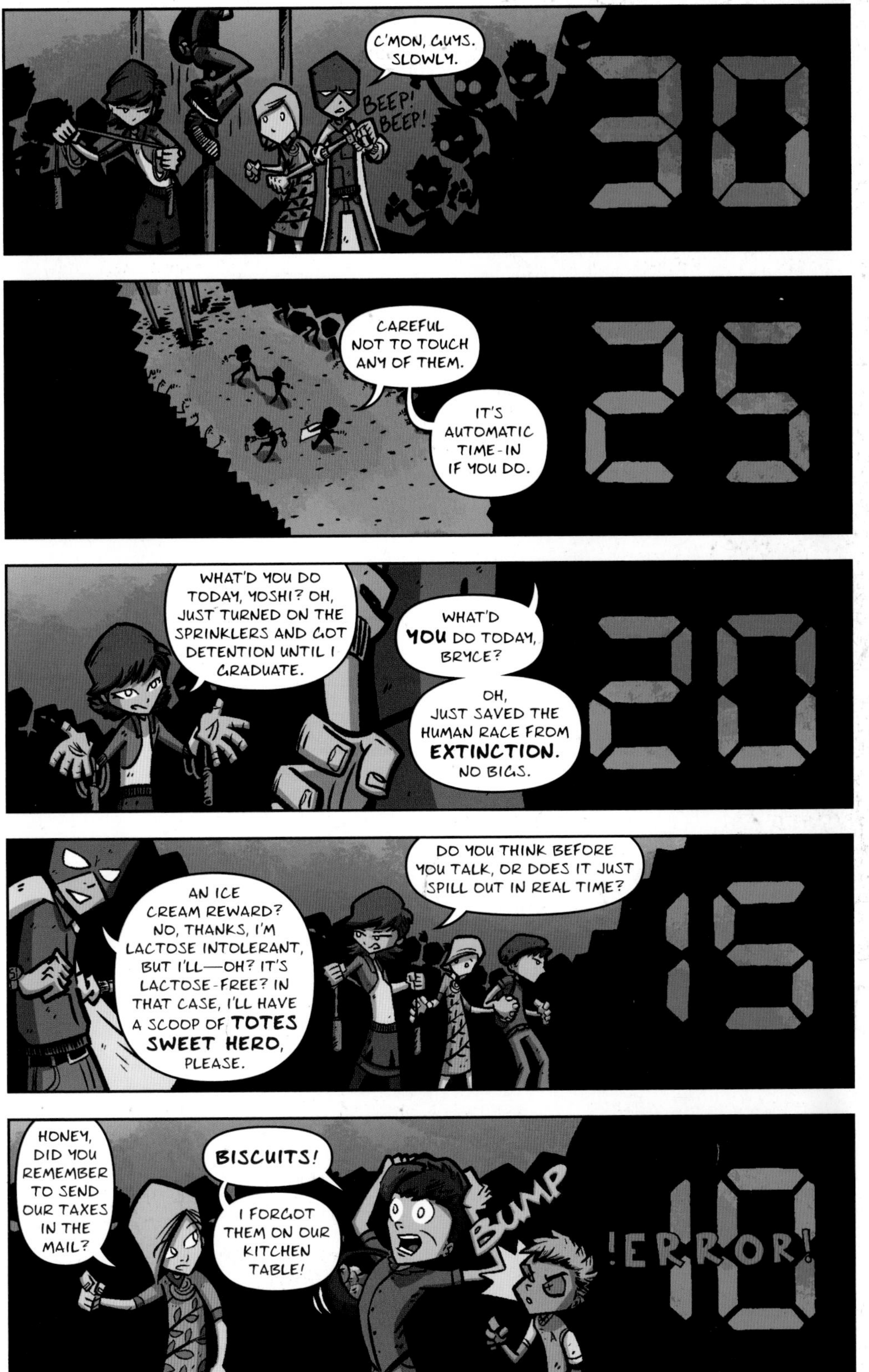
C'MON, GUYS. SLOWLY.
BEEP! BEEP!
30
CAREFUL NOT TO TOUCH ANY OF THEM.
IT'S AUTOMATIC TIME-IN IF YOU DO.
25
WHAT'D YOU DO TODAY, YOSHI? OH, JUST TURNED ON THE SPRINKLERS AND GOT DETENTION UNTIL I GRADUATE.
WHAT'D YOU DO TODAY, BRYCE?
OH, JUST SAVED THE HUMAN RACE FROM EXTINCTION. NO BIGS.
20
AN ICE CREAM REWARD? NO, THANKS, I'M LACTOSE INTOLERANT, BUT I'LL—OH? IT'S LACTOSE-FREE? IN THAT CASE, I'LL HAVE A SCOOP OF TOTES SWEET HERO, PLEASE.
DO YOU THINK BEFORE YOU TALK, OR DOES IT JUST SPILL OUT IN REAL TIME?
15
HONEY, DID YOU REMEMBER TO SEND OUR TAXES IN THE MAIL?
BISCUITS!
I FORGOT THEM ON OUR KITCHEN TABLE!
BUMP
10
!ERROR!

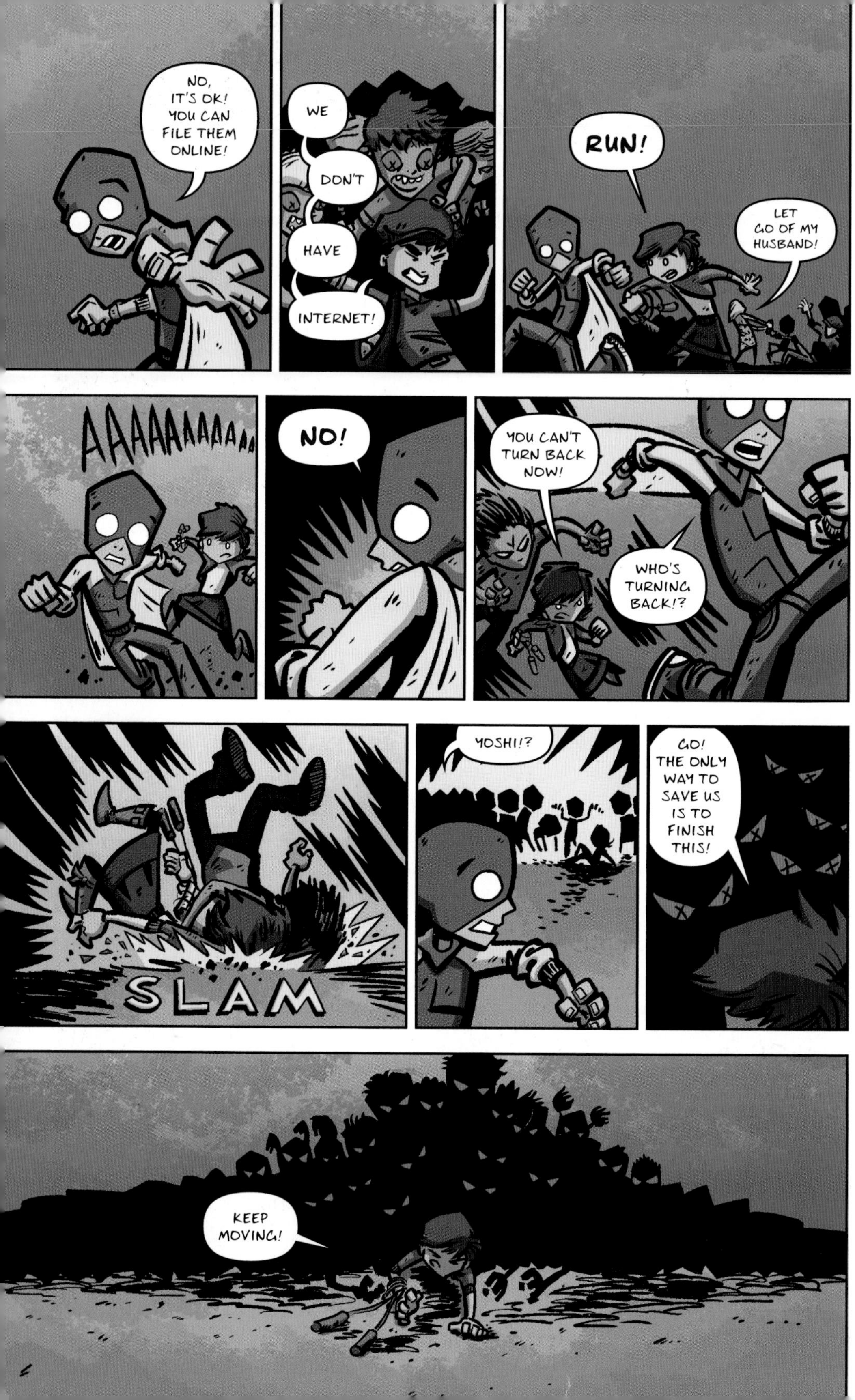
NO, IT'S OK! YOU CAN FILE THEM ONLINE!
WE
DON'T
HAVE
INTERNET!
RUN!
LET GO OF MY HUSBAND!
AAAAAAAAAA
NO!
YOU CAN'T TURN BACK NOW!
WHO'S TURNING BACK!?
SLAM
YOSHI!?
GO! THE ONLY WAY TO SAVE US IS TO FINISH THIS!
KEEP MOVING!

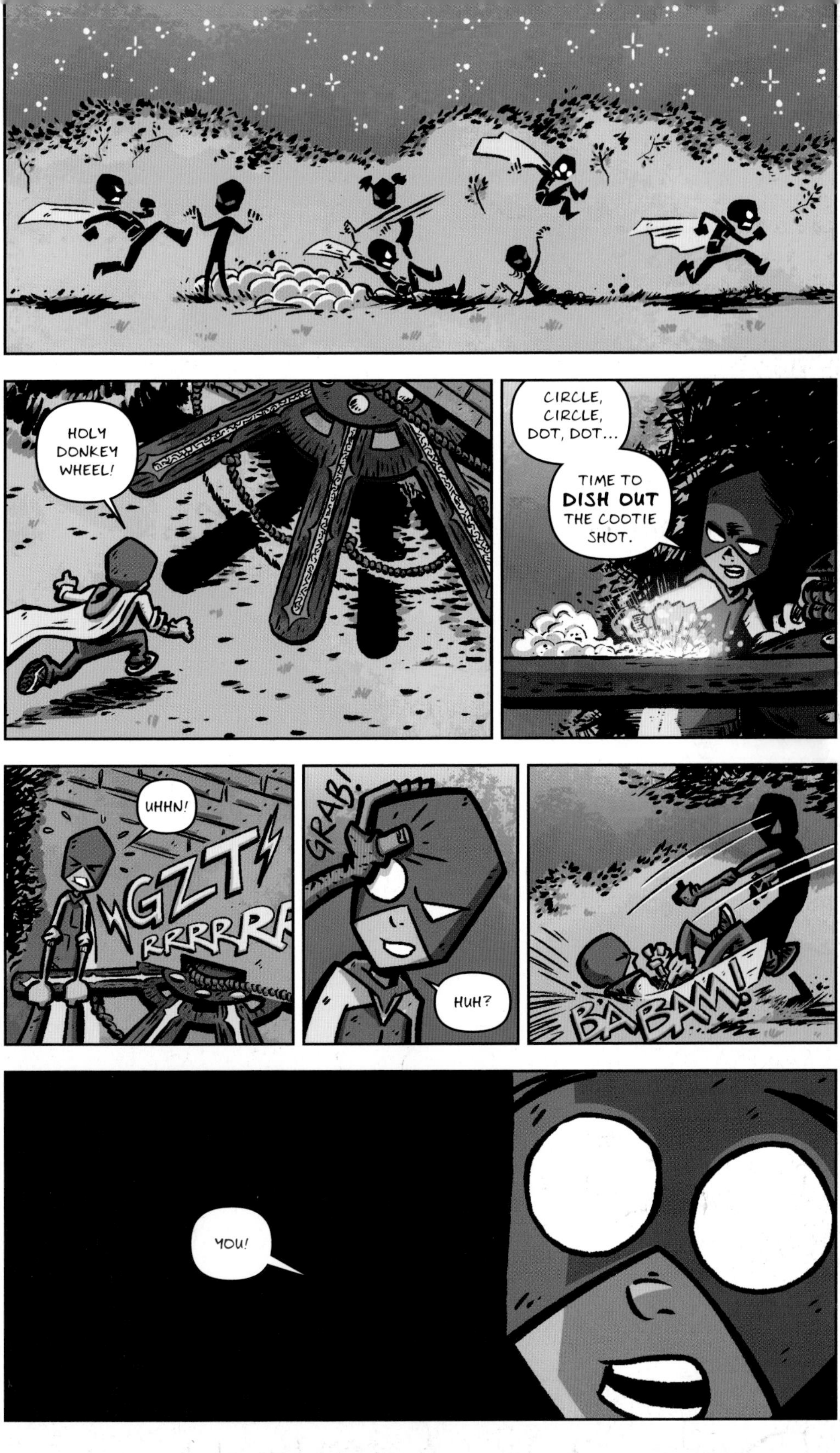
HOLY DONKEY WHEEL!
CIRCLE, CIRCLE, DOT, DOT...
TIME TO **DISH OUT** THE COOTIE SHOT.
UHHN!
GZZT
RRRRRR
GRAB!
HUH?
BABAM!
YOU!

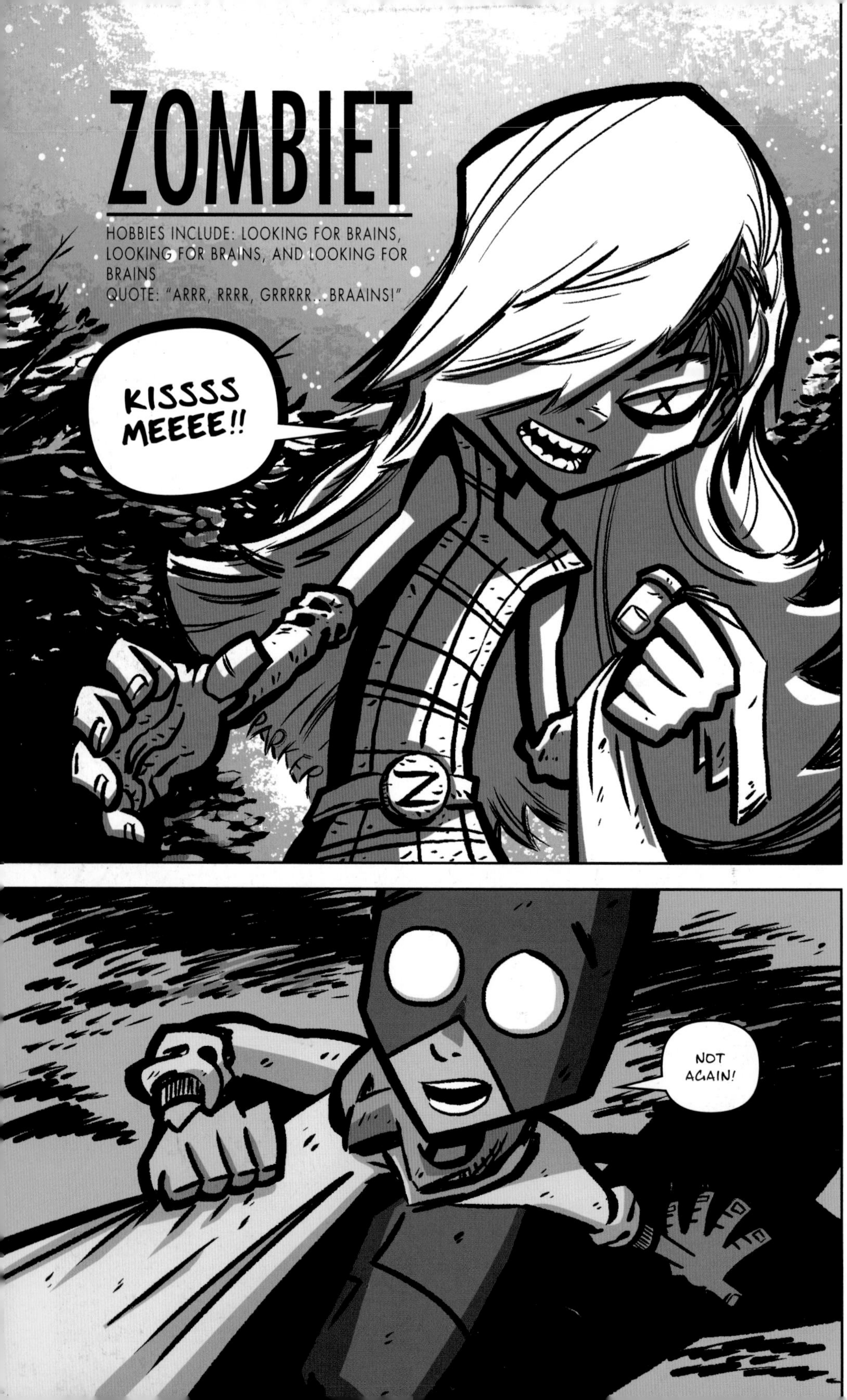
ZOMBIET
HOBBIES INCLUDE: LOOKING FOR BRAINS, LOOKING FOR BRAINS, AND LOOKING FOR BRAINS
QUOTE: "ARRR, RRRR, GRRRRR...BRAAINS!"
KISSSS MEEEE!!
PARKER
NOT AGAIN!

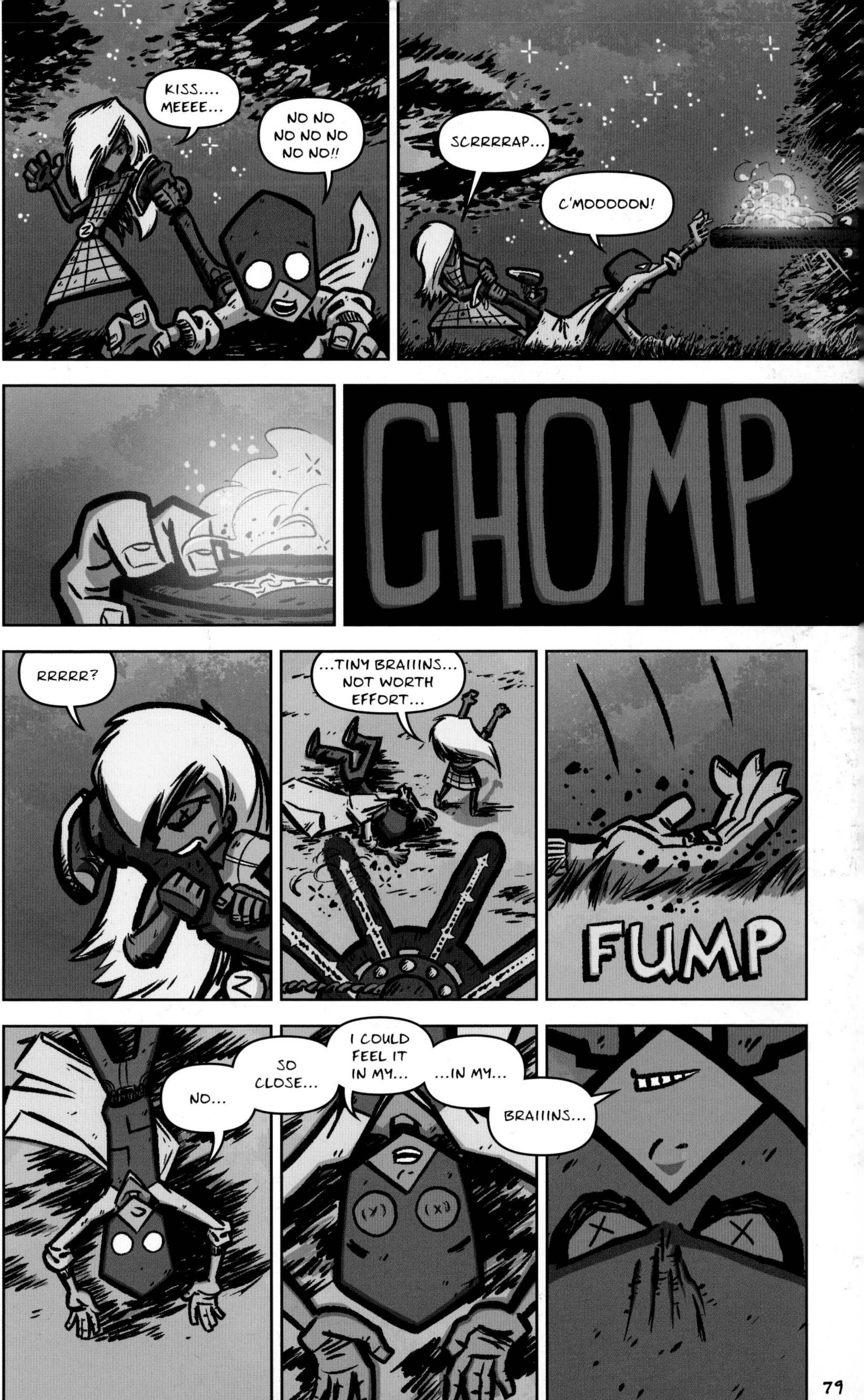
KISS.... MEEEE...
NO NO NO NO NO NO NO!!
SCRRRRAP...
C'MOOOOON!
CHOMP
RRRRR?
...TINY BRAIIINS... NOT WORTH EFFORT...
FUMP
NO...
SO CLOSE...
I COULD FEEL IT IN MY...
...IN MY...
BRAIIINS...

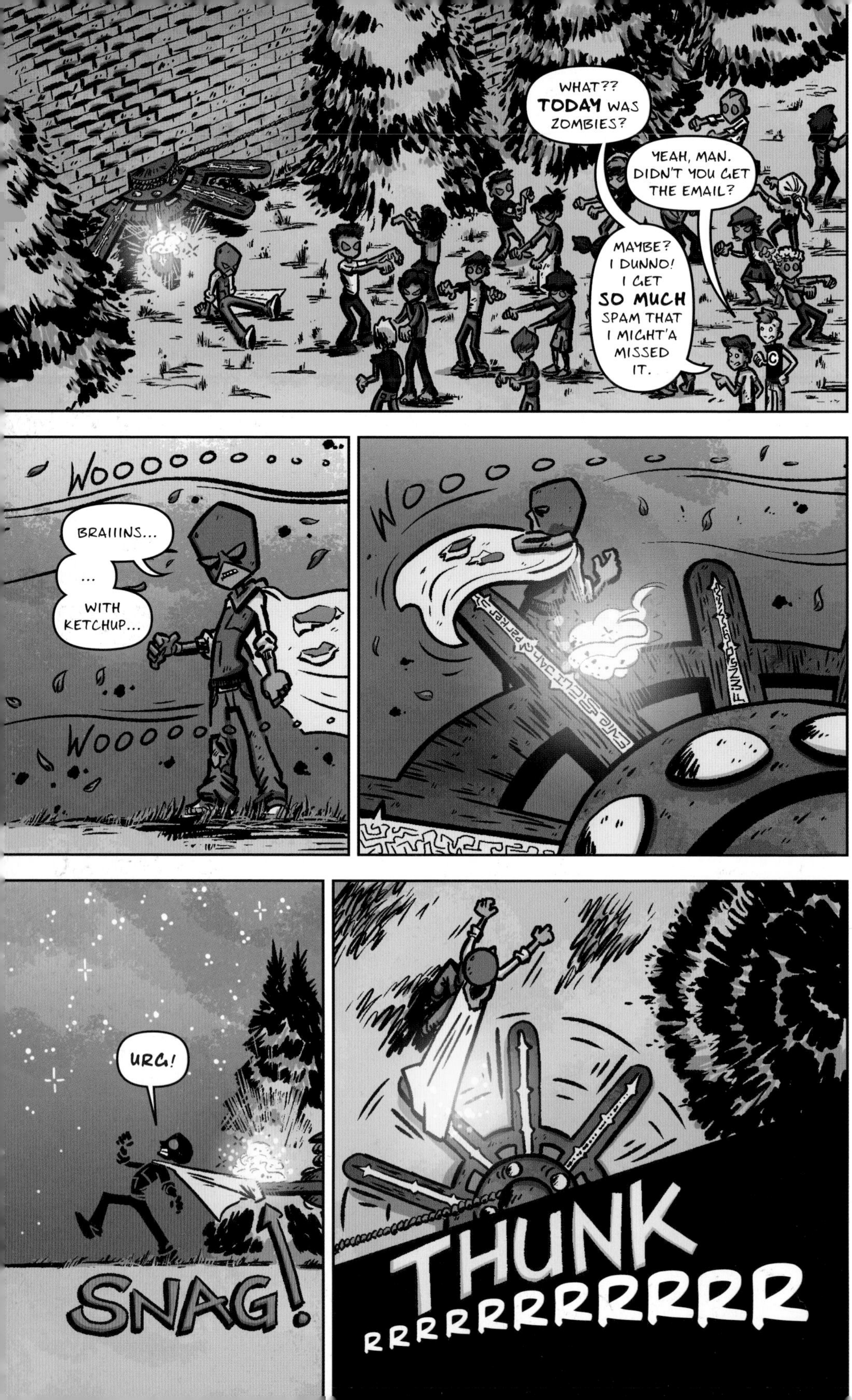
WHAT?? **TODAY** WAS ZOMBIES?
YEAH, MAN. DIDN'T YOU GET THE EMAIL?
MAYBE? I DUNNO! I GET **SO MUCH** SPAM THAT I MIGHT'A MISSED IT.
WOOOOOOOOOO
BRAIIINS...
...
WITH KETCHUP...
WOOOOOO
WOOOOOOOOO
URG!
SNAG!
THUNK
RRRRRRRRRRRR

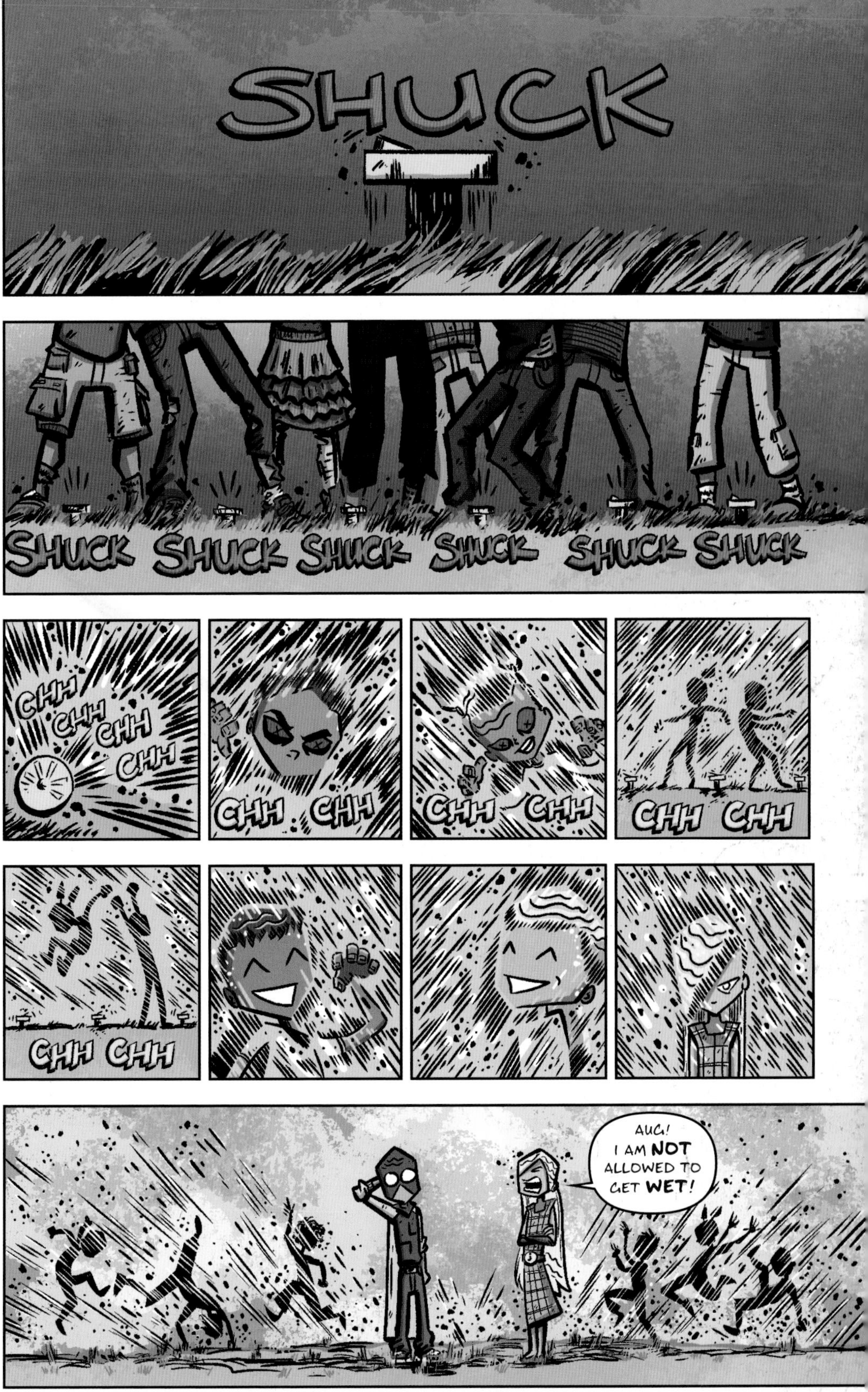
SHUCK
SHUCK SHUCK SHUCK SHUCK SHUCK SHUCK
CHH CHH CHH CHH
CHH CHH
CHH CHH
CHH CHH
CHH CHH
AUG! I AM **NOT** ALLOWED TO GET **WET**!

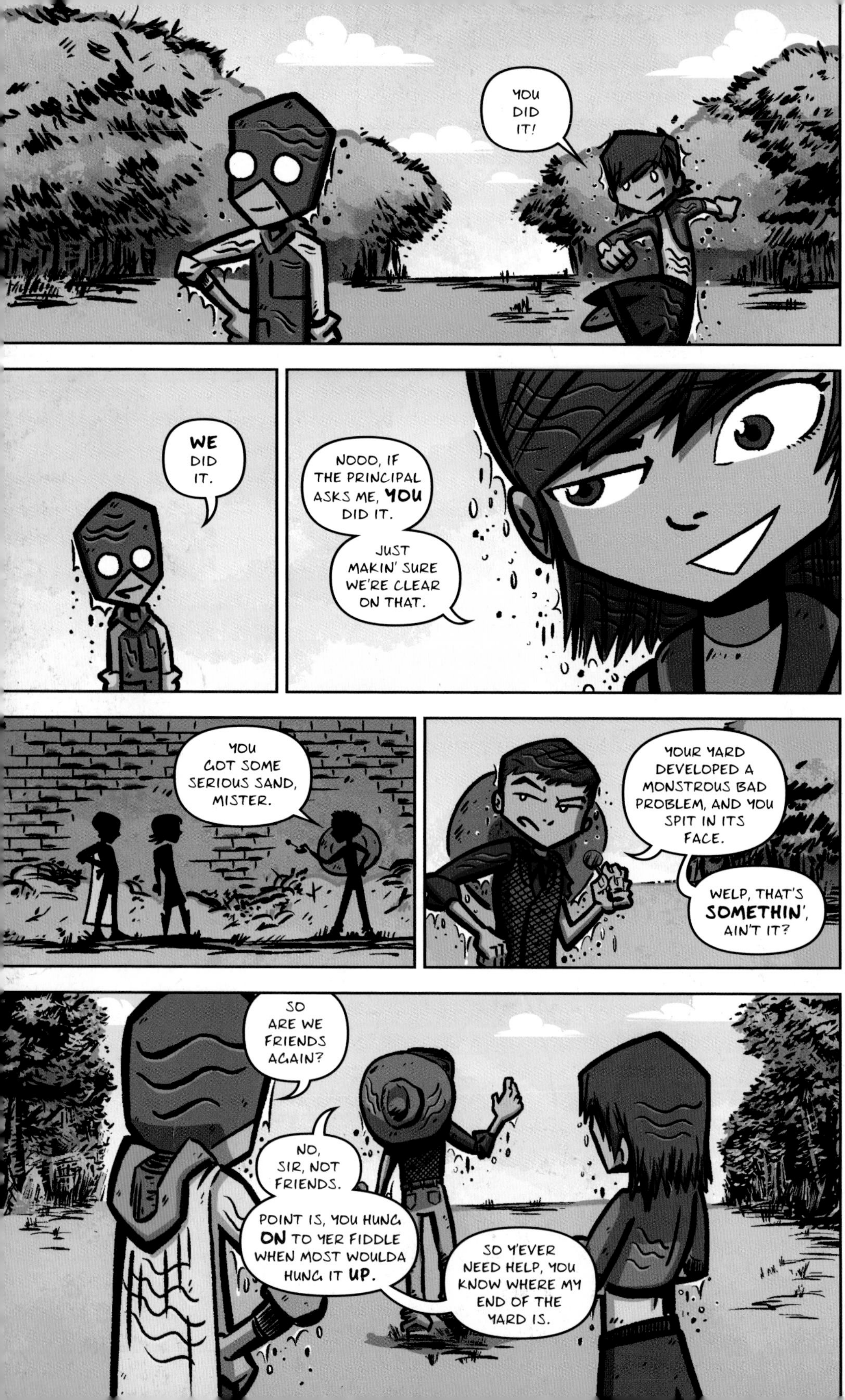
YOU DID IT!
WE DID IT.
NOOO, IF THE PRINCIPAL ASKS ME, YOU DID IT.
JUST MAKIN' SURE WE'RE CLEAR ON THAT.
YOU GOT SOME SERIOUS SAND, MISTER.
YOUR YARD DEVELOPED A MONSTROUS BAD PROBLEM, AND YOU SPIT IN ITS FACE.
WELP, THAT'S SOMETHIN', AIN'T IT?
SO ARE WE FRIENDS AGAIN?
NO, SIR, NOT FRIENDS.
POINT IS, YOU HUNG ON TO YER FIDDLE WHEN MOST WOULDA HUNG IT UP.
SO Y'EVER NEED HELP, YOU KNOW WHERE MY END OF THE YARD IS.

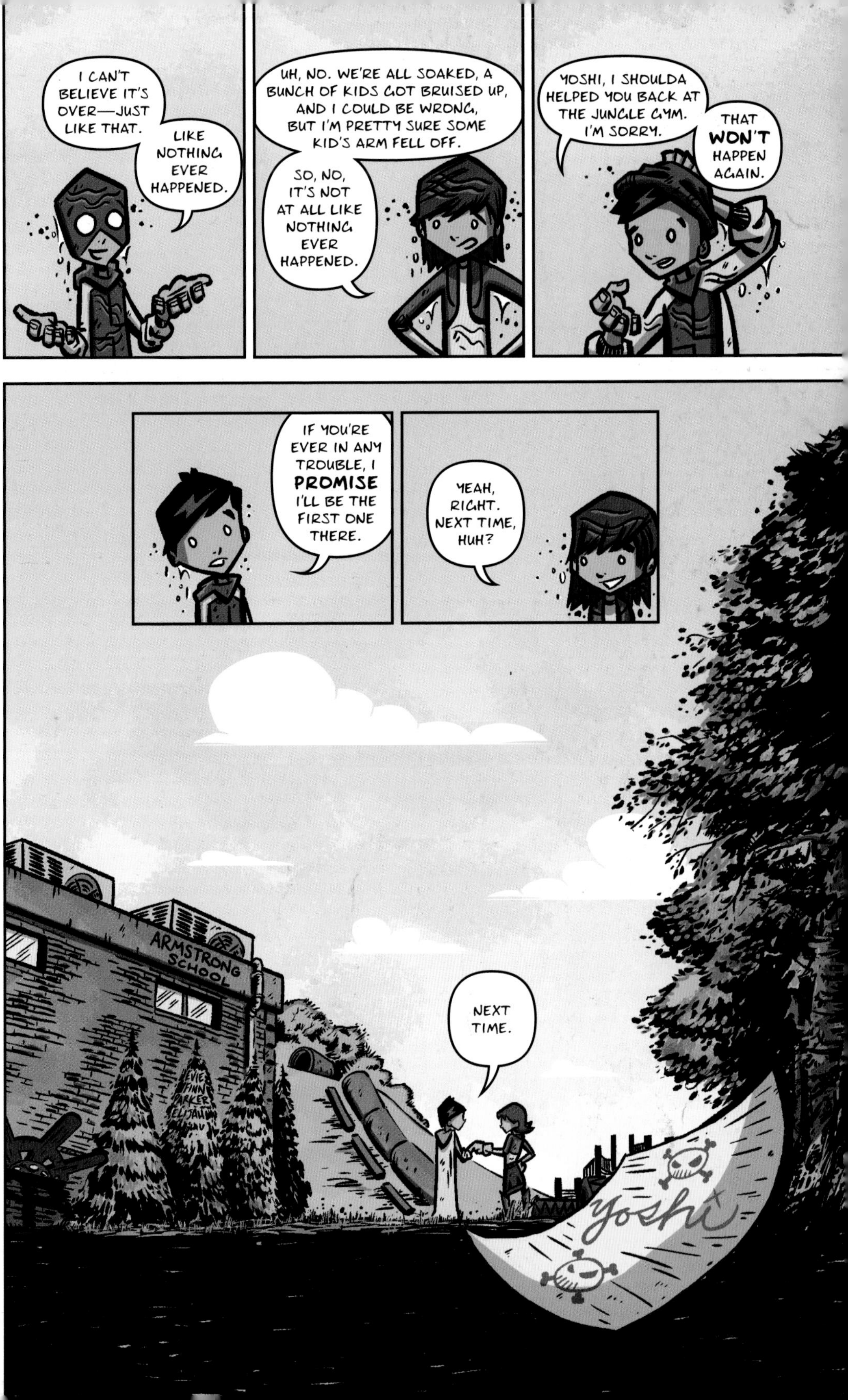
I CAN'T BELIEVE IT'S OVER—JUST LIKE THAT.
LIKE NOTHING EVER HAPPENED.
UH, NO. WE'RE ALL SOAKED, A BUNCH OF KIDS GOT BRUISED UP, AND I COULD BE WRONG, BUT I'M PRETTY SURE SOME KID'S ARM FELL OFF.
SO, NO, IT'S NOT AT ALL LIKE NOTHING EVER HAPPENED.
YOSHI, I SHOULDA HELPED YOU BACK AT THE JUNGLE GYM. I'M SORRY.
THAT WON'T HAPPEN AGAIN.
IF YOU'RE EVER IN ANY TROUBLE, I PROMISE I'LL BE THE FIRST ONE THERE.
YEAH, RIGHT. NEXT TIME, HUH?
ARMSTRONG SCHOOL
NEXT TIME.
yoshi

03 THE LIGHT AT THE EDGE OF THE WRECKYARD

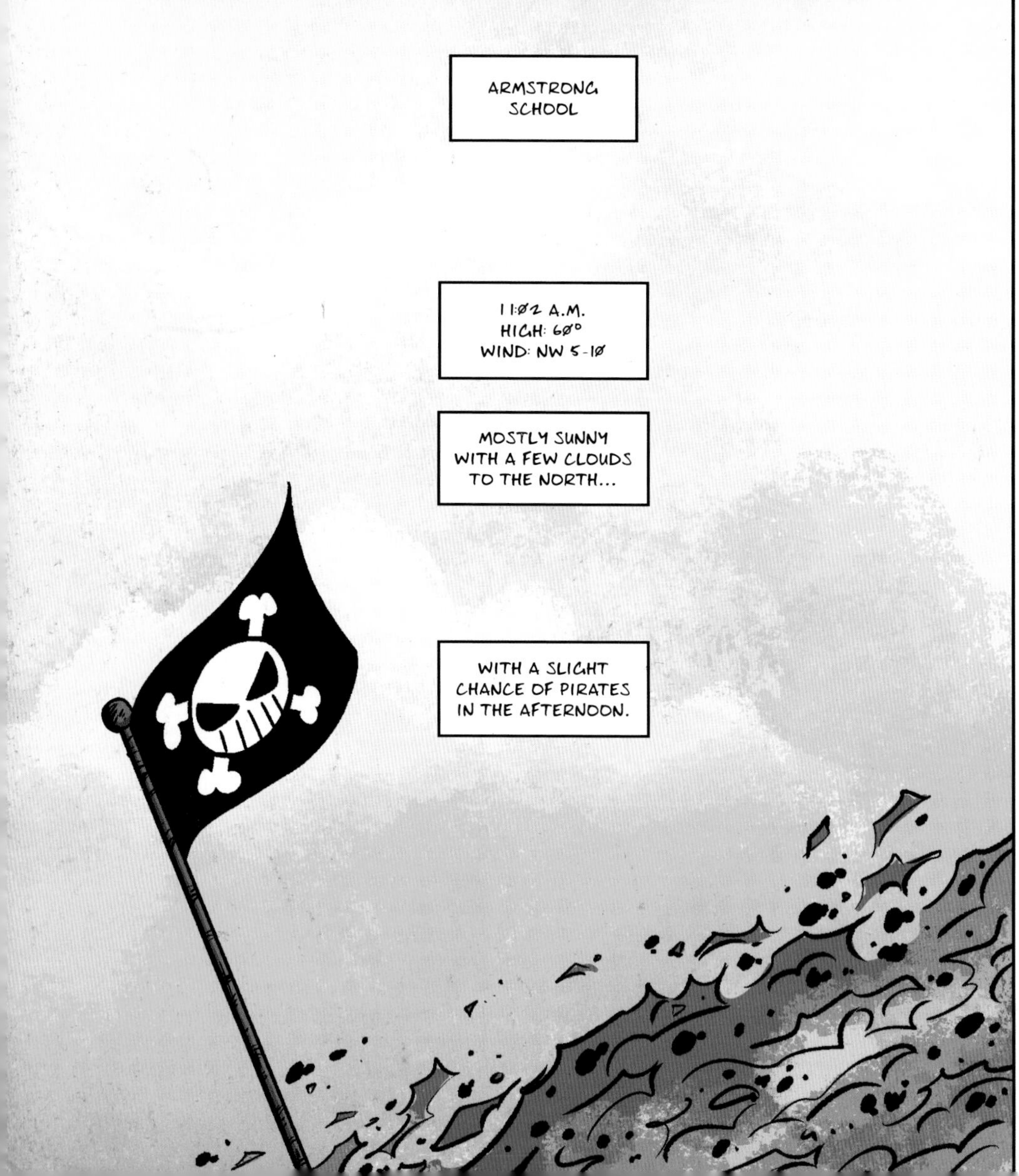
ARMSTRONG SCHOOL
11:02 A.M. HIGH: 60° WIND: NW 5-10
MOSTLY SUNNY WITH A FEW CLOUDS TO THE NORTH...
WITH A SLIGHT CHANCE OF PIRATES IN THE AFTERNOON.

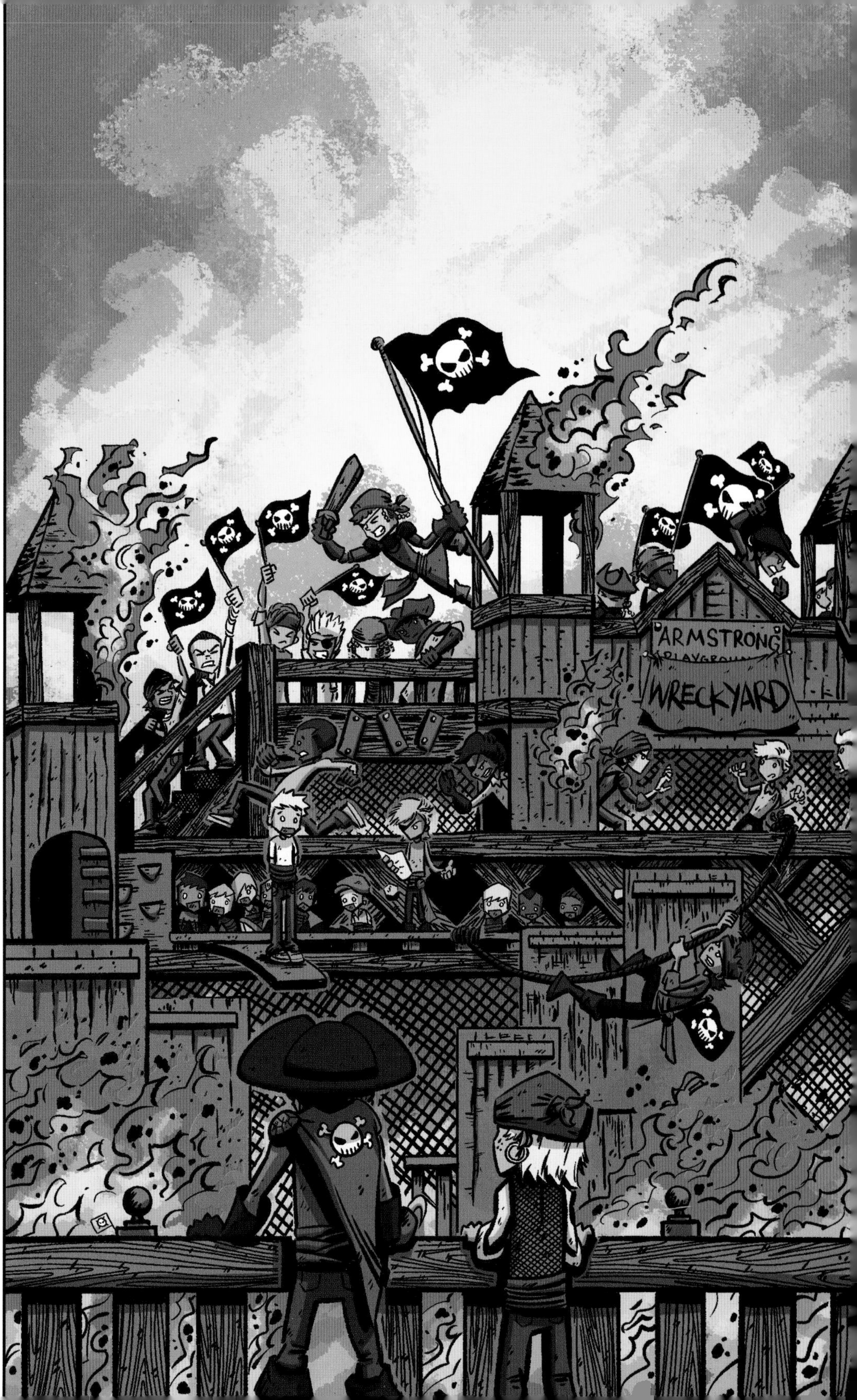
ARMSTRONG
WRECKYARD

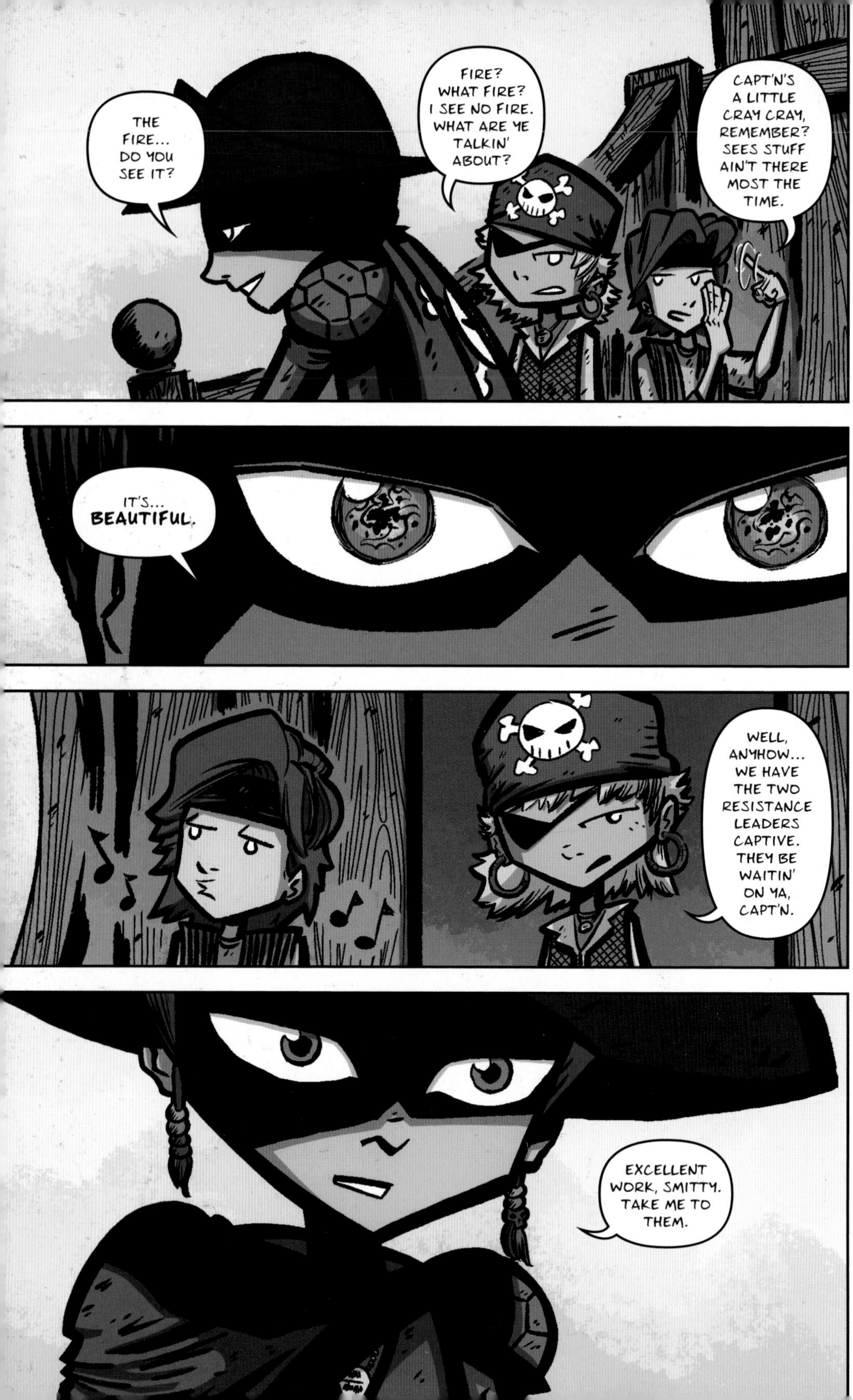
THE FIRE... DO YOU SEE IT?
FIRE? WHAT FIRE? I SEE NO FIRE. WHAT ARE YE TALKIN' ABOUT?
CAPT'N'S A LITTLE CRAY CRAY, REMEMBER? SEES STUFF AIN'T THERE MOST THE TIME.
IT'S... BEAUTIFUL.
WELL, ANYHOW... WE HAVE THE TWO RESISTANCE LEADERS CAPTIVE. THEY BE WAITIN' ON YA, CAPT'N.
EXCELLENT WORK, SMITTY. TAKE ME TO THEM.

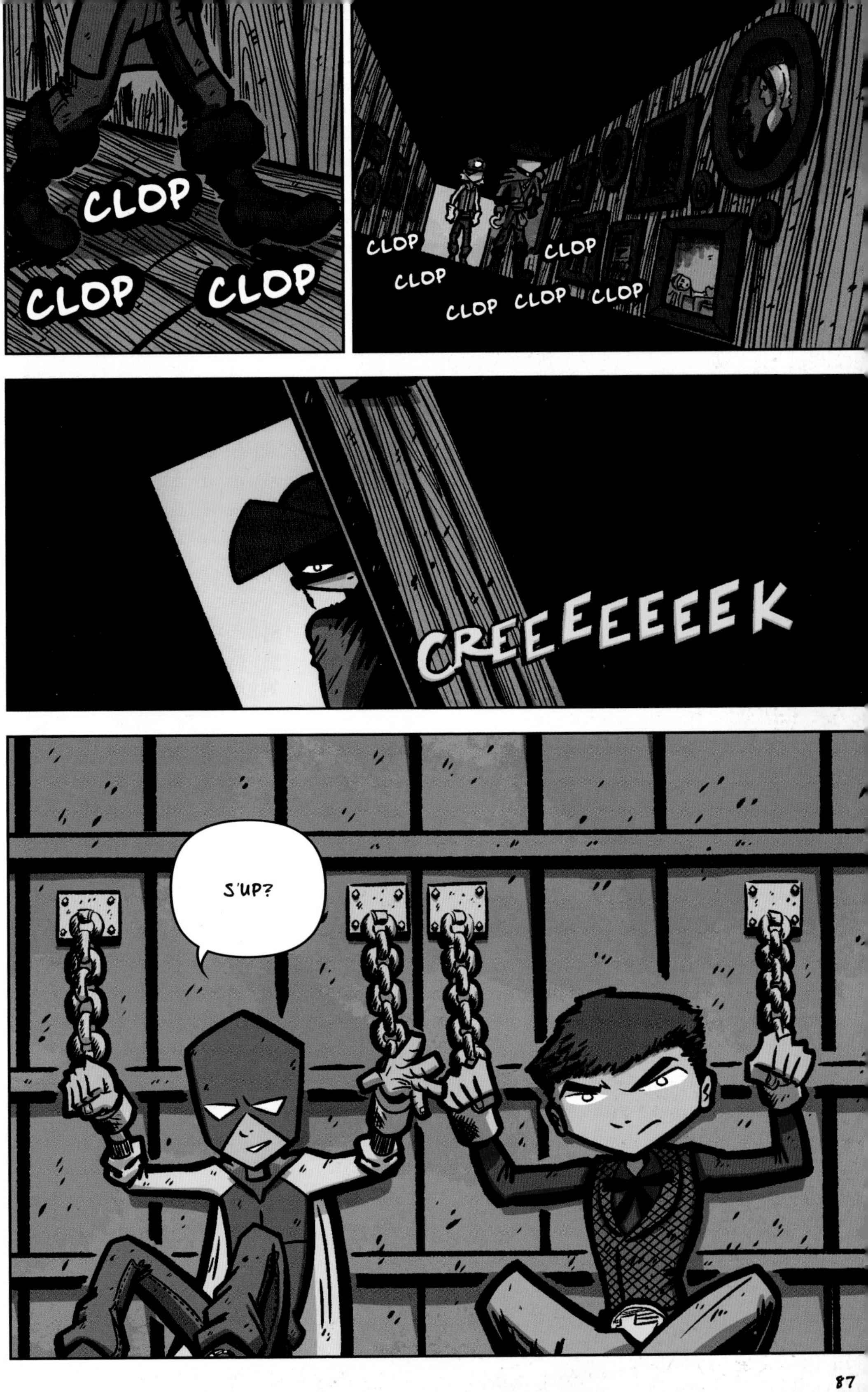
CLOP
CLOP
CLOP
CLOP
CLOP
CLOP
CLOP
CLOP
CLOP
CREEEEEEEK
S'UP?

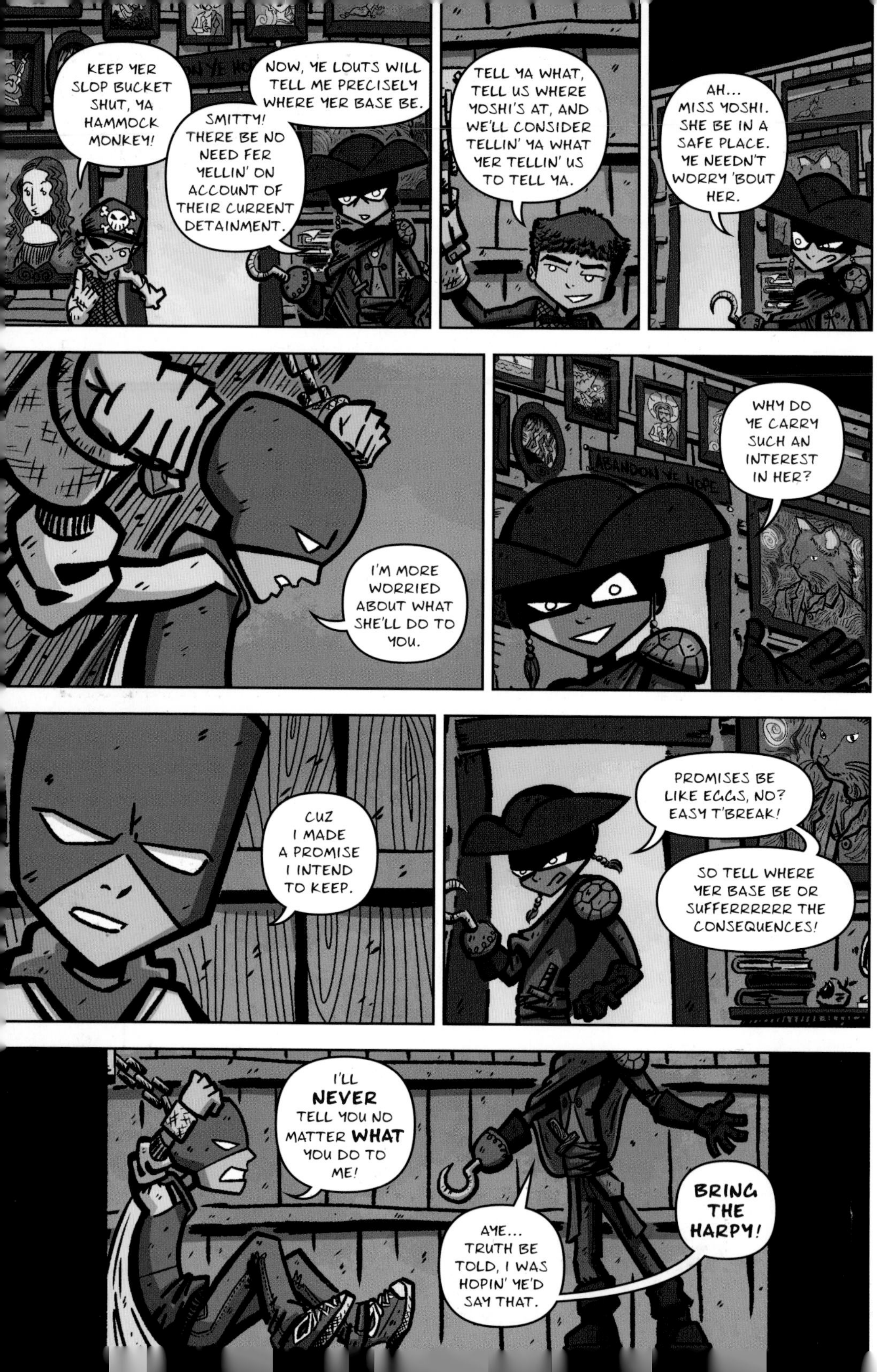
KEEP YER SLOP BUCKET SHUT, YA HAMMOCK MONKEY!
NOW, YE LOUTS WILL TELL ME PRECISELY WHERE YER BASE BE.
SMITTY! THERE BE NO NEED FER YELLIN' ON ACCOUNT OF THEIR CURRENT DETAINMENT.
TELL YA WHAT, TELL US WHERE YOSHI'S AT, AND WE'LL CONSIDER TELLIN' YA WHAT YER TELLIN' US TO TELL YA.
AH... MISS YOSHI. SHE BE IN A SAFE PLACE. YE NEEDN'T WORRY 'BOUT HER.
I'M MORE WORRIED ABOUT WHAT SHE'LL DO TO YOU.
ABANDON YE HOPE
WHY DO YE CARRY SUCH AN INTEREST IN HER?
CUZ I MADE A PROMISE I INTEND TO KEEP.
PROMISES BE LIKE EGGS, NO? EASY T'BREAK!
SO TELL WHERE YER BASE BE OR SUFFERRRRRR THE CONSEQUENCES!
I'LL **NEVER** TELL YOU NO MATTER **WHAT** YOU DO TO ME!
AYE... TRUTH BE TOLD, I WAS HOPIN' YE'D SAY THAT.
BRING THE HARPY!

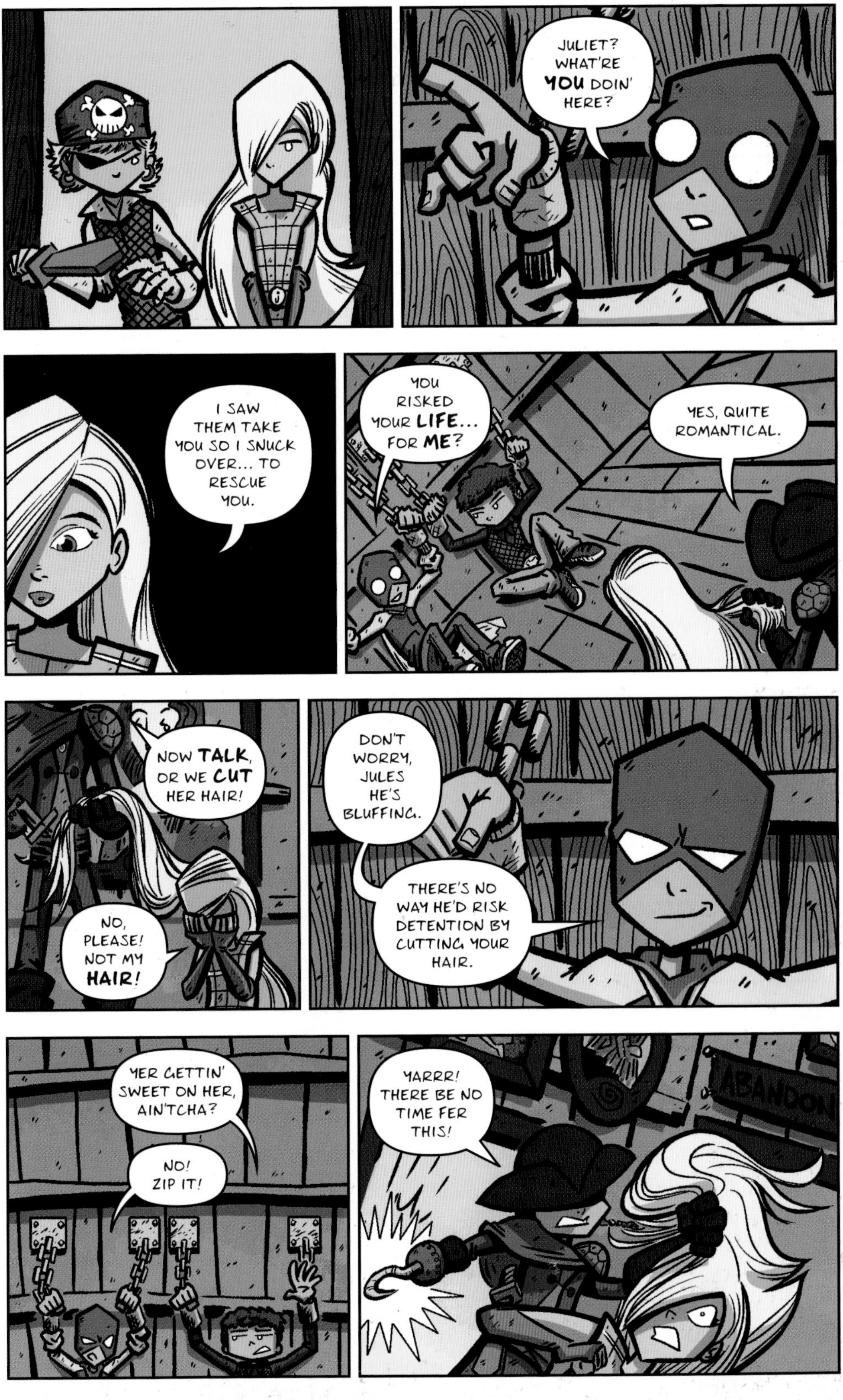
JULIET? WHAT'RE **YOU** DOIN' HERE?
I SAW THEM TAKE YOU SO I SNUCK OVER... TO RESCUE YOU.
YOU RISKED YOUR **LIFE**... FOR **ME**?
YES, QUITE ROMANTICAL.
NOW **TALK**, OR WE **CUT** HER HAIR!
NO, PLEASE! NOT MY **HAIR**!
DON'T WORRY, JULES HE'S BLUFFING.
THERE'S NO WAY HE'D RISK DETENTION BY CUTTING YOUR HAIR.
YER GETTIN' SWEET ON HER, AIN'TCHA?
NO! ZIP IT!
YARRR! THERE BE NO TIME FER THIS!
ABANDON

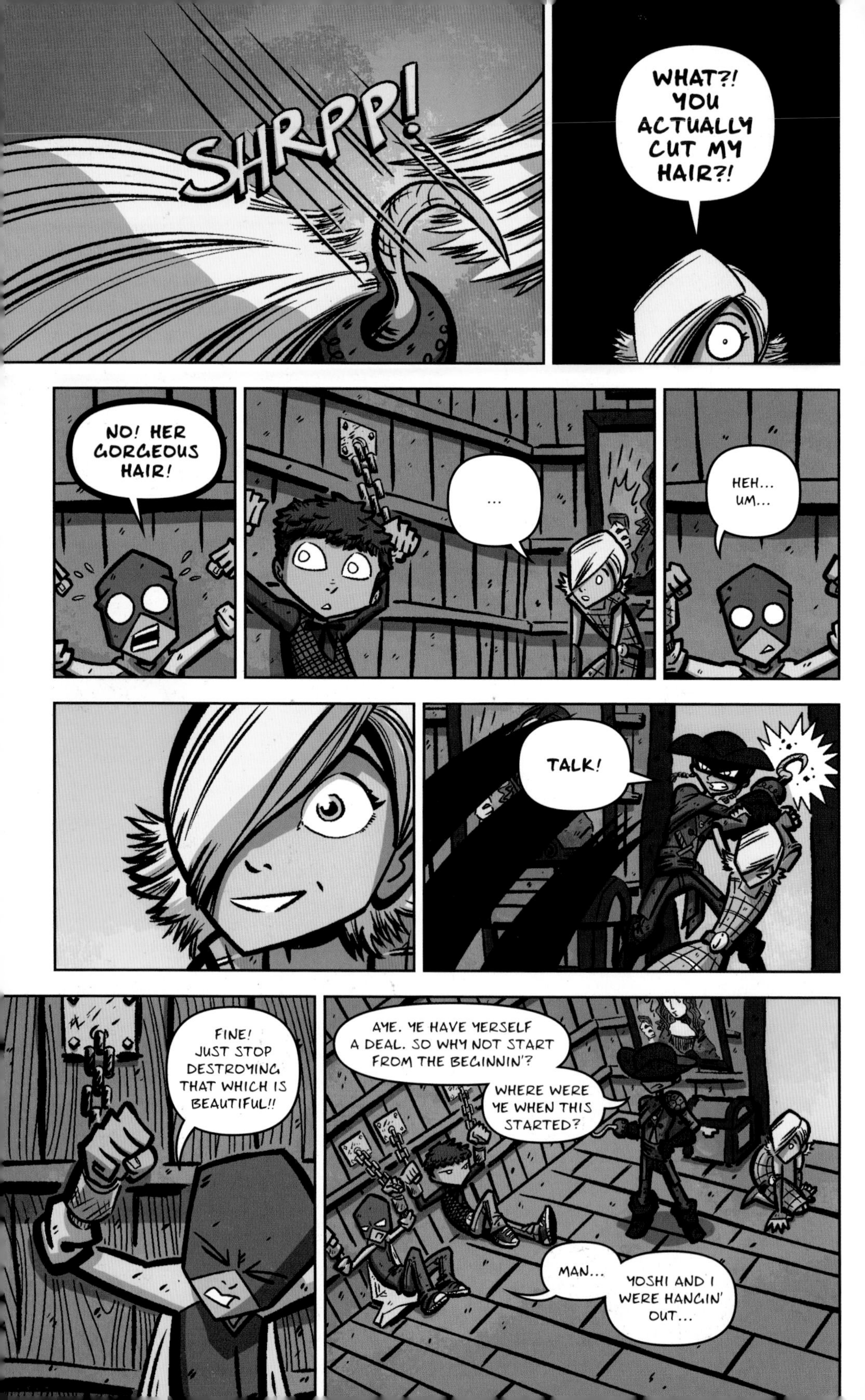
SHRPP!
WHAT?! YOU ACTUALLY CUT MY HAIR?!
NO! HER GORGEOUS HAIR!
...
HEH... UM...
TALK!
FINE! JUST STOP DESTROYING THAT WHICH IS BEAUTIFUL!!
AYE. YE HAVE YERSELF A DEAL. SO WHY NOT START FROM THE BEGINNIN'?
WHERE WERE YE WHEN THIS STARTED?
MAN...
YOSHI AND I WERE HANGIN' OUT...

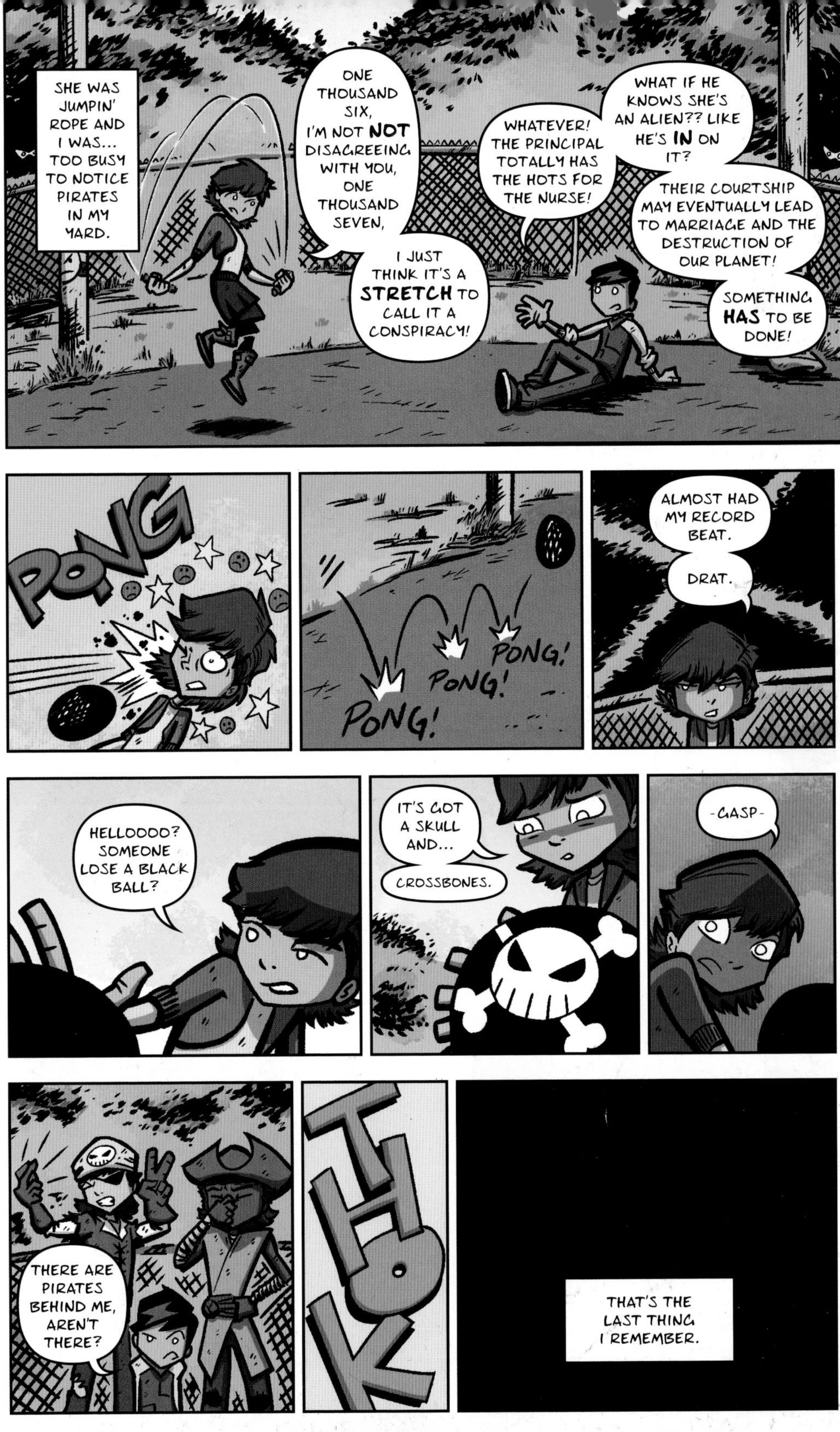
SHE WAS JUMPIN' ROPE AND I WAS... TOO BUSY TO NOTICE PIRATES IN MY YARD.
ONE THOUSAND SIX, I'M NOT **NOT** DISAGREEING WITH YOU, ONE THOUSAND SEVEN,
I JUST THINK IT'S A **STRETCH** TO CALL IT A CONSPIRACY!
WHATEVER! THE PRINCIPAL TOTALLY HAS THE HOTS FOR THE NURSE!
WHAT IF HE KNOWS SHE'S AN ALIEN?? LIKE HE'S **IN** ON IT?
THEIR COURTSHIP MAY EVENTUALLY LEAD TO MARRIAGE AND THE DESTRUCTION OF OUR PLANET!
SOMETHING **HAS** TO BE DONE!
PONG
PONG!
PONG!
PONG!
ALMOST HAD MY RECORD BEAT.
DRAT.
HELLOOOO? SOMEONE LOSE A BLACK BALL?
IT'S GOT A SKULL AND...
CROSSBONES.
-GASP-
THERE ARE PIRATES BEHIND ME, AREN'T THERE?
THOK
THAT'S THE LAST THING I REMEMBER.

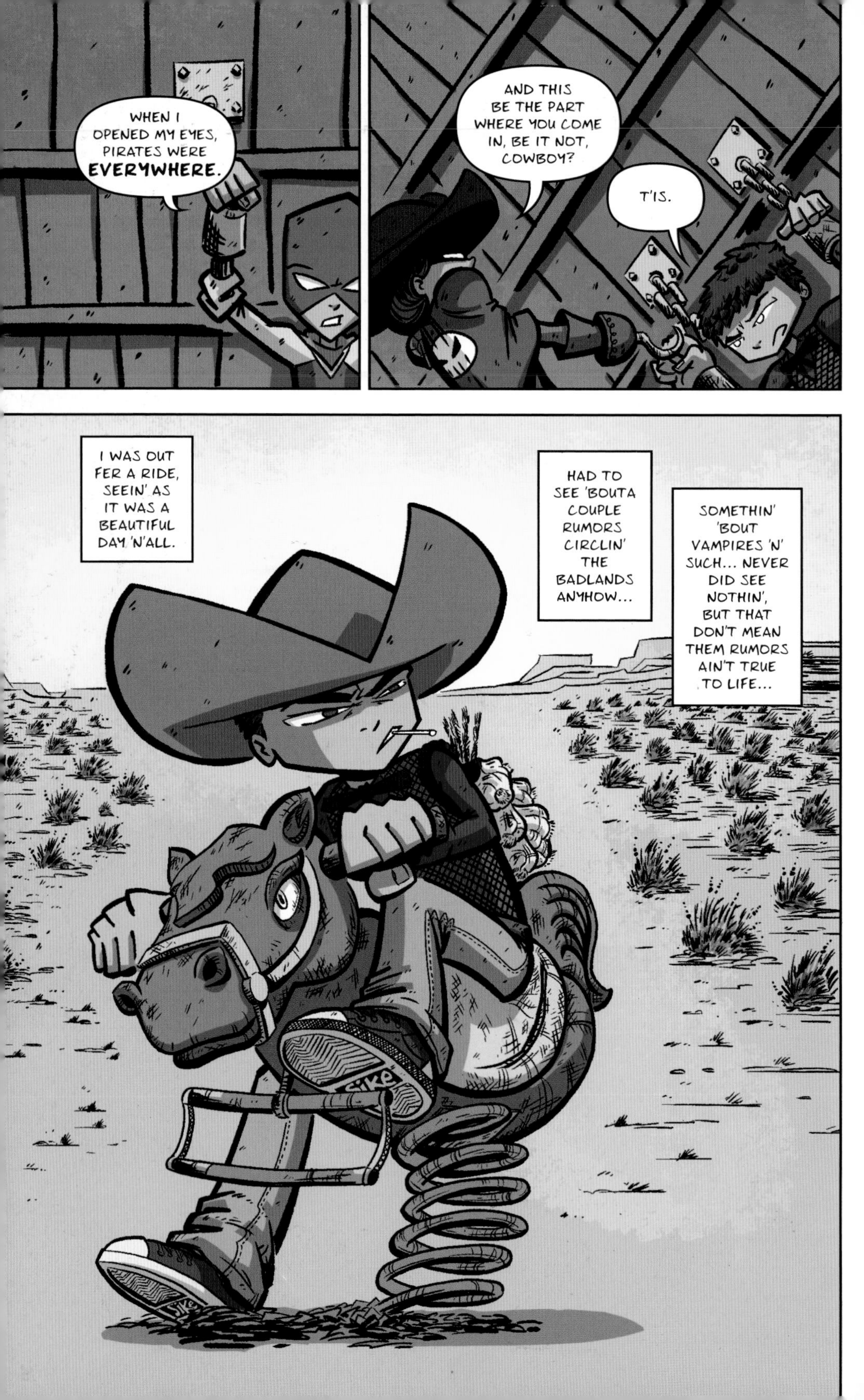
WHEN I OPENED MY EYES, PIRATES WERE **EVERYWHERE.**
AND THIS BE THE PART WHERE YOU COME IN, BE IT NOT, COWBOY?
T'IS.
I WAS OUT FER A RIDE, SEEIN' AS IT WAS A BEAUTIFUL DAY 'N'ALL.
HAD TO SEE 'BOUTA COUPLE RUMORS CIRCLIN' THE BADLANDS ANYHOW...
SOMETHIN' 'BOUT VAMPIRES 'N' SUCH... NEVER DID SEE NOTHIN', BUT THAT DON'T MEAN THEM RUMORS AIN'T TRUE TO LIFE...

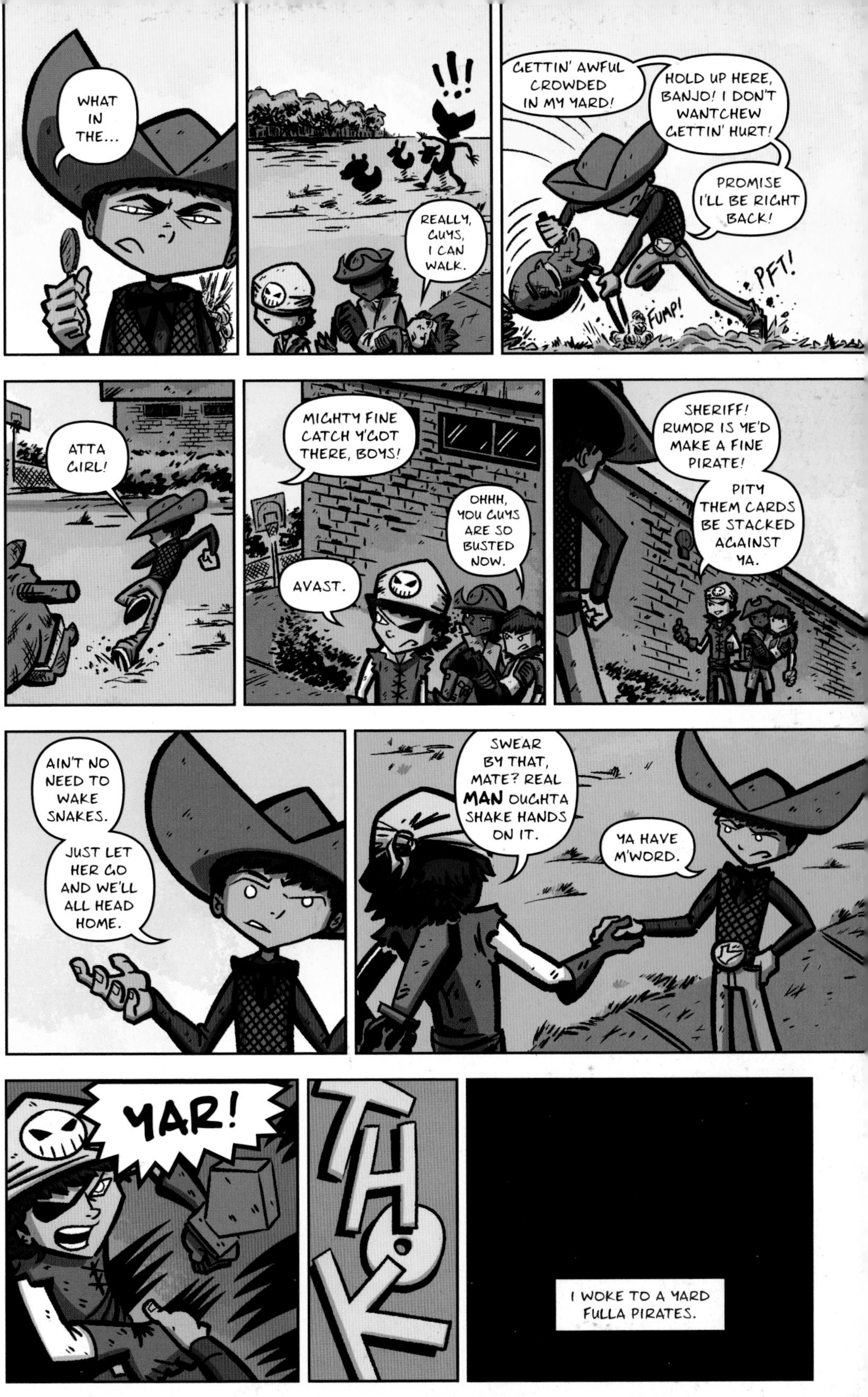

WHAT IN THE...
!!!
REALLY, GUYS, I CAN WALK.
GETTIN' AWFUL CROWDED IN MY YARD!
HOLD UP HERE, BANJO! I DON'T WANTCHEW GETTIN' HURT!
PROMISE I'LL BE RIGHT BACK!
FUMP!
PFT!
ATTA GIRL!
MIGHTY FINE CATCH Y'GOT THERE, BOYS!
OHHH, YOU GUYS ARE SO BUSTED NOW.
AVAST.
SHERIFF! RUMOR IS YE'D MAKE A FINE PIRATE!
PITY THEM CARDS BE STACKED AGAINST YA.
AIN'T NO NEED TO WAKE SNAKES.
JUST LET HER GO AND WE'LL ALL HEAD HOME.
SWEAR BY THAT, MATE? REAL MAN OUGHTA SHAKE HANDS ON IT.
YA HAVE M'WORD.
YAR!
THOK!
I WOKE TO A YARD FULLA PIRATES.

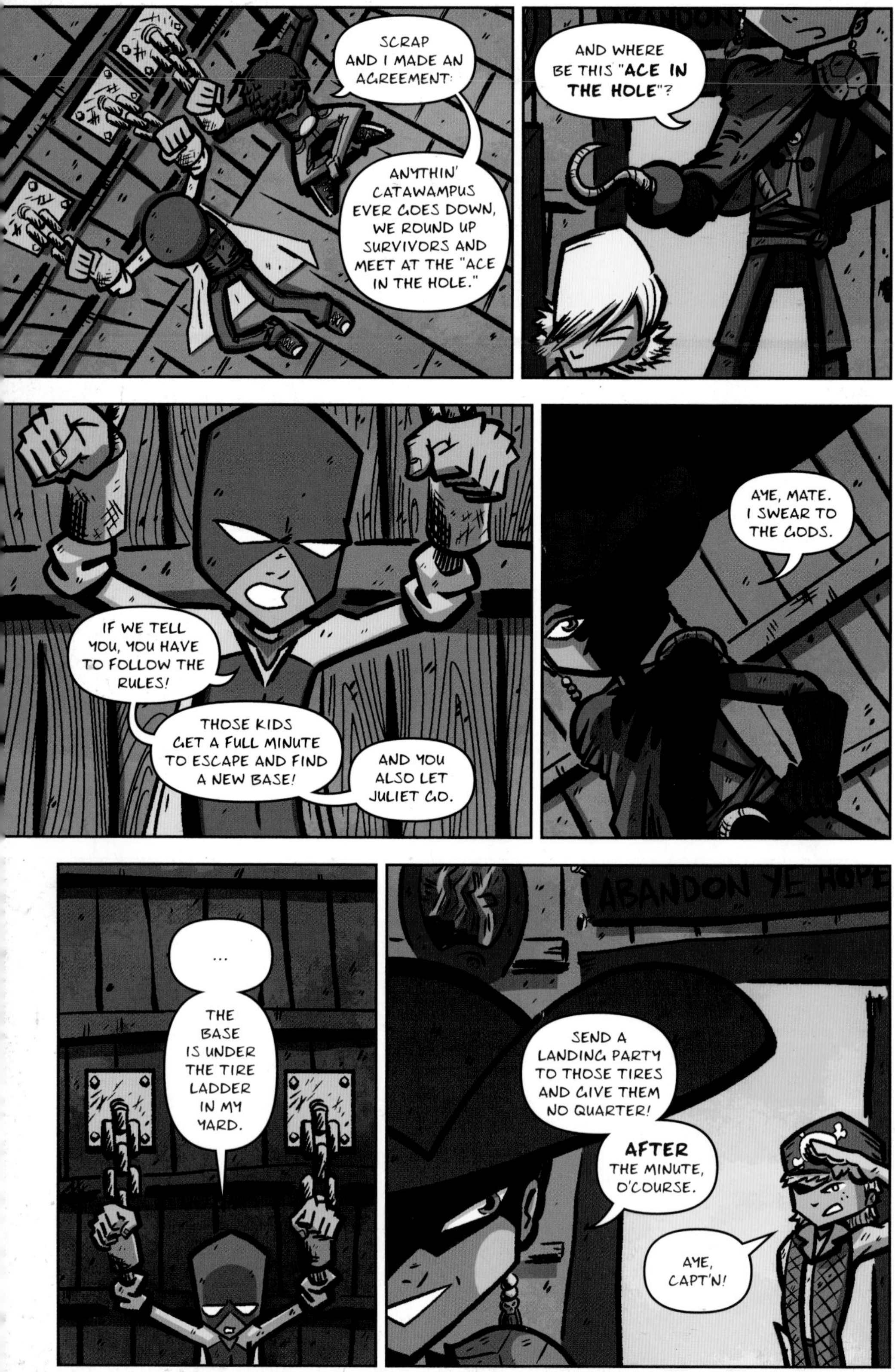
SCRAP AND I MADE AN AGREEMENT:
ANYTHIN' CATAWAMPUS EVER GOES DOWN, WE ROUND UP SURVIVORS AND MEET AT THE "ACE IN THE HOLE."
AND WHERE BE THIS "**ACE IN THE HOLE**"?
IF WE TELL YOU, YOU HAVE TO FOLLOW THE RULES!
THOSE KIDS GET A FULL MINUTE TO ESCAPE AND FIND A NEW BASE!
AND YOU ALSO LET JULIET GO.
AYE, MATE. I SWEAR TO THE GODS.
...
THE BASE IS UNDER THE TIRE LADDER IN MY YARD.
ABANDON YE HOPE
SEND A LANDING PARTY TO THOSE TIRES AND GIVE THEM NO QUARTER!
AFTER THE MINUTE, O'COURSE.
AYE, CAPT'N!

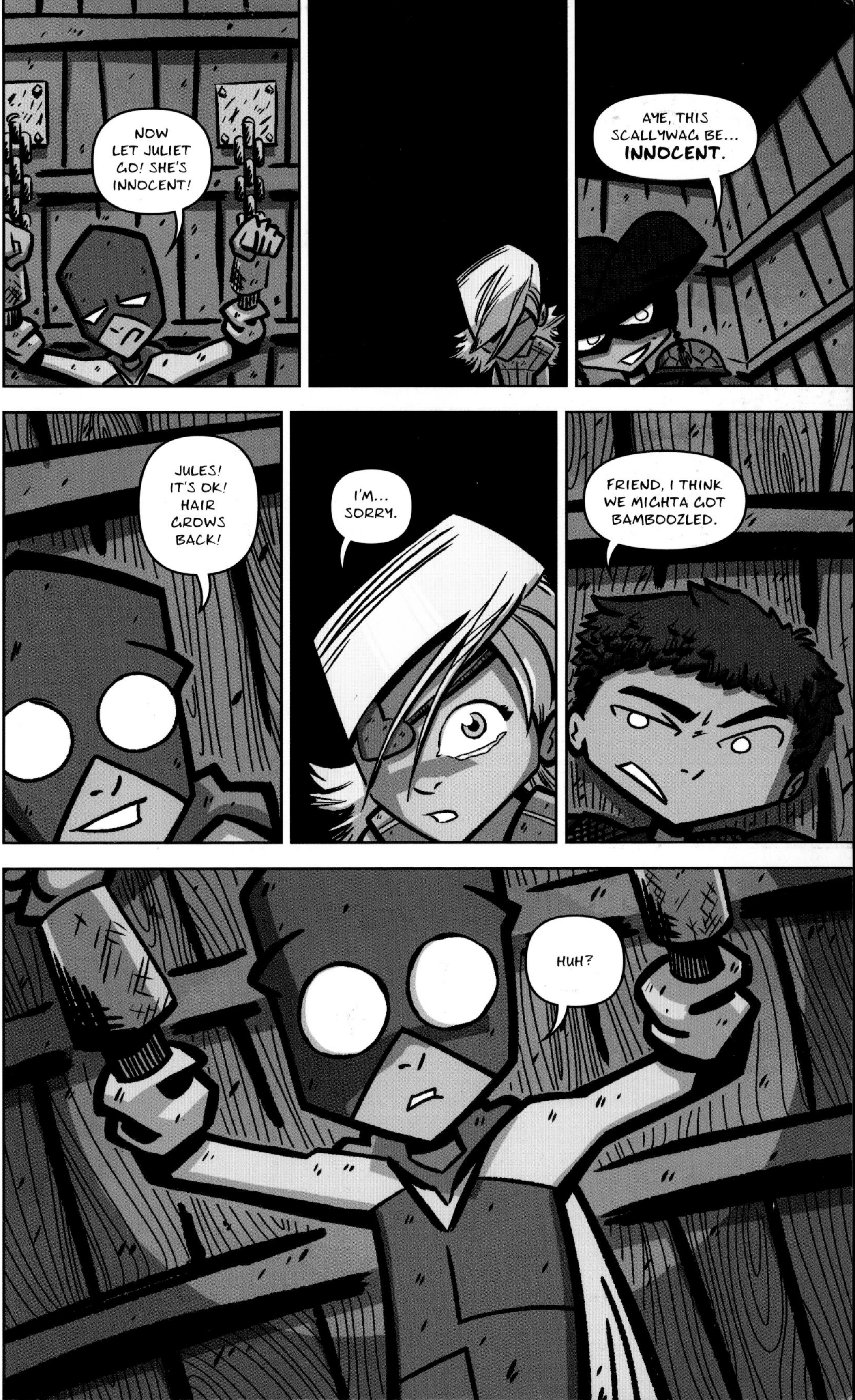
NOW LET JULIET GO! SHE'S INNOCENT!
AYE, THIS SCALLYWAG BE... **INNOCENT**.
JULES! IT'S OK! HAIR GROWS BACK!
I'M... SORRY.
FRIEND, I THINK WE MIGHTA GOT BAMBOOZLED.
HUH?

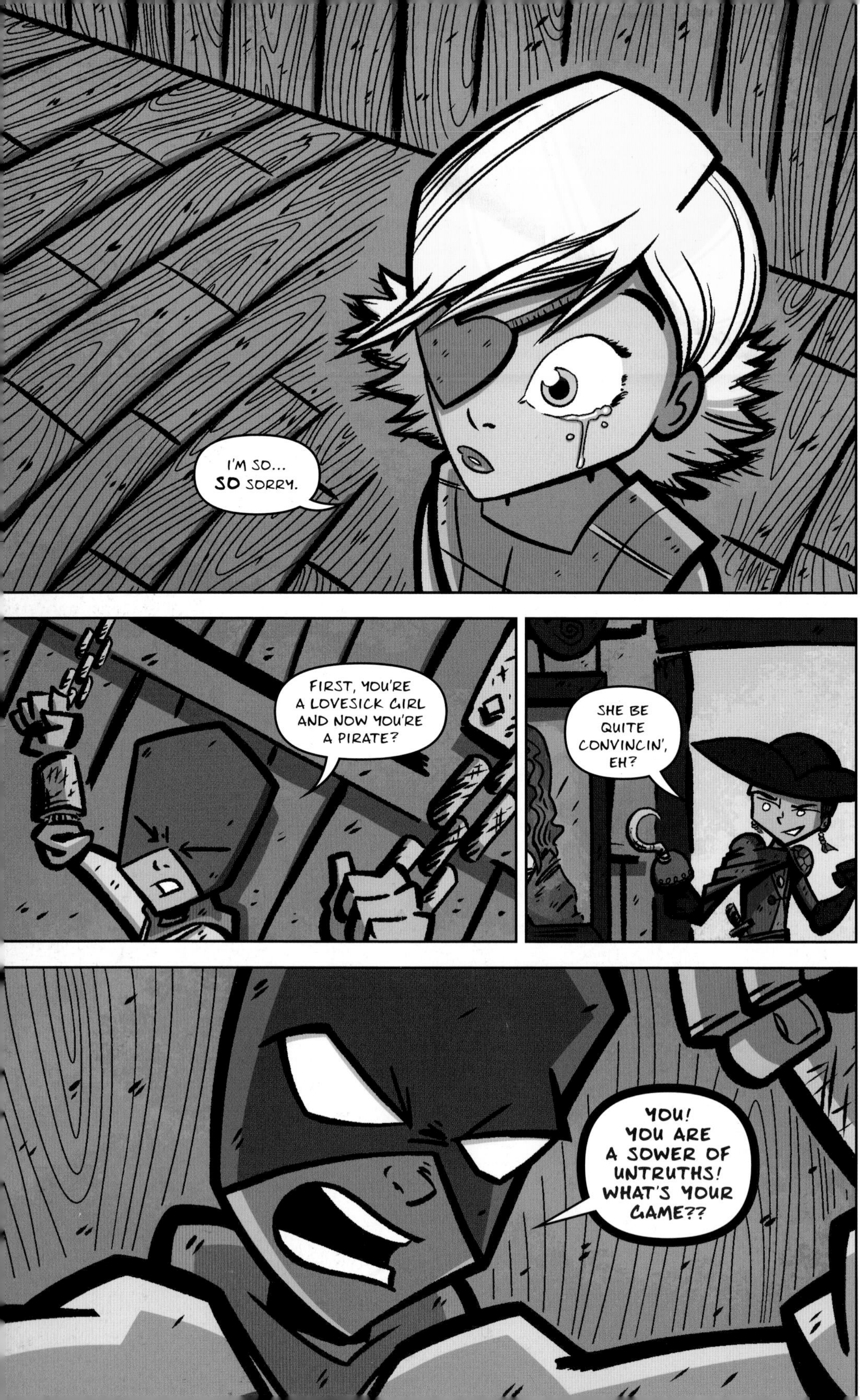
I'M SO... SO SORRY.
FIRST, YOU'RE A LOVESICK GIRL AND NOW YOU'RE A PIRATE?
SHE BE QUITE CONVINCIN', EH?
YOU! YOU ARE A SOWER OF UNTRUTHS! WHAT'S YOUR GAME??

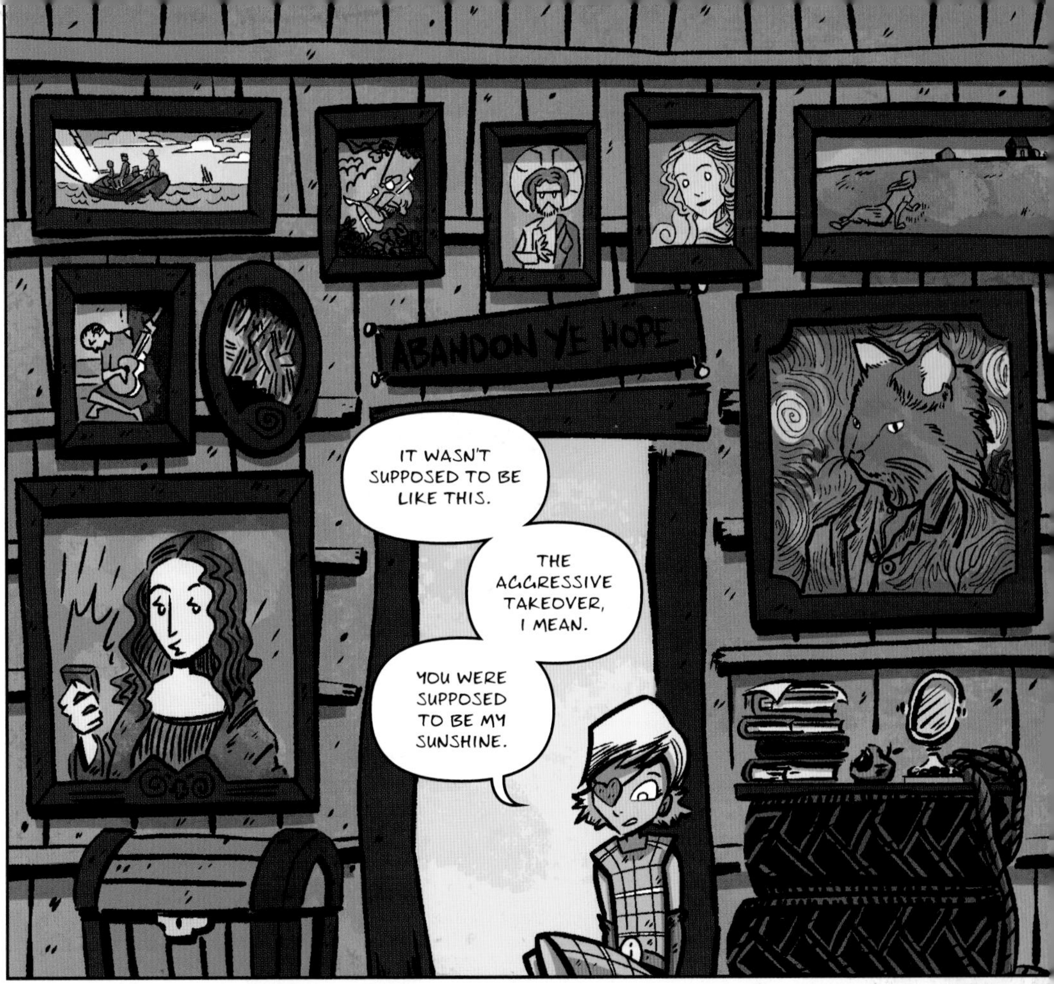
ABANDON YE HOPE
IT WASN'T SUPPOSED TO BE LIKE THIS.
THE AGGRESSIVE TAKEOVER, I MEAN.
YOU WERE SUPPOSED TO BE MY SUNSHINE.

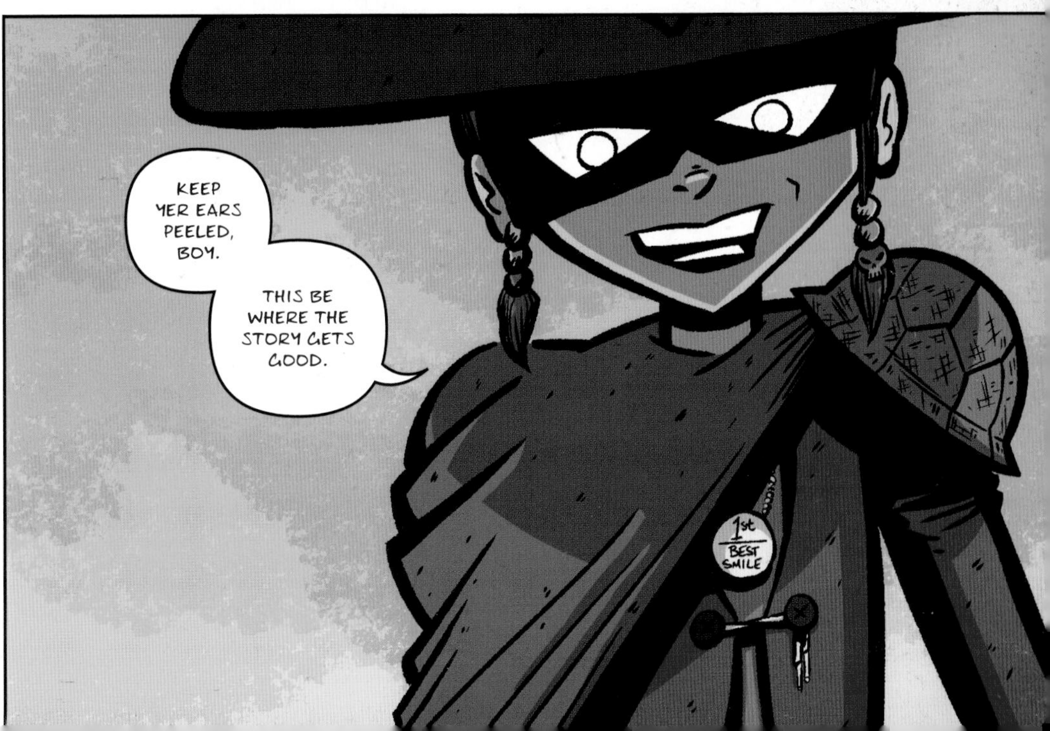
KEEP YER EARS PEELED, BOY.
THIS BE WHERE THE STORY GETS GOOD.
1st BEST SMILE

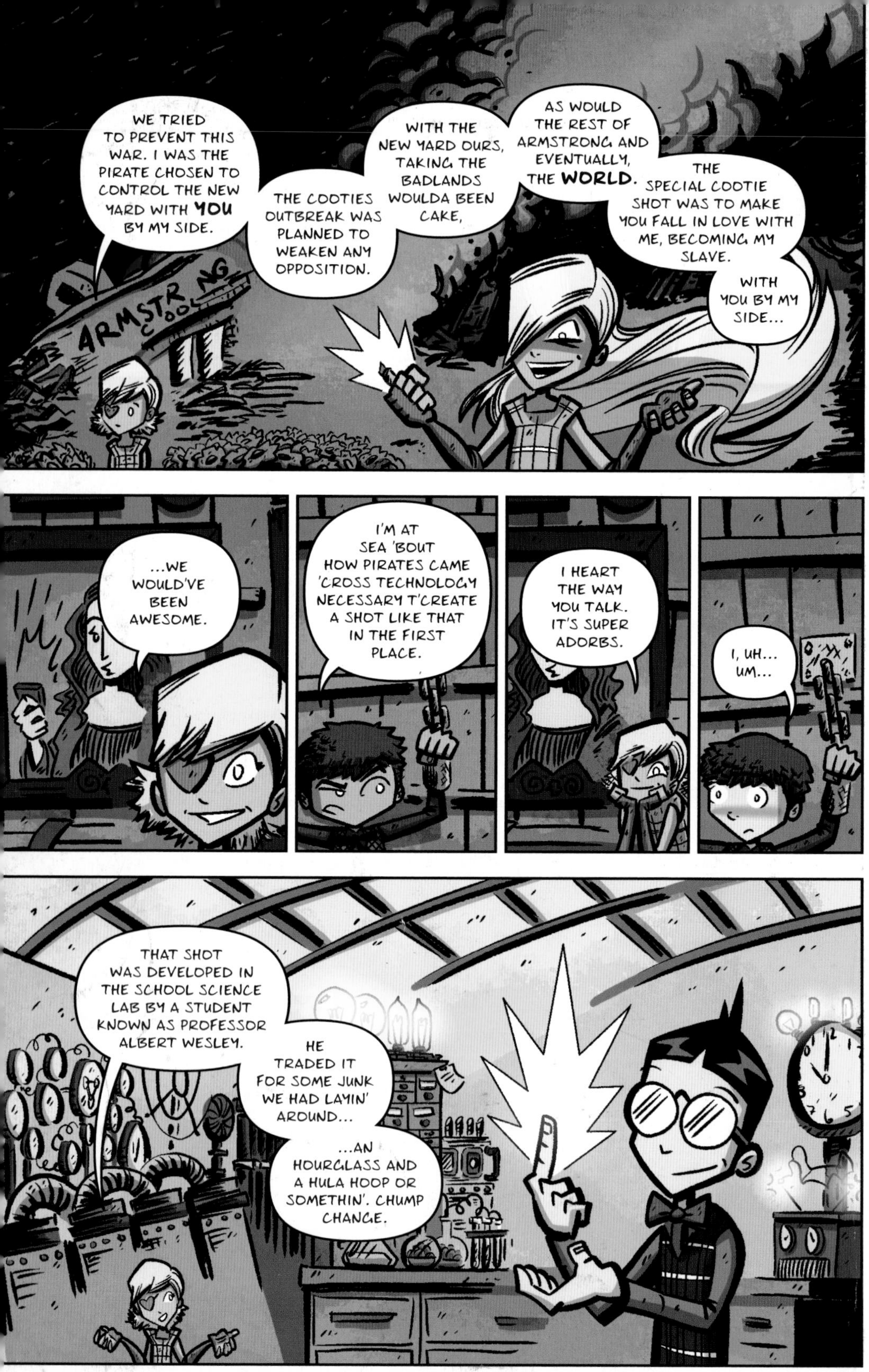
WE TRIED TO PREVENT THIS WAR. I WAS THE PIRATE CHOSEN TO CONTROL THE NEW YARD WITH **YOU** BY MY SIDE.
THE COOTIES OUTBREAK WAS PLANNED TO WEAKEN ANY OPPOSITION.
WITH THE NEW YARD OURS, TAKING THE BADLANDS WOULDA BEEN CAKE,
AS WOULD THE REST OF ARMSTRONG AND EVENTUALLY, THE **WORLD**.
THE SPECIAL COOTIE SHOT WAS TO MAKE YOU FALL IN LOVE WITH ME, BECOMING MY SLAVE.
WITH YOU BY MY SIDE...
...WE WOULD'VE BEEN AWESOME.
I'M AT SEA 'BOUT HOW PIRATES CAME 'CROSS TECHNOLOGY NECESSARY T'CREATE A SHOT LIKE THAT IN THE FIRST PLACE.
I HEART THE WAY YOU TALK. IT'S SUPER ADORBS.
I, UH... UM...
THAT SHOT WAS DEVELOPED IN THE SCHOOL SCIENCE LAB BY A STUDENT KNOWN AS PROFESSOR ALBERT WESLEY.
HE TRADED IT FOR SOME JUNK WE HAD LAYIN' AROUND...
...AN HOURGLASS AND A HULA HOOP OR SOMETHIN'. CHUMP CHANGE.

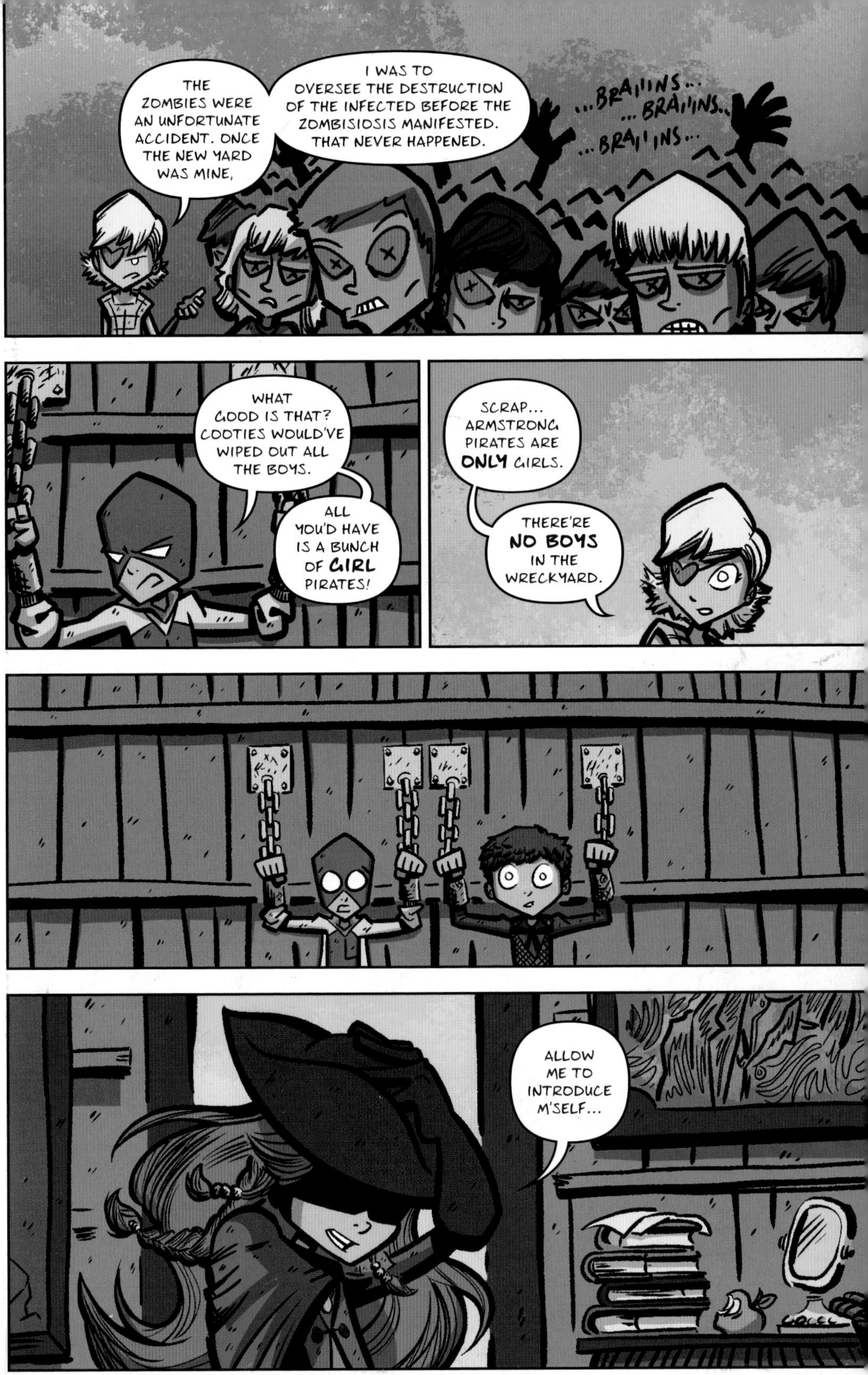
THE ZOMBIES WERE AN UNFORTUNATE ACCIDENT. ONCE THE NEW YARD WAS MINE,
I WAS TO OVERSEE THE DESTRUCTION OF THE INFECTED BEFORE THE ZOMBISIOSIS MANIFESTED. THAT NEVER HAPPENED.
...BRAIIINS...
...BRAIIINS...
...BRAIIINS...
WHAT GOOD IS THAT? COOTIES WOULD'VE WIPED OUT ALL THE BOYS.
ALL YOU'D HAVE IS A BUNCH OF **GIRL** PIRATES!
SCRAP... ARMSTRONG PIRATES ARE **ONLY** GIRLS.
THERE'RE **NO BOYS** IN THE WRECKYARD.
ALLOW ME TO INTRODUCE M'SELF...

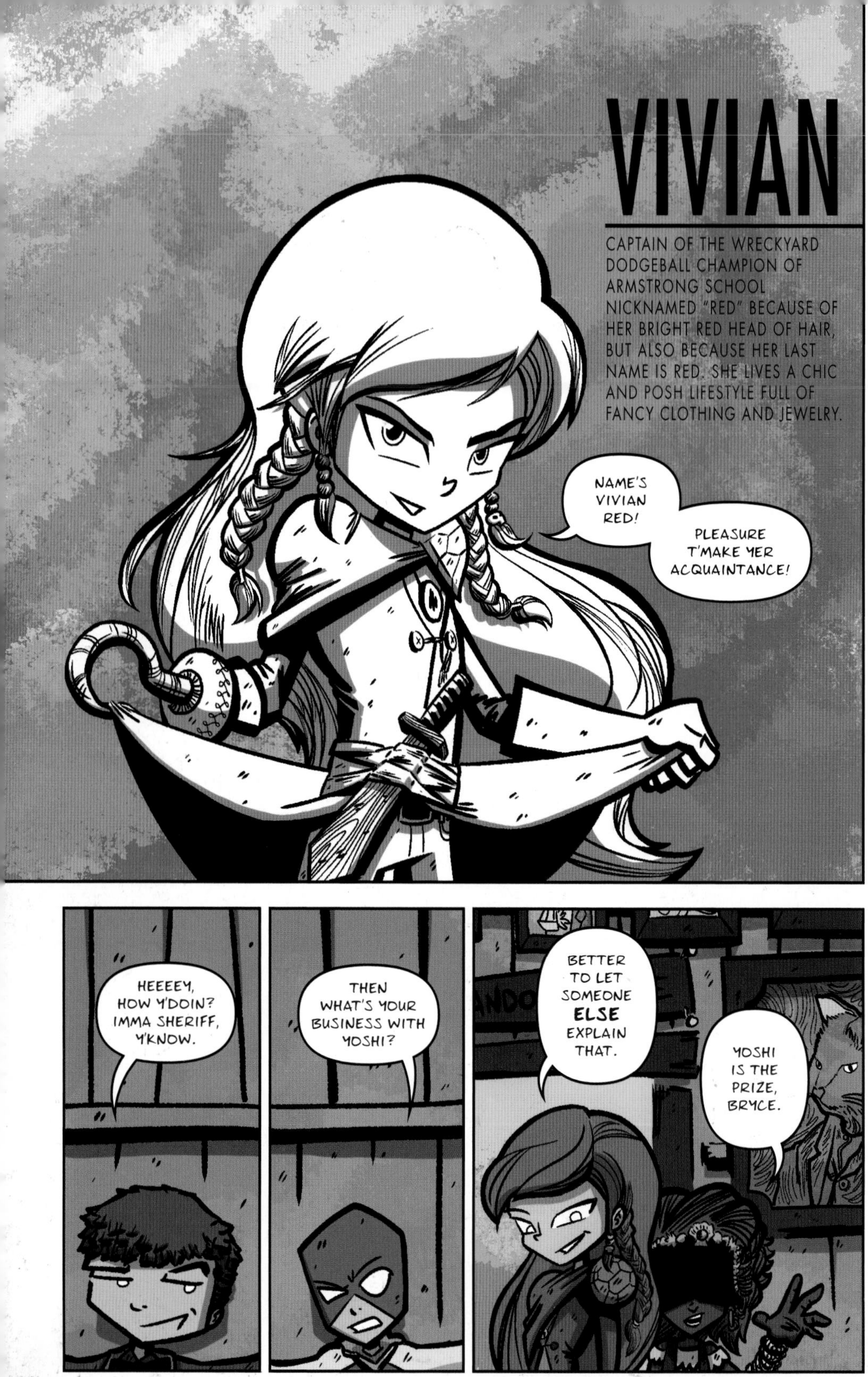
VIVIAN
CAPTAIN OF THE WRECKYARD DODGEBALL CHAMPION OF ARMSTRONG SCHOOL
NICKNAMED "RED" BECAUSE OF HER BRIGHT RED HEAD OF HAIR, BUT ALSO BECAUSE HER LAST NAME IS RED. SHE LIVES A CHIC AND POSH LIFESTYLE FULL OF FANCY CLOTHING AND JEWELRY.
NAME'S VIVIAN RED!
PLEASURE T'MAKE YER ACQUAINTANCE!
HEEEEY, HOW Y'DOIN? IMMA SHERIFF, Y'KNOW.
THEN WHAT'S YOUR BUSINESS WITH YOSHI?
BETTER TO LET SOMEONE ELSE EXPLAIN THAT.
YOSHI IS THE PRIZE, BRYCE.

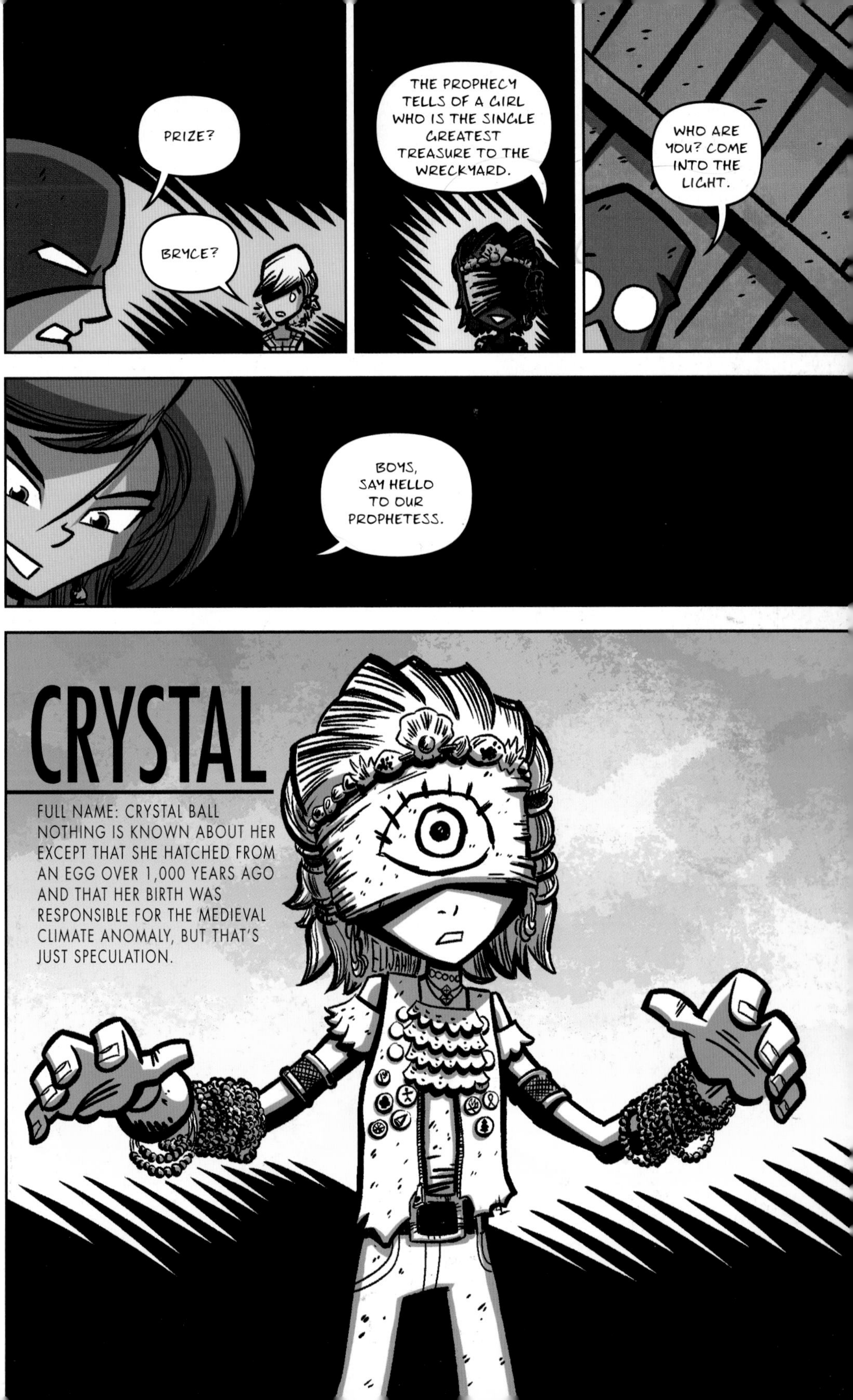
PRIZE?
BRYCE?
THE PROPHECY TELLS OF A GIRL WHO IS THE SINGLE GREATEST TREASURE TO THE WRECKYARD.
WHO ARE YOU? COME INTO THE LIGHT.
BOYS, SAY HELLO TO OUR PROPHETESS.
CRYSTAL
FULL NAME: CRYSTAL BALL
NOTHING IS KNOWN ABOUT HER EXCEPT THAT SHE HATCHED FROM AN EGG OVER 1,000 YEARS AGO AND THAT HER BIRTH WAS RESPONSIBLE FOR THE MEDIEVAL CLIMATE ANOMALY, BUT THAT'S JUST SPECULATION.

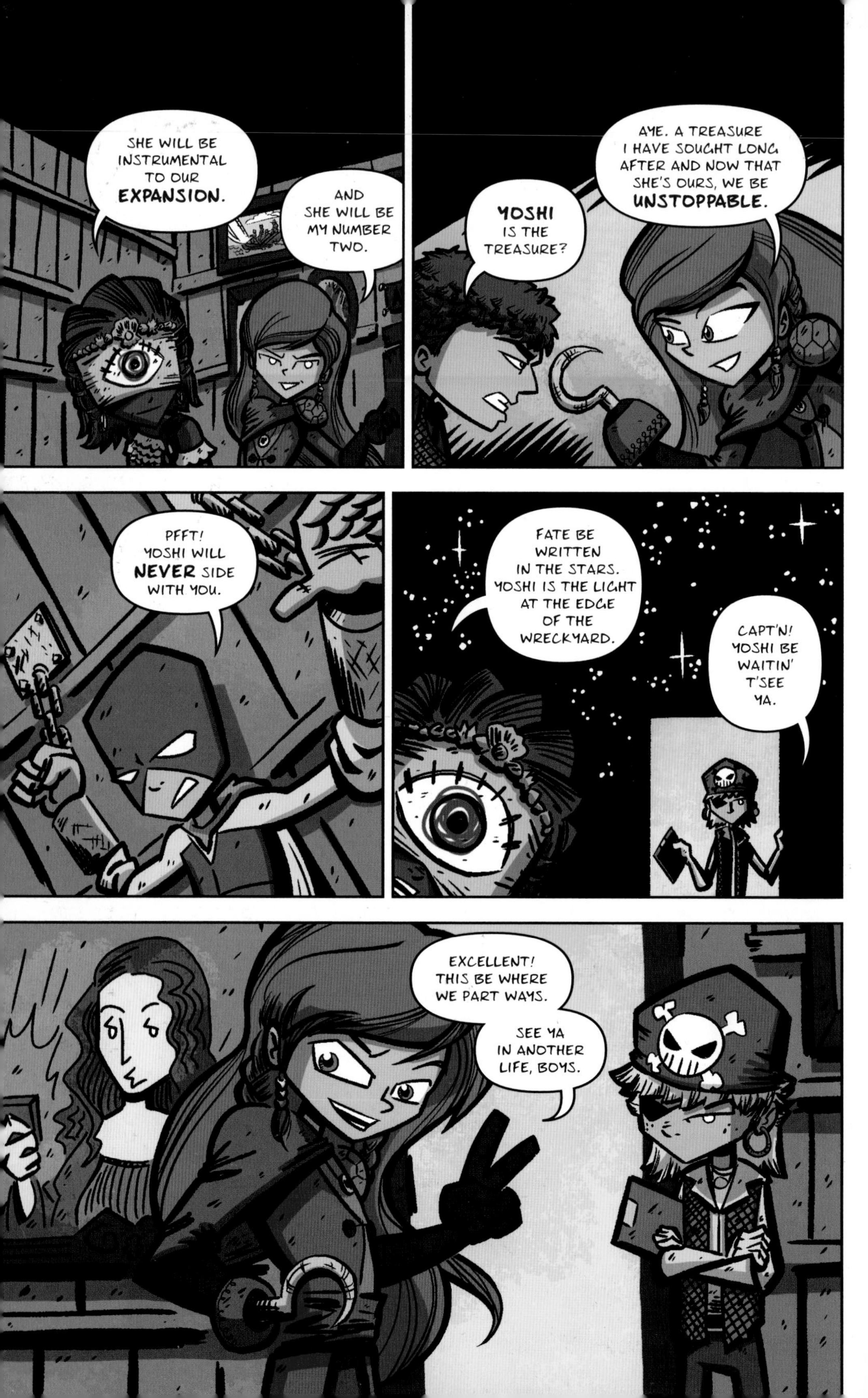
SHE WILL BE INSTRUMENTAL TO OUR **EXPANSION**.
AND SHE WILL BE MY NUMBER TWO.
YOSHI IS THE TREASURE?
AYE. A TREASURE I HAVE SOUGHT LONG AFTER AND NOW THAT SHE'S OURS, WE BE **UNSTOPPABLE**.
PFFT! YOSHI WILL **NEVER** SIDE WITH YOU.
FATE BE WRITTEN IN THE STARS. YOSHI IS THE LIGHT AT THE EDGE OF THE WRECKYARD.
CAPT'N! YOSHI BE WAITIN' T'SEE YA.
EXCELLENT! THIS BE WHERE WE PART WAYS.
SEE YA IN ANOTHER LIFE, BOYS.

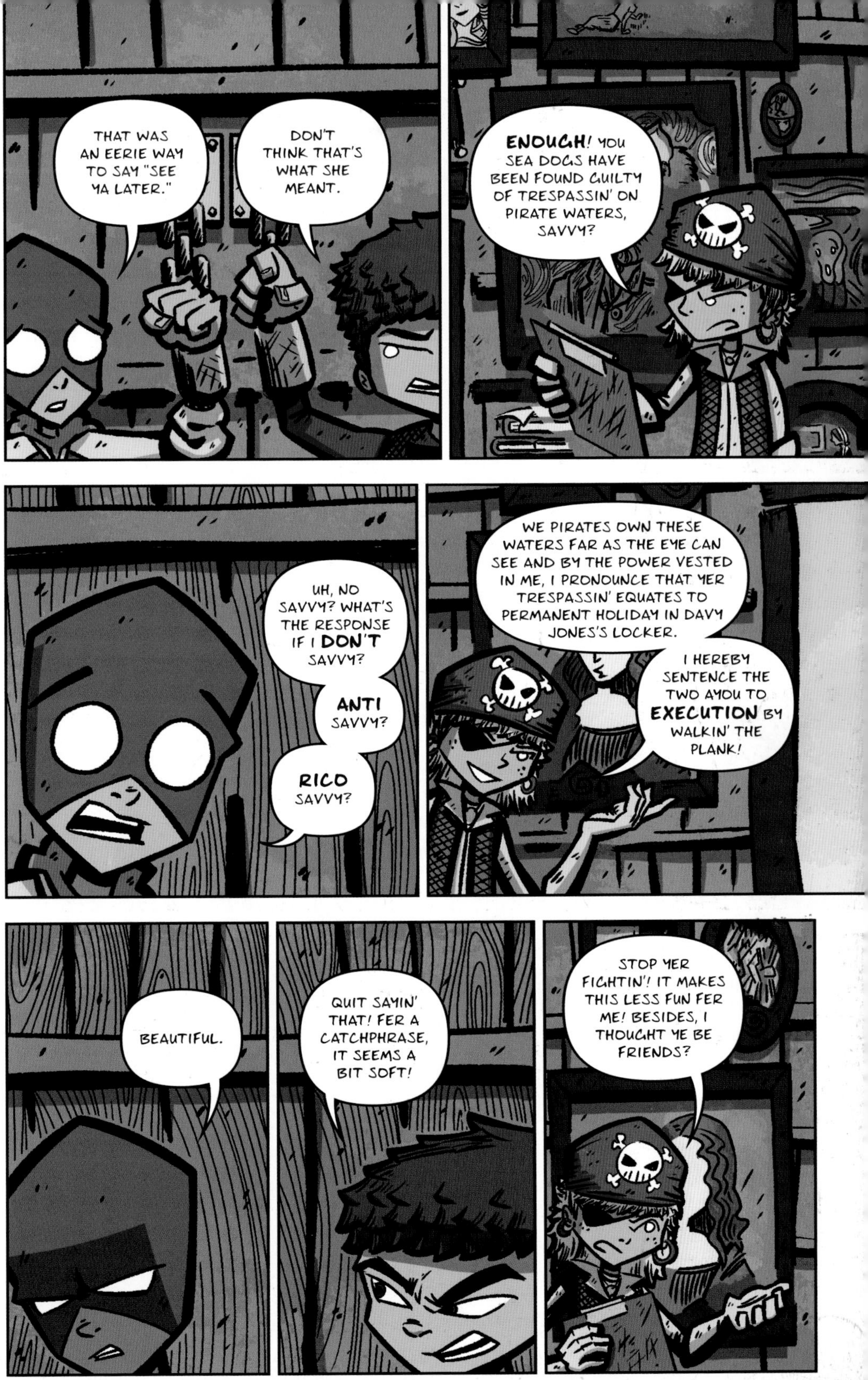
THAT WAS AN EERIE WAY TO SAY "SEE YA LATER."
DON'T THINK THAT'S WHAT SHE MEANT.
ENOUGH! YOU SEA DOGS HAVE BEEN FOUND GUILTY OF TRESPASSIN' ON PIRATE WATERS, SAVVY?
UH, NO SAVVY? WHAT'S THE RESPONSE IF I **DON'T** SAVVY?
ANTI SAVVY?
RICO SAVVY?
WE PIRATES OWN THESE WATERS FAR AS THE EYE CAN SEE AND BY THE POWER VESTED IN ME, I PRONOUNCE THAT YER TRESPASSIN' EQUATES TO PERMANENT HOLIDAY IN DAVY JONES'S LOCKER.
I HEREBY SENTENCE THE TWO AYOU TO **EXECUTION** BY WALKIN' THE PLANK!
BEAUTIFUL.
QUIT SAYIN' THAT! FER A CATCHPHRASE, IT SEEMS A BIT SOFT!
STOP YER FIGHTIN'! IT MAKES THIS LESS FUN FER ME! BESIDES, I THOUGHT YE BE FRIENDS?

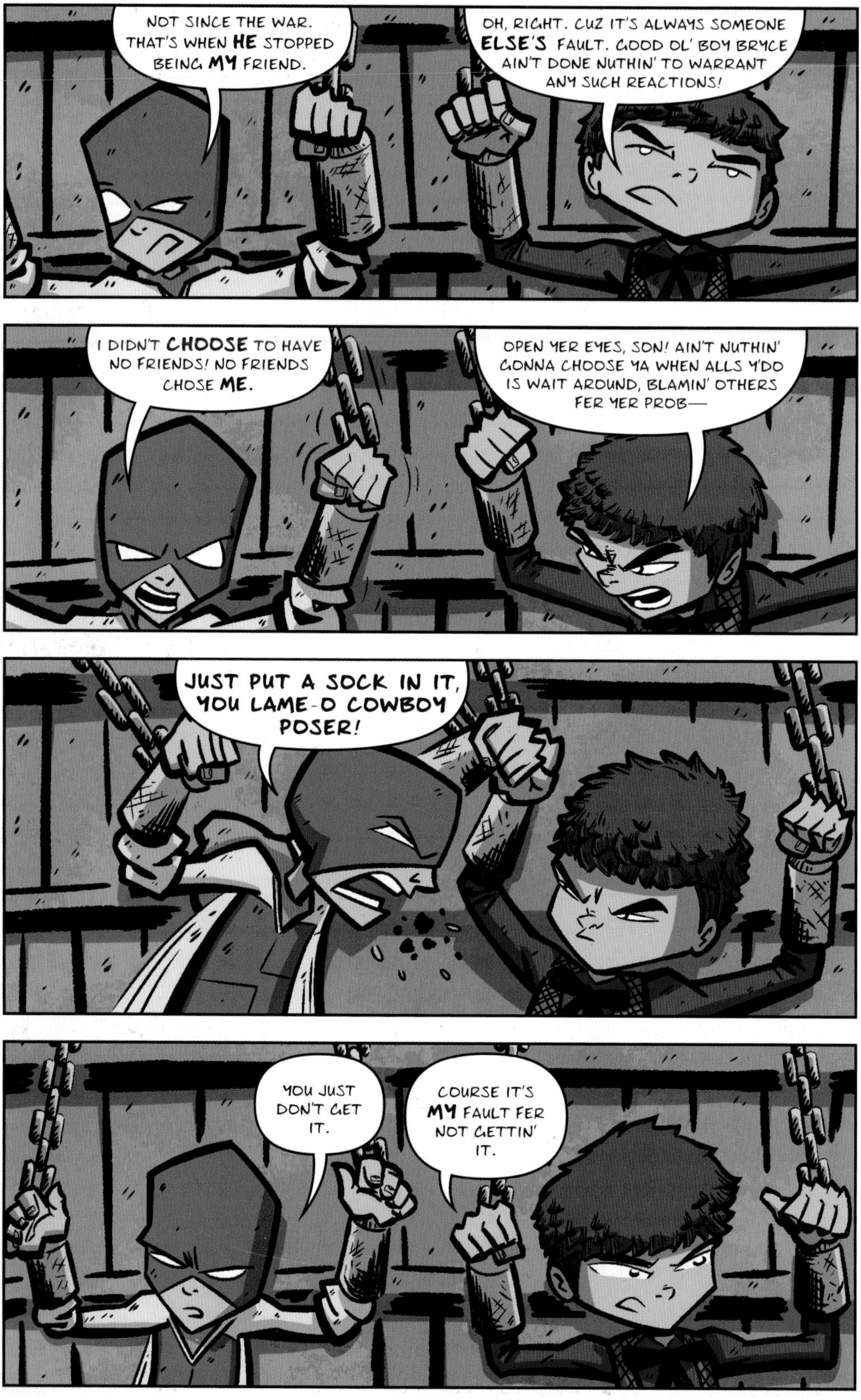
NOT SINCE THE WAR. THAT'S WHEN HE STOPPED BEING MY FRIEND.
OH, RIGHT. CUZ IT'S ALWAYS SOMEONE ELSE'S FAULT. GOOD OL' BOY BRYCE AIN'T DONE NUTHIN' TO WARRANT ANY SUCH REACTIONS!
I DIDN'T CHOOSE TO HAVE NO FRIENDS! NO FRIENDS CHOSE ME.
OPEN YER EYES, SON! AIN'T NUTHIN' GONNA CHOOSE YA WHEN ALLS Y'DO IS WAIT AROUND, BLAMIN' OTHERS FER YER PROB—
JUST PUT A SOCK IN IT, YOU LAME-O COWBOY POSER!
YOU JUST DON'T GET IT.
COURSE IT'S MY FAULT FER NOT GETTIN' IT.

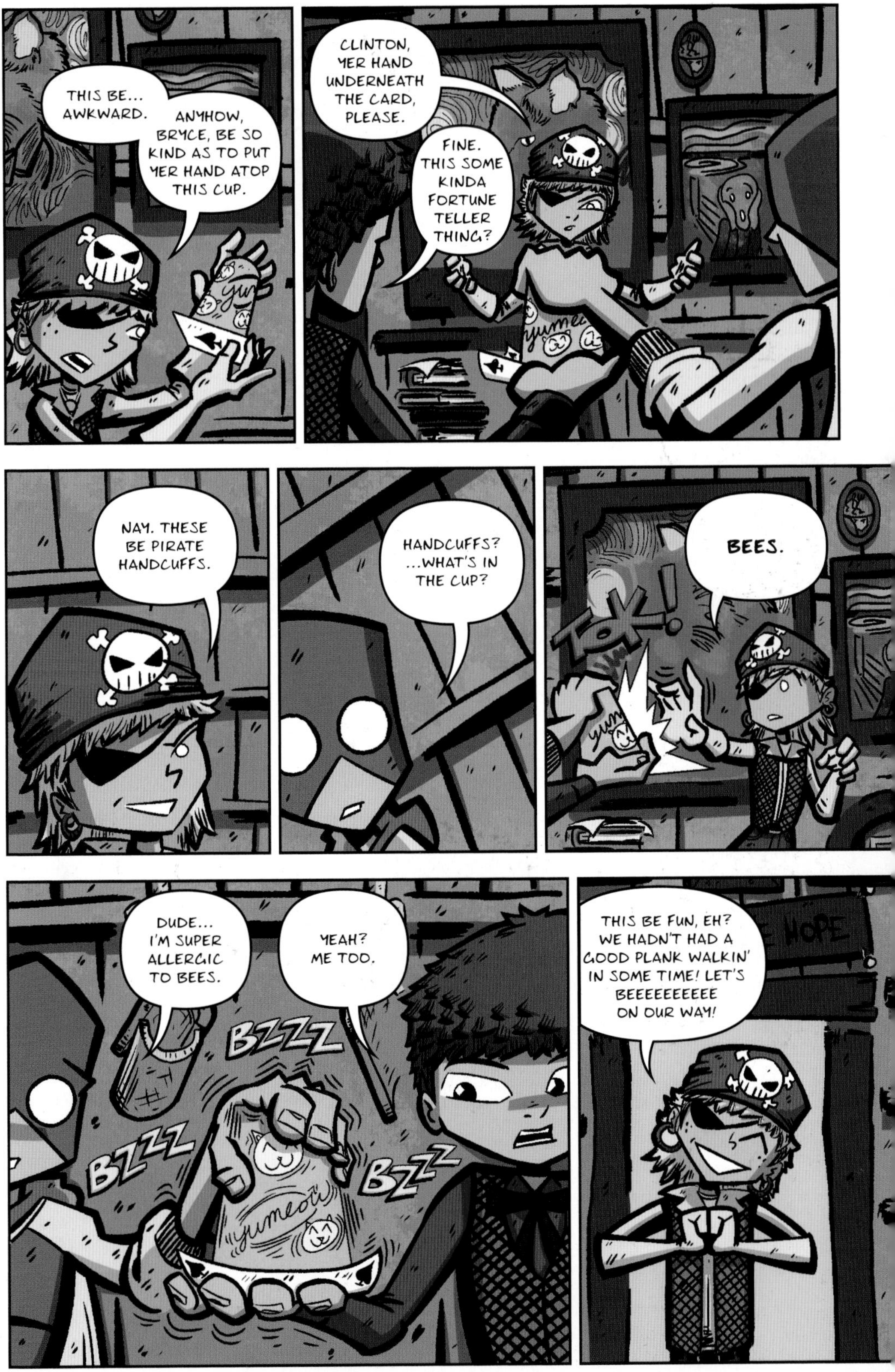

THIS BE... AWKWARD.
ANYHOW, BRYCE, BE SO KIND AS TO PUT YER HAND ATOP THIS CUP.
CLINTON, YER HAND UNDERNEATH THE CARD, PLEASE.
FINE. THIS SOME KINDA FORTUNE TELLER THING?
NAY. THESE BE PIRATE HANDCUFFS.
HANDCUFFS? ...WHAT'S IN THE CUP?
TOK!
BEES.
DUDE... I'M SUPER ALLERGIC TO BEES.
YEAH? ME TOO.
BZZZ
BZZZ
BZZZ
THIS BE FUN, EH? WE HADN'T HAD A GOOD PLANK WALKIN' IN SOME TIME! LET'S BEEEEEEEEEE ON OUR WAY!

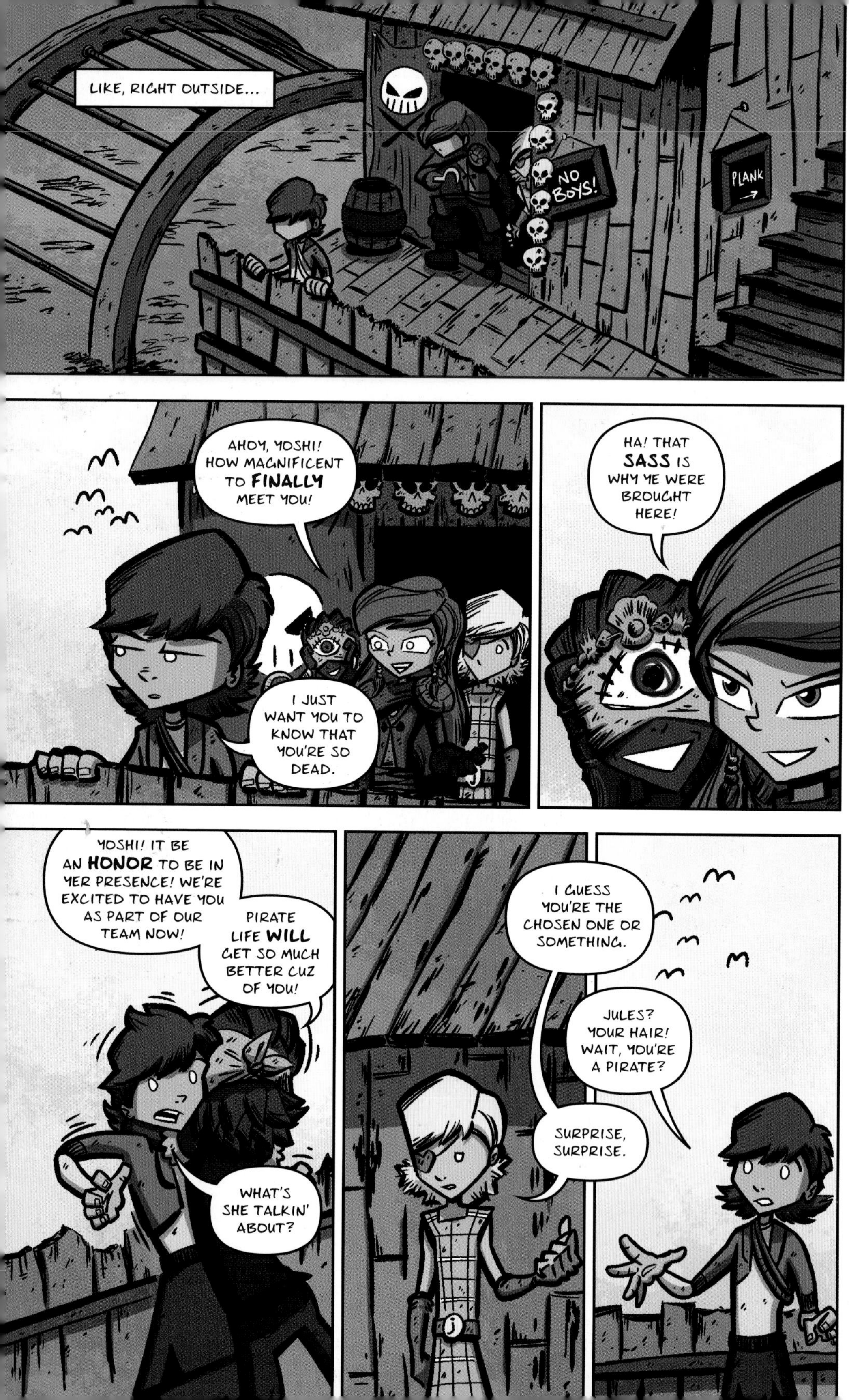
LIKE, RIGHT OUTSIDE...
NO BOYS!
PLANK →
AHOY, YOSHI! HOW MAGNIFICENT TO FINALLY MEET YOU!
I JUST WANT YOU TO KNOW THAT YOU'RE SO DEAD.
HA! THAT SASS IS WHY YE WERE BROUGHT HERE!
YOSHI! IT BE AN HONOR TO BE IN YER PRESENCE! WE'RE EXCITED TO HAVE YOU AS PART OF OUR TEAM NOW!
PIRATE LIFE WILL GET SO MUCH BETTER CUZ OF YOU!
WHAT'S SHE TALKIN' ABOUT?
I GUESS YOU'RE THE CHOSEN ONE OR SOMETHING.
JULES? YOUR HAIR! WAIT, YOU'RE A PIRATE?
SURPRISE, SURPRISE.

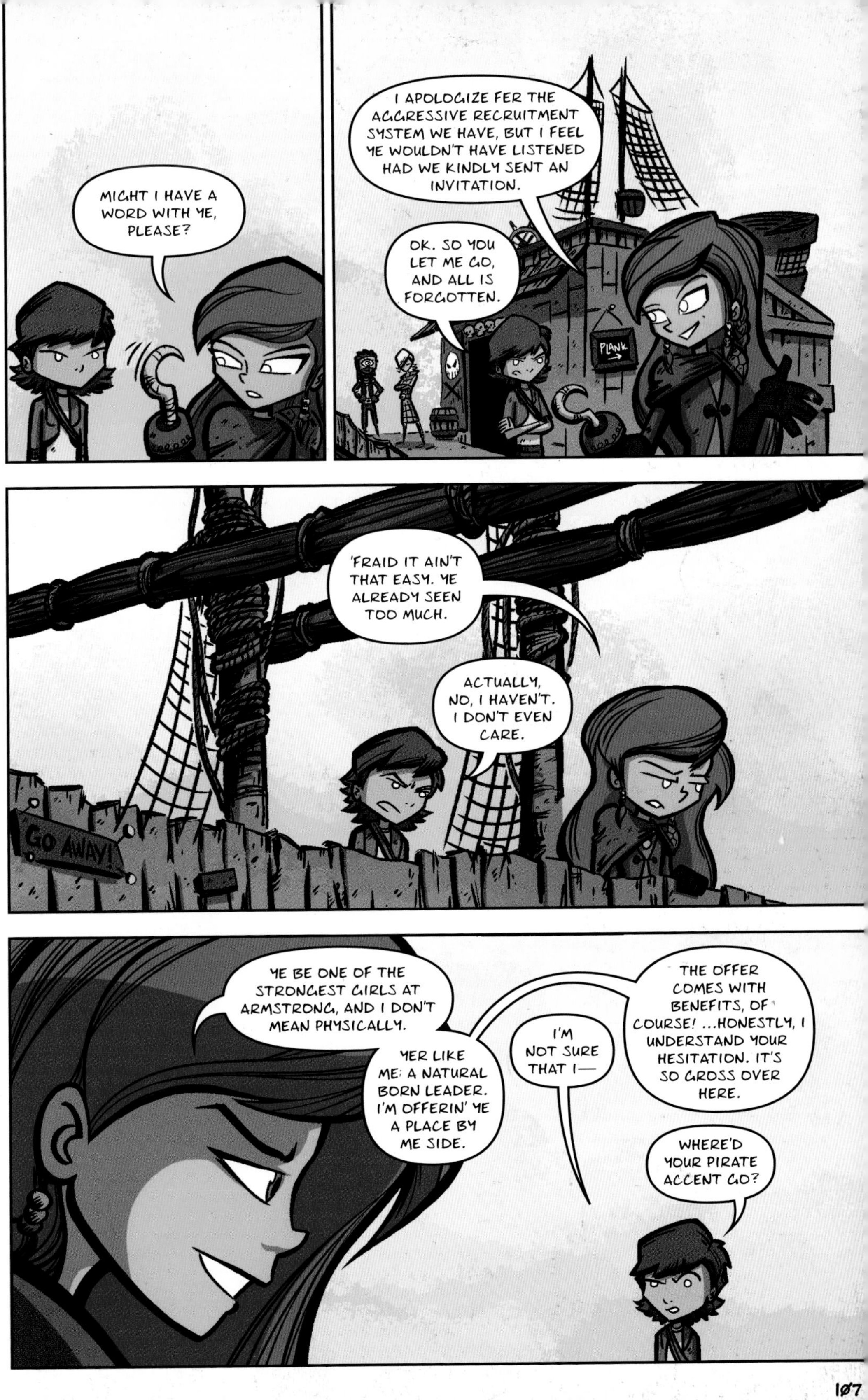
MIGHT I HAVE A WORD WITH YE, PLEASE?
I APOLOGIZE FER THE AGGRESSIVE RECRUITMENT SYSTEM WE HAVE, BUT I FEEL YE WOULDN'T HAVE LISTENED HAD WE KINDLY SENT AN INVITATION.
OK. SO YOU LET ME GO, AND ALL IS FORGOTTEN.
PLANK
'FRAID IT AIN'T THAT EASY. YE ALREADY SEEN TOO MUCH.
ACTUALLY, NO, I HAVEN'T. I DON'T EVEN CARE.
GO AWAY!
YE BE ONE OF THE STRONGEST GIRLS AT ARMSTRONG, AND I DON'T MEAN PHYSICALLY.
YER LIKE ME: A NATURAL BORN LEADER. I'M OFFERIN' YE A PLACE BY ME SIDE.
I'M NOT SURE THAT I—
THE OFFER COMES WITH BENEFITS, OF COURSE! ...HONESTLY, I UNDERSTAND YOUR HESITATION. IT'S SO GROSS OVER HERE.
WHERE'D YOUR PIRATE ACCENT GO?

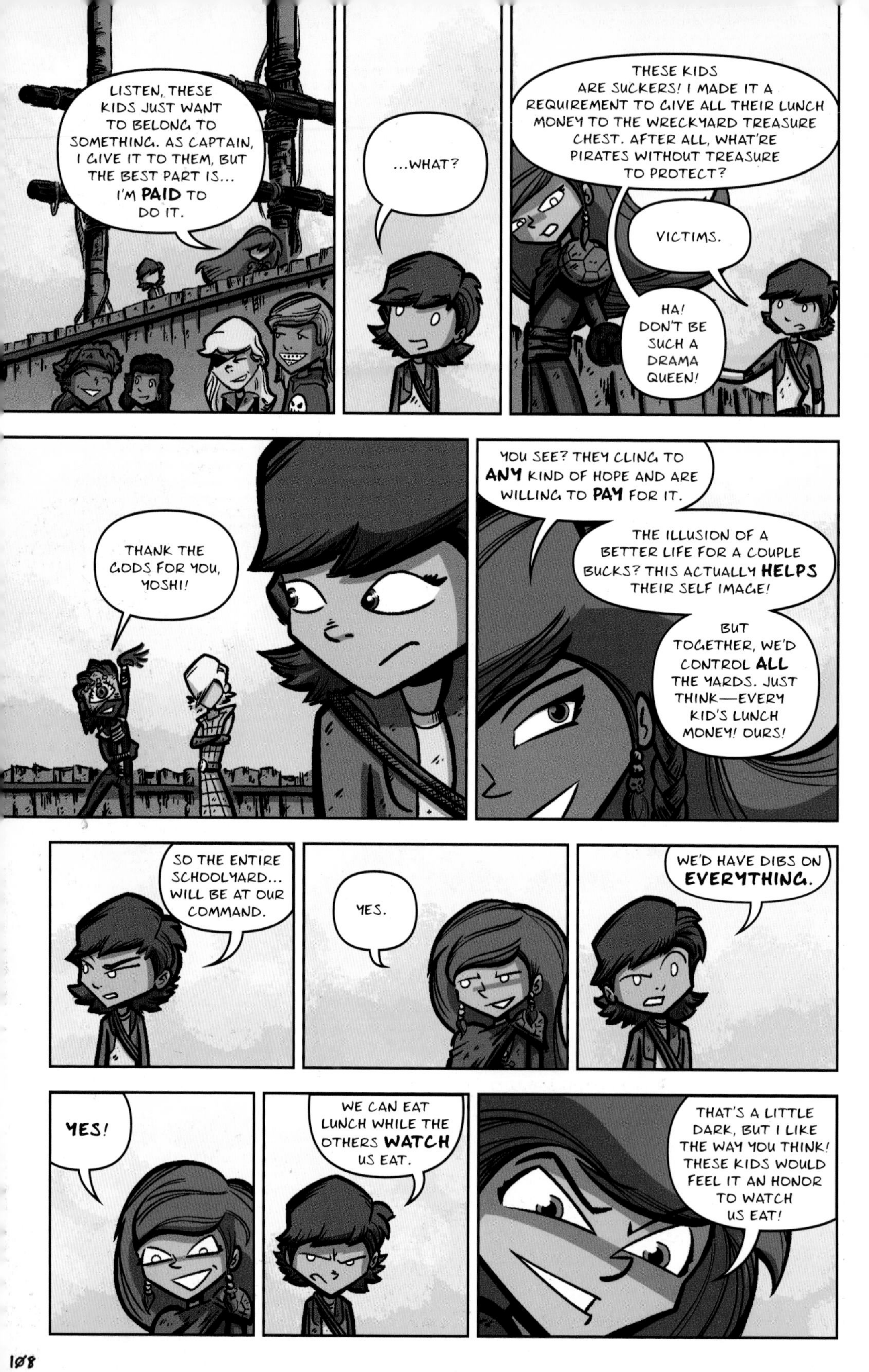

LISTEN, THESE KIDS JUST WANT TO BELONG TO SOMETHING. AS CAPTAIN, I GIVE IT TO THEM, BUT THE BEST PART IS... I'M PAID TO DO IT.
...WHAT?
THESE KIDS ARE SUCKERS! I MADE IT A REQUIREMENT TO GIVE ALL THEIR LUNCH MONEY TO THE WRECKYARD TREASURE CHEST. AFTER ALL, WHAT'RE PIRATES WITHOUT TREASURE TO PROTECT?
VICTIMS.
HA! DON'T BE SUCH A DRAMA QUEEN!
THANK THE GODS FOR YOU, YOSHI!
YOU SEE? THEY CLING TO ANY KIND OF HOPE AND ARE WILLING TO PAY FOR IT.
THE ILLUSION OF A BETTER LIFE FOR A COUPLE BUCKS? THIS ACTUALLY HELPS THEIR SELF IMAGE!
BUT TOGETHER, WE'D CONTROL ALL THE YARDS. JUST THINK—EVERY KID'S LUNCH MONEY! OURS!
SO THE ENTIRE SCHOOLYARD... WILL BE AT OUR COMMAND.
YES.
WE'D HAVE DIBS ON EVERYTHING.
YES!
WE CAN EAT LUNCH WHILE THE OTHERS WATCH US EAT.
THAT'S A LITTLE DARK, BUT I LIKE THE WAY YOU THINK! THESE KIDS WOULD FEEL IT AN HONOR TO WATCH US EAT!

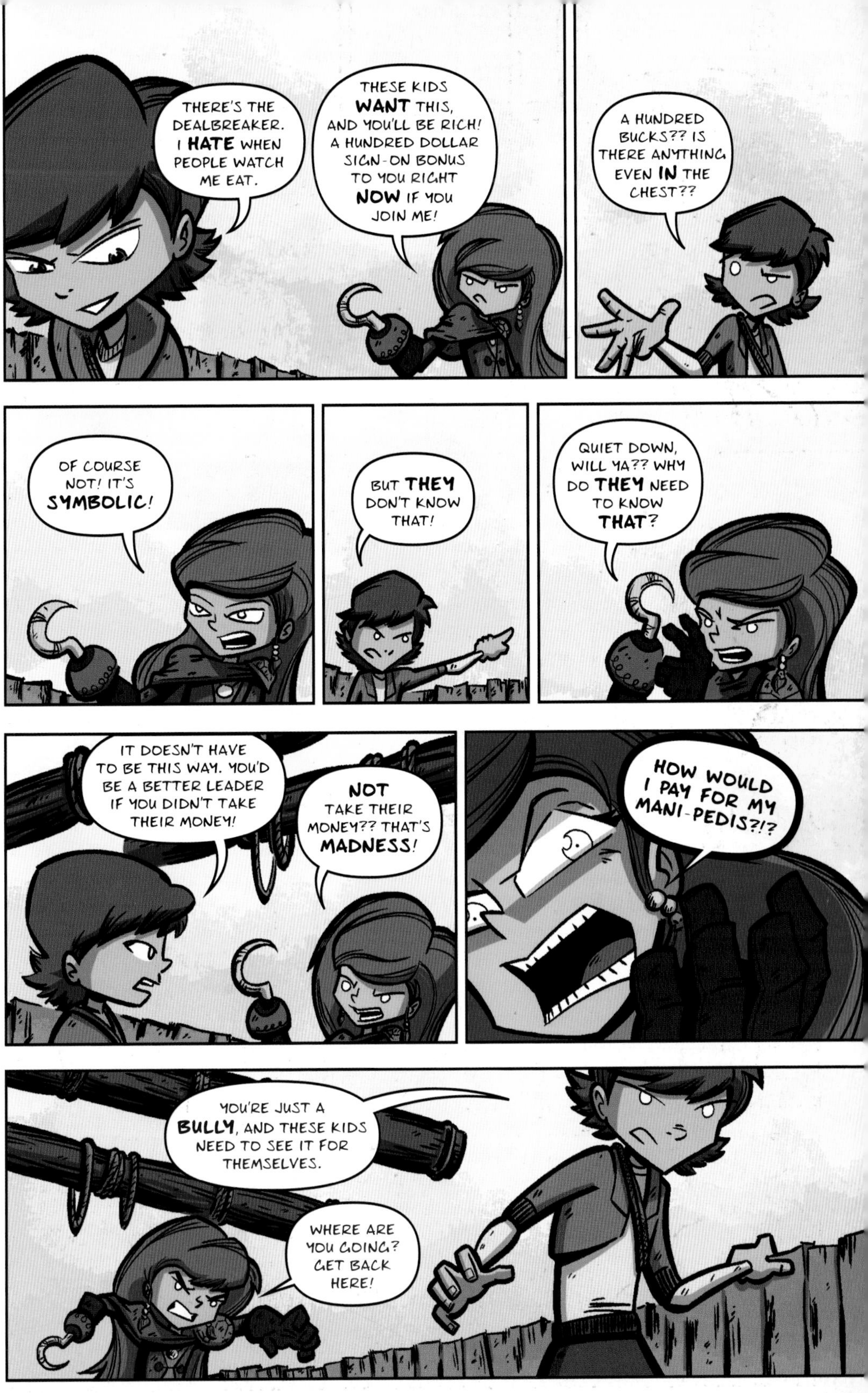
THERE'S THE DEALBREAKER. I **HATE** WHEN PEOPLE WATCH ME EAT.
THESE KIDS **WANT** THIS, AND YOU'LL BE RICH! A HUNDRED DOLLAR SIGN-ON BONUS TO YOU RIGHT **NOW** IF YOU JOIN ME!
A HUNDRED BUCKS?? IS THERE ANYTHING EVEN **IN** THE CHEST??
OF COURSE NOT! IT'S **SYMBOLIC**!
BUT **THEY** DON'T KNOW THAT!
QUIET DOWN, WILL YA?? WHY DO **THEY** NEED TO KNOW **THAT**?
IT DOESN'T HAVE TO BE THIS WAY. YOU'D BE A BETTER LEADER IF YOU DIDN'T TAKE THEIR MONEY!
NOT TAKE THEIR MONEY?? THAT'S **MADNESS**!
HOW WOULD I PAY FOR MY MANI-PEDIS?!?
YOU'RE JUST A **BULLY**, AND THESE KIDS NEED TO SEE IT FOR THEMSELVES.
WHERE ARE YOU GOING? GET BACK HERE!

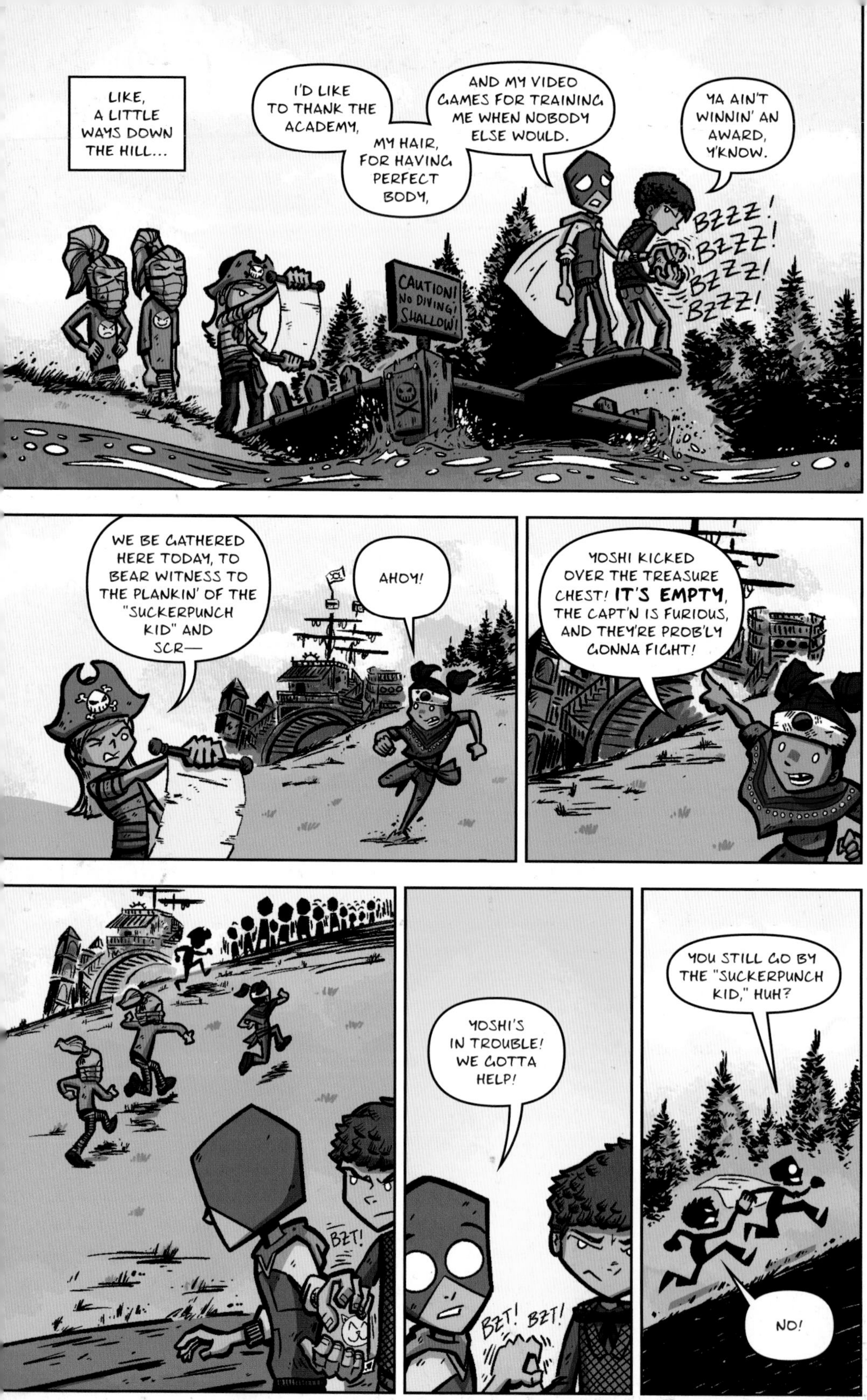
LIKE, A LITTLE WAYS DOWN THE HILL...
I'D LIKE TO THANK THE ACADEMY,
MY HAIR, FOR HAVING PERFECT BODY,
AND MY VIDEO GAMES FOR TRAINING ME WHEN NOBODY ELSE WOULD.
YA AIN'T WINNIN' AN AWARD, Y'KNOW.
BZZZ! BZZZ! BZZZ! BZZZ!
CAUTION! NO DIVING! SHALLOW!
WE BE GATHERED HERE TODAY, TO BEAR WITNESS TO THE PLANKIN' OF THE "SUCKERPUNCH KID" AND SCR—
AHOY!
YOSHI KICKED OVER THE TREASURE CHEST! IT'S EMPTY, THE CAPT'N IS FURIOUS, AND THEY'RE PROB'LY GONNA FIGHT!
BZT!
YOSHI'S IN TROUBLE! WE GOTTA HELP!
BZT! BZT!
YOU STILL GO BY THE "SUCKERPUNCH KID," HUH?
NO!

WHAT!? IT'S EMPTY??

ARE YOU KIDDING?!

ZOMG!

BY ODIN'S BEARD!

ARRR! YER MONEY BE IN A **SAFE** PLACE! I'D BE A BAD CAPTAIN HAD I KEPT IT IN THE OPEN!

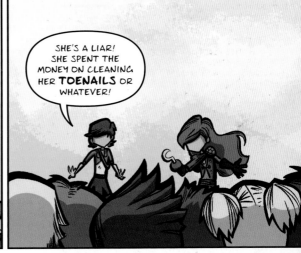

SHE'S A LIAR! SHE SPENT THE MONEY ON CLEANING HER **TOENAILS** OR WHATEVER!

I AIN'T ONE TO WITHDRAW ME PARTNERSHIP OFFER, BUT ANOTHER **WORD** FROM YA AND I'LL HAVE T'SERIOUSLY WEIGH THE OPTION!

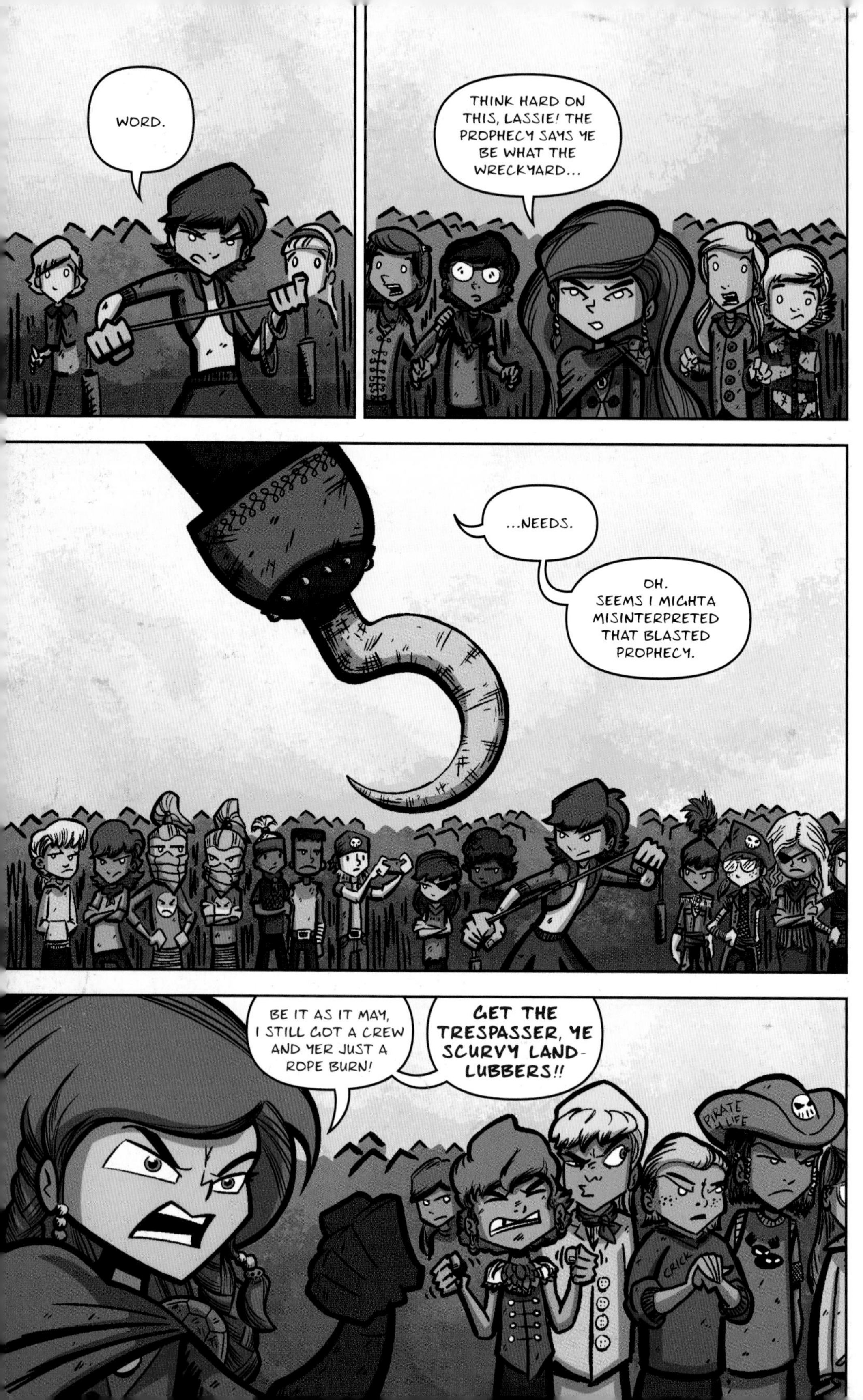
WORD.
THINK HARD ON THIS, LASSIE! THE PROPHECY SAYS YE BE WHAT THE WRECKYARD...
...NEEDS.
OH. SEEMS I MIGHTA MISINTERPRETED THAT BLASTED PROPHECY.
BE IT AS IT MAY, I STILL GOT A CREW AND YER JUST A ROPE BURN!
GET THE TRESPASSER, YE SCURVY LAND-LUBBERS!!
PIRATE LIFE
CRICK

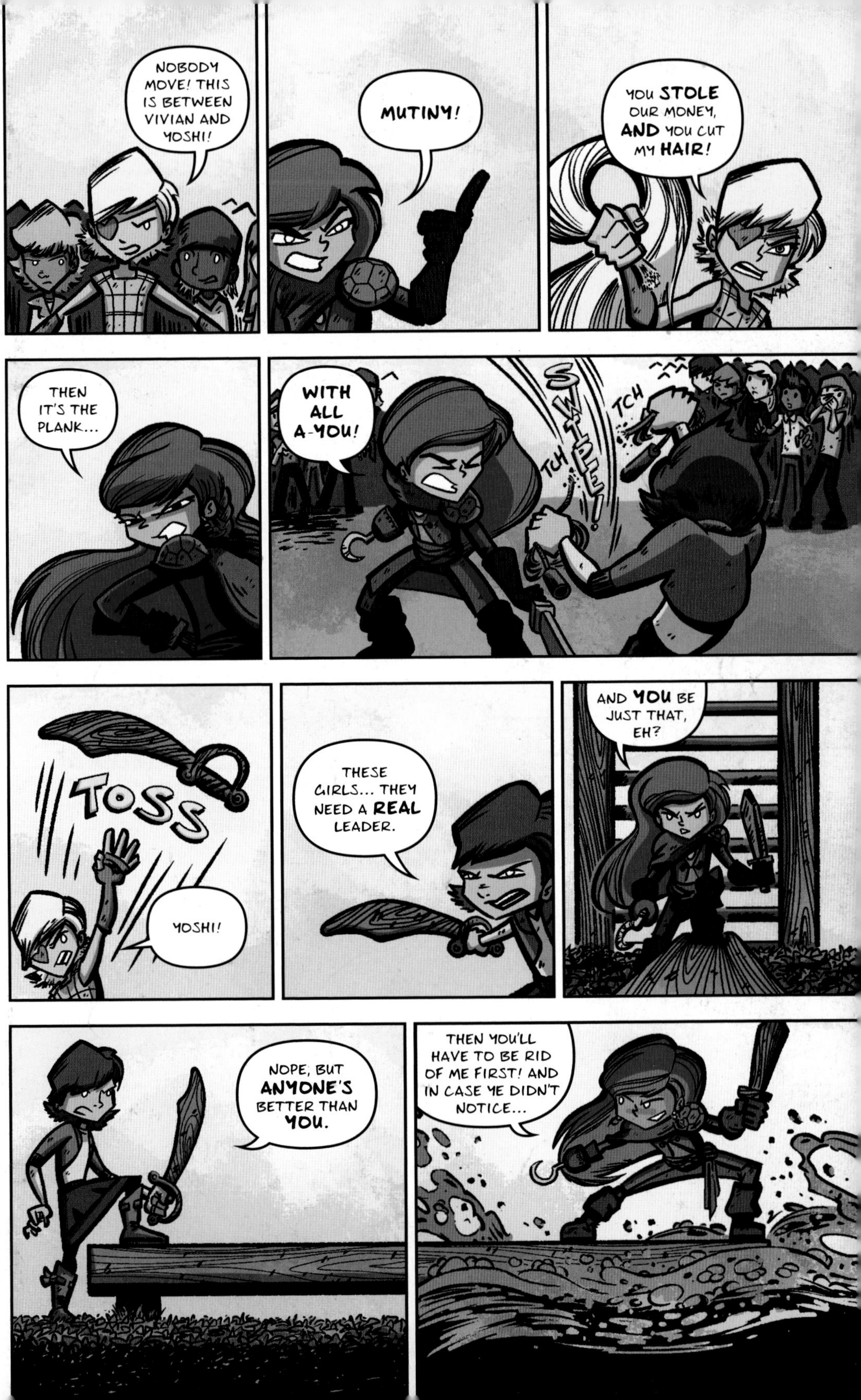
NOBODY MOVE! THIS IS BETWEEN VIVIAN AND YOSHI!
MUTINY!
YOU STOLE OUR MONEY, AND YOU CUT MY HAIR!
THEN IT'S THE PLANK...
WITH ALL A-YOU!
SWIPE!
TCH
TCH
TOSS
YOSHI!
THESE GIRLS... THEY NEED A REAL LEADER.
AND YOU BE JUST THAT, EH?
NOPE, BUT ANYONE'S BETTER THAN YOU.
THEN YOU'LL HAVE TO BE RID OF ME FIRST! AND IN CASE YE DIDN'T NOTICE...

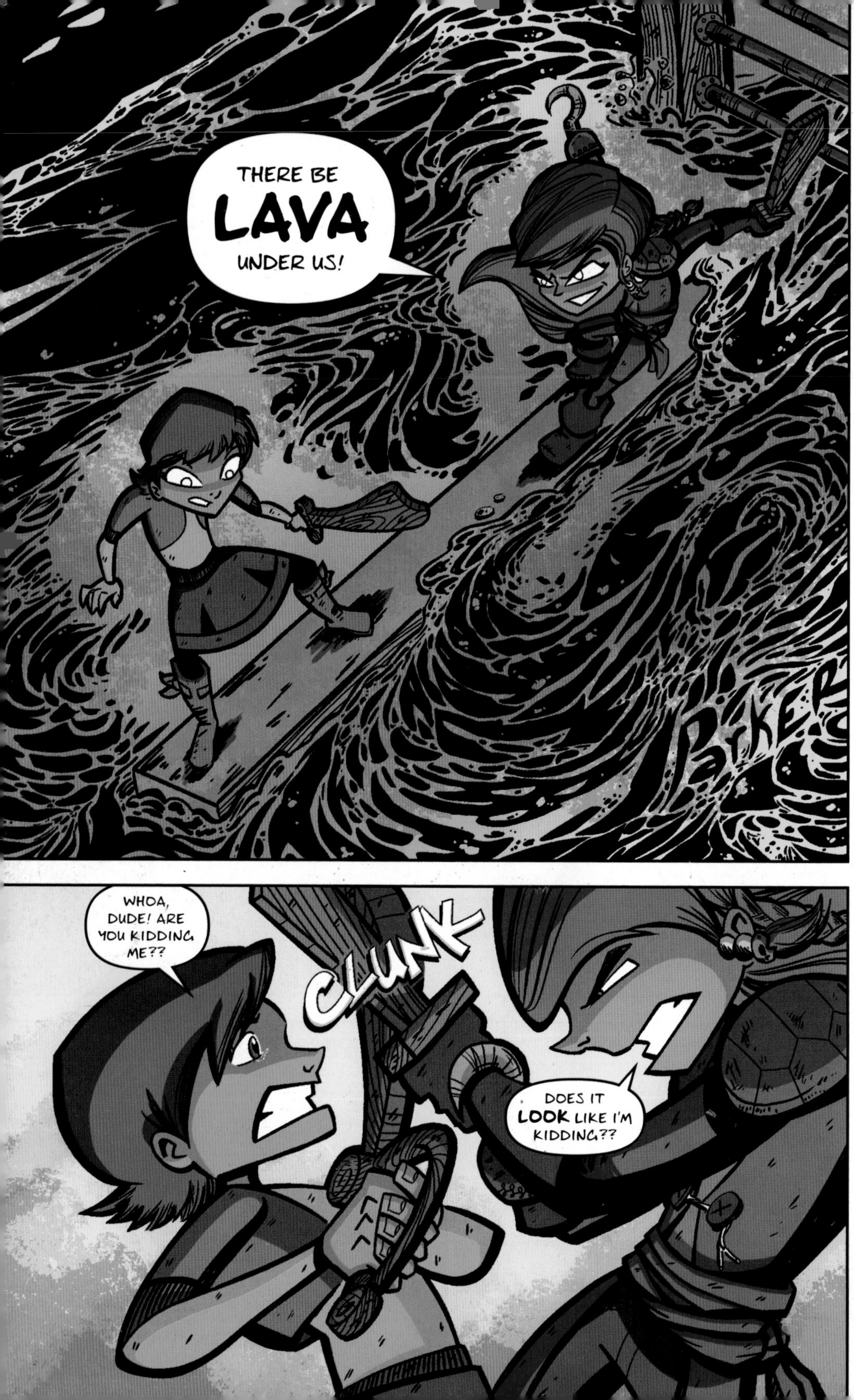
THERE BE LAVA UNDER US!
WHOA, DUDE! ARE YOU KIDDING ME??
CLUNK
DOES IT LOOK LIKE I'M KIDDING??

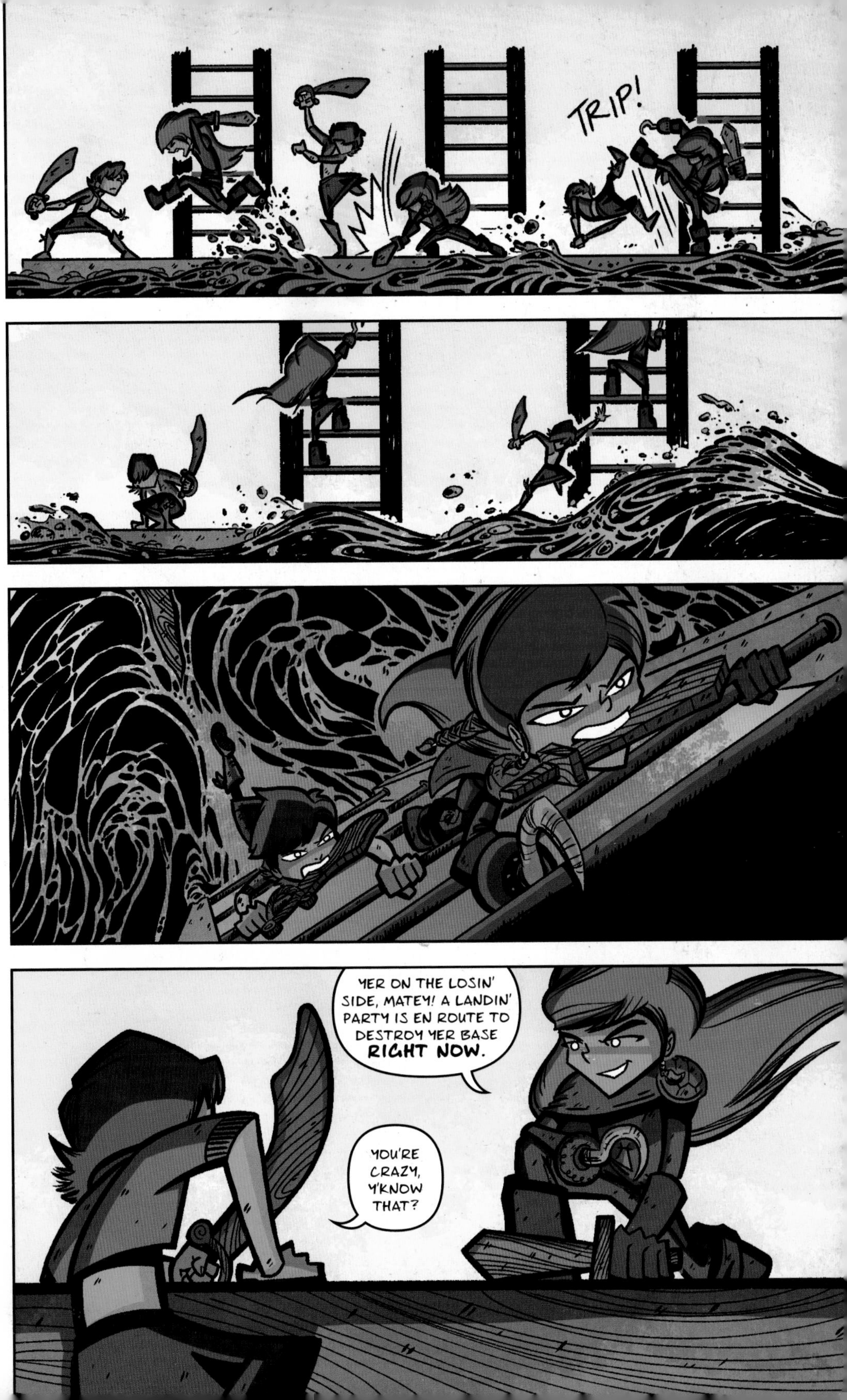
TRIP!
YER ON THE LOSIN' SIDE, MATEY! A LANDIN' PARTY IS EN ROUTE TO DESTROY YER BASE **RIGHT NOW.**
YOU'RE CRAZY, Y'KNOW THAT?

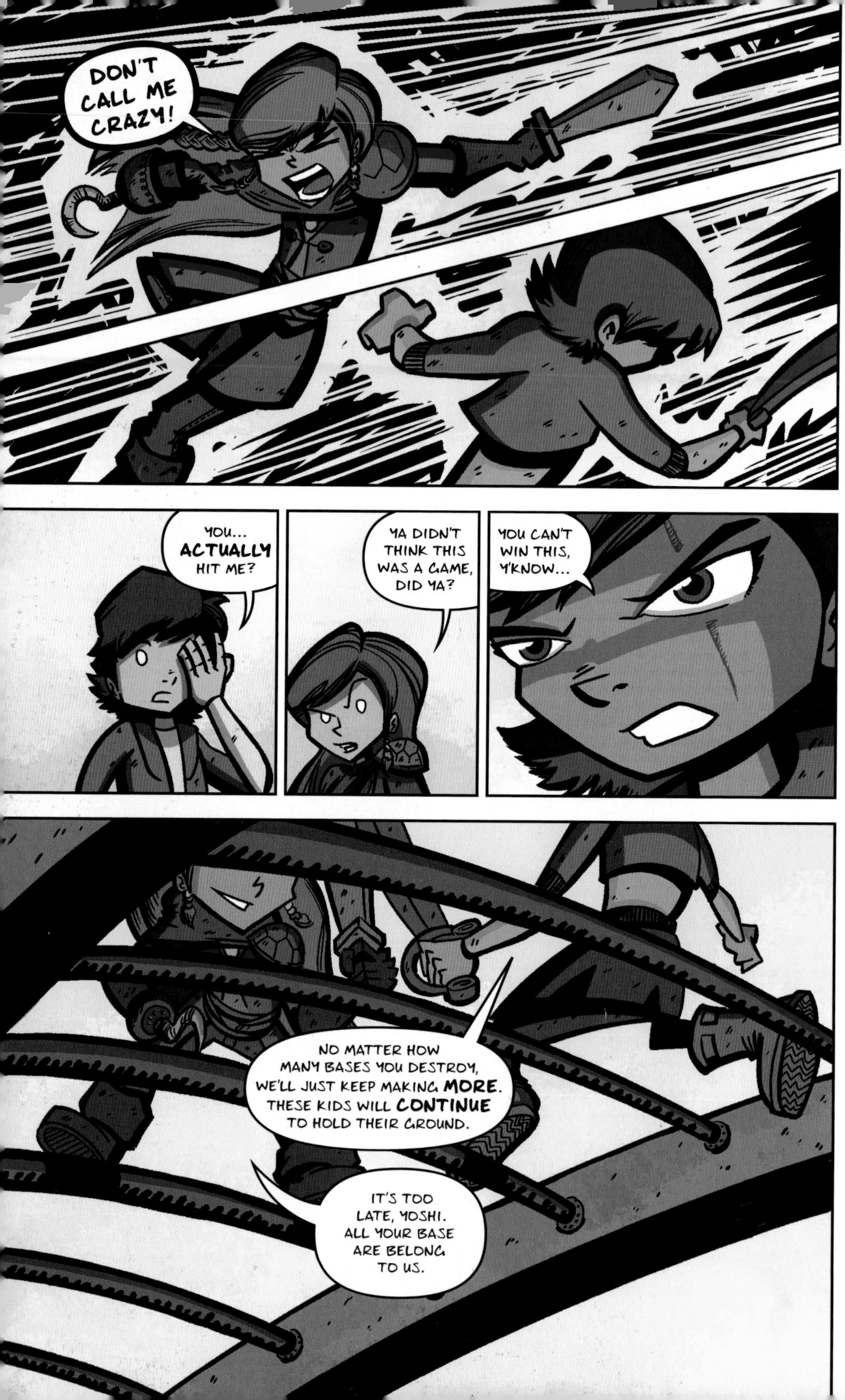
DON'T CALL ME CRAZY!
YOU... ACTUALLY HIT ME?
YA DIDN'T THINK THIS WAS A GAME, DID YA?
YOU CAN'T WIN THIS, Y'KNOW...
NO MATTER HOW MANY BASES YOU DESTROY, WE'LL JUST KEEP MAKING MORE. THESE KIDS WILL CONTINUE TO HOLD THEIR GROUND.
IT'S TOO LATE, YOSHI. ALL YOUR BASE ARE BELONG TO US.

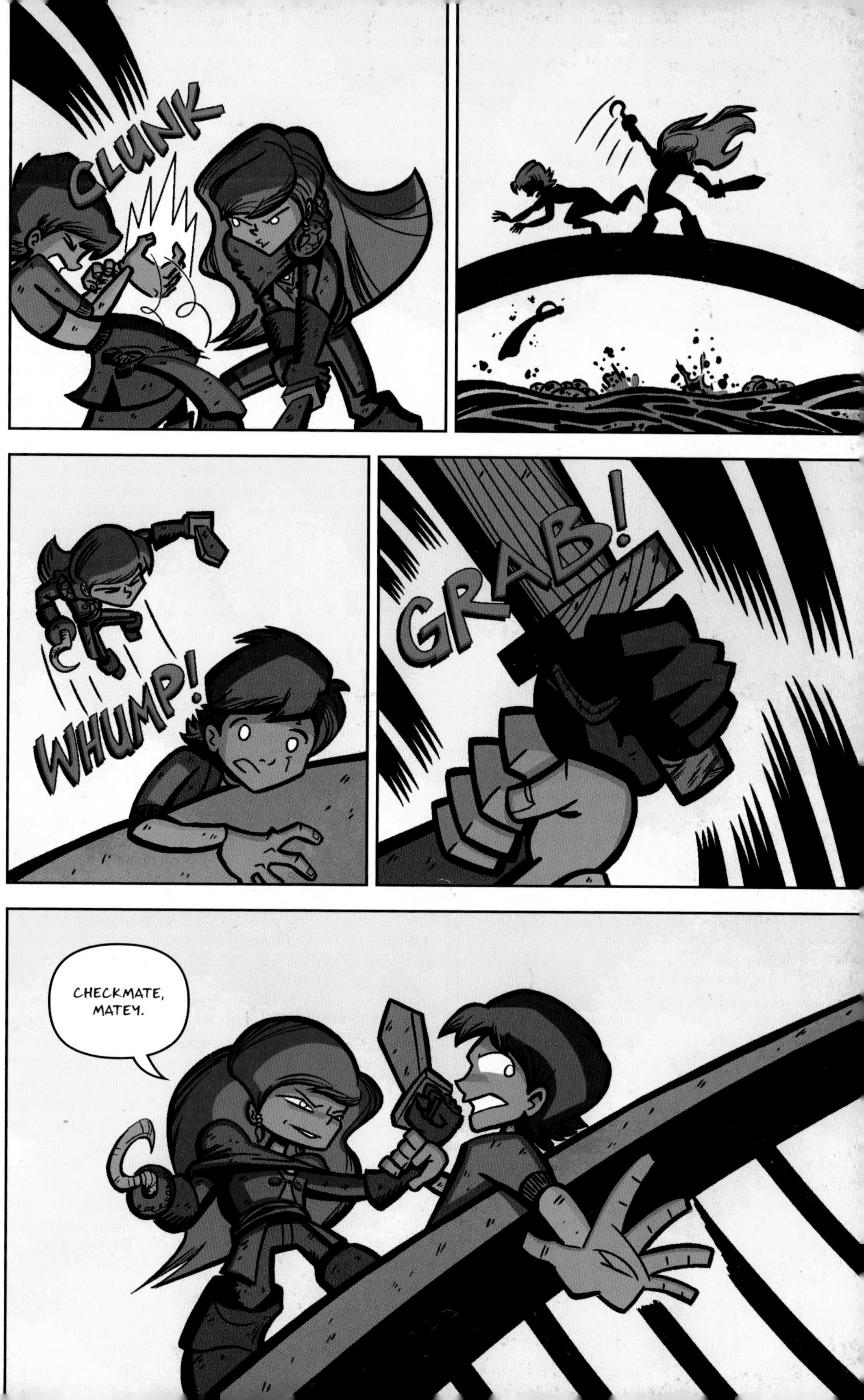
CLUNK
WHUMP!
GRAB!
CHECKMATE, MATEY.

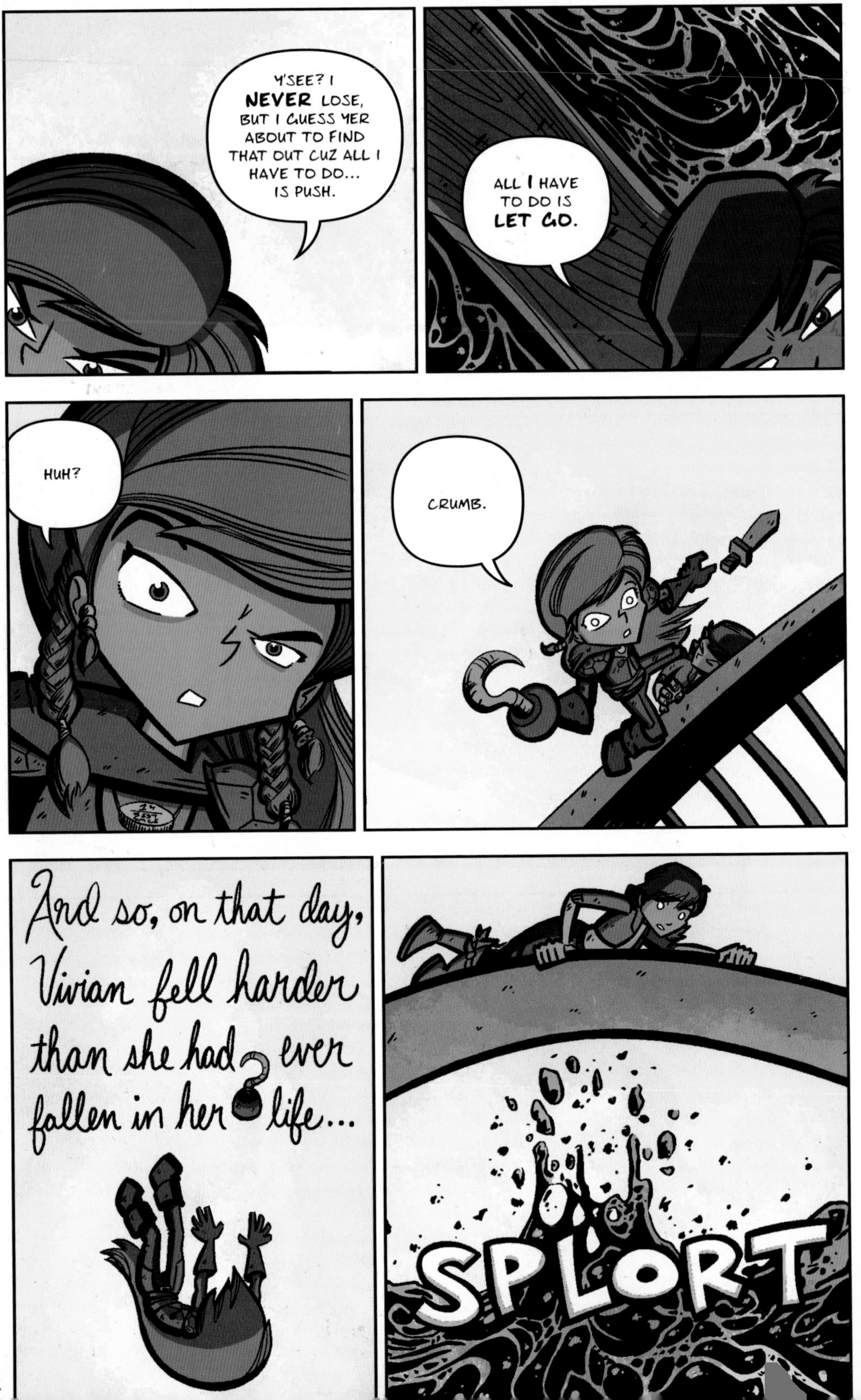
Y'SEE? I NEVER LOSE, BUT I GUESS YER ABOUT TO FIND THAT OUT CUZ ALL I HAVE TO DO... IS PUSH.
ALL I HAVE TO DO IS LET GO.
HUH?
CRUMB.
And so, on that day, Vivian fell harder than she had ever fallen in her life...
SPLORT

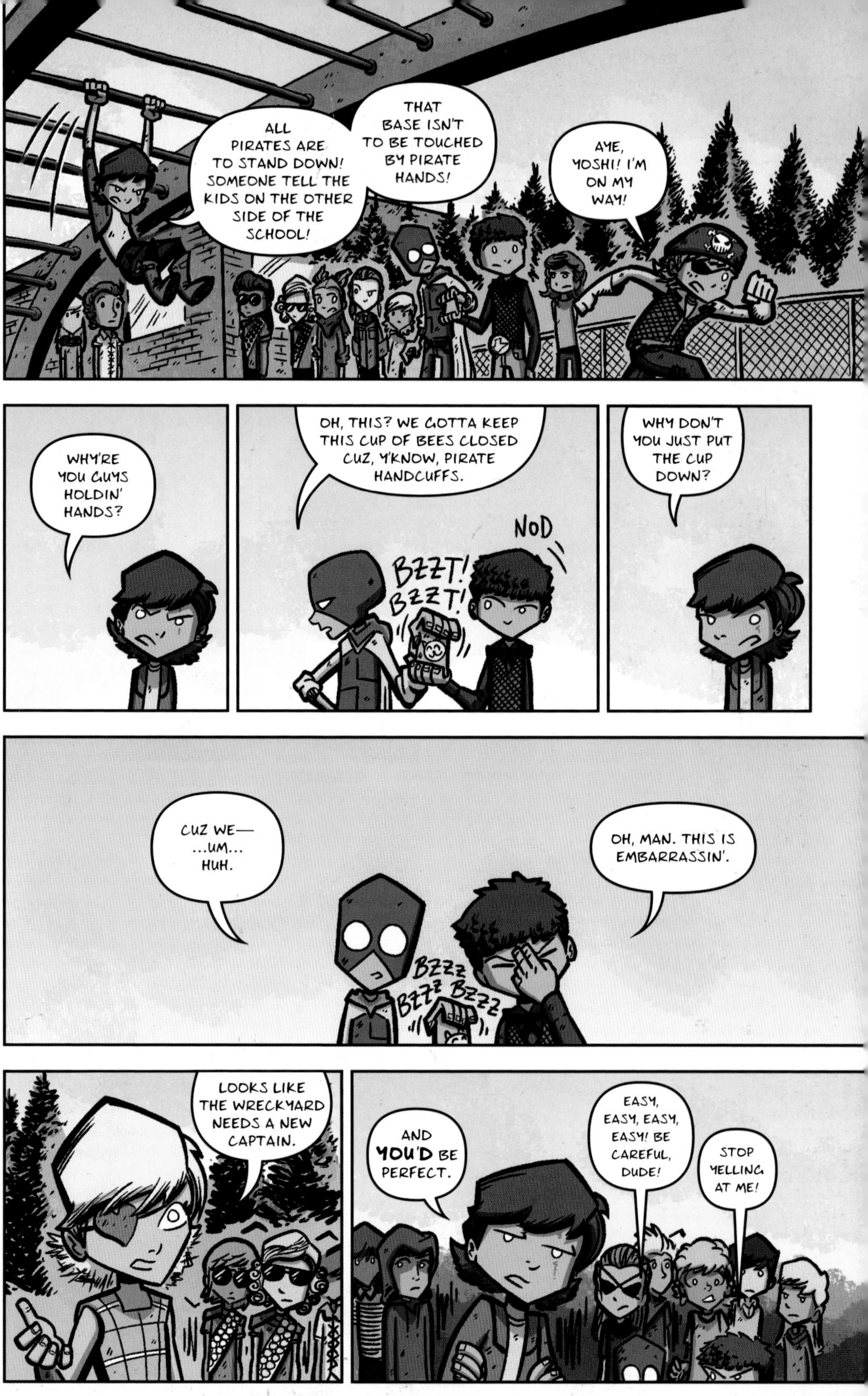
ALL PIRATES ARE TO STAND DOWN! SOMEONE TELL THE KIDS ON THE OTHER SIDE OF THE SCHOOL!
THAT BASE ISN'T TO BE TOUCHED BY PIRATE HANDS!
AYE, YOSHI! I'M ON MY WAY!
WHY'RE YOU GUYS HOLDIN' HANDS?
OH, THIS? WE GOTTA KEEP THIS CUP OF BEES CLOSED CUZ, Y'KNOW, PIRATE HANDCUFFS.
BZZT! BZZT!
NOD
WHY DON'T YOU JUST PUT THE CUP DOWN?
CUZ WE— ...UM... HUH.
OH, MAN. THIS IS EMBARRASSIN'.
BZZZ BZZZ BZZZ
LOOKS LIKE THE WRECKYARD NEEDS A NEW CAPTAIN.
AND **YOU'D** BE PERFECT.
EASY, EASY, EASY, EASY! BE CAREFUL, DUDE!
STOP YELLING AT ME!

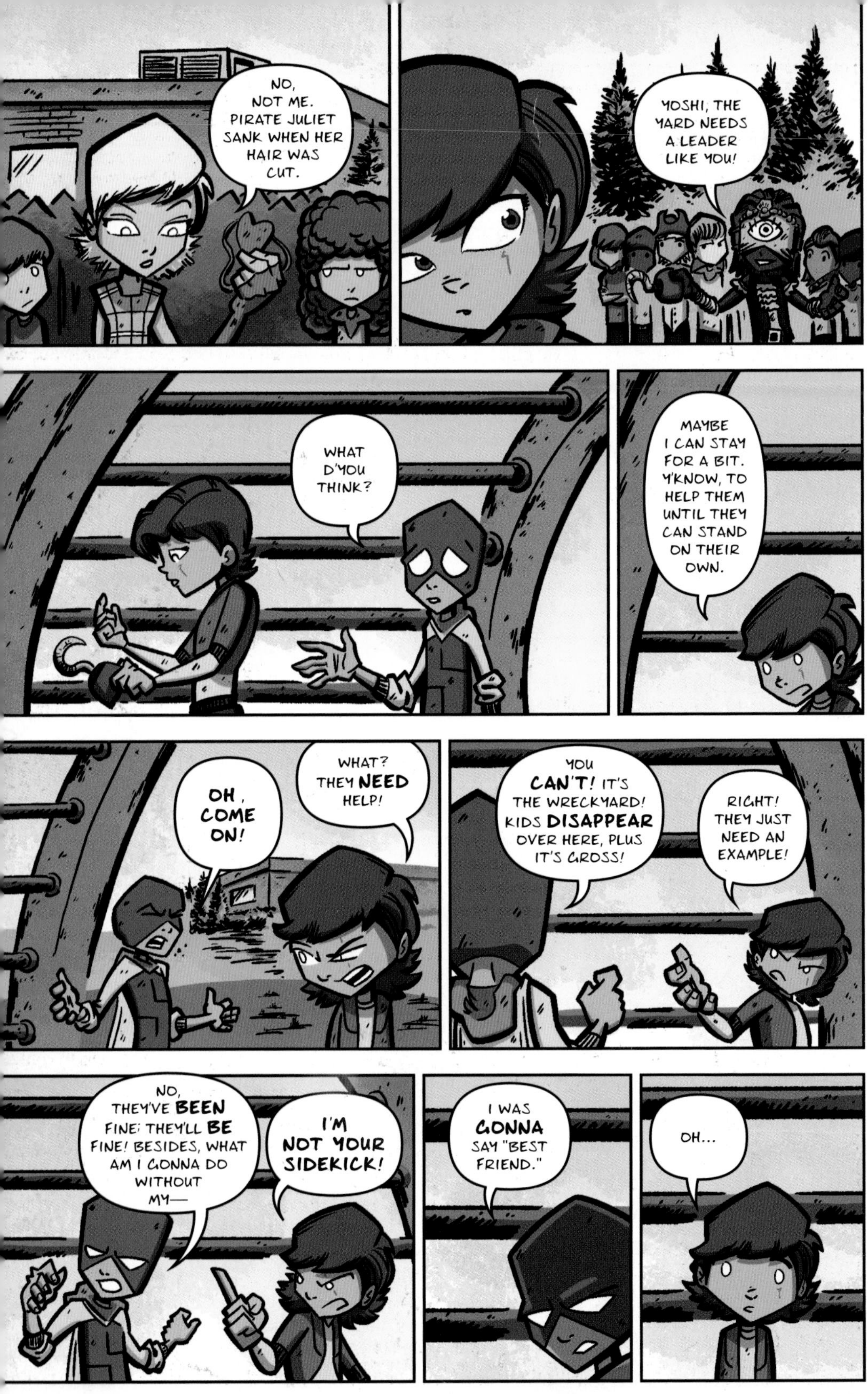
NO, NOT ME. PIRATE JULIET SANK WHEN HER HAIR WAS CUT.
YOSHI, THE YARD NEEDS A LEADER LIKE YOU!
WHAT D'YOU THINK?
MAYBE I CAN STAY FOR A BIT. Y'KNOW, TO HELP THEM UNTIL THEY CAN STAND ON THEIR OWN.
WHAT? THEY **NEED** HELP!
OH, COME ON!
YOU **CAN'T!** IT'S THE WRECKYARD! KIDS **DISAPPEAR** OVER HERE, PLUS IT'S GROSS!
RIGHT! THEY JUST NEED AN EXAMPLE!
NO, THEY'VE **BEEN** FINE; THEY'LL **BE** FINE! BESIDES, WHAT AM I GONNA DO WITHOUT MY—
I'M NOT YOUR SIDEKICK!
I WAS **GONNA** SAY "BEST FRIEND."
OH...

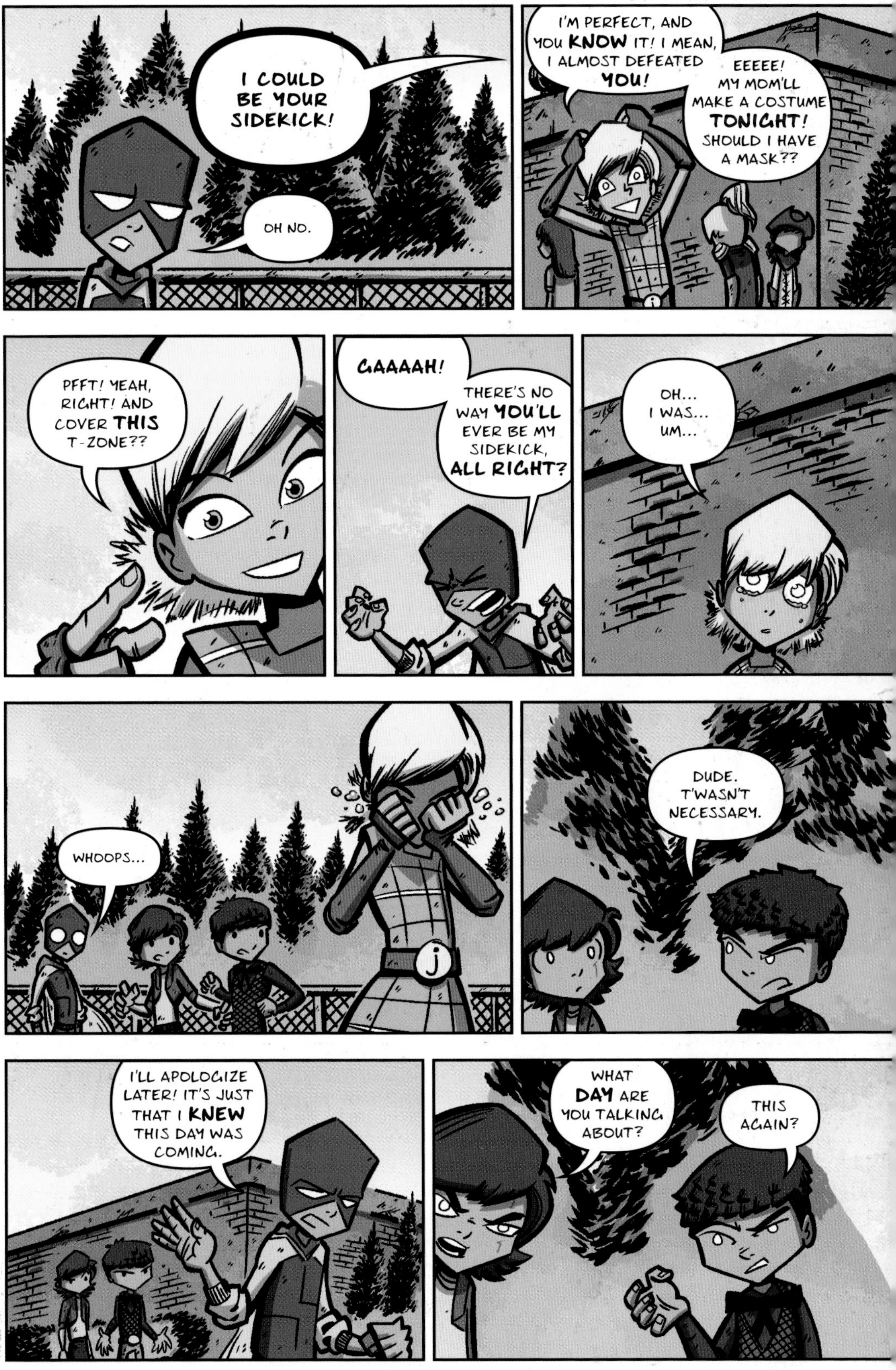
I COULD BE YOUR SIDEKICK!
OH NO.
I'M PERFECT, AND YOU KNOW IT! I MEAN, I ALMOST DEFEATED YOU!
EEEEE! MY MOM'LL MAKE A COSTUME TONIGHT! SHOULD I HAVE A MASK??
PFFT! YEAH, RIGHT! AND COVER THIS T-ZONE??
GAAAAH!
THERE'S NO WAY YOU'LL EVER BE MY SIDEKICK, ALL RIGHT?
OH... I WAS... UM...
WHOOPS...
DUDE. T'WASN'T NECESSARY.
I'LL APOLOGIZE LATER! IT'S JUST THAT I KNEW THIS DAY WAS COMING.
WHAT DAY ARE YOU TALKING ABOUT?
THIS AGAIN?

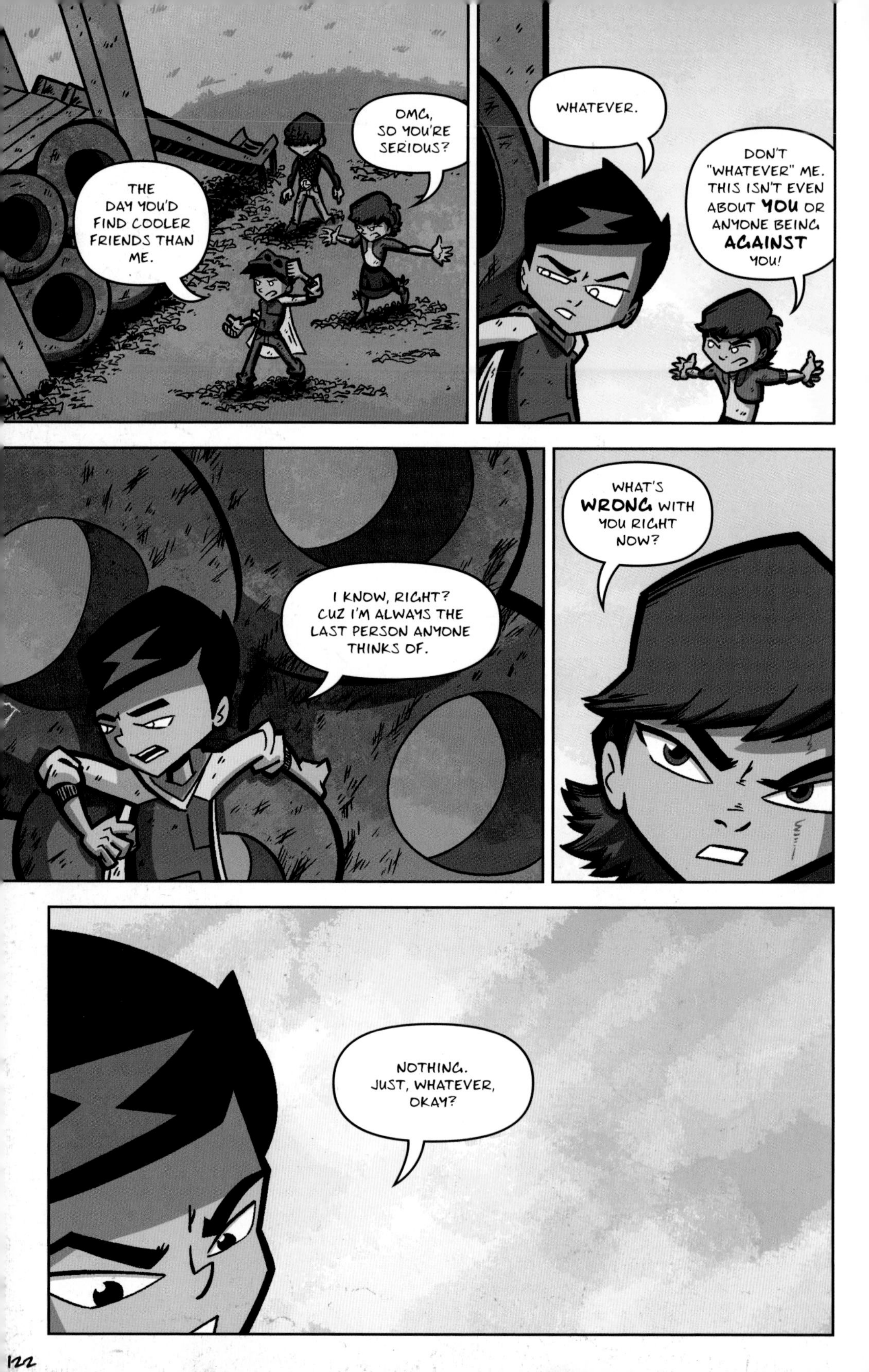
OMG, SO YOU'RE SERIOUS?
THE DAY YOU'D FIND COOLER FRIENDS THAN ME.
WHATEVER.
DON'T "WHATEVER" ME. THIS ISN'T EVEN ABOUT YOU OR ANYONE BEING AGAINST YOU!
I KNOW, RIGHT? CUZ I'M ALWAYS THE LAST PERSON ANYONE THINKS OF.
WHAT'S WRONG WITH YOU RIGHT NOW?
NOTHING. JUST, WHATEVER, OKAY?

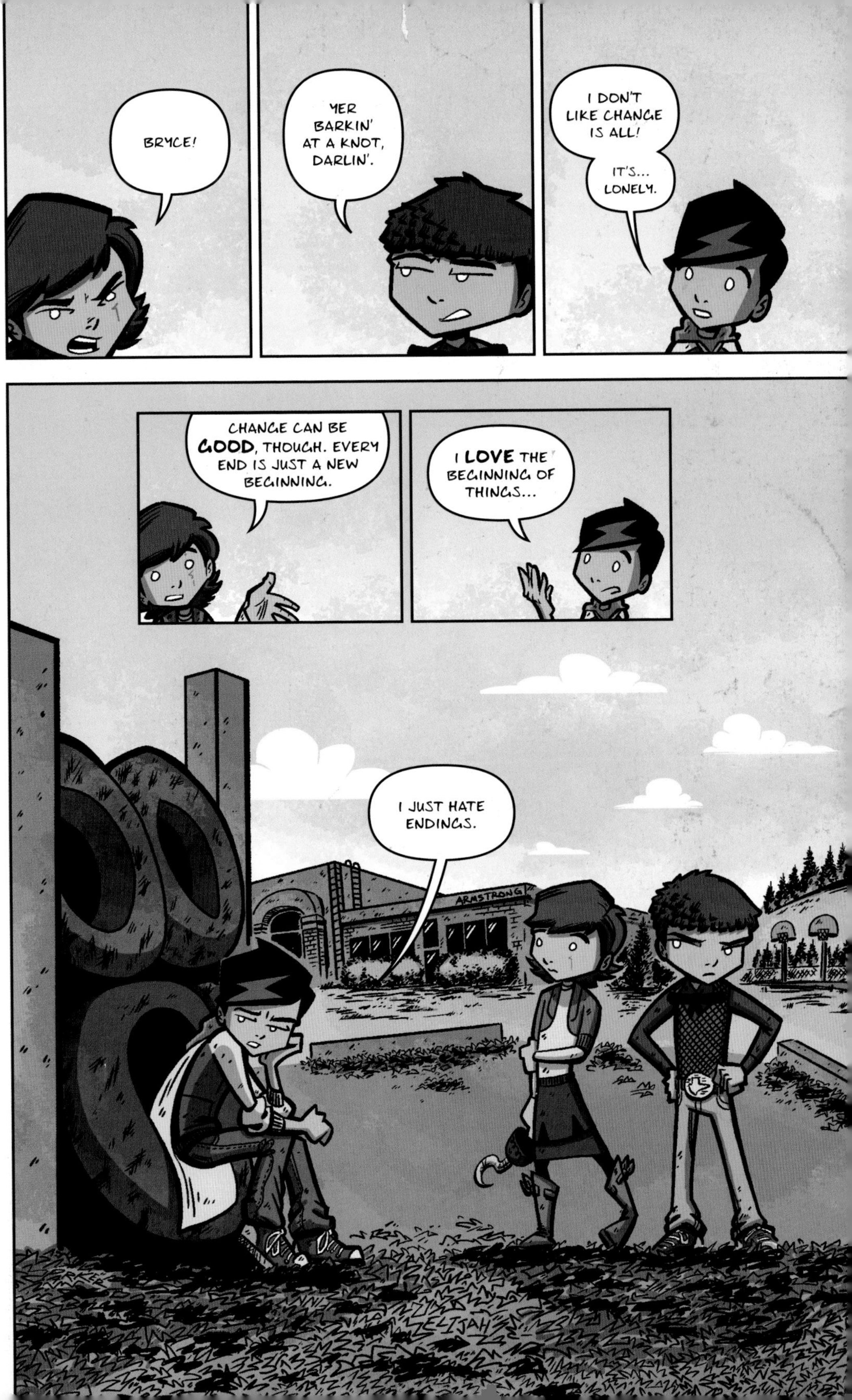
BRYCE!
YER BARKIN' AT A KNOT, DARLIN'.
I DON'T LIKE CHANGE IS ALL!
IT'S... LONELY.
CHANGE CAN BE GOOD, THOUGH. EVERY END IS JUST A NEW BEGINNING.
I LOVE THE BEGINNING OF THINGS...
I JUST HATE ENDINGS.
ARMSTRONG
ELIJAH

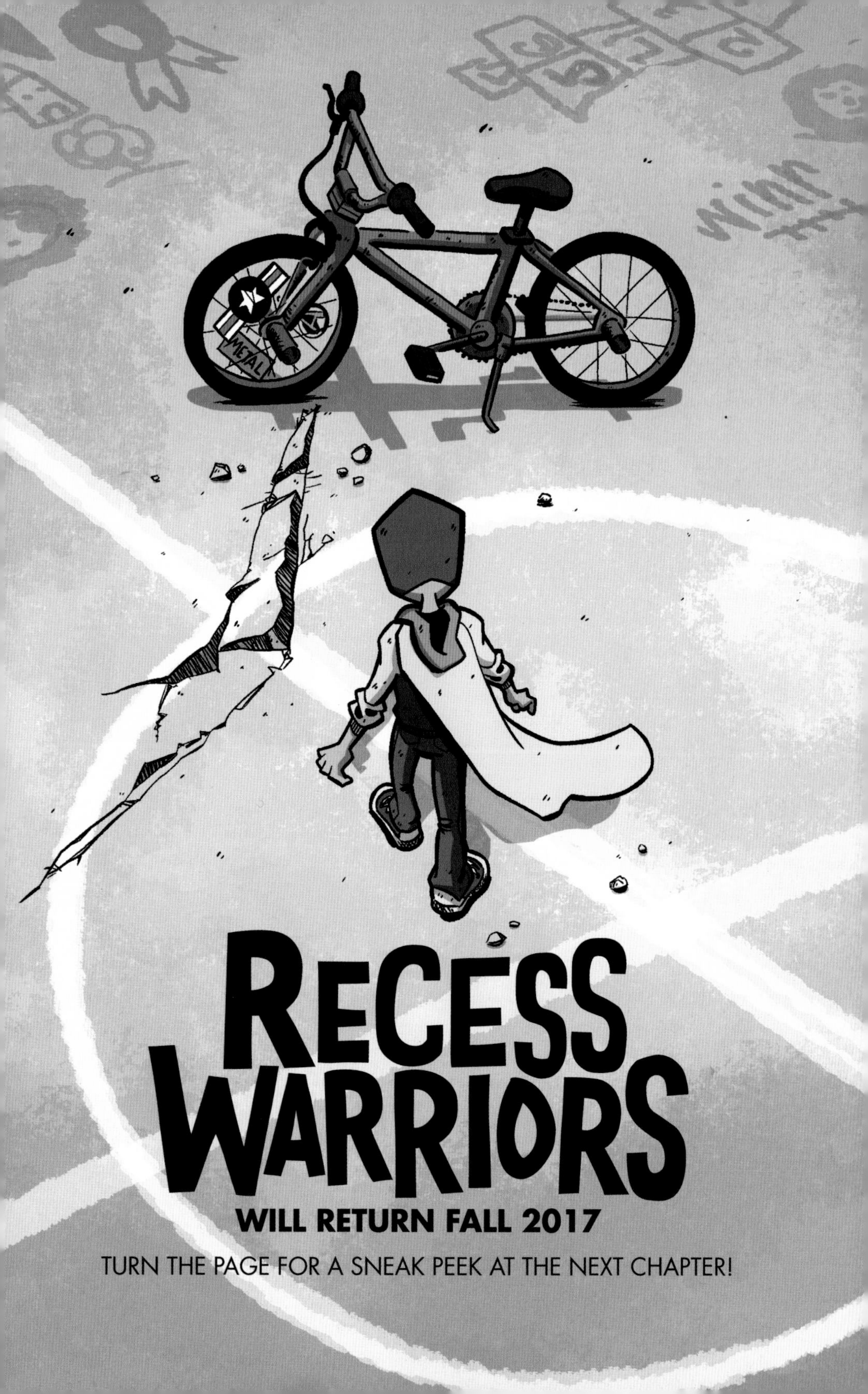
RECESS WARRIORS
WILL RETURN FALL 2017
TURN THE PAGE FOR A SNEAK PEEK AT THE NEXT CHAPTER!

04 THE [illegible]ALLAD OF SHERIFF DAVENPORT

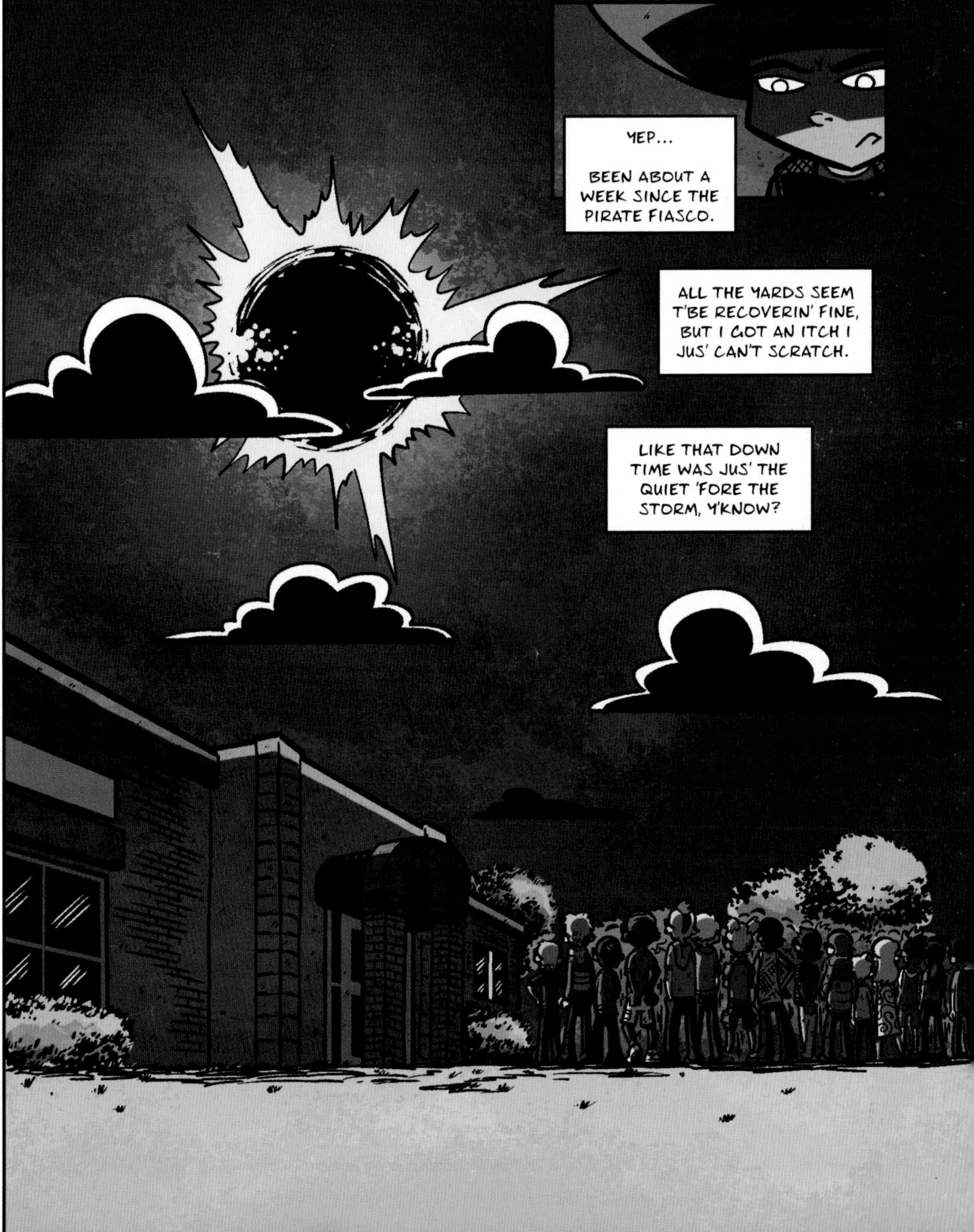
YEP...
BEEN ABOUT A WEEK SINCE THE PIRATE FIASCO.
ALL THE YARDS SEEM T'BE RECOVERIN' FINE, BUT I GOT AN ITCH I JUS' CAN'T SCRATCH.
LIKE THAT DOWN TIME WAS JUS' THE QUIET 'FORE THE STORM, Y'KNOW?

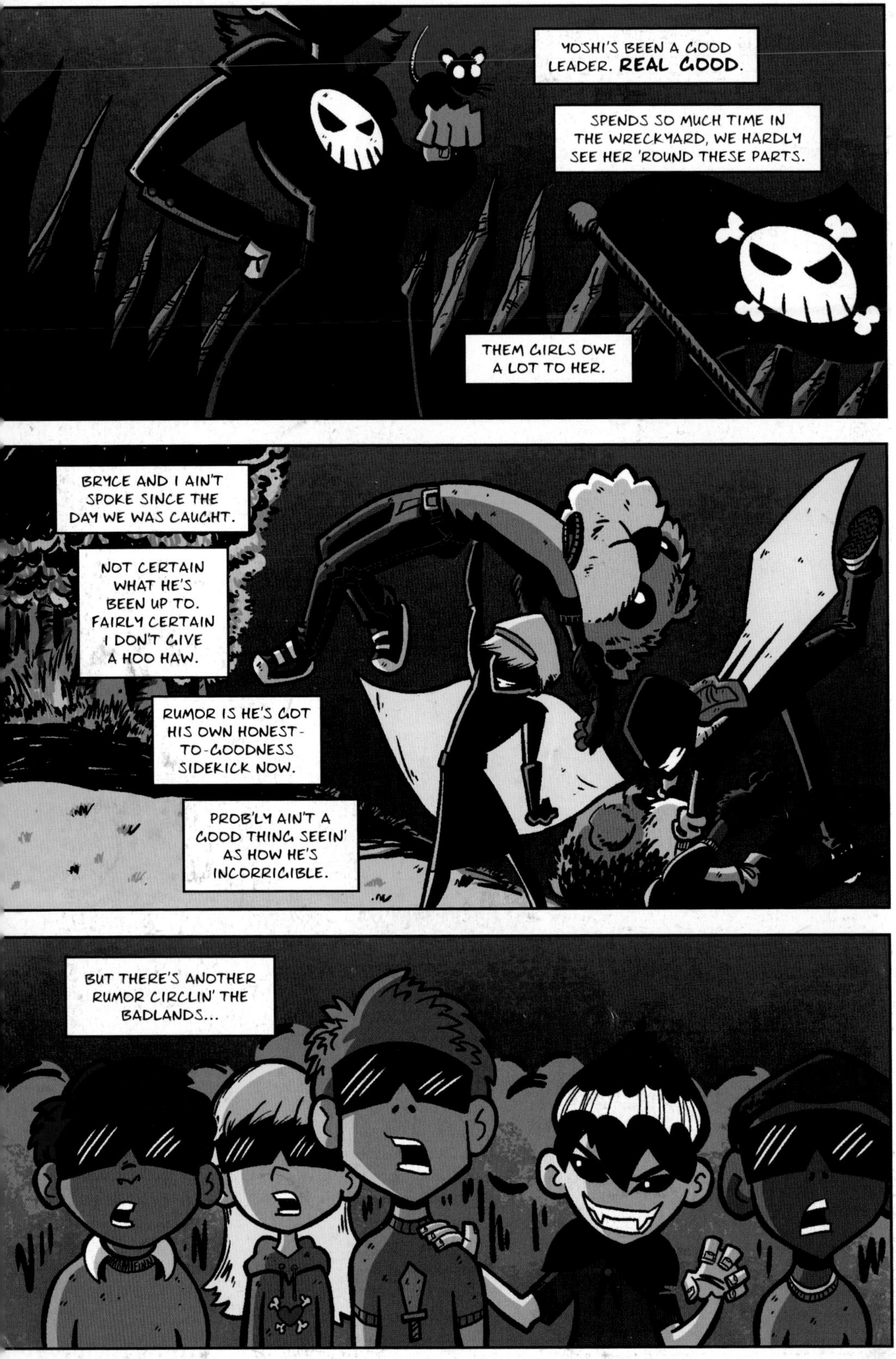
YOSHI'S BEEN A GOOD LEADER. REAL GOOD.
SPENDS SO MUCH TIME IN THE WRECKYARD, WE HARDLY SEE HER 'ROUND THESE PARTS.
THEM GIRLS OWE A LOT TO HER.
BRYCE AND I AIN'T SPOKE SINCE THE DAY WE WAS CAUGHT.
NOT CERTAIN WHAT HE'S BEEN UP TO. FAIRLY CERTAIN I DON'T GIVE A HOO HAW.
RUMOR IS HE'S GOT HIS OWN HONEST-TO-GOODNESS SIDEKICK NOW.
PROB'LY AIN'T A GOOD THING SEEIN' AS HOW HE'S INCORRIGIBLE.
BUT THERE'S ANOTHER RUMOR CIRCLIN' THE BADLANDS...

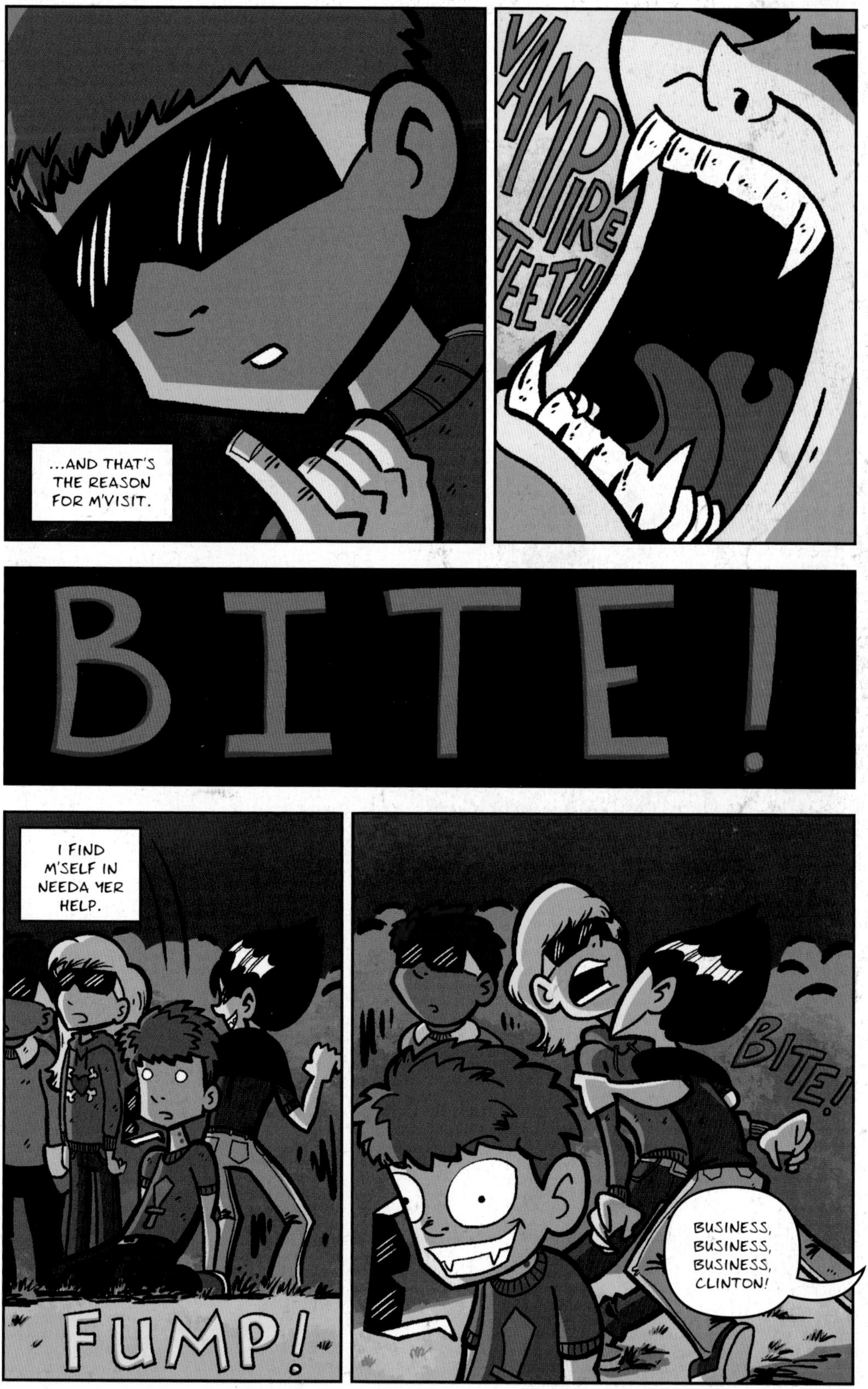

...AND THAT'S THE REASON FOR M'VISIT.
VAMPIRE TEETH
BITE!
I FIND M'SELF IN NEEDA YER HELP.
FUMP!
BITE!
BUSINESS, BUSINESS, BUSINESS, CLINTON!

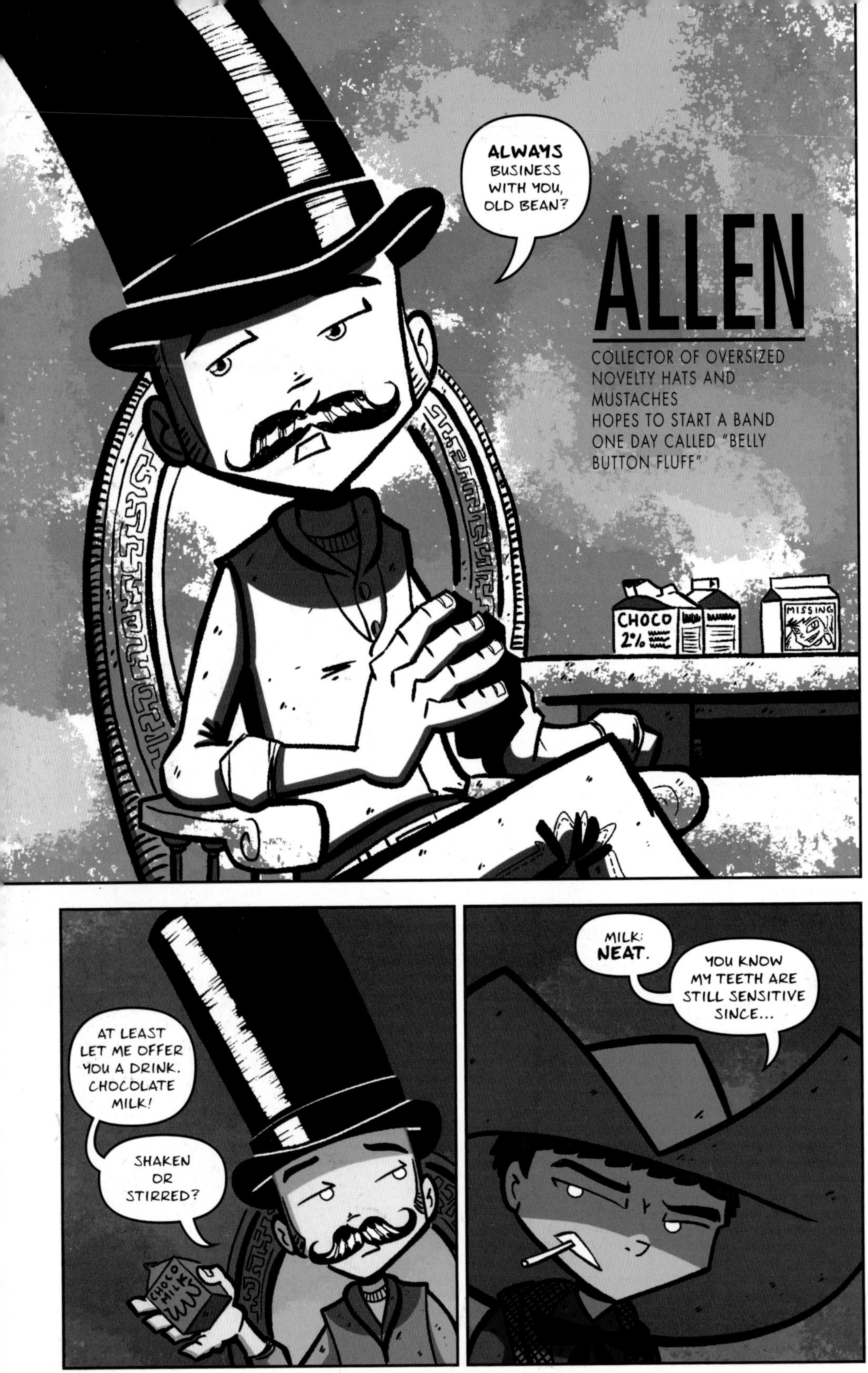
ALWAYS BUSINESS WITH YOU, OLD BEAN?
ALLEN
COLLECTOR OF OVERSIZED NOVELTY HATS AND MUSTACHES
HOPES TO START A BAND ONE DAY CALLED "BELLY BUTTON FLUFF"
CHOCO 2%
MISSING
AT LEAST LET ME OFFER YOU A DRINK. CHOCOLATE MILK!
SHAKEN OR STIRRED?
CHOCO MILK
MILK; NEAT.
YOU KNOW MY TEETH ARE STILL SENSITIVE SINCE...

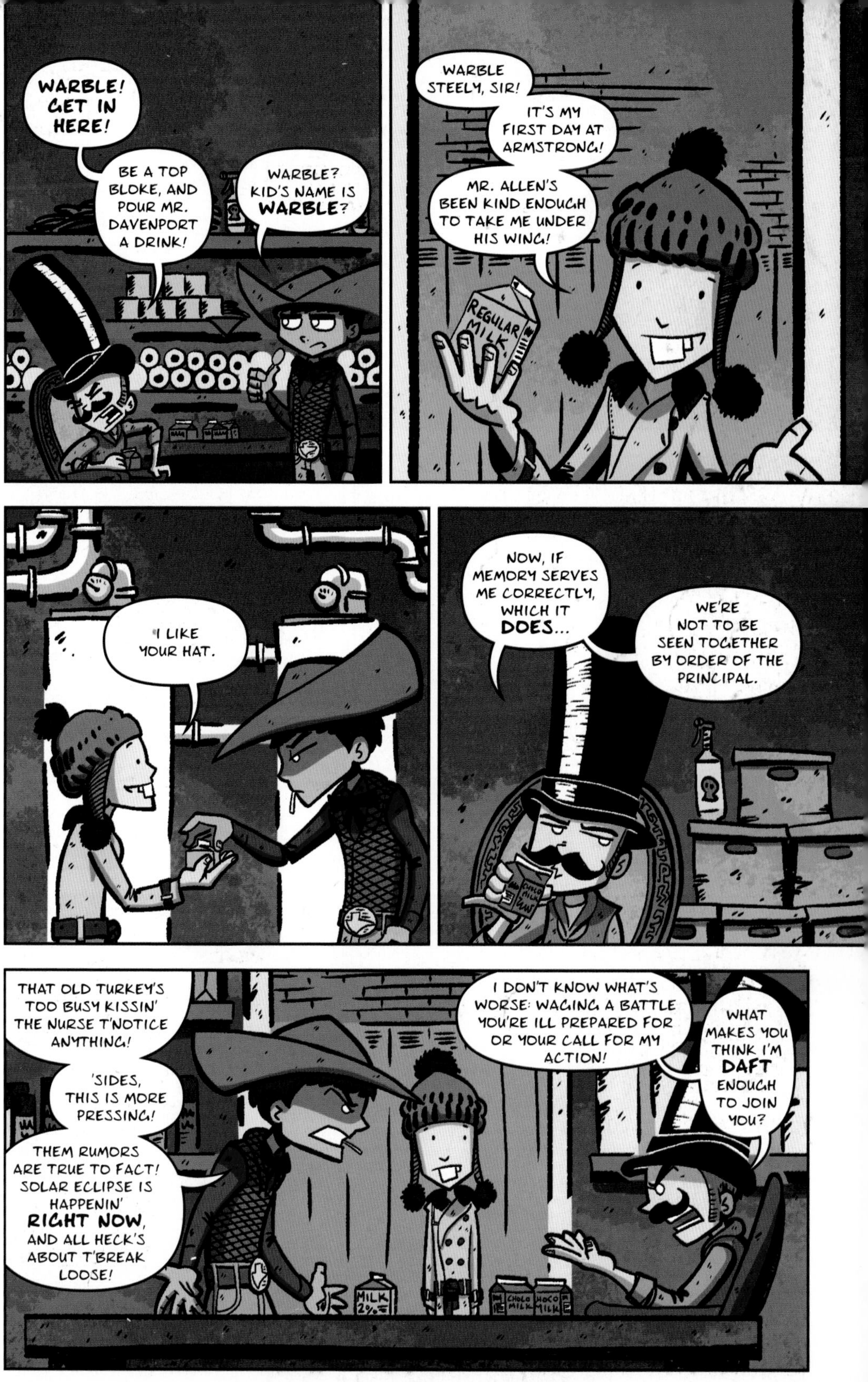
WARBLE! GET IN HERE!
BE A TOP BLOKE, AND POUR MR. DAVENPORT A DRINK!
WARBLE? KID'S NAME IS WARBLE?
WARBLE STEELY, SIR!
IT'S MY FIRST DAY AT ARMSTRONG!
MR. ALLEN'S BEEN KIND ENOUGH TO TAKE ME UNDER HIS WING!
REGULAR MILK
I LIKE YOUR HAT.
NOW, IF MEMORY SERVES ME CORRECTLY, WHICH IT DOES...
WE'RE NOT TO BE SEEN TOGETHER BY ORDER OF THE PRINCIPAL.
THAT OLD TURKEY'S TOO BUSY KISSIN' THE NURSE T'NOTICE ANYTHING!
'SIDES, THIS IS MORE PRESSING!
THEM RUMORS ARE TRUE TO FACT! SOLAR ECLIPSE IS HAPPENIN' RIGHT NOW, AND ALL HECK'S ABOUT T'BREAK LOOSE!
I DON'T KNOW WHAT'S WORSE: WAGING A BATTLE YOU'RE ILL PREPARED FOR OR YOUR CALL FOR MY ACTION!
WHAT MAKES YOU THINK I'M DAFT ENOUGH TO JOIN YOU?
MILK 2%
CHOCO MILK
CHOCO MILK

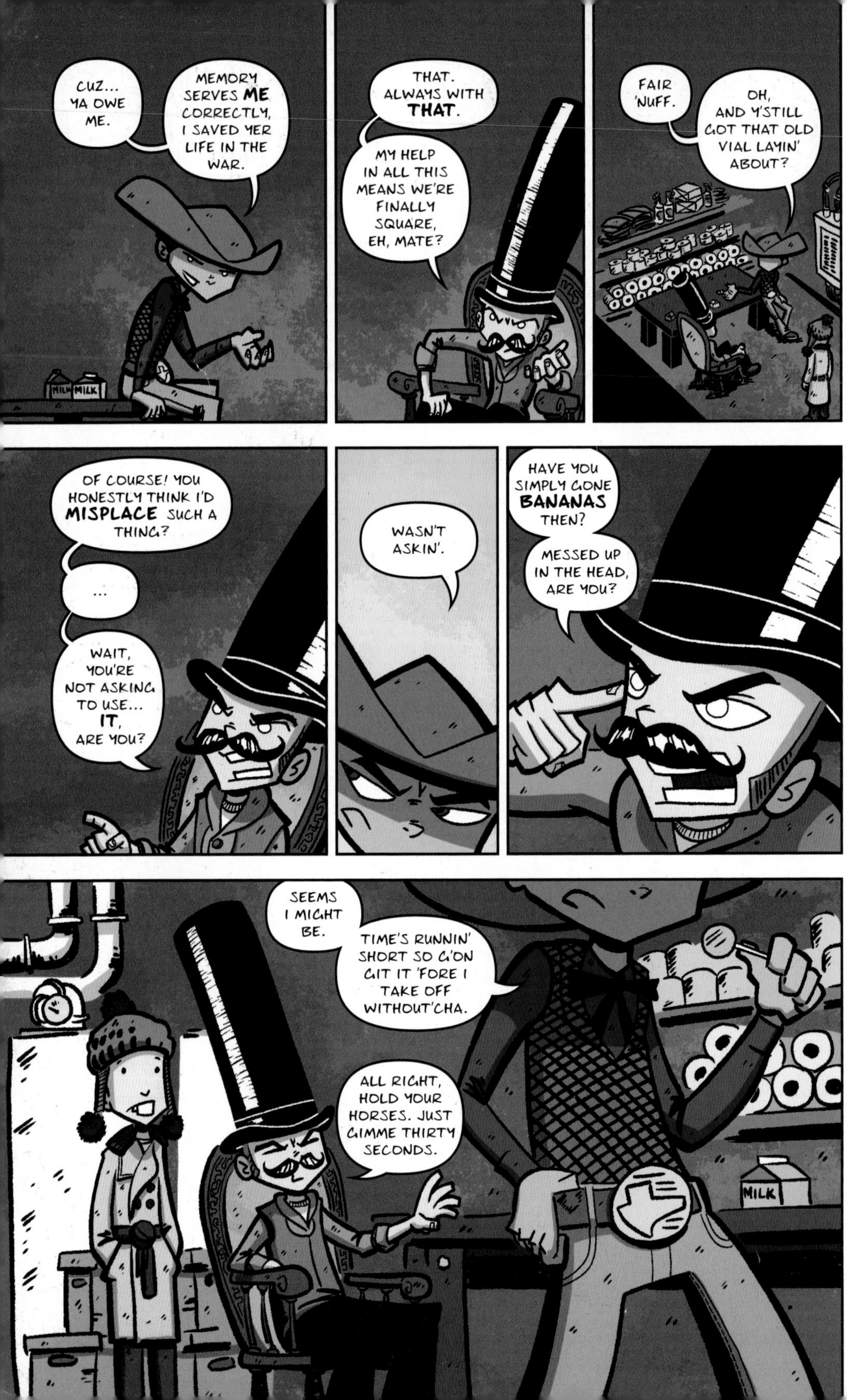

CUZ... YA OWE ME.
MEMORY SERVES **ME** CORRECTLY, I SAVED YER LIFE IN THE WAR.
THAT. ALWAYS WITH **THAT**.
MY HELP IN ALL THIS MEANS WE'RE FINALLY SQUARE, EH, MATE?
FAIR 'NUFF.
OH, AND Y'STILL GOT THAT OLD VIAL LAYIN' ABOUT?
MILK
MILK
OF COURSE! YOU HONESTLY THINK I'D **MISPLACE** SUCH A THING?
...
WAIT, YOU'RE NOT ASKING TO USE... **IT**, ARE YOU?
WASN'T ASKIN'.
HAVE YOU SIMPLY GONE **BANANAS** THEN?
MESSED UP IN THE HEAD, ARE YOU?
SEEMS I MIGHT BE.
TIME'S RUNNIN' SHORT SO G'ON GIT IT 'FORE I TAKE OFF WITHOUT'CHA.
ALL RIGHT, HOLD YOUR HORSES. JUST GIMME THIRTY SECONDS.
MILK

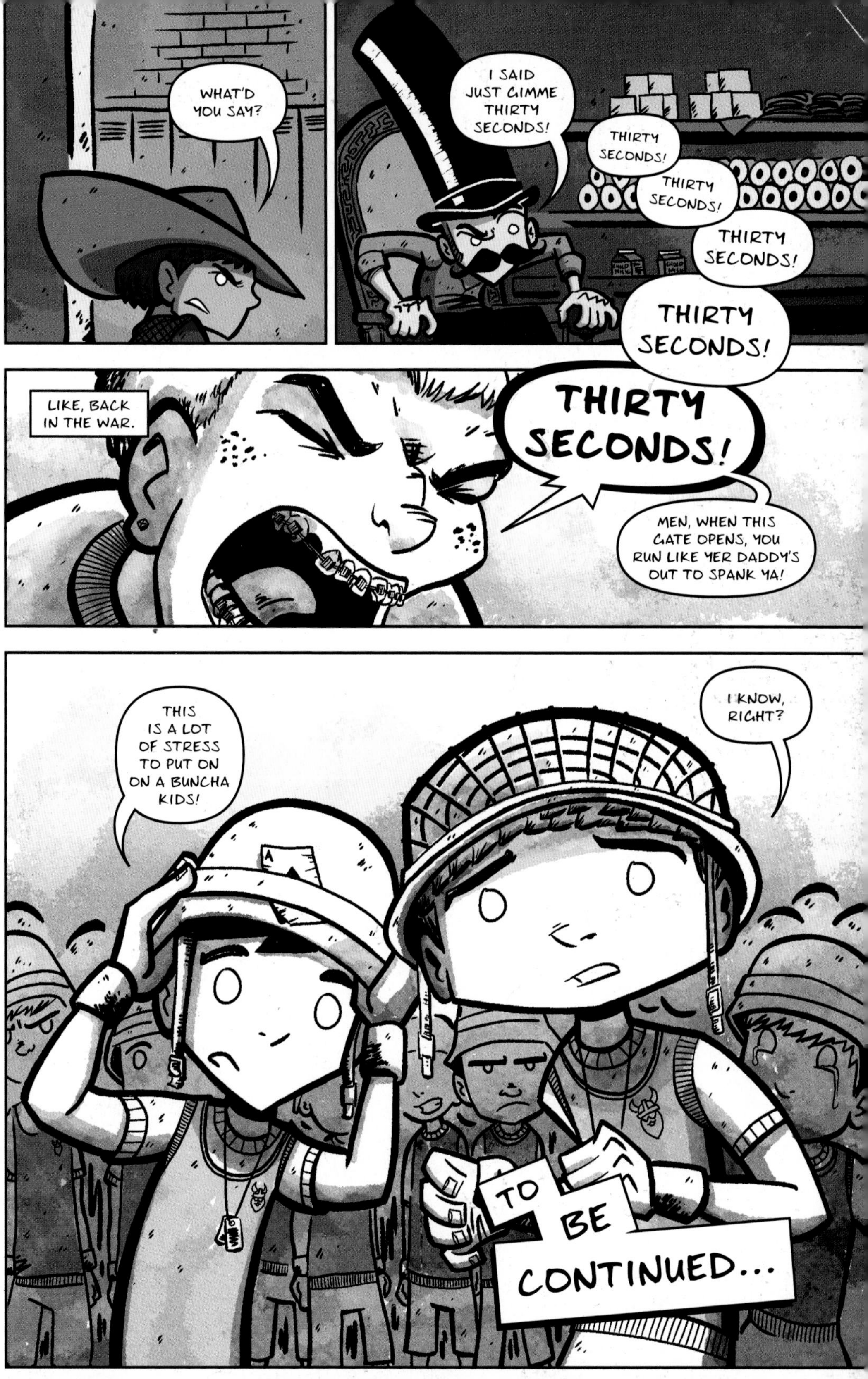
WHAT'D YOU SAY?
I SAID JUST GIMME THIRTY SECONDS!
THIRTY SECONDS!
THIRTY SECONDS!
THIRTY SECONDS!
THIRTY SECONDS!
LIKE, BACK IN THE WAR.
THIRTY SECONDS!
MEN, WHEN THIS GATE OPENS, YOU RUN LIKE YER DADDY'S OUT TO SPANK YA!
THIS IS A LOT OF STRESS TO PUT ON ON A BUNCHA KIDS!
I KNOW, RIGHT?
TO BE CONTINUED...

ARMSTRONG SCHOOL HIGHLIGHTS

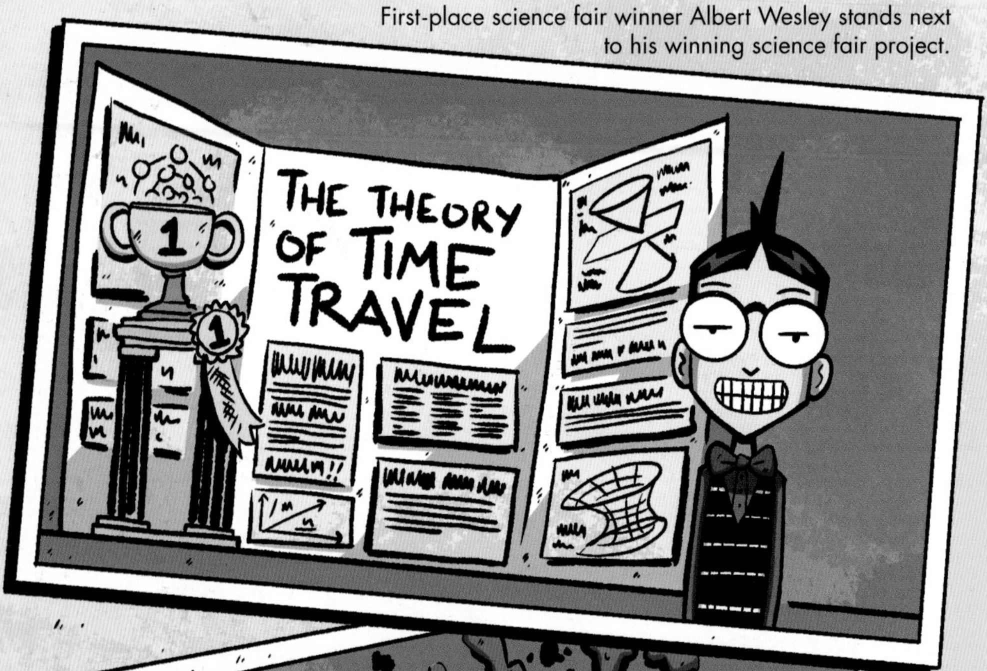
THE THEORY OF TIME TRAVEL

First-place science fair winner Albert Wesley stands next to his winning science fair project.

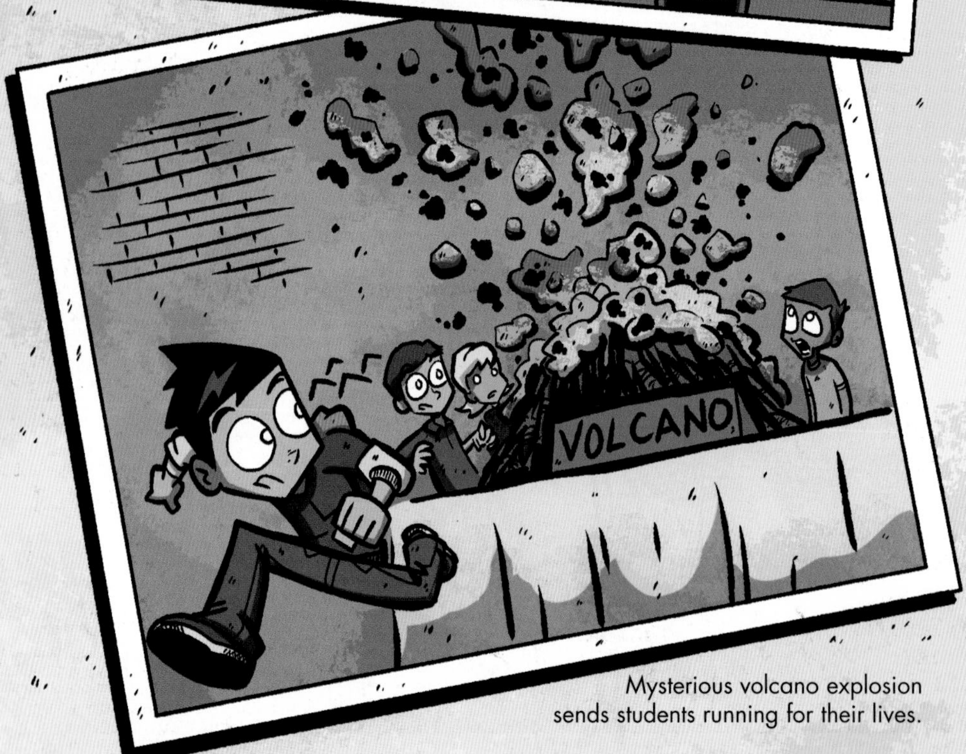
VOLCANO

Mysterious volcano explosion sends students running for their lives.

The Dodgeball Game Heard 'Round the World.

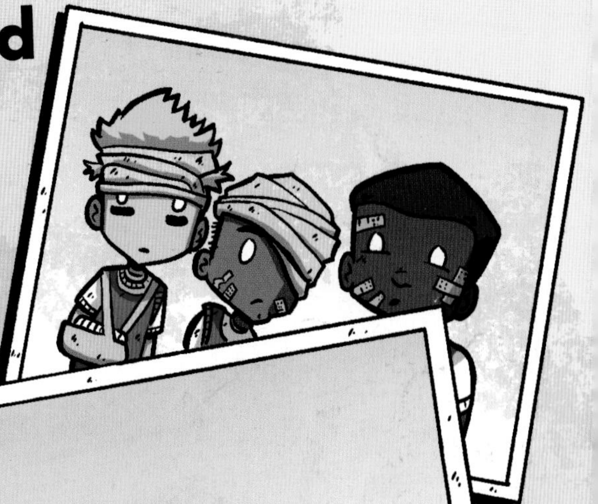

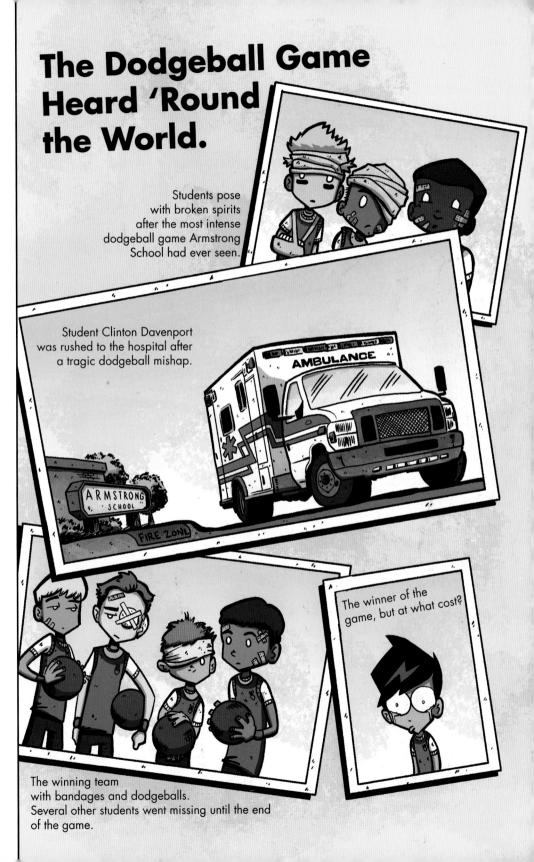

Students pose
with broken spirits
after the most intense
dodgeball game Armstrong
School had ever seen.

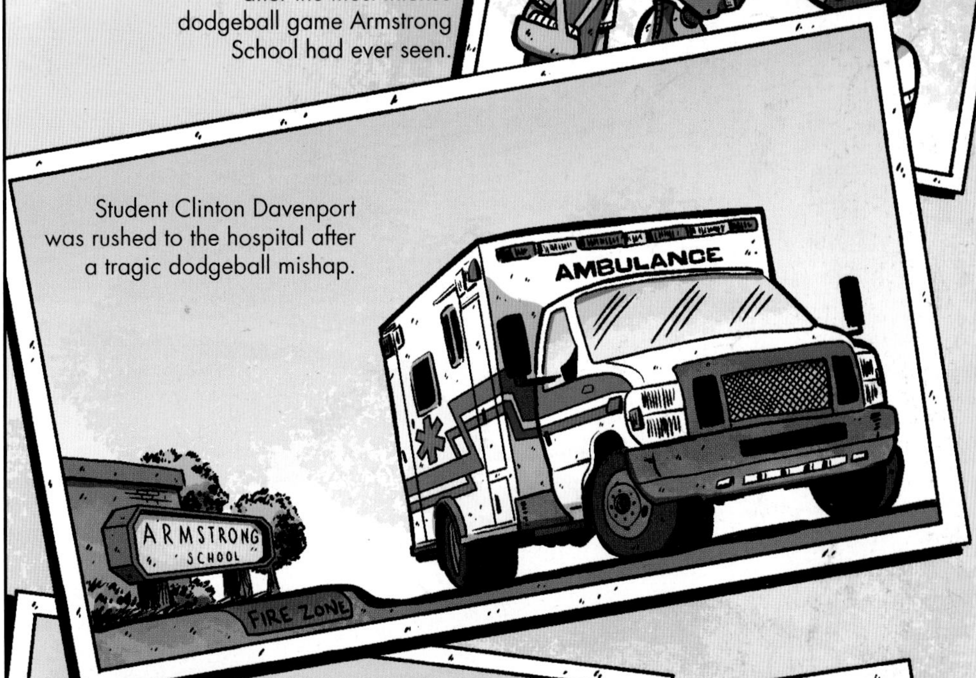
AMBULANCE
ARMSTRONG
SCHOOL
FIRE ZONE

Student Clinton Davenport
was rushed to the hospital after
a tragic dodgeball mishap.

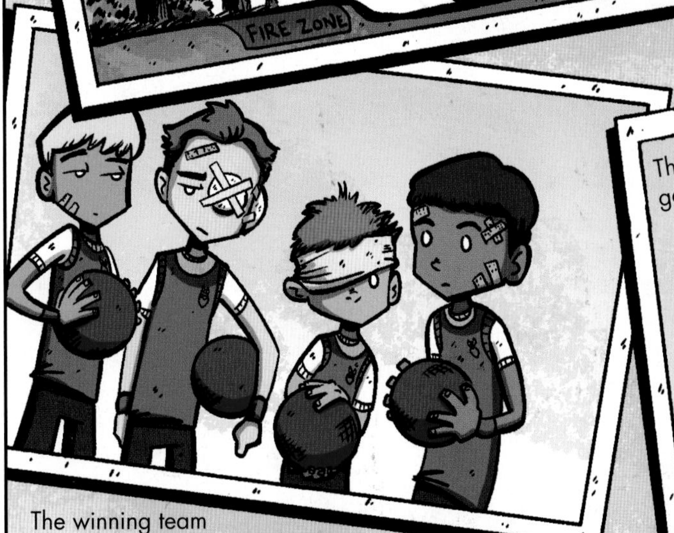

The winning team
with bandages and dodgeballs.
Several other students went missing until the end
of the game.

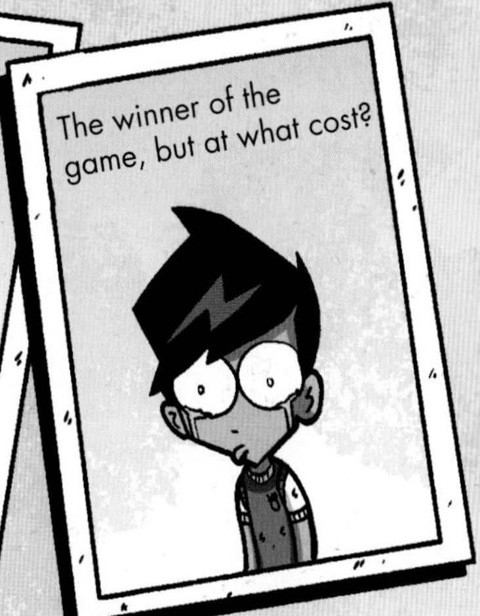

The winner of the
game, but at what cost?

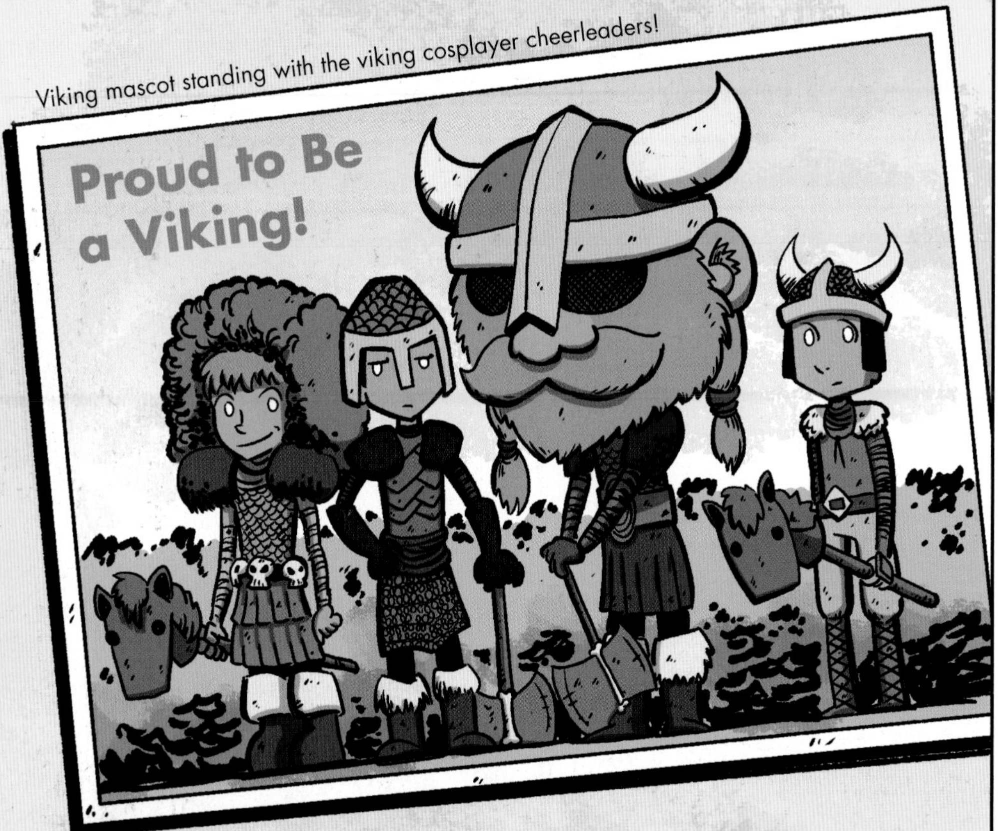
Viking mascot standing with the viking cosplayer cheerleaders!
Proud to Be a Viking!

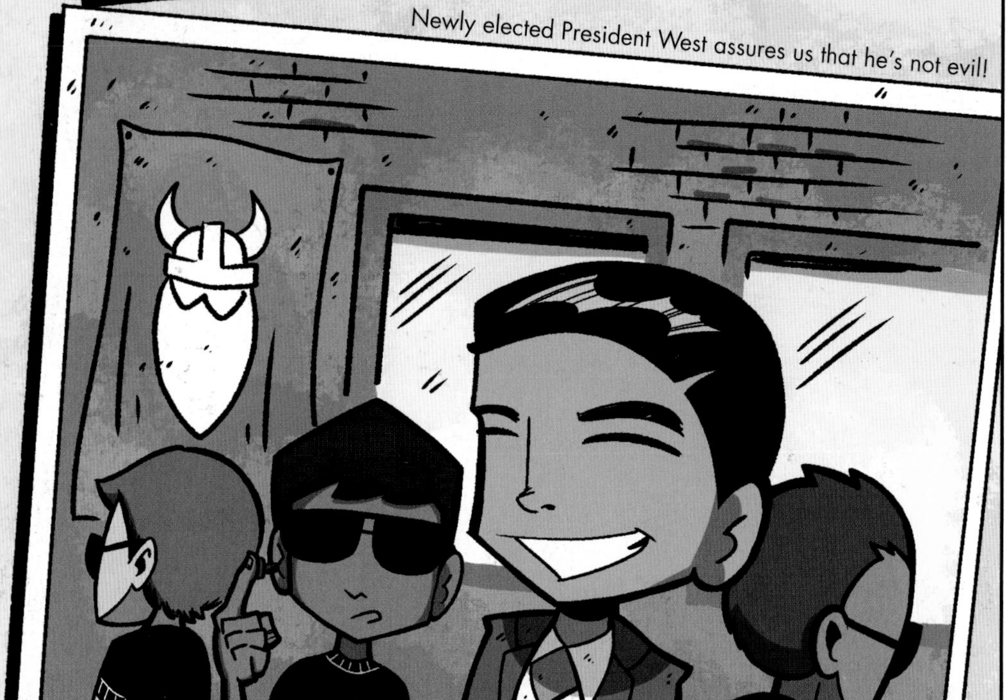
Newly elected President West assures us that he's not evil!

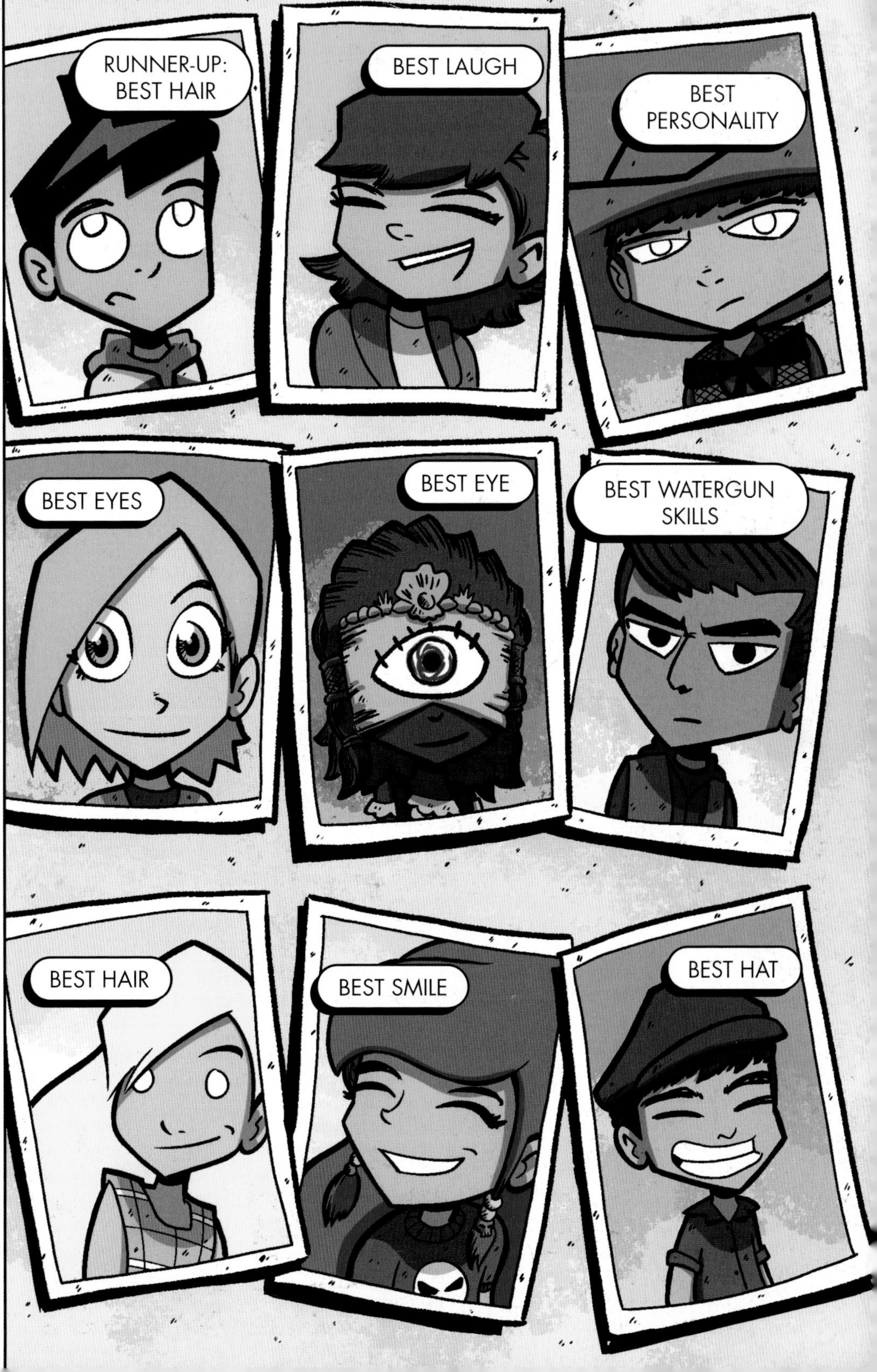
RUNNER-UP: BEST HAIR
BEST LAUGH
BEST PERSONALITY
BEST EYES
BEST EYE
BEST WATERGUN SKILLS
BEST HAIR
BEST SMILE
BEST HAT

EXTRAS

Scrap's design and demeanor came quickly because I already knew exactly who he was when I wrote *Recess Warriors*. It was Bryce's design that was difficult, and I had to get it right because Scrap without his mask only occurs on a few pages in the book.

A lot of the characters changed when I actually started drawing the book. It was a lot easier to find the right direction as soon as I saw them in the world of *Recess Warriors*.

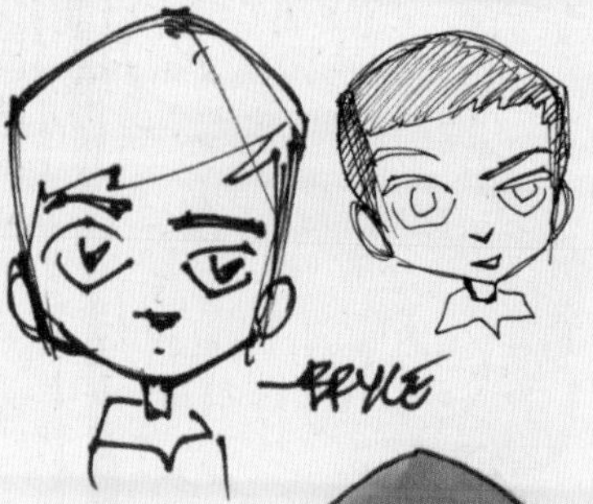
BRYCE

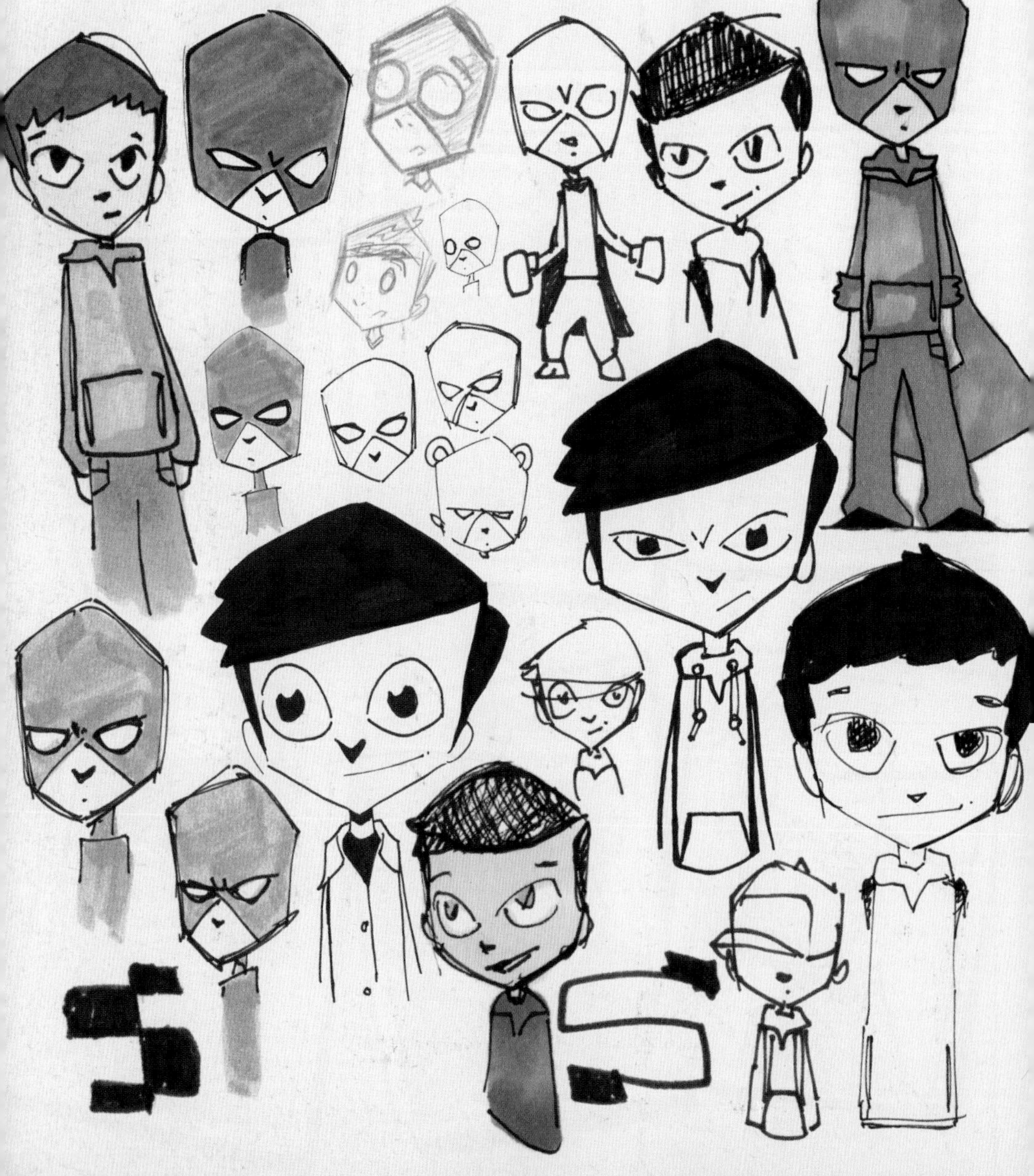

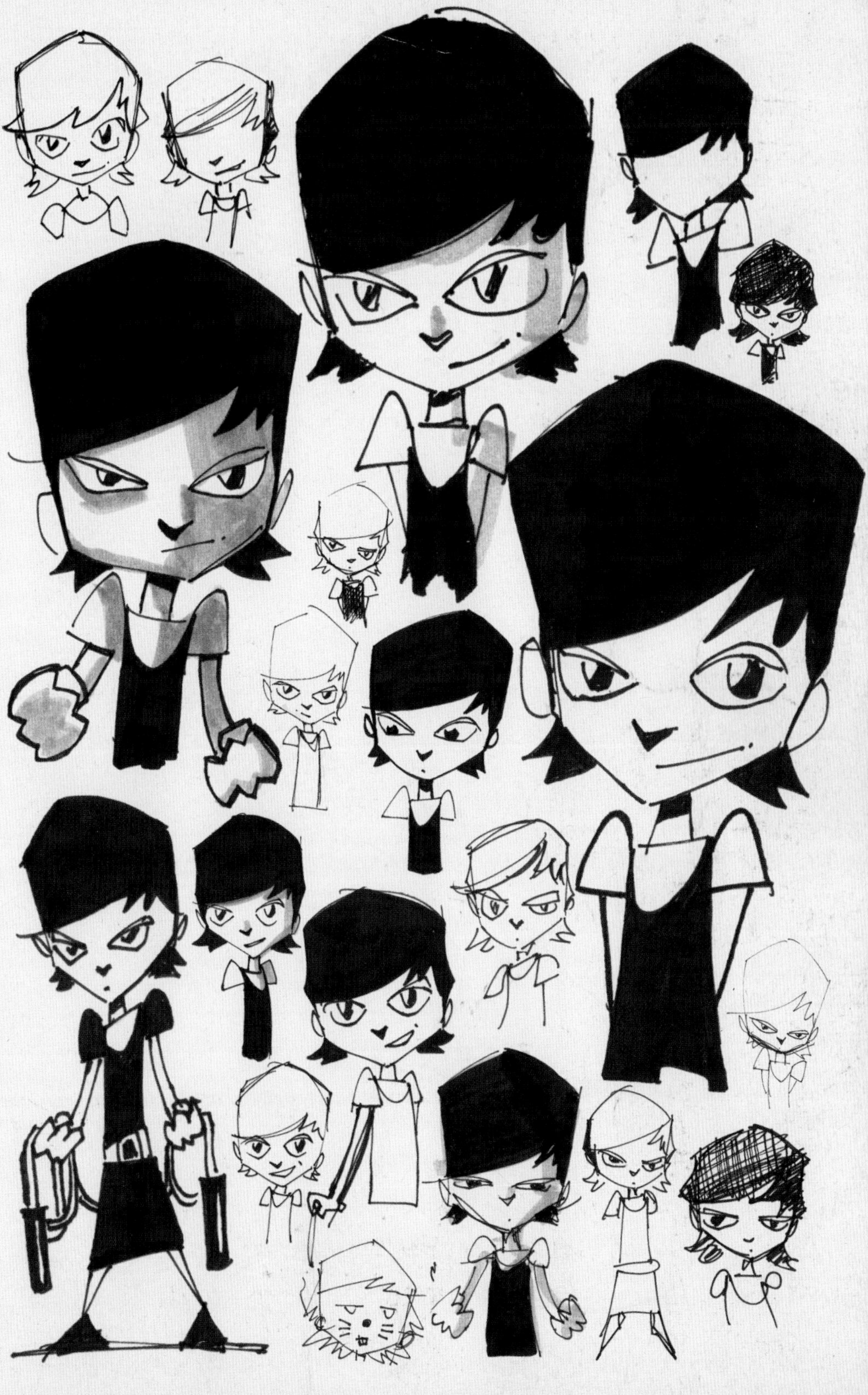

PROCESS

A look at the steps in creating a comic book page.

STEP ONE—THUMBNAILS

I sketch quick thumbnails of every page from the script to get a good idea for the layout. It's a lot of tiny drawings done super fast. This is also the only part of the process when I use an actual pencil and paper. The thumbnails are about two inches tall.

I use blue or red pencil lead during this stage for no other reason except that I like how it looks. Sometimes doing things differently than how you normally do them helps you to see it differently, too.

Traditionally, an artist uses colored pencils because they're easier to erase after scanning the art into a computer.

STEP TWO—PENCILS

Because I work digitally (using a Cintiq screen—a special computer screen I can draw on!), my pencils aren't actually "pencils."

At this stage, I draw the larger version of the comic page, but I still keep my lines very loose (you can see the bushes behind Clinton are just ovals). Doing this helps me see how the scene will look before I start drawing the black lines.

Drawing digitally also makes it so I can make as many mistakes as I need since there's an "undo" button.

Sometimes it'll take me eight or nine times drawing someone's face before I'm happy with how it looks. On an actual sheet of paper, I'd probably have erased right through the page.

STEP THREE—INKS

This is where I start drawing the "inks" right on top of the "pencils."

When working digitally, you can create separate layers for each step in the art process. Pencils are one layer—inks are on their own layer above it.

Once I'm done and happy with how the "inks" look, I delete the "pencils" layer, which leaves a clean black-and-white drawing of the comic page.

STEP FOUR—FLAT COLORS

Everything is colored with solid flat colors. With *Recess Warriors*, I colored all the flats in the entire book first before moving on to shading and textures.

Just like the "pencils" and "inks," these pages are also done digitally and on their own separate layers using Adobe Photoshop. I'm basically coloring behind the "inks."

I'm able to experiment by quickly changing colors if I need to.

I went through several different colors before settling on a blue I liked for Clinton's horse.

STEP FIVE—SHADOWS

After the flats are finished, I start working on shadows.

This is where the characters come to life for me because they feel like they're actually in their own physical environment.

Moods can be set using shadows as well. Clinton's hat usually casts his eyes in shadow, making him slightly mysterious—it's the same with Captain Red before the reveal.

And back in chapter 1, I used shadows to make Juliet look downright insane when she's monologuing to Scrap.

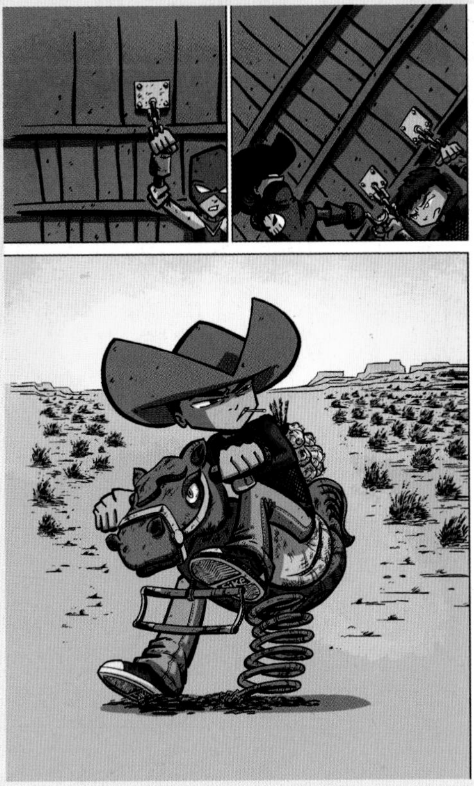

STEP SIX—TEXTURES

After the shadows are finished, textures are added to help the scene feel more complete and alive.

I only use textures on backgrounds and never on the characters themselves. This helps the kids pop out a little more. There are also times when textures subtly guide the reader's eyes to important parts of a panel.

I try not to overdo it on the textures because they're not there to catch attention. They're just a little bit of extra flair on the page.

Once textures are complete, I'll adjust the colors once more until they feel more balanced and complete, leading to the finished comic book page.

MY STUDIO

This is where all that stuff I just talked about happens. It's *never* this clean.

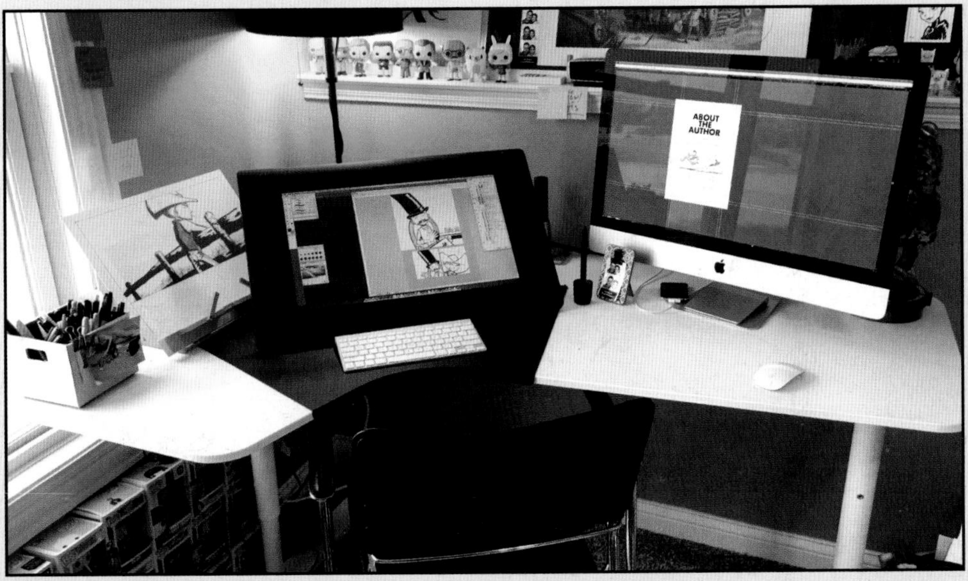
ABOUT THE AUTHOR

ABOUT THE AUTHOR

Marcus Emerson is the author of several highly imaginative children's books. His goal is to create children's books that are engaging, funny, and inspirational for kids of all ages—even the adults who secretly never grew up.

Marcus Emerson is currently having the time of his life with his beautiful wife and their four amazing children. He still dreams of becoming an astronaut someday and walking on Mars.

Stories—what an incredible way to open one's mind to a fantastic world of adventure. It's my hope that this story has inspired you in some way, lighting a fire that maybe you didn't know you had. Keep that flame burning no matter what. It represents your sense of adventure and creativity, and that's something nobody can take from you. Thanks for reading!

M.E.

—Marcus Emerson
m@MarcusEmerson.com